WHITE HUNTER, BLACK HEART

PETER VIERTEL

"Its incidental pictures of African scenery and colonial society, both British and Belgian, are vividly those of a first-rate observer and reporter. So, too, is the London background of hotels and restaurants, and the financial shenanigans that precede and accompany the making of a motion picture."

—James Hilton, *Book Week*

"Viertel is a strong writer; his characters are real people, his dialogue is flawless."

—*The Oakland Press*

"[WHITE HUNTER, BLACK HEART] was published in 1953, when Viertel's emotions about working with [John] Huston on the rewrite of the script for *The African Queen* (1951) were still raw: Huston is its hero and its villain. The portrait of him is marvellously, scathingly full, and convincing."

—Pauline Kael, *The New Yorker*

QUANTITY SALES

WHITE HUNTER, BLACK HEART

PETER VIERTEL

Published by
Dell Publishing
a division of
The Bantam Doubleday Dell Publishing Group, Inc.
666 Fifth Avenue
New York, New York 10103

FOR MY MOTHER AND FATHER

ISBN: 0-440-39809-6

Reprinted by arrangement with the author.

Printed in the United States of America

One Previous Edition

September 1987

10 9 8 7 6 5 4 3

WFH

"*They are insane. Gutshot and dying, one of them kept me in a tree for eleven hours with water only a little distance away. It was an insane performance. It is the insanity of the animal that makes him magnificent.*"

(A white hunter speaking of buffalo; overheard in Nairobi, May 1951.)

1

When I think back now, I realize that the only thing John Wilson and I actually ever had in common was the fact that at one time or another each of us ran over someone with an automobile. The victim of his accident died; mine lived on to sue the insurance company for a good many years. The great difference between the end results of these two very similar happenings seems fairly symptomatic to me, for it somehow symbolizes the essential difference between Wilson and myself. Things that happened to me always simmered down and became mild little adventures, hardly worth remembering. Things that happened to Wilson exploded. Most people attributed this directly to his nature, but I prefer to think that chance had something to do with it. It is true that Wilson was always a violent man, given to violent actions. Some of my friends called him a spoiler, and ascribed his wild, troubled life directly to his personal mania for destruction and disaster, but these generalizations always seemed inaccurate to me, for although he certainly contributed to the trouble that always sprang up around him, I cannot believe that he caused it all. Violent, irresponsible personalities seem to attract similar personalities and very often it is hard to put your finger on who is cause and who is effect. That was certainly true of Wilson. I say was, not because he is dead, but because I think our long friendship is over. The end of love always gives you a momentary over-all look at life, and you can see the past in a cold, true light. That's why I can write all this about John.

A very talented, intelligent actor I know said that Wilson was the leading exponent of the "screw-you-all" type of personality. He also always added that in order to survive with that particular type of personality one had to be born rich or very, very talented. The latter was true of

John. He had and still has a great amount of talent. He made a career, despite the basic attitude so aptly described by my friend, by continually violating all the unwritten rules that govern the motion picture business. He told his bosses what he thought of them (and he was always right), he publicly abused all the women he was involved with (which is dangerous, for Hollywood is a very moral, middle-class town), he supported doubtful political causes (on the basis of integrity and not because of a romantic, adolescent political conviction), he drank to excess (and he certainly became less charming when he did so), he made a great many wonderful pictures, very few of which made any money at the box office (which is the most dangerous thing a man can do in Hollywood), and he spent all his money (which is a dangerous thing to do anywhere). All of these violations of the tribal rules, for which I admired him, did him no harm. Instead they helped him. There have been a great many imitations of his style of living. Actors, writers, and even producers have occasionally tried what he did day in and day out and they have all ended badly: in jail or in hock or as recipients of the Motion Picture Relief Fund. Perhaps they lacked his talent, but I don't think that is it. I think they lacked the magic, almost divine ability he had to land on his feet.

I knew him for many years. I met him in the thirties after my first novel was published. He admired it, and took a lot of time to tell me so. From that rather solid beginning we went on to discover that we both loved horses. From that he went on to suppose that we were both capable of a wild, dangerous life. The war cemented our friendship. Vainglory and pride made me join the Marine Corps, which I regretted twenty-five minutes after I had done so. Wilson interpreted my actions as those of a kindred spirit, and although we met only a few times during the war while we were both on leave, the fact that I wore the green uniform of the "attack force" helped maintain our friendship. He was in the Air Corps, as a photographer, and he flew a great many dangerous missions, and made two very solid documentary movies which helped his career no little bit. I mention this as another example of the screw-you-all spirit which motivated him, and which catapulted him upward.

After the war we saw a lot of each other. Both of us were practiced listeners, having survived a good many story conferences prior to surviving World War II, and we were able to spend days and days together on the company payroll, lying to each other about our various exploits. Actually I think I know his war stories as well as I know my own, and although he usually elaborated my tales of fear and suffering, I know he could tell any one of my stories as well as I could. He would tell them slower, that's all, because that was and is his style of storytelling. His movies are fast and brilliant. His after-dinner stories are slow and tortured affairs. However, they usually have a very good ending—that is, if he hasn't had too much to drink and remembers everything properly.

A few years after our return to civilian life we made our first movie together. It was not one of Wilson's best pictures, but apart from the writing of the script, it was one of the best times he ever had. Everything went wrong, and so he thoroughly enjoyed himself, somehow pulling it all together in the end and making a critical success of what had seemed a frightening disaster. I made enough money out of the venture to be able to go to Europe, where I intended to write a novel. Instead I learned to ski, and became one of the best skiers in the Screen Writers' Guild, if not the best. Once the snow began to melt I realized that I had succeeded at the wrong thing, and I faced a dismal spring of frustration and guilt. It was at this moment that Wilson telephoned. I was sitting in the bar of the small Swiss hotel where I had frittered away just about as much time as I had wasted on the slopes, when the barman turned to me and said that someone in London was asking for me on the telephone.

I couldn't imagine who was calling me, and so the first two minutes of our conversation were spent as fruitlessly as my two months in Switzerland.

"Pete . . ." a voice seemed to be calling dimly over the noise of the piano and the static of the Channel.

"Yes, who is it?"

"I can't hear you, Pete."

"I said who is it?"

"Hello, Pete," the voice repeated. I asked Willy the bartender to subdue the pianist and then I heard Wilson's voice come unmistakably into the small, hot room.

"Hello, Pete . . . this is John. John Wilson."

"John! Where the hell are you?"

"Well, I'm in London, kid, where are you?"

"In Switzerland."

"Well, for God's sake."

We both sounded like happy idiots. Hearing his voice again seemed to have cured me of my mountain fever, and I was delighted. It was like hard reality coming to one after an endless pleasant dream which has turned into a nightmare.

"What are you doing in London?" I asked.

"What are you doing in Switzerland?" he replied.

"Skiing."

"You are, eh? Well, for God's sake." He chuckled happily, as did I. We both felt childishly impressed to be talking to each other from such strange locales. He had always called from Burbank, and I had always been in Santa Monica.

"Why don't you come over?" I asked.

"I can't, kid. But I've got something to ask you."

"Shoot. What is it?"

He seemed to be talking slower than ever, and then as I realized that it was seven-thirty in the evening I knew what the cause of it was.

"I've got a little proposition to make you," he said, enjoying the moment. "How would you like to go to Africa?"

"Sure," I said, living up to his notion of me. "Where in Africa?"

"Darkest Africa," he said. "The very darkest bloody corner of Africa we can find."

I confess that I felt immediately dismayed. "For a trip?" I asked.

"Well, of course," he said.

"Who's going to pay?"

"Not us, kid. You know that. What a damned fool thing to ask. I'm going to make a movie down there."

"And what am I suppose to do?"

"Help me. Keep me company. There's a little work to be done on the script, and then you can stay on and we'll hunt."

"Hunt what?"

"Everything. Haven't you always wanted to shoot an elephant?"

"No, I don't think so," I said.

"Well, a buffalo, or a lion. We'll have a safari, kid, the real thing. Hell, we'd never be able to afford it ourselves."

"How's the script we'll have to work on?"

"Not bad," he said. "Not any worse than the last one, and we'll be in Africa."

I had looked forward to some spring touring on the high snowfields of the Alps, and Africa seemed like a hot, uncomfortable alternative. I also felt an ominous foreboding about going off into the wildest corner of the world with John Wilson. He had always made Sunset Boulevard seem perilous enough to me.

"What's the matter with you?" he asked, sounding truly worried about his friend.

"I'm trying to make up my mind."

"What?" He was amazed.

"I'm trying to make up my mind," I said.

"Oh, for God's sake," he said, sounding disgusted. "Look, I'll have my secretary give you my address. You cable me what time tomorrow you'll arrive."

"Not tomorrow," I shouted. "The day after."

"O.K., but hurry up, kid."

"Why don't *you* give me your address?"

"I don't know it," he said. "Not tonight, anyway. Just hold on."

A very crisp English voice came onto the phone. "This is Jean Wilding, Mr. Wilson's secretary," the voice said. "Just wire us at Claridge's when you'll arrive."

"Is that where Mr. Wilson is staying?" I asked.

"Well, not tonight," she said. "But they'll forward all our messages for us."

"Where are you now?" I asked, out of idle curiosity.

"We're in Dorset," the girl said. "Mr. Wilson's been hunting with the Dorset's Blues, you know."

"Well, of course. I should have guessed it. I'll wire you."

"Thank you very much, Mr. Verrill."

"Are you going to Africa too?" I asked. It all sounded like one of Wilson's tiresome practical jokes.

"Well, I hope to," the girl said, and giggled. "We're working on Mr. Landau, and I hope he'll give in."

"He's not hunting, is he, Mr. Landau?"

"No, he's in London."

I heard Wilson say, "Give me the phone, honey," and then I heard his voice again: "Why ask so many damn fool questions? Get on the plane."

"All right, John," I said. Even if it was a joke, it would be worth the trip to see him again.

"Hurry up, kid. I'm anxious to see you."

"I'll be there," I told him, and hung up. The piano started immediately, continuing "La Vie en Rose" from the place where it had stopped. Well, I said to myself, I'll soon be away from all this anyway, away from the same songs and the same faces. Africa will be a change if nothing else. I had felt the mountains closing in on me for some time.

2

There was a chauffeur-driven Rolls-Royce waiting for me at Heath Row, and of course Miss Wilding. She was a pale, almost pretty English girl with bad teeth and a very jaunty, efficient manner.

"Isn't the weather lovely?" she said as we walked out to the car. "Did you have a pleasant flight?"

"Very pleasant." I must not become too British while I'm here, I told myself.

"Good," Miss Wilding said. "Now actually we thought about putting you up at Claridge's, but Mr. Wilson said he would rather have you stay with him, and so unless you have some objection . . ."

"I thought Mr. Wilson was staying at Claridge's."

"Well, he was," she laughed, pleased by some secret joke, "but he's got a house now. Someone loaned it to him. One of his social friends. You know John . . . I mean Mr. Wilson."

So he had already established his usual relationship with his secretary, I thought to myself. It didn't take him long. They were always in love with him, before they became the victims of his daily torture. Obviously Miss Wilding was just approaching the torture stage. That usually came immediately after they began calling him by his first name.

"Where to, miss?" the chauffeur asked.

"Eggerton Court. I hope you won't mind there not being too much hot water today," she said to me. "The boiler's on the blink."

"I guess I'll bear up," I answered, and thought longingly of Claridge's. One of the only pleasant things about working for the movies was that they always put you up at the best hotels, and now I was being denied that advantage.

"I wanted to hold your room at Claridge's, but Mr. Wilson was so adamant about canceling it . . . I think he's lonely, you know."

"It doesn't really matter."

"Well, I wouldn't say that. You see, there's another gentleman staying with Mr. Wilson . . ."

"But the room at Claridge's is no longer available, is it?"

"No, it isn't."

"Then let's not discuss it."

We drove on in silence. I offered her a piece of the chocolate bar I had brought with me from Switzerland, which she accepted eagerly.

"How is Mr. Landau?" I asked.

"Oh, he's fine."

"Is he getting along with Mr. Wilson?"

"Fairly well," she said. Landau was another one of Wilson's manifestations of character. After his most successful picture, when every studio in Hollywood had been after him, he had suddenly signed a contract with this mysterious Hungarian producer and founded his own company. It was another instance of his thumbing his nose at the mores of the community in which he lived. Once you had a hit, you always signed with a big studio for a lot of money and thereby insured your future. Wilson had signed with a man hardly anyone had ever heard of outside Budapest, whose financial background was one of the great mysteries of our time. Landau always ate in the best restaurants, rhumbaed in the most fashionable night clubs, and never allowed anyone else to pick up the check. However, it was quite commonly known that he usually had trouble paying the grocer and the butcher bills at the end of each month. Wilson had signed with him for four very theoretical pictures, the first one of which we had collaborated on. The name of their company was Sunrise Productions, although everyone always referred to it as Sunset, because it was obviously going down. I once asked him why he had signed with Landau and Sunrise, and he smiled his most affable, vague smile, and said: "Because it's the wrong thing to do, that's all," and there the matter had rested.

Later on, when I got to know Landau, I began to understand the whole thing a little better. Besides helping him along with his private program of self-destruction, Landau amused Wilson. He was a good target for practical jokes, and he had a truly charming manner, a sad continental grace and polish. He had the elaborate manners of a Hungarian cavalry officer, which he maintained despite his having survived a truly perilous past. The early Hungarian pogroms, as well as Hitler, had missed him by a hair, and although he now operated like a movie big shot, evidences of what had almost happened to him were constantly coming to the surface. Furthermore, he had one sterling quality which we all appreciated. Wherever he went, Landau always had access to four or five very beautiful girls, and he was never selfish about them.

"Are they really going to make a picture together?" I asked.

"I certainly hope so," the girl said, sounding very astonished. "And I can tell you that Mr. Reissar and Mr. Anders hope so too."

"Who are they?"

"The British producers," she said. It was obvious that she was not very impressed with my intelligence. "Have you worked in the film industry before?"

"Oh yes. Just not in England."

"Well, they're just about the best people we have left," she said haughtily.

"And they're putting up the money?"

"The British half, Mr. Landau is the American producer. It's the first interallied deal that's ever been made."

"Oh, I see. And how's the story?"

"Frightfully good." She sounded more surprised with

each one of my questions. "Haven't you read the book?"

"I think I have. What's it called again?"

The Trader."

"Oh yes. . . . It's about the racial problems in Africa, isn't it?"

"Not at all," she said. "It's a love story that plays among traders. The script is better than the novel. I have a copy for you, by the way, at the office."

"That's fine." We settled back in silence once more. "Would you like another piece of chocolate?" I asked after a while. We were rolling smoothly through the depressing outskirts of London.

"I would, rather," she said.

I broke off the second bribe. Then I waited while she munched on the chocolate. "Has Mr. Wilson been working hard on the script?" I asked then.

"Quite hard," she answered. "He's a man of very irregular habits, you know, and people don't think he's working, when actually he's thinking about the script all of the time. He's much the most fascinating man I've ever worked for."

"Has he been drinking a lot?"

"Not a lot," she said.

"Seeing many people?"

"Well, mostly the hunting crowd. He's very keen on it, you know. And he did jolly well up in Dorset."

"Did he stay on?"

"Well, he had one fall," she said in that wonderful, hollow British voice that makes all disaster sound trivial. "Got right up again, though, and caught up with the pack."

"That's not quite right, miss," the chauffeur said, leaning back through the glass partition. "He had another one after that, and we had a devil of a time catching his mount."

"Were you there, Ronald?" she asked haughtily.

"Yes'm. I drove him."

"H'mm, anyway, he did jolly well. Two falls are not so bad for the first hunt."

"He's a game chap, he is," Ronald observed.

"H'mm, yes." She made a face which indicated that she had had enough of Ronald's conversation. "Are we nearly there?"

"About ten more minutes, miss."

"Fine. Please hurry, will you, Ronald."

"I'm doing the best I can, miss."

He was doing jolly well, I thought, maneuvering the enormous, antiquated car through the narrow streets, backing up occasionally to let smaller, more mobile vehicles squirm around him like sardines passing a whale in a narrow, rocky corner of the ocean.

"He always knows everything better," Miss Wilding confided in a low voice. "But he *is* a good driver."

And he's not quite as much in love with Wilson as you are, I almost remarked. But I refrained from the observation. After all, I was in a foreign country, and furthermore we had arrived.

There was a slim park in the center of a small square of houses, and there were no shops. It was obviously an elegant district. Ronald held open the door of the car, and with Miss Wilding leading the way, we crossed a narrow sidewalk to a small wooden door with a very shiny brass knocker. Miss Wilding rang, and almost immediately a thin, gray-haired man in a white serving jacket opened for us.

"Hullo, George," Miss Wilding said. "This is Mr. Verrill. Is Mr. Wilson up?"

"Good morning, sir," George said very formally to me, and then to the secretary: "I don't believe so, madam. He had his breakfast, though."

We went up a steep stairway into a dark gray room which was incredibly furnished with ancient gold mirrors and white statuettes. It was Roman in spirit and Georgian in atmosphere, and smelled of stale cigarette smoke. On a pale silken couch a man in a dark blue suit was reading the morning paper. He got up and stared nervously at me through steel-rimmed glasses.

"This is Mr. Jules Randsome, Mr. Verrill," the girl said breezily. "You'll be seeing a lot of each other."

I shook hands with Mr. Randsome. He was a tall, haunted-looking man. He wore a blue shirt and a dark red tie, and he looked as if he had slept in his clothes on the very couch from which he had just risen.

"Have a good trip?" he asked.

"Yes, fine, thank you."

"Looks awfully well, doesn't he, Jeanie? Brought the

mountain air right with him into this room."

I wanted to say that I thought the room could well afford a little mountain air, but again I refrained. I was a guest in the house, and I wanted to get started on the right foot.

"John's upstairs waiting," Randsome said.

"Fine. We'll go up," Miss Wilding replied briskly. We started out of the room, toward the next stairway. "Any mail, Jeanie?" Randsome called after us.

"Nothing for you, Jules. Sorry."

We stopped, somewhat breathless, outside a cream-colored door, and Miss Wilding knocked.

"Come in," John's voice called faintly to us.

The first thing I saw was the bed. It was shaped like a coliseum cut in half, and was painted a very shiny silver, its walls rising upward in small, undulating silver waves. John Wilson was seated in the center of the curve of the coliseum, hunched over his breakfast tray and the morning paper. He wore a red silk pajama top which hung from his gaunt shoulders. His fine, graying hair was tousled on his head. He didn't look up.

"Mr. Verrill is here, Mr. Wilson," the girl said.

He glanced up quickly and grinned, and immediately I felt what I had felt so often on seeing him again: Here was a truly wonderful fellow, the best friend I had, delightful, entertaining, wise, perceptive, warmhearted. I even forgot that I had often had exactly the same feeling toward him before, only to want to escape him desperately not more than two weeks later.

"Well, Pete," he said. "For God's sake."

"Johnny." We shook hands and pounded each other's shoulders.

"Well, how the hell are you, kid?"

"I'm fine. How are you?"

"You look pretty good. I'd say you looked better than ever," he went on, scratching his head with a long, thin hand. "What the hell have you been doing with yourself?"

"Skiing. Sitting in the sun."

"Well, isn't that just swell." He grinned. "I've missed you, kid."

"I've missed you too, old boy."

"Well, what do you know. Old Pete," he said. "It's been a hell of a long time, hasn't it?"

"It certainly has."

"Well, what do you know." He rubbed his head again, grinning. "Want some coffee?"

"No, thanks."

"Well, what do you know?" He seemed content to beam and repeat himself. We both grinned at each other. "This is some joint," I said.

"Terrific, isn't it?" He smiled happily. "Have you seen the living room?"

"I sure have."

"Isn't it the most hideous place you've ever seen?"

"Fantastic."

"I'm just crazy about it," he said. Then suddenly an urgent thought seemed to take hold of his mind. "Go through that door over there into the closet, and have a look. Go on. Right away. And, Jeanie, you get the hell out of here. No work today." Miss Wilding withdrew petulantly.

"Right now?" I asked.

"Yes, right now. Go ahead."

I was mystified, but I did as I was told. I opened the closet door and there was a rather plain dressing room, with a mirror and a clothing rack.

"See anything?" he called after me.

"No."

"Look on the floor, kid."

I looked down at the floor. There was a saddle lying on its back, and a pair of black boots, and a pink coat, and cream-colored breeches.

"Your gear?"

"That's right. Bring me the coat and the hat." I found the black hunting cap and picked up the coat. He didn't say anything when I gave them to him. He put on the cap and slipped into the pink coat. Then he pushed his tray aside and got up. He had on white shorts. His long thin legs were slightly bowed.

"Isn't this the goddamnedest outfit you ever did see?" he asked.

"You look just great."

"You've got to get a suit like this."

"For Africa?"

"Well, of course." He climbed back into his bed. "I've been hunting every weekend. It's just wonderful, kid, and let me tell you something . . . these English fellows can't teach us anything. Not a damn thing."

Slowly and methodically, choosing his words with a great deal of thought, he told me about the hunt. At first the English people who had invited him had looked down their noses at him, and then ultimately they had been impressed. It had obviously been a weekend of conquest for Wilson.

"Sounds great," I said, once he had finished.

He lit a cigarette and shook his head. "Just terrific, kid," he said. "Now what about you? What about the book?"

"I didn't do much on it."

"Why not, kid? Or would you rather not talk about it?"

"I don't mind talking about it. I just couldn't get started . . . and then I got into trouble with a dame . . ."

"You did, eh?" he asked with concern. "Well, what do you know?" Then he roared with laughter. He felt a kindred spirit was there in the room facing him, only fifteen years younger, and all the troubles he had been in seemed to come back comically into his memory. "Bad trouble?"

"Unpleasant," I said. It was the understatement of the year.

"You don't say." He shook his head, and then he laughed again. "Good old Pete. It's just hell, isn't it, the whole thing."

"Not worth it," I said. "After it's all over you can never understand why it seemed so damn important."

"No, you can't," he said. "Nothing is tougher than remembering what made you chase the dame once you've had her."

"It was a lousy winter," I said. "I couldn't work, and I spent too much money and I didn't have a good time. I didn't even get to ski very much."

"Well, that's a shame, Pete," he said, exploding into laughter once again. "There's only one solution . . . Africa for you, kid." When he said Africa he seemed to give the word a greater meaning than it had ever had for me. He twisted his face slightly, and overpronounced it, and I had the spontaneous feeling of darkness and evil. Everything Conrad had said in thousands of words about the black stagnant river where Kurtz had died was echoed in Wilson's pronunciation of the name of that continent. I saw

twisted trees and jungle and black rivers, and I felt quite
strongly that I really didn't want to go there at all.

"You really think it'll help me with my problems?"

"Even if it doesn't, you've got to go." He straightened
in bed. "There are times in your life when you can't even
ask yourself is this wrong or right, clever or dumb. Not
guys like you and me, kid. You've just got to pack up and
go, that's all."

"What about my book?"

"Well, if you didn't write it last winter, you just weren't
ready to write it, that's all."

He always managed to make me feel better about myself, made me find new hope. "You really think so, John?"
I asked doubtfully.

"I know so," he said. "You see, someday you'll write
that book. But you'll have to give up thinking about everything else, about form or story or if people will want to
read it. You'll just have to risk all those things and just
put down what you know. That's all. All the things you've
learned. And then it'll be something . . . believe me, kid.
The other stuff is all phony; the slick, carefully planned
jobs. Phony as far as you're concerned anyway. You're
the kind of writer that just has to jump into it, try to fly,
or crawl or sing or Christ knows what."

I felt fine. Form had always baffled me. What he suggested is what I always hoped would happen to me, exactly as it had happened with my first book. I had simply
written it. It had just happened. By suggesting a similar
treatment now, he managed to cure all the doubts that
the winter in the snow had caused me to have about myself. He also made me forget my fears about Africa. He
was right about my work. He would probably be right
about my life.

"When would we leave?" I asked hesitantly.

"Well, we'll work here for a week or ten days, and then
perhaps I'll go ahead on a survey trip while you do a little work on the script. Two weeks after I'm down there
you'll join me, and that's it."

"How long will we stay?" I asked.

"Long as it takes to make the picture and do some hunting. Three months, four months . . . maybe longer than
that."

April May, June, July, I counted mentally. I would come

straight from the heat of Africa to the heat of Europe. No spring touring in the Alps, no Paris in May and June.

"Are you worried about staying too long, kid?" he asked me.

"No," I lied. "I was just trying to figure out my schedule."

"We'll be back here in August," he said. "Then I'll get Laurene and we'll take a couple of cars and we'll drive all over Italy and cure our marriages."

"All right," I said doubtfully, "but I'll have to make some kind of a financial arrangement with Landau."

"Oh, that's no problem," he said, laughing happily. "You know Paul."

"I know Paul," I said gloomily.

"It'll just be a great thing to have done, kid," he said. He obviously didn't want to dwell too long on the financial end of the affair.

"You think he'll want to pay my way and my salary?"

"Oh sure. There's no problem."

"How do you stand financially?"

"Nothing has changed."

"Are you very broke?"

"Well, that all depends on what you mean by very broke, kid," he said with mock seriousness. "I owe about a quarter of a million dollars. Now for a guy like Baruch that would seem like nothing at all."

"A quarter of a million dollars?"

"Closer to three hundred thousand."

I was amazed. I knew he wasn't lying. "Does it worry you?" I asked.

"Yes, I think about it every once in a while."

"Do you see a way out of it?"

"This picture, maybe. And if not this one, maybe the next one."

"Holy smoke, John," I said.

He grinned suddenly. "You see why I want to go to Africa, kid. I've got very little to lose. Even if a lion does get me, or a buffalo, my last minute on earth will be a very happy one. I'll think of all my creditors back in the States when they hear I've been eaten alive. That'll make it all seem worth while."

3

My heart sank a little. There was an element of truth in what he said. He was accustomed to being reckless; and I knew that part of his reason for going to Africa was a secret desire to risk his life. Like most of us, he had read Hemingway and had been influenced by him, had accepted the romanticism of that style of living. John Wilson wanted to prove himself, and to disprove others; I was almost certain of that. I had known a few men like that during the war, most of whom had not read Hemingway, but who had been constantly tempted by the same illusion, and the thing that had struck me about almost all of their ultimate fates was that they usually survived, and that the people who went with them very often didn't make it back. I knew a major in a Marine parachute battalion who was like that. He had volunteered time and again for the most dangerous assignments, and a good many of the boys had been caught up by his spirit of daring and had gone with him and had not returned. I thought about him now, as I watched John dress.

"Are you sure I can be of some use on the picture?" I asked. "I don't want to just go along for the ride."

"Why not?"

"I wouldn't feel right about taking the money."

"Oh, you've changed, kid," Wilson said. "That Alpine scenery has done things to you."

"I'm not kidding, John."

"I'm not either," he said seriously. "You think I'd ask you to go along just for the ride?"

"I'm not sure."

"Oh, for God's sake, Pete." He pulled a light pink shirt over his thin shoulders. "You must think I've lost my mind. Sure you can help me."

"Have you got a copy of the script here?"

"I'm not sure."

"I'd better read it, I guess."

"Well, it might throw you off, altogether."

"Is it any good, John?"

"Well, you read it. Then we'll talk about it."

But he couldn't find a copy anywhere in the house once he was dressed. Jules Randsome wandered around trying to help him with the search, as did Miss Wilding. Wilson grew irritable.

"You're a hell of a secretary, Jeanie. What do you do all day long?"

"I've been typing your letters, as a matter of fact," she said in an injured voice, "and I've been answering the phone."

"Balls."

"I have, haven't I, Jules?"

"Yes, she has, John. She's been awfully busy," Randsome mumbled.

"Don't help the bitch lie," Wilson said. He was enjoying his little torture treatment. "God damn it, when you came here you were a competent secretary," he went on. "Now you're just a lazy slut, hanging around here all day spying on me for Landau . . ."

"That isn't true, Mr. Wilson," the girl said heatedly. "I don't spy for anyone, especially not Mr. Landau."

"Well, find the script, then, for God's sake," he said, searching through an enormous pile of submitted manuscripts. "Don't just follow me around apologizing for yourself."

The search went on for another few minutes and then Wilson gave up. He told Miss Wilding to get several new copies, and to be sure to give one to me.

"Well," he said with a satisfied air once this had been decided upon, "shall we all go out and have a little drink?"

"You've got an appointment at a quarter to twelve, Mr. Wilson," Miss Wilding said sternly.

"Have I? Where?"

"You told me not to make public gossip out of your life."

"That was in reference to Landau. Don't make a mystery of things in front of my friends."

"I'm not making a mystery of things," the girl said. "You're to be at your tailor's."

"Well, we've got time for one drink, for God's sake."

"I know that."

"Well, then why did you bring it up? The little bitch is just getting to be impossible, isn't she, Jules?"

"H'mmm, quite difficult."

"All right for you, Jules," Miss Wilding said. She went upstairs to get her things. Wilson put on a tweed hacking coat and a small tweed cap.

"Just look at this, kid," he said, adjusting the angle of the cap in front of the hall mirror.

"Holy God," I said. "We'll have to fight our way out of the house."

He grinned happily. "Isn't it just swell," he said. "You've got to get one, kid."

"I guess I do," I said, "if I want to go anywhere with you."

"It's the new look," Randsome mumbled incoherently. "Drainpipe trousers and flaring coats."

"If you're an officer in the Guards," I said, "but not if you're a Hollywood movie director."

"Don't argue with him, Jules," John said imperiously. "The poor ignorant bastard will be wearing something like this himself before long."

We went to the local pub and had a drink. Everyone stared at us, and I couldn't blame them. Randsome looked like a hobo, while Wilson looked like an American version of a spiv. Miss Wilding and I just looked as if we didn't belong.

We ignored the stares of the natives and drank warm beer. Wilson continued to bait his secretary. Once we had finished the first round, two or three more of Wilson's acquaintances turned up. They all had one thing in common: the glazed early morning look of people who have spent the night drinking.

"You look a sight, John old boy," one of them said. Wilson told me that he was a movie columnist on a London paper. To me he looked like a refugee from a saber duel. His face was full of cuts, partially healed.

"I'm glad you approve," Wilson told him. "What the hell happened to your face?"

"Forgot to screw in the blade on my bloody razor," the Englishman replied. "Suddenly saw I was all over blood. Couldn't have been more surprised."

Wilson roared with laughter. They continued talking about how drunk they had all been the previous night. "Aren't these just a bunch of wonderful guys," Wilson said enthusiastically to me out of the corner of his mouth.

"Characters," I answered. I was longing to get out of there. "What about your tailor?"

"That's right. We've got to go."

"Shall I come with you?" Miss Wilding asked.

"What the hell for?" Wilson asked.

"Well, Mr. Landau said I was responsible for you to-day. That if you didn't turn up at Claridge's at six for the meeting I'd be fired."

"You know what you should tell Mr. Landau?"

"That's all very well for you to say," the girl whined, "but I'm the one that's for it every time you don't turn up."

"You tell me the next time Landau makes trouble," Wilson said menacingly. "Come on, Pete, let's go."

We walked to the tailor's. On the way Wilson told me about the early years of his life, which he had spent in London. He had been terribly poor and out of a job, and had taken to rolling drunks and fairies in Hyde Park. I had heard the stories before, but they sounded much better told in their actual locale.

"Why didn't you write home for money?" I asked him. I knew that his father had been a fairly wealthy business-man in Ohio.

"Have *you* ever done that?" he asked me.

"No, but I've never rolled drunks, either."

"But you would, wouldn't you, kid, if you had to. You'd do that rather than ask your father for help?"

"I don't know."

He thought I was trying to provoke him. "Oh, come on," he said. "You know you would. *I* know you would." It was just another instance of his being persistently mistaken about me. I let the matter rest.

We went into Tautz's, where a rather elegantly dressed lady was sitting, obviously waiting for someone. She rose when she saw Wilson.

"Irene," Wilson said with surprise. "Well, for God's sake." He introduced me.

"I suppose you forgot that we had a date to meet here," the lady said.

"Not at all, honey. Not at all." She turned out to have a title, and she looked fabulously wealthy.

"You're a terrible liar, John," she said.

He ignored her. He was already fascinated by the various bolts of material on the table in front of him. He waved us over to him. "Now come on, guys, help me choose."

He ordered three suits, all with drainpipe trousers and flaring hacking coats. Then he tried on a pair of riding breeches, which he had ordered before. I watched him as he stood in front of the mirror in the half-finished riding breeches, his thin legs sticking out like matchsticks. He seemed not at concerned that he looked ridiculous.

"You've got to get some of this stuff," he said to me. "You've just got to."

"Not today," I answered.

"He's really one of the best sporting tailors in the world," the lady said.

"*The* best," Wilson added. The tailor looked pleased. I hoped the little man would remember this pleasant hour later on while he was waiting to be paid.

"Now there's one more thing I'd like you to make for me," Wilson said, once he had changed back to his street clothes. "I want three pair of very light breeches made of twill, to be worn with leggings. I'm going to Africa, you see . . ."

"Very well, sir," the tailor said. "I'll show you the material I have."

I was busy making mental calculations of what Wilson had just spent. It was probably right around five hundred dollars.

"You should really have a couple of light shooting jackets," the lady said, "of the same material. They'll be awfully comfortable."

"H'mm, that's true," he answered. "Can you get all of it ready in time?"

"We'll do our best," the little man answered.

"I know you will." John smiled. Their one-sided love affair was progressing nicely.

We left the tailor, and John decided it was time to have lunch. I agreed with him. It was after one-thirty. John suggested going to the Caprice.

"All you picture people like only two places in every city of the world," the lady complained. "In New York it's Twenty-one and the Cub Room. In Paris it's the Tour d'Argent and La Méditerranée, and in London it's Les Ambassadeurs or the Caprice."

John winked at me, and gave me a very obvious poke with his elbow. "You can tell this broad has been around," he said, and then turning to her with an equally obvious smile, he asked: "And where would you like to go, dear?"

She shook her head, smiling. "You're really awful, John," she said. "But there are a lot of nice places in London. The Ward Room, for instance. I'm a member there."

"All right," John said. "Let's go to your joint." He had shifted into his role of the tough. "Anything you say, doll, is okay with my pal and me."

The lady was not enjoying herself. We went to the Ward Room and John continued with his act. He said pal to the headwaiter, and asked to have the word "entrecôte" explained to him.

"Well, why don't they say steak, if that's what it is. What a phony front they got in this joint."

"John, really," the lady said. She was scarlet. "He's not actually like this," she said to the headwaiter.

"Yeah, I'm usually a right guy, but all this fancy stuff throws me."

After we had ordered, which was a long, complicated performance, in which every plate on the menu was discussed and which ended with John choosing grapefruit and steak, he started to move in on the lady, who seemed to regret her invitation thoroughly by now. He made an obvious play for her, including me as a partner in his performance.

"Isn't she just the swellest-looking broad you ever did see, Pete?" he would ask again and again.

She could only say: "Really, John," and look nervously around the room. She didn't understand why he was suddenly behaving this way. I knew. He was punishing her for complaining about his choice of restaurant.

Finally coffee arrived. John took one sip and shook his head. "Damnedest stuff I ever had in my mouth," he said. "They musta just scooped it up out of the gutter."

He snapped his fingers at the headwaiter. "Say, pal, I'd like to ask you something," he said. The headwaiter came over to our table rather reluctantly. "What do they get for this brew?" Wilson asked.

"Excuse me, sir?"

"What's the rap for the coffee?"

"I'm afraid I don't quite understand," the headwaiter said.

"I'm speaking English, ain't I, Pete?" Wilson asked aggressively.

"Sure you are. You're speaking U.S.A.," I said.

"Mr. Wilson is joking," the lady explained weakly. "He would like to know how much the coffee is. The price."

"The price, madam?"

"Forget it, pal," Wilson said, enervated.

The headwaiter moved away. Wilson doubled up with laughter. "Oh, God, isn't he wonderful?" he said. "I'm sure he's called the bobby, just to be on the safe side."

"I don't think it's as funny as all that," the lady said.

"Would you like it to stop?"

"I certainly would."

"O.K., we stop."

Accent and act vanished. The lady began to thaw visibly. Wilson looked at his watch.

"Good God, is it almost three o'clock?"

"Sure, we only started to eat at one-thirty."

"Well, we've got to run, kid. Get the check."

I coughed self-consciously. "I only arrived this morning," I said. "I have no pounds."

"You haven't?" He looked truly dismayed, and began to search through his pockets. "I've only got about thirty shillings."

"Maybe they'll let you sign," I suggested.

"Oh sure. They're bound to. Or we'll break up the joint."

The lady was pretending that she had not heard our conversation. John realized that she had. He moved closer to her, playing the coquette. "Honey," he said, "are you any good at washing dishes?"

"What, John?" She spoke rather sharply to him now.

"My pal and I are busted, flat broke. Could you advance us ten pounds?"

"John, are you joking?"

He laughed helplessly. "I wish I were. I came out without any money."

"I have no money either," she said. "But I can sign."

"I thought you could," John said. He winked at me. "Real class," he said. "I told you so."

"John, please don't start that again," the lady said. She called for the check and signed it. John gave the head-waiter a pound note.

"That's because you've been such a brick," he said.

"Excuse me, sir?"

"I thought sure you said 'brick,' John," I added. We roared; two happy idiots. Our hostess was already flee-ing across the thick crimson carpet. We caught up with her on the ground floor. The manager was just bowing her out of the place. John put on his tweed cap.

"Dear," he called after her. "Just a minute."

"What is it, John?"

"We'd like cigars, and then I wonder if you couldn't get me a guest membership here?"

"I don't think so, John."

"Oh, it could be arranged, madam," the manager said. He had not witnessed our performance upstairs. John was inscribed as a temporary member of the club, and we each got a cigar.

We lit them outside on the sidewalk, very pleased with ourselves.

"You're awful, both of you." The lady smiled. "Really, John. I've never been so embarrassed in my life."

"Really, dear? I thought it was a lovely lunch, didn't you, Pete?"

"Smashing."

"First-rate." He took off his cap and bowed elaborately. "Thank you so much, dear."

"Don't you want a cab?" she asked.

"We can't afford it," he said.

The doorman opened the door of a taxi for her. She got in, looking more confused than ever.

"I'll call you," John said. She didn't answer. She waved vaguely and was gone. John grinned happily. "Isn't that just a swell gal?" he said.

"Very nice, but I'm afraid you've seen the last of her."

"Not a chance," he said confidently. "She just won't take us to any place where she's known after this."

"Well, where to now?" I asked.

"Let's go back in and have a drink," he said. "I can sign now."

We had a brandy at the bar downstairs and then walked briskly through the London streets. In a few minutes we were lost. John was telling me one of his war stories as we moved deeper and deeper into unknown territory. It was getting dark when Wilson finally became concerned with our geographic position. He scratched his head.

"Where the hell are we?" he asked, puzzled.

"I haven't any idea, but I know that it's after six and you're supposed to be back at the hotel for a conference."

We hailed a taxi and asked the driver to take us to Claridge's. The hotel turned out to be less than five blocks away.

"You know, if they put out all the lights in this damn city," Wilson said to me, "I could find my way around again."

The conference in Landau's suite had not started as yet, although a few people were already there having drinks. I was introduced to two very nice-looking Englishmen, who turned out to be Anders and Reissar, the producers. They shook hands politely, and said that they were glad to see me. I was amazed that anyone should have mentioned my name to them. Anders was the older one of the two. He looked like a lawyer, with a thin, intelligent face and dark, carefully combed hair. Reissar was obviously the artist of the combination. He had soft brown eyes and wavy blond hair. He could be a young poet, I thought to myself. How different it was from Hollywood, where the producers were always overly elegant and sunburned and usually not too pleased to see any intruder.

Landau was puffing on a cigar. He was as elegant as ever in a dark blue suit with a shiny blue tie held in a rippled gold tie clasp; the whole outfit a little too neat, too tailored, and too new. He put a large, warm hand on my arm and drew me off to one side. I remembered that this was a distinguishing characteristic of the man. He always had to hold onto anyone with whom he spoke, for fear that he would somehow get away from him before he was quite finished, a habit undoubtedly acquired because people had walked away from him so often.

"I'm so glad to see you, Pete . . . I can't tell you," he said.

"I'm glad to see you too, Paul."

"You can save all our lives."

"Really? How?" I was astonished by such an abrupt, tragic beginning.

"The ogre," he said. It was his nickname for Wilson. "I think he's losing his mind."

"Don't be ridiculous. He seems in great shape."

"You've only been with him one day," Landau said, his voice rising perceptibly. "You don't know what he's like."

"He hasn't changed, Paul. You're just getting tired, that's all." I could see Wilson mixing a cocktail across the room. More men were arriving every minute.

"He's changed, I tell you," Landau said. "I'm sure of it. He's changed and it isn't for the better."

"What has he done?"

"Everything," Landau said, breathing heavily. "He's almost killed the deal five times. The only reason it's still going is because of me."

"And because he wants to go to Africa."

"That's right. But still I'm working like a dog to keep it from blowing up. You have no idea of what's gone on. No idea . . ."

"He doesn't work."

"Of course not. But that's not the worst of it. He's just crazy, I tell you. He looks at me with open hatred, and whatever I say he's automatically on the other side. I can't stay in the same room with him for more than an hour. And the strange thing is I'm beginning to hate him too. You know how it was a few years ago when we made the picture in Hollywood. We were all friends. Sure, he tortured me . . . but we were friends. Now he loathes me. That's why I had the idea to call you. To take my place. To be my representative in Africa." He pushed me away with his clutching hand. Wilson was approaching.

"Hello, Paul," he said pleasantly.

"Hello, Johnny boy," Landau replied, his voice full of love and tenderness. "Did you have a good day? Get a lot done?"

"Well, Pete and I had a long talk," Wilson said.

"What do you think of the script?" Landau asked me.

"I'll talk to you about it later," I said. Wilson and I had always operated behind a united front. We covered for each other automatically, sensing the necessity whenever it arose. That's why I was amazed that Landau had consented to having me work on the picture. He was not gaining an ally, he was hiring an accomplice for his enemy.

"I think it's awfully good," Landau said.

"You do, eh?" Wilson said. "You really do, Paul? Isn't it a shame you don't know a damn thing about it." He turned and walked away. Landau's mouth tightened as he tried to control his temper.

"You see," he said in a low voice, clutching me again. "Exactly what I told you."

"But that's nothing new," I replied. "He's always been like that."

Landau shook his head. "No, he's worse than ever. You've got to understand that, or you won't be able to help me at all. He's insane. In a well-ordered society he'd be in a strait jacket right now."

4

The conference began in a most gentlemanly fashion. I was amazed once more at what a wonderfully polite people the British were. Everyone waited for his turn to speak. No one interrupted anyone else. It didn't matter whether the man who had the floor was a technician or a producer, the others listened attentively and waited until he was finished to express their doubts or convictions. Fielding, the cameraman, talked a little too much and made his points too slowly, but everyone bore up just the same. Basil Owen, the unit manager, on the other hand, was cold and precise in his statements and it was obvious from the start that he had done a good deal of thinking about all of the problems that were now being discussed.

At first there was a short debate about the size of the crew that was to go to Africa. John referred all questions back to whatever technical department heads were present, and agreed with whatever they asked for. They liked him for it. I remember that the crews in Hollywood had always loved Wilson and had worked themselves half to death whenever he had asked them to do so. In that he was the new type of movie director, in direct contrast to the old-fashioned sound-stage dictator that the early years of the movies had made popular. A good many people in Hollywood felt that he was too nice to the crews, that he spent too much time amusing them with practical jokes, and catered too much to their whims, but I must say I always felt that in this respect he was a model director. He was nice to everyone and everyone who worked with him was eager to do so again. At the same time he was definite and unwavering in what he wanted. He was like a perfect company commander. The troops loved him, but they never took advantage of his seemingly lax discipline. He relegated authority and was usually correct in his estimate of the people in whom he put his trust. And when the critical battle came, everyone was willing to die for him. It was obvious that even if Landau's accusations of his growing madness were true, they did not influence this phase of his work.

The conference branched out into the financial complications, which were still in the hands of the lawyers. Someone brought up the question of hiring a well-known English actor for a supporting part, and Anders stated that they were not yet in a position to make financial commitments with actors. Wilson looked amazed.

"Well, why is that, Roger?" he asked in his most agreeable voice. "I thought all that had been straightened out."

"The American backers still insist on some kind of war-protection clause," Anders said. "Of course the British backers can't give way on that. They're not frightened of the possibility of war, but they can't guarantee that it won't happen."

"H'mmm," John said. "When will that be settled?"

"We're working on it," Landau interrupted nervously. "I guarantee that it will be settled this week."

"You do, eh, Paul?" Wilson said. I could tell that there was a certain bite in his voice. "Are you going to give Stalin a piece of the picture?"

There was general laughter. Landau blushed. "I tell you it will be attended to," he said firmly.

"All right, Paul," Wilson said falsely, "we'll depend on you." He turned to the rest of the room. "It's wonderful the influence Paul has everywhere in the world. He's just the best kind of partner a man could have."

There was more laughter. Then Reissar brought up the

question of color. Immediately the room grew tense. Color was a tremendous extra expense and, as far as the British partners were concerned, of questionable value at the box office. Landau wanted color. It was worth half a million dollars at least, he explained.

"That's unimportant," Wilson said. "What I want to hear from Ralph Fielding is whether color complicates our operation."

"I'm afraid it does, John," Fielding said. "The camera is much heavier, and there are many more light problems, of course."

"That's what I thought," Wilson said. "I've never made a picture in color, but I've been told it makes things much more difficult."

The English producers exchanged meaningful glances.

"Color is essential to the success of the picture," Landau said heatedly.

"In America," Anders said.

"We're not concerned with the success of the venture as yet," Wilson said pointedly. "I know how easy it is to get bogged down on location . . ."

"Bogged down?" the English partners said in one unified, horror-stricken voice.

"Yes. That's the biggest danger that confronts a company on location. I know how it is . . ."

"Have you ever been bogged down, John?" Landau asked rhetorically.

"No, but I've never worked with Technicolor either," Wilson said.

"But why bring it up, if it's never happened to you?" Landau asked angrily.

"Because it could happen."

"I think it's a very valid point," Reissar said above the murmurings of the others.

"I don't think so," Landau maintained.

"I know you don't think so," Wilson snapped back at him. "It won't affect you. We'll be down in the heart of Africa, sweating and killing ourselves, and you'll be in Paris sending cables."

"That's not true. How can you say that?" The two American partners had risen, and were pacing angrily around the room. "I'll be right there in Africa with you."

"You will, eh?" Wilson snarled. "Like hell you will."

"If the picture were to be shot on a river in England, and a second unit were sent to Africa," Fielding said timorously, "the risk of using color would be greatly minimized."

"Well, in that case you'll all have to look for another director," Wilson said.

The English partners rose now. The entire deal was slowly blowing up into thin air.

"But we've discussed doing just that," Anders said with surprise.

"Without me, God damn it," Wilson replied.

"John," Landau said firmly. "Will you come into my bedroom for just a minute."

Wilson looked poisonously at his partner. "Sure," he said. "I'd hate to punch you in the nose in front of all these people."

He started toward the nearest door. "That's a closet," someone warned, and he turned away just in time.

"Pete," Landau called out. "You come with us." The Imperial Powers were calling for Italy's entry into the First World War, I thought glumly to myself.

"Why me?" I asked.

"I said come with us," Landau insisted.

I rose and smiled at the astonished Englishmen present. "American conference of three," I announced. Everyone laughed nervously.

"God help the Empire," Anders said.

We went into the bedroom. Landau's bed was turned down. A pair of white silk pajamas with red trimmings were lying on the chair beside the bed. Wilson went into the bathroom, leaving the door open. Landau followed him. Most of their quarrel took place there, with Wilson standing with his back to his partner.

"What the hell is the matter with you?" Landau said in a guarded voice, controlling his anger. "You want to kill the deal?"

"No, I don't want to kill the deal," Wilson said. He seemed strangely calm. But then he was busy.

"Then why bring up the possibility of bogging down? You scared the bejesus out of them. And telling them you'll quit if the picture is made partly in England. Good God, John."

"If the picture is to be shot in England, I will quit," Wilson said. "I'll put it in writing if you like."

"But it won't be."

"You discussed the possibility of it . . . behind my back, you son of a bitch."

"I didn't mention it to you because there isn't a chance in the world that it will be done that way."

"You guarantee it, I suppose."

"Yes, God damn it, I guarantee it."

"Well, your guarantee doesn't mean a damn thing to me," he said, turning angrily, and adjusting his trousers. "I'm not going to make a fake, crappy mess just to please you. I don't care if it's in black or white or in sepia or if we have to make the whole damn thing in animation, we're going to Africa."

"I tell you you'll get your way. Only don't screw up everything and talk about bogging down and quitting."

"We might bog down!"

"A snake might bite the leading lady, too, but why mention it now!"

"That's what this conference was called for, wasn't it? To discuss the difficulties we might encounter."

"Sure it was, but we're still not going to give way on color. If you want to throw a million dollars out of the window. . ."

"Don't give me that crap, Paul, God damn it," Wilson screamed, clenching his fists. "Don't try to soft-soap me. Just tell me what gives, that's all. If we're trying to put one over on these guys, just say so, and I'll know to keep my mouth shut, but don't try to rope us all in with your goddam lies."

"I didn't lie."

"You discussed making the thing in England behind my back!"

"And you took their side against me in the color question. You're supposed to be my partner!"

"Don't think I'm not sorry about it!"

"Hey, fellows," I said, "I think you'd better lower your voices." There was a brief silence.

"You behave like a goddam maniac," Landau said, and sat down on his bed.

"You behave like a goddam crook," Wilson replied. He moved forward threateningly. "I'm not going to play the fall guy for you, Paul," he warned. It was a line out of one of his best pictures.

"You won't have to," Landau said. "I took the fall when I signed our contract."

"Let's join the gentlemen," I said. "We've been gone an awfully long time."

Wilson unclenched his fists. "Pete's right," he said. "Come on. But next time you try to put one over on me and I find it out, I'm going to bust you, so help me God, in front of everyone."

"You bust me and I'll sue you for every cent you have," Landau said. "Or every cent you'll ever make," he corrected himself. He got up slowly and followed Wilson into the other room. I went in after them.

"Well, how about a drink all around, and then a little dinner," I heard Wilson say in his most charming voice. Everyone agreed that this was an excellent idea.

I think none of the difficulties that face us are insurmountable," Anders said calmly.

"Of course not," Landau agreed.

"Don't you think we have a chance to make a wonderful picture, Mr. Verrill?" Reissar asked me.

"If you make it in Africa," I answered. Italy, for what she was worth, had joined the side of the Allies.

Dinner was served. As usual, Landau had arranged everything beautifully. There was a long table presided over by the British producers. The rest of the technicians and department heads were ranged along both sides. Wilson was seated near the head of the table. I was down at the far end, next to Landau. Although the food was not brilliant, it was quite good, and the wine was excellent. Landau proposed a toast.

"To our British co-workers and friends," he said. Everyone raised his glass. It was really quite a nice gesture. "Hands across the sea." Landau added after he had sipped his wine.

Wilson rose. I could see that he was not entirely sober. He swayed a little. "I want to propose a toast too," he said. There was a silence, as he raised his glass. "I want to drink . . . to my partner," he said. "I hope I don't have to kill the son of a bitch before it's all over."

Landau sat blushing among the laughter of the guests. Despite the vague threat, he was touched and pleased. He had obviously chosen to disregard the sarcasm with which the toast had been proposed.

"We've come through a lot together, Paul old boy,

haven't we," Wilson called across the table.

"We certainly have, baby," Landau called back. They seemed both to be caught up in a vague kind of nostalgia that rekindled their love momentarily.

"Old Paul and I have taken some of the biggest guys for the biggest rides," Wilson went on. There was more laughter. "Never got a chance to operate in England, did we, Paul?"

"No. We never did. But we're here now," Landau chuckled. He was very ill at ease.

"Let's drink to Old Bailey, then," Wilson said.

Everyone except Landau was enjoying himself immensely. They had all come out of fairly well-regulated pasts. They had not been menaced by concentration camps and secret police, and so joking about jail was easy for them. I noticed that Landau seemed to have lost his appetite. He devoted himself entirely to directing the waiters, disregarded his own plate in front of him. The conversation at the other end of the table turned once more to the adventure that lay before them all.

I was struck again by the cheerful spirit that existed among the entire company. They all faced hard work, separation from their families, and possible dangers, and yet they all seemed eager to start on the project. I was used to Hollywood, which has a much more professional atmosphere. At a dinner or a conference like this one, nobody would be wildly enthusiastic or gay. They would all have had too many memories of strenuous locations to be fooled by false enthusiasm.

"I think you've got a great crew, Paul," I said to Landau.

He nodded. "If the captain of the ship were not nuts, I wouldn't be worried at all," he replied in a low voice.

"That's a thing with you, Paul," I said. "Get over it. He's one of the best in the business. And he's brilliant and talented to boot. You're just sour on him, that's all."

"I know him," Paul said pessimistically.

Wilson's voice floated down toward our end of the table. "Look at my partner now," he said, "trying to turn one of my oldest friends against me. Look at the bastard. My own sleek Cassius there, with a hungry look. Hungry, but he can't eat."

There was more laughter. Wilson was enjoying a great success at the cost of his associate.

"See what I mean?" Landau said to me.

"It's a good line, though," I said. "Hungry but he can't eat."

"Better than any line in the script," Landau said. He had obviously forgotten that he had told me that he thought it was an excellent adaptation.

We finished dinner, and the conference broke up. Quite a bit had been accomplished. The entire crew had been decided on; the color issue was going in Landau's favor, and the venture itself seemed really to be getting under way. Reissar and Anders invited us out for a drink.

We went to a night club. That was another important aspect of the London period, as I remember it now. We always seemed to end our evenings in night clubs, always as the guests of the two Englishmen. They probably thought that Hollywood people expected to end their every day in that fashion.

The place we went that first night of my brief stay in England was somehow strangely symbolic, for the high point of the floor show was a weird, awful act in which an enormous ape chased a beautiful half-naked girl around the dark interior of the club. She ran screaming through the maze of tables, and finally the ape caught her, in the center of the floor, and pulled off her veils. Primitive nature vanquished beautiful civilization, violated her, and carried her off to his lair. It was awful and funny. Wilson enjoyed himself immensely. The extreme bad taste of the act convulsed him with laughter.

"Wasn't that something, kid?" he grinned, once the lights were turned on again, and the better-dressed apes of London night life had taken over the floor. "Doesn't that just make you long for the dark continent?"

"Oh sure," I said. "We'll have something like that going night and day."

"That's right," Wilson said in mock seriousness. "You know, kid, we may like it so much down there, we may never want to come back."

"Well, some of us, anyway," I told him. I was only worried that the one who would not come back might be me.

He stretched. An ape on skis was chasing me down an endless mountain, and when he finally caught me he looked like a weird combination of Wilson and Landau. I woke with a start, and tried to remember just where I was. He was cold and hungry and uncomfortable. I was in London, of course, I said to myself, and closed my eyes.

5

The script with a note attached to its cover was lying next to my bed when I got home. Miss Wilding had done her job. "I hope you like it as much as I do," her note to me said, but I was much too tired to investigate this. I stretched out between the cold sheets on the converted couch and went to sleep. I had a nightmare, which was to be expected. An ape on skis was chasing me down an endless mountain, and when he finally caught me he looked like a weird combination of Wilson and Landau. I woke with a start, and tried to remember just where I was. I was cold and hungry and uncomfortable. Oh yes, London, of course, I said to myself, and closed my eyes.

The butler woke me at eight-fifteen with a cup of hot tea. A few minutes later John appeared. He was fully dressed, neat and sober-looking in a tweed jacket and gray flannel trousers.

"I'm shooting a color test this morning at the studio," he said. "Want to go?"

"I'd better not. I'll stay and read the script."

"O.K. But there's no hurry, you know."

"There is if you want to start shooting May first," I replied.

He shrugged. "That's a date Paul made up," he said.

"I think I'll stay here anyway. What time will you be back?"

"Oh, about one," he said. "There's a girl coming to lunch. Talk to her in case I'm late, will you?"

Miss Wilding appeared in the room. "We're all ready, Mr. Wilson," she said.

"That bitch is still tailing me," he said. "All right, dear. I'm coming."

"Will you be needing a secretary today?" she asked me.

"Of course he won't," Wilson said. "He's just going to read the damn thing."

"I thought he might want to dictate his criticism."

"Stop thinking. That's not what you're being paid to do."

"God, he's difficult," the girl said.

He gave her a long, doubtful look, and began playing a small scene for my benefit. "That's because I'm so nuts about you," he said. "I'm hiding my true feelings." He leaped at her, and she screamed. He roared with laughter.

"Oh, you are a beast," she said, laughing halfheartedly.

He put his arm affectionately around her shoulders. "Poor little Jeanie. Would you rather go back and work for Landau?"

"Not for all the money in the world," she said. "Do hurry, please."

I watched them get into the Rolls-Royce that was waiting for them in front of the house. Wilson allowed her to get into the limousine first, which gave him the opportunity to look carefully and lovingly at her behind. Then he winked at the chauffeur and jumped in after her. The chauffeur shook his head, grinning, and closed the door. They drove off.

I shaved and dressed and went upstairs into the living room. Randsome got up slowly from the couch.

"Have a good night's sleep?" he asked.

"Fair," I said. "What about you?"

"All right. Went to bed awfully late. John insisted on playing poker with Jeanie and me until three-thirty this morning."

"Was she waiting here for him last night?"

"Yes. He told her he might want to work after the conference, and so the poor child waited. I suppose he forgot all about her during the day."

That was typical of Wilson. He had probably intended to work but had forgotten, and finding the secretary there late at night, he had felt guilty. In order to make up for his rudeness and indifference he had played poker with her and Randsome.

"Where did Jeanie stay, then?"

"On the couch, here."

"The poor girl."

"Oh, I think she likes it," Randsome said. "She's lonely, you know, and quite smitten with John, and an hour spent with him is worth twelve hours of waiting."

"She'll collapse before the picture is finished."

"Oh, I don't think so. She's quite strong, really." He stood hesitantly in front of the couch, waiting to see what I was going to do. I stood well away from him, rather undecided myself.

"Will you have a little drink," he asked me, "or are you starting to work this morning?"

"I don't think I'm ready for a drink yet. I'm going to read the script."

"Well, then let's plan to go to the pub around twelve after you've finished."

"We'll see," I said. "I think there's a friend of John's coming to lunch."

He was obviously a lonely man, and quite broke. John very often had friends hanging around the house, feeding them and drinking with them while they tried to get back on their feet. Ultimately he always helped them at great expense to himself, which was one of the many ways in which he increased his enormous debts. Randsome was obviously a part of Wilson's London past, a bum who had not succeeded, and so he had to be loyal to him.

"Well, I'll let you go to work," Randsome said. "I have a bit of writing to do myself."

"Are you working on a book?"

"Yes, hasn't John told you? He's helping me. He thinks we might be able to peddle it in Hollywood. Trouble is he has very little time these days."

That was true. The tailors and the titled ladies and the hunting week ends obviously kept him pretty busy. And of course there was the picture.

"Well, I'll leave you now," Randsome said hesitantly. He went to a small table where the drinks were kept and poured himself a tall glass of gin, with which he went upstairs. I tried to make myself comfortable in an impossible gilt chair, and started to read the screenplay of *The Trader*.

It was a strange manuscript, full of brilliant scenes and endless descriptions of life along an African river. Some of it sounded completely unlike Wilson. I looked at the title page. There was another name on the script besides his. It was a name that was vaguely familiar to me: a journalist I seemed to have heard mentioned in some of John's stories. I read on.

Usually reading a motion picture scenario is a fairly simple thing. Most of the situations that one finds are recognizable, and the structure of the story is easily discernible. That was not true of *The Trader*. It was a period romance of a young American woman who marries an adventurer and goes off to Africa with him. She has the usual nineteenth-century prejudices against Negroes, but when she discovers that her husband is involved in the slave trade and witnesses the cruelty of this profession, she undergoes a change of heart. Her revulsion against the slave trade as she sees it practiced was the theme of the story.

It was a very simple story, told in a complex manner. The woman's reactions to Africa made up most of the opening scenes. The thing that made it unusual was the mixture of enchantment and horror with which she accepts the country and the people. I could see what Wilson was trying to do. He wanted to fill the white audience with guilt for what their ancestors had done to the colored race, and yet he wanted to make the actions of his leading characters entirely plausible. He seemed also to want to show the romance that was part of the slave trade. All this he had more or less accomplished. Only the ending of the story seemed not to be quite right. The trader and his wife see the true nature of the crimes they have committed, and try to atone for them by releasing the Negroes in their stockade. The Negroes then go berserk and destroy the grass-hut village that the trader has built, and kill the man who has mistreated them.

It was a logical ending, but it seemed to have too much of a sardonic twist. It left me feeling limp and hopeless. I sat for a long time in the gloomy living room with the manuscript lying next to my chair. The pessimistic ending of the story was depressing. And yet it had the strange quality of integrity that most of Wilson's work always had. I tried hard to think of what I should say to him. I saw a dozen technical things that must be done to the story, but I saw no way out of the end. It was logical. Awful and logical. And still it seemed wrong. I suddenly felt that I was a Hollywood writer in the worst sense of the word. I desired a solution that was not hopeless, and yet this story seemed to demand a hopeless ending.

I began thinking about Wilson's other pictures. Nearly all of them ended this way. They were the stories of great endeavors that finished in futility. That was undoubtedly

his view of life, and I was certainly not the one to argue
with him about that. Still I knew that if he wanted to
avoid another artistic failure something would have to be
done to make *The Trader* finish on a note of hope. "It
has no lift, it's downbeat," a thousand voices seemed to be
calling out to me from Vine Street and Sunset Boulevard.
"But you're not one of the backers," another voice said.
"You're not a banker, or a producer; you're a writer."
Still I couldn't help wanting the woman and the trader
to survive. I didn't want them to die in the flames of the
grass village on the banks of the upper Nile.

The telephone rang. It was Landau.

"Pete?"

"Yes, Paul?"

"What do you think?"

"What do I think about what?"

"The script."

"Oh . . . well, I've just finished reading it."

"I thought as much."

"I haven't got an opinion yet." I felt irritated with myself and Landau. I knew which side he would be on. I
knew he would plead for a happy ending. He would quote
Somerset Maugham, and Aristotle, and Thalberg the way
he had done when we made our first picture together.
And although I was basically on his side, I felt I couldn't
really take my stand with him.

"Well, what are your first impressions?" he asked.

"It's a little too long," I said.

"I know, I know." He sounded impatient. "But what
do you think of it generally?"

"I think it's very good. It can be improved, sharpened,
made much more exciting. And I think you must make it
in Africa."

"What about the ending?" the voice from the studio
asked.

I hesitated. "I'm not sure about it," I said.

"I'm delighted to hear you say so. I can't tell you how
much I agree with you. It's downbeat. It has no lift. It
will be just another wonderful financial failure."

"Are you sure, Paul?"

"Positive. It doesn't matter so much to me . . . but
John needs a hit. He needs one badly. Outside of his own
financial situation, people are beginning to be leery of his
artistic failures. The banks . . ."

"The banks feel he's a bad risk."

"Exactly."

"You know how I feel about the banks, don't you, Paul?" I said. "They're 'private people.' They're not in show business. They haven't got the faintest idea of what will go and what will fail. They only judge everything by what has been successful in the past. To hell with the banks."

"Don't give me a lecture on what's wrong with American cinematographic art," he shouted. "You sound like Wilson. Face reality. If you make a flop, you're no good. That's a rule of show business too."

"Are you so damn sure it'll *be* a flop if it ends the way it does?"

"I'm sure."

"You give me your personal guarantee?"

There was a long silence. "If you start that I'll send you back to Switzerland," Landau said slowly. "One maniac is enough."

"O.K., Paul, we'll talk about it. But don't threaten me. Switzerland isn't so bad, you know."

"Don't get hurt now, for God's sake."

"You started it."

"Because you started to ape Wilson."

All conversations with Landau always seemed to end with mutual recrimination. Mine were no exception to the rule.

"I'll see you tonight," I said.

"All right. But talk to John. Tell him what you think. Tell him that the ending is wrong, dangerous."

"I'll see you tonight," I said, and hung up.

I got up and went over to Randsome's little table and poured myself a drink. It turned out to be aquavit. It made me feel no better. Damn it, I said to myself. Damn the banks and the audience and Landau. I remembered a plan a friend of mine had devised after his fourth talented play had been badly received. He wanted to bring the curtain of his next venture up on an empty stage, on which a heavy machine gun had been set up facing the audience. Then as the first-night crowd settled noisily in their seats he wanted to open fire with live ammunition. A hell of an idea, I thought. Teach theatregoers the world over a good lesson.

The doorbell rang. I heard the butler open the front

door, and a few minutes later he ushered a fading blonde into the living room. Deus ex machina, I thought. You've come just in time, lady.

She introduced herself. Her name was Sylvia Lawrence, and she seemed not at all surprised that Wilson wasn't there.

"He never is, you know," she said in a very broad Mayfair accent. "He's kept me waiting for years and years. In bars, and hotels . . . just anywhere."

"I don't think he'll be very late today," I said. "Won't you have a drink?"

"You've just had one, haven't you?"

"Yes, I have."

"Well, then I suppose I might as well have one too. Terrible vice, drinking alone. Wouldn't encourage it for anything in the world."

"Would you like a martini?"

"No, I think I'll have what you're having."

"Aquavit?"

"Why not?" She wandered nervously around the room, slapping her left hand with her leather gloves, and finally dropped onto Randsome's couch. I noticed that she had very nice legs. Remnants of a better time, I thought, and gave her a glass of liquor.

She noticed the script on the floor. I told her I hadn't read it as yet, but she told me that she had and thought it was wonderful.

"Most everything he does is wonderful, dear old Johnny," she said.

"Are you an old friend of his?" I asked politely.

"Very old; and very tired today."

"What's the matter?"

"Life, in one word. The thing we all run after so madly, night and day. The fun's gone out of mine. Only the running remains. A lot of us are like that, I suppose. Only good old Johnny seems to be always pleased about what he's running after."

There are people you meet occasionally with whom you find no barriers. Usually they are in trouble of some kind, and their trouble makes them speak frankly, without pretensions, and you avoid the initial meaningless exchanges that dominate most of our talk. Sylvia Lawrence was one of these.

"John does manage to keep amused and interested in things," I said, deciding that she must have been a ravishing beauty not too long ago.

"It's the most rare and wonderful thing about him. I haven't seen him in years and years, and finding him here again is really the only solace I have. I do love him, dear old Johnny."

"He's a wonderful guy."

"He's unique. Absolutely unique. Such a lamb. He's the only person in the world I think can still help me. The only one."

"Are you having troubles?" I asked.

"The most real, the most awful trouble, my dear Mr. Verrill . . ." Despite her broad, languorous pronunciation of words, she did sound upset. "The kind of trouble which haunts you night and day, follows you everywhere. I've just come from the hairdresser, and sitting there under that awful drier, I suddenly felt I should go mad, stark raving mad . . ."

"I'm very sorry . . . can I do anything . . . if it's urgent . . ."

"No, you can't really do anything. I don't think anyone can, except my Johnny perhaps." She drank a big gulp, and showed no signs of feeling the burning liquor pass down her throat. "My husband's just gone off with another woman," she said. "My dear silly Francis has fallen madly and hopelessly in love with an utter little slut, and there's nothing I can do. I've tried everything, you know. Sex, tears, the children. I've told him about all the men she's slept with, but nothing seems to help. He's gone off with her, and he hates me. All of the wonderful years we've had together are vanished in thin air. It's too awful."

"What do you think John will be able to do?" I asked doubtfully.

"Talk to me. Give me some advice. He's so clever about people, Johnny."

"He'll probably tell you to go off with someone yourself. That's usually the quickest way to bring a husband back to his senses."

"Do you think so really?" she slurred, smiling charmingly at me. "I might try it, but I'm afraid. Francis is so terribly in love. Of course, I don't mind his sleeping with the girl and spending his money on her, but he wants to divorce now. It's just awful. And if I do what you say he might just be delighted, that's all."

"Oh, he'll probably get over it," I said. I was starting to worry about the script again.

"I don't know, oh, I don't really know anything any more," she moaned.

I heard a car door slam outside. "Here's John now," I said.

He appeared a few moments later. "Well," he said, "for God's sake . . . Sylvia." They embraced each other tenderly.

"For God's sake yourself, Johnny," the woman said. "You're late again, and I'm in such a frightful mess. I've been telling this young man all about it."

"Well, that's fine," Wilson said. "Was he helpful?"

"He was awfully sympathetic and he gave me a drink," she wailed, "but, Johnny, that isn't enough, darling."

"Francis?" he asked, starting to make himself a martini.

"Yes. Just as I wired you. He's gone off with that ghastly little slut Marcia. Isn't it too awful for words, Johnny."

"Just terrible," Wilson said, grinning. He came over to me. "Have you read the script, kid?" he asked.

"Yes. I think most of it is swell, but I'd like to talk to you about it."

"You're not listening to me," Sylvia Lawrence wailed. "You don't give a damn about what happens to me."

"Sure I do, honey," Wilson said. "I'm all ears. Francis went off with Marcia and you want to get him back."

"Don't make it sound so placid and unimportant, Johnny. This is the worst thing that's ever happened to me in my entire life."

"Poor old Sylvia," Wilson said. He went over and kissed her tenderly on the forehead. She clung to his neck for an instant. "Well, now," he said, straightening. "What is there we can do?"

"I don't know, my darling. I've tried everything."

"Everything?"

"Yes. Sex, tears, the children. Dear Mr. Verrill suggested I go off with someone else, but I'm not sure that would make any impression at all."

"No, that's no good," Wilson said, dismissing my idea.

He began walking slowly around the room. "Now, let's see . . . have you made a scene?"

"Of course. The most frightful scene. Quite a few of them. Was that wrong, Johnny darling?"

"No, I don't think so," he said thoughtfully. He lit a cigarette. "Have you tried violence?"

"Violence, Johnny? I don't understand."

"Violence. Physical violence."

"You mean strike Francis? But he's ever so much stronger than I am."

"I don't mean hit him with your fist," Wilson said, laughing happily to himself. "Just be there waiting for him when he gets home . . ."

"He doesn't come home," she wailed.

"Well, go to her place and wait for him there. Have a poker in your hand, or any blunt, heavy object. Don't say anything, just let him have it when he comes into the room."

"Oh, Johnny," she said, "do you really think so?"

"Why sure," he said with mock seriousness. "That's the answer."

"I've bought a pistol," she said.

"That's no good; you'll kill him, and then where will you be?" He went to the fireplace and picked up a pair of tongs. "Just let him have it, without even saying hello," he suggested. "Crack him . . . hard. When he picks himself up let him have it again." He played the scene, complete with business. " 'Is that blood on your ear, darling?' you say. 'I'm so sorry.' Bang . . . you let him have it again."

"Oh, Johnny," she said. "Do you really think so? Perhaps it would be better to strike her."

"No, for God's sake don't do that. He'll leap to her defense. Go after him. With the poker, or a heavy malacca cane. But don't kill him. Just beat the hell out of him."

"And you think that'll make him come back?" she asked, worried.

"Well, it's the only thing you haven't tried," he said in a false matter-of-fact tone of voice.

"I'm so frightened, darling. I think I might lose him forever."

"You won't lose him. I know Marcia. She likes her men all in one piece. By the time he's out of the hospital she'll be off with someone else."

"Couldn't you kind of seduce her, Johnny? She's mad to be in pictures, you know."

"She's already part of my past," Wilson said ruefully.

"Oh, that's awful, Johnny. Is she wonderful? I mean from a man's point of view? The love department?"

Wilson chuckled. "She's all right, but she's nothing like you."

"She's young, darling," Sylvia Lawrence wailed.

"That's why she'll never stand by a cripple," Wilson said. "Now, honey, I've given you my advice. You can take it or leave it. Pete and I unfortunately have some work to do, else we could discuss the whole thing with you some more."

"I know you do. And you have been sweet." She got up to go.

"You want lunch, dear?" Wilson asked her, remembering that he was the host.

"No, I'm not hungry at all. I'll press on, and leave you two to work. You've been lambs, both of you." She kissed Wilson tenderly, and shook my hand.

"Call me. We'll be dying to know how it turns out."

"I will, darling." She blew us both a kiss from the door. "Work well. Make another wonderful, wonderful film."

"We'll do that," Wilson said. "Good-by, dear." She was gone. He dropped weakly in a chair, roaring with laughter. "Oh, Jesus," he said, his thin body shaking. "What a gal!"

"Part of your past?" I asked.

"Past and present. She was beautiful years ago. Just beautiful."

"What's he like? Francis."

"A little jerk. An idiot. Funny thing is last time she was here we renewed our acquaintance. She didn't know about Marcia then." He shook his head and sighed. "Oh boy," he said. "What a strange bunch they are, our English cousins." He poured himself another drink. "Well, now, Pete," he said seriously, "let's talk a little about the script. Just talk. Spend the rest of the day on it."

"O.K., John," I said. "Here goes."

6

His manner changed abruptly. The tone of half-serious mockery left him at once. There were no artificial gestures, no faces to be made. The clownish side of his nature had gone out of the house with the girl, and he sat down opposite me, as plain a John Wilson as I had ever seen. His elbows rested on his bony knees, while one hand was buried in his hair. In the other one he held a pencil with which he sketched vaguely on a pad in front of him.

"Tell me what you feel about it," he said. "Don't try to be systematic if you find that difficult. Just say what you thought about when you read it."

"Well, it isn't as easy as that," I said. "I don't want to start criticizing it right away because that will give you a wrong impression of what I actually feel, and it'll get your back up, if I may say so."

"Go ahead, go ahead, I'm listening."

"All right. Well, first of all I liked most of it very much. I think it's original, and moving, and it has something to say."

"That was true of the book too."

"I haven't read the book."

"You should."

"I will as soon as I get a copy." I felt a slight wave of resistance starting, rolling toward me.

"Go ahead, kid. Never mind the asides."

"I thought I was just supposed to talk," I said.

"Sure, I'm sorry."

He seemed to be more nervous than I had ever seen him during a story conference. His face twitched impatiently when I dwelt too long at any one point of my critique. He looked seriously alarmed when I attacked specific lines in the script.

"You didn't like that, eh?"

"No, I'm sorry, I didn't."

"Well, go ahead, kid."

He went on listening attentively. I had often talked story with him, and I knew exactly when his interest was waning and when I was making sense to him. I also knew when what I was saying was falling on absolutely deaf ears, or driving squarely into the most obstinate facet of his nature. This time I was amazed to find him quite willing to give way on almost every point I brought up. He understood all of my reasoning, and very often anticipated what I was going to say.

"You're quite right. It's too long, and there's no point to the scene. Go on to the next one," he said time and time again. Very often he even seemed to know the true reason why my objections were justified better than I did. I was impressed again by his talent and intelligence. The clowning, the impossible things he said half in jest throughout the day, had made me forget what his values really were. Now in less than an hour I felt reassured. There was a lot I could learn from Wilson, and most of it had nothing to do with the movies. His talent was not necessarily limited to that. Economics had made him a movie director. If his father's fortune had been large enough to resist the frenzied assaults he made on it during his youth, he would undoubtedly have become a really good writer. The movies had been an easy way out of his personal crash and depression, and although he had worked in them with great integrity they had finally spoiled him. All of the easy solutions that talent finds spoil it, I moralized to myself. Wilson had become spoiled. He had made a long series of practical jokes out of his life, had associated with the wrong people, had failed to grow. And more than that, I felt that he was ashamed of what he was, ashamed of his trade. Although no one in Hollywood had done more to have the movies taken seriously as an art form, no one in Hollywood really doubted them more than Wilson did. That seemed to me to be the reason for his absurd working habits and his even more absurd private life.

I passed quickly over the last few objections I had to the script. He nodded and continued scribbling on the pad in front of him.

"Now we come to the ending," I said.

"The ending?" He looked startled, and frowned. "You

mean you don't like the ending?"

"Well, it isn't as simple as that. It isn't that I don't like it. It's that I'm not sure it's the right one."

He got up abruptly and began to pace the room, glancing down at his jodhpur boots when he turned. He obviously liked their maroon color, and the way the folds of the leather clung to his feet. He seemed hardly to be listening to me.

"Are you listening, or are you thinking of your boot-maker?" I asked.

"I'm listening. Go on."

Most people argue when you attack their work. John had always done exactly that. His silence now worried me.

"Go ahead," he said. "Don't stall. It's too late now."

"Well, my objections may sound like front-office objections to you, but I don't think they're exactly that. Furthermore, it seems to me that there's always a grain of truth in what the front office has to say."

"Well, spit out your grain of truth."

"I'll say it in Hollywood terms. Close your eyes and you'll think you're back in Burbank, with the dry hills right outside your window. I think the ending is down-beat. It has no lift, no hope. With the death of the trader and his wife, you're slugging the audience on the head. They've sweated these two people out for nine or ten reels. They've seen them through every kind of danger: black mambas, cataracts, poisoned arrows shot by Pygmies, elephant stampedes . . ."

"I know the script, kid."

"I presume you do. Anyway they've gone through hell with these two people, and finally, once you've improved their characters, made them see life with a humane, decent point of view, then you kill them. And you kill them brutally, uselessly. I don't think an audience can stand up under that."

"There's a saying that God makes a man just before he kills him," Wilson said. "I suppose you've heard it."

"I have. It's trite, and perhaps even true, but I don't think people go to the theatre to be lectured to."

"Tell me something, Pete," he mused. "When you made your deal with Paul, did you take a percentage of the profits of this picture?"

"I haven't made my deal with Paul as yet," I said.

"Well, is that what you intend to do?"

"No. I'll take the cash and let the credit go."

He turned on me then. His face was agitated, distorted by the belief that what he was saying was true and unanswerable.

"Well, why the hell do you worry about the profits of the goddamned thing, then? Why do you worry about the audience? Why do you even think about what's going to make them spend their lousy eighty-five cents?"

"Because if you make a flop you've failed," I said, trying out Landau's pet argument. "If you make a picture that no one goes to see you're not a professional, you're a charlatan, a dilettante . . ."

"How often do you think people said that to Stendhal, to Beethoven?"

"Movies aren't like literature," I argued, "nor are they like music. They're theatre, and theatre has to play to the people that are currently alive. It's no use even releasing a picture if people will only be able to enjoy it in a hundred years. There's always a partner in with you, whom you must consider: not Paul or Reissar or Anders, but the audience. That's what makes it tough. That's what makes show business such a rat race . . . that's why . . ."

"Listen," he interrupted angrily, "I'm not in show business. And neither are you while we're working together. We're gods, see, lousy little gods who control the lives of the people we've created. We sit up in this heavenly place," he indicated the room, "and we decide who's to live and die. That's the only way to play this game. We decide on their merits, on what they've done in reel one and two and three et cetera, and we decide if they've got a right to live. That's the only way to arrive at an ending. You don't know what'll succeed. Neither does Paul. Neither does Jack Warner. You're all guessing. You're all gambling on eighty million people you don't know. They're like this, and that, they want love to triumph or to fail, you say, but that's a lot of crap. You don't *know* them. But *I* know the people I'm involved with. I know the trader and I know the woman. I know what course they're supposed to run. Before the main title goes on I've had as intimate a relationship with them as I have with you. I've been off for weeks in the jungle with the guy. I've slept with the dame more than a dozen

times. I know they're both predestined to come to a bad
end. I know *they* know it. Then when the picture starts I
hear them talking. I hear the death they're heading toward in every one of the scenes. When they're making
love to each other I can sense their knowledge that it's a
temporary love. I know they'll never leave Africa alive,
and I know that both of them are convinced of this. So
don't come to me with your eighty million unknown friends, all of whom you despise, and try to tell
me they should live because these eighty million characters want them to. Don't try to tell me that kind of hooey,
kid. Because when you do you're just talking like a crook
who wants to cheat at the game; but this is no game you
can cheat at. You're a god, and if you cheat, you're a
lousy god."

"That's what you say," I argued. "I say I'm a kind god,
and you're a wild, vengeful one. I say I'm going to let
them live because they've seen the light. I say I'm going
to save them temporarily because the world isn't hopeless
and lousy, because we're not all doomed to die of radium
poisoning in a year or two. Maybe I'm kidding myself, but
that's what makes me such a hell of a swell god."

"It makes you mortal. It makes you a flea on an elephant's ass. Everything will turn out great, you scream,
and the elephant has already got his trunk full of muddy
water with which he's going to wash you off into the
mud. Balls, I say, because I sit well away from everything,
and because I can see it all clearly, just the way it's going
to go."

"And I say balls to your supermystical pessimism."

He grinned. "You do, eh, kid?" he laughed. "Well, let
me tell you something. If you go on, if you persist on sitting on the elephant's rump and screaming hurray, you're
never going to be a good writer, a movie writer or a nov-
elist or anything. You might turn out a couple of nice
poems, but that's the all-time limit. You've got too soft a
nature. You let eighty million popcorn-eating idiots blow
the cards out of your hands. You let them influence you,
push you this way or that, and that's no good. If you write
you've got to forget that anyone is ever going to read it.
If you make a movie you've got to forget that anyone is
ever going to see it."

"You're making sure of that," I laughed.

"Maybe I am; so what?" he said aggressively. "I believe there are two ways to live. One is to crawl, and kiss ass, and try to please. Write their happy endings, sign their long-term contracts. Never take a chance on anything. Worry your way through life. Take the train and the boat. Never fly. Never drive faster than thirty-five miles an hour even with Life Guard inner tubes. Never leave Hollywood. And save your goddam money. Save every cent you can. And then when you're a healthy-looking fifty you'll die of a stroke because whatever was wild inside you has eaten away the muscles of your heart. That's one way. It's nice and comfortable and safe. You'll always sleep in a clean bed, and you'll never catch syph, and you'll never create anything better than slick two-sided figures that can't cast a shadow. The other is my way, or at least I've tried to make it my way most of the time. To hell with the consequences, I say. Let the chips fly and fall where they may. Spend the money. Take Air France because they serve champagne. Refuse the contracts. Tell off the guy who can cut your throat, and flatter the helpless little bastard who's hanging by the string *you* hold."

"If that's your way of living, you shouldn't be in the movie business," I said.

"Maybe I shouldn't be," he answered. He paused, and then started pacing even more quickly. "I guess I shouldn't be. That's where I compromised. You're right. I should have wandered around the world, gambling on oil wells. I should have stolen diamonds, pimped for maharajas, played it as hard and dirty as I knew how."

"But you didn't because you don't really believe it *is* all hard and dirty. You compromised because you had a little hope left inside you. Hope took you to Hollywood instead of Timbuktu, because the other way to live is based on not having any hope at all. It's dog eat dog, you say, and you start right in on the closest guy to you."

He stopped in the middle of the room. "Now wait, now wait," he said. "You're getting it all confused. I don't think integrity necessarily means becoming a crook."

"It does if you believe the world is hopeless," I said. "If you believe that, then you've got to get in and scrap every way you know how. You can't settle for anything. As an artist you've got to say things just the way you see them. But *then* I say as an artist you shouldn't be in the movies."

"That's where you're only half right. Anyway I'm *in* the movies. I don't know about art, but I'm in the movies, and I have to play it as straight as I can, no matter what happens."

"Still you can give these two characters a chance to live," I said. "Don't be so goddam moral with them. Don't make them good, just to kill them. They'll die ultimately anyway."

"Pete," he said, pausing to change his attack. "Shall we examine our lives and try to find two endings? Wouldn't that be a good way to settle it? Wouldn't that illustrate the differences between our styles and point us down the right road?"

"I guess so," I said. "I'll work on yours."

"No, that's wrong. Each guy works on his own."

"All right."

"Go ahead. But use whatever integrity you have left inside you."

"I will," I said. "I'm a writer," I began. "I work in the movies to make enough money so that I can write books. But because I have a little integrity, I try to work on those movies that won't necessarily violate my sense of what's good and bad. Just making dough is too immoral, and I know that. If I whore around with my typewriter long enough I'll ruin myself for my novels. So the pictures I work on are usually pretty good . . ."

"What about the books?"

"Well, I haven't managed to write one for a while."

"Why, do you suppose?"

"I don't know."

"I'll tell you why. Because you don't really whore. So you love, or half love, the wrong things, and you get back to your books all used up by false love, and you can't get them going. Your end is simple. You'll write quite a few pretty good movies, and about fifteen half-finished novels. You'll die bitter and disillusioned, or you'll die filling everyone full of crap that the movies are really just as worth while and that you spent your life on the right thing after all. One way you'll die bitter. The other way you'll die a liar."

"Thank you very much, Dr. Wilson. Now what about you?"

"I'm different. I realized that you can't serve two masters very early in life. Money or art, I said to myself.

Money *and* art, I answered, just as you did. But I knew immediately that I couldn't keep the two separated. I had to make art and money at the same time, and I knew that could only work in Hollywood. And it did. I became a success. Artistically, that is. However, my pictures don't make money. In the years to come I will make five, or six, or ten critical triumphs that will fail at the box office and the banks will ultimately say, 'Throw that bastard out or we'll grow mushrooms in those sound stages.' The bosses will oblige. Landau, who'll be the head of MGM by that time, will fire me. As a parting shot I'll punch him in the nose. Then I'll try to write a novel. I won't be able to do it either, because I'll be too busy borrowing money from all of my ex-friends. I'll die in a downtown Los Angeles flophouse, but I won't be bitter. I'll have contributed ten damn good pictues. A special Academy Award will be named after me, and all the wrong guys will get it, and I'll sit in hell, laughing my head off."

"Romantic futility. Your one true love," I said.

"Well, that's nothing to be ashamed of, kid."

I sighed deeply. "O.K.," I said. "The wife dies. The trader burns in a grass hut."

"I knew you'd ultimately see it my way, Pete." He grinned. "How about a drink?"

"Why not? If I'm going to die as a bitter, frustrated writer of unfinished novels, I might as well become a lush."

He laughed delightedly. "That's not certain. You're young yet. You can still change."

"I'm thirty-one," I said.

"It *is* getting late." He grinned. "Wouldn't you like a stick of tea instead?"

"If you've got one."

"I'm sure Randsome has." He called loudly in the direction of the stairs. "Jules!"

Randsome appeared. "Yes, John?"

"Have you got a stick of tea, old man?"

"What?"

"A pipe of opium, perhaps."

"You're both mad." He came quickly into the room. He had obviously spent a lonely day.

"Now here's the only one of the three of us who's doing it right," Wilson announced. "Jules is not selling out. He's writing his book, and he doesn't give a damn if anyone reads it. He doesn't need money. He lives in the same clothes for months on end. We'll drink to Jules."

"This is all I brought with me from Scotland," Rand-some apologized. Then turning to me: "He made me leave on five minutes' notice, and told me he was sure he could get Landau to take an option on my novel. Nothing has happened as yet."

"Landau has no money," Wilson explained. "He's operating on his charm."

"That's great," I groaned.

"Oh no. Anders and Reissar have money. Millions and millions of pounds. All we have to do is separate them from it."

"The hard, untraveled road again," I said. "You'll never make it, John."

"Paul will. He'll do it for us. He doesn't have art to worry about."

There was a knock on the door, and Landau entered.

"On cue," Wilson said. He moved threateningly toward his partner, his fist raised. "Shall I poke him now, for what's coming?" He grabbed Landau by one of his lapels and got ready to swing.

"John, come on. Please try to act like a human being," Landau pleaded. It was obvious that he had had a rough morning.

Wilson released him. "You don't understand. You see, Pete and I worked out the endings of our lives. I'm going to die in a flophouse after you, as the boss of Metro, fire me. I poke you in the snoot once more before they throw me off the lot. So I thought I'd do it while I'm still in my prime."

"I'm glad to see you boys have been working," Landau said with great dignity.

"We have, curiously enough," I said.

He gave me a disgusted look. "John," he said, "I think the entire financial deal has finally been settled. Isn't that wonderful?"

"Great," Wilson said. "Where's my part of the take?"

"You'll get it, brother, you'll get it," Landau said, forcing a grin. "Now, really . . . while I was working my ass off, was anything accomplished here?"

"You were at your tailor's this morning, you lying bastard," Wilson said, "and at the barber's this afternoon, and in between times you probably had three or four dames in for interviews. Jeanie told me."

"She's lying," Landau said, blushing. "I spent six hours locked up with the lawyers. If you think that's fun . . ."

"We didn't have much fun either," Wilson said. "We had to help a desperate woman get her man back. And we talked about the script, and, Paul, let me tell you there isn't a duller subject to be found anywhere. Furthermore this morning, while you were still lying warm and safe in your bed, I was out on the Thames in a leaking kayak shooting a color test."

"Did you accomplish anything on the story?" Landau asked me.

"Don't tell him," John commanded.

"Please, John. Stop all this nonsense," Landau pleaded. "Did you do anything about the ending?"

There was a long silence. Wilson looked at his partner and shook his head.

"Well, did you?"

"You son of a bitch," Wilson said. "You've been intriguing against me again. You lousy, Hungarian, flesh-peddling pimp."

"John, really," Landau said. He looked with embarrassment in the direction of Randsome.

"We talked about the ending," Wilson said, "and I discovered to my absolute horror that you have had a filthy, demoralizing effect on my young friend over there. You're going to go to jail for corrupting the morals of a major. You're going to be hung for violating the pure-art law. You're obscene, Paul. A man like you, who has witnessed the disintegration of the entire central European artistic world, persists in following the cheap, disastrous course that led to Hitler over Europe, World War II and the atom bomb . . ."

"God, I'm tired," Landau said, sitting down. "I suppose the ending stays as it is."

"That's right," Wilson said. "With one slight change. You burn in the last grass hut as well. That's the end title."

"John, can you be serious for a little while?" Landau asked.

"I've never been more serious in my whole life."

"All right. Anders and Reissar are worried about the ending too. They are putting up the money. They only ask that you think about saving the girl. They're willing to lose the trader."

"Tell them to put their money in government bonds if they're worried about it," Wilson said. "If anything, I'd save the trader and burn the dame."

"Is that your final opinion?"

"That's my final decision, not opinion."

"Pete, have you told him what you felt about it?"

"I've argued with him, and I've been defeated," I said. "On personal grounds."

"You realize, John, that you're risking the success of the entire venture?"

"I realize that, Paul."

"You realize also, of course, that your share of the proceeds from this picture is based mostly on the profits we might or might not make?"

"I realize that as well."

"You remember that you have various responsibilities remaining in California?"

"If you're talking about my wife and two kids, I faintly remember them. Less faintly than usual today, because I just received a cable." He took it out of his coat pocket. " 'Situation desperate,' " he read. " 'Paul's lawyer had not yet, repeat, not yet, paid rent, or food bills.' " He looked up. "I've been meaning to talk to you about this. If they're not paid by the end of the week, I'll return to the States and get a job there."

"The deal isn't signed yet," Landau moaned. "We get no money until it is."

"You just said it was settled today."

"Settled, but not sighed."

"Well, my statement holds. I have my return ticket."

"John, you talk to me as if I were an enemy, or your boss, or the backer of this venture. I'm your *partner*, John."

"Get the dough, partner, is all I have to say," Wilson replied.

"Well, I think you're behaving in an impossible manner. I really do." He got up, momentarily forgetting his fatigue.

"I think *you're* behaving in an impossible manner. *I* really do."

"I can't get the money until the deal is signed. I'm in debt too, you know."

"I don't give a damn. Get the dough or I leave."

"Is that your final word?"

"Absolutely. I'll book a reservation tomorrow."

"All right," Landau sighed. "I've done everything I could to keep the deal alive. I can't do any more. If you go . . . well, I've faced worse crises than this in my life."

"O.K.," Wilson said. "The meeting is adjourned." He started toward the stairs.

"We're having dinner with Reissar and Anders," Landau reminded him. "They've invited a girl for you."

"Are we? Well, good," Wilson said. "Are they paying again?"

"What difference does that make?"

"None, I suppose. Only it's getting a little embarrassing. They always pay. I think it's your turn soon."

"Not ours? Mine? Is that right?" Landau asked rhetorically.

"Well, I have no money," Wilson replied, "and Pete seems to have even less."

Landau sighed heavily. "For one day in my life," he said, "I'd like to have your sense of responsibility. We'll call for you at eight."

He moved wearily across the room. " 'By, Paul," Wilson called after him, cheerfully.

"Good-by," Landau mumbled. At the door he turned to face Wilson once again. "You know you're supposed to leave for Africa on Saturday on the location trip. Shall I cancel your reservation?"

"Why do that?" Wilson asked. He seemed perturbed. I felt great admiration for Paul.

"Because you may be going back to the States."

"Well, that's up to you."

"Not altogether."

"You're supposed to get the dough to my wife."

"And if I'm a day late?"

"A day? Well, a day's not so bad. She's waited this long."

"All right. Then I won't cancel your reservation. See you later, Pete."

He left the room. Wilson looked after him and shook his head. "You know," he said slowly, "I really can't help liking Paul. He's such a desperate man."

7

The dinner the British producers gave was not an unqualified success. The food was excellent, and the lady who had been invited for Wilson turned out to be a charming young actress. Even the night club we went to after dinner was quite entertaining. But Wilson unfortunately failed to play the role assigned to him. Instead of devoting himself to the young actress, he turned all of his attention to the girl who had come with Reissar. He talked only to her, turning his back on the rest of the table. Landau grew more and more nervous. He didn't dance with the tall English chorus girl he was with, which was a sure sign that he was feeling the strain. Finally he beckoned to me, and we both went to the men's room.

"You've got to do something about John," he said, once we were alone.

"Why? What's the matter?"

"What's the matter?" he puffed. "He's making an obvious play for Reissar's girl."

"Oh, I don't think so," I lied. "He's just talking to her."

"Now come on, Pete. Don't pretend you don't know our friend. He's turning on the full blast of his charm."

"Well, what do you want me to do about it? Drag him home?"

"If necessary, yes."

"He's not drunk enough, yet."

"Well, then get him drunk."

"At the beginning of the evening you told me to keep him sober so that we could work in the morning," I complained. "Make up your mind."

"Get him drunk."

"At the expense of the script?"

"What's the use of having a script if we have no producer?" Landau said.

I laughed. He shook his head. "You're no better than he is," he said.

"Why don't you tell your girl to make a big play for him? He's always willing to give up a sure thing for a maybe."

"She's not that kind of a girl," Landau said. He shook his head. "Oh, God, what have I done to deserve a partner like this?" he asked the shining lavatory wall.

"We all get what we deserve in life," I said. "However, I'll do what I can." We went back into the main room of the night club. But long before we had arrived back at our table I knew that the issue was lost. Wilson and Reissar's girl had disappeared. Everyone else sat in mute discord.

"Where's John?" I asked.

"Where's Adelaide, that's the really important question," Reissar said agreeably.

"With John, I believe," Anders said. He was holding the hand of the girl who had come with him in an unmistakably frightened clutch.

"I doubt that," I said.

"Well, it doesn't really matter," Reissar said. He was being terribly nice about it. He didn't want to spoil the evening for us just because he had a broken heart.

"Would you like a little more champagne?" Anders asked with his faint, pleasant smile.

"Thank you. I don't think so."

"Oh yes, do have some more," Reissar said. He called for the waiter. "And, Paul, what on earth is the matter with you? They're playing a rhumba and you're not dancing."

And so we stayed on and had more champagne and waited for Wilson to return. He didn't come back, of course, and neither did Reissar's girl. We left the night club at two-thirty and went home. I awoke the next morning at ten, and Wilson still had not returned. Randsome and I sat around all morning discussing Irish writers and why they all had such a great gift for the English language. Miss Wilding had joined us at eleven o'clock, and had started telephoning everyone she knew to try to find

Wilson. I kept my mouth shut as to where I thought he was probably to be found. At twelve-thirty we went to the neighborhood pub and had a drink. Then we came back to the house again and ate lunch. At two forty-five Wilson arrived. He was still in evening clothes.

"Hello, guys," he said, grinning happily as he took off his white silk muffler.

"Hello, John. We sure got a lot of work done this morning."

"We sure did," he grinned.

"What happened to you?" Miss Wilding asked.

"I don't know," he said. "You know this girl who came with Reissar last night suddenly felt ill, and so I took her home. Then I stopped in at some other joint and had a drink. When I came back to look for you guys, you'd gone. . . . I stayed on with some Navy officers who were there, and holy smoke, I really got blind. I woke up on a submarine tender this morning."

He was being gallant, and I was not the one to interfere with such a rare manifestation of his character.

"Will you have a little lunch?" I asked him.

"I sure will, kid," he said. He sat down and began to eat hungrily.

"You might have called," Miss Wilding said bitterly. "We were worried half to death."

"Jeanie was worried," Randsome said. "Pete and I had a rather good morning."

"Poor old Jeanie," Wilson said. He patted her cheek, and the girl recoiled. "Are you sore at me, honey? Aw, come on now, that's no way to be."

"There's a trick to working with John," I explained. "You must never expect him to show up. Then if he does, you're pleasantly surprised. The same rule can be adopted by hostesses who invite him, and girls who have dates with him."

"Thank you, Pete," he said with a false grin. "Doesn't what Pete said make you feel better, dear?" he asked Jeanie.

"I don't care what you do with your life as long as you get the script done," the girl said furiously. "That's all that really matters. If you think all of your smart friends will stick to you once you've made a couple of failures, you're sadly mistaken."

"Uh-huh," John gulped. "Now what about you, Jeanie? Will you stick to me?"

She started to answer him and then thought better of it. "You make me so cross," she said weakly.

He chuckled. "I'm sorry if I do, dear, but I asked you a question. Are you going to answer me or not?"

"It's a ridiculous question."

"No, it's not. To try and find out who your real friends are is very important."

"How would you propose to go about doing that, John?" Randsome asked.

"Well, I don't know. It's kind of difficult. I think the perfect test would be to go to your friends and tell them you've just committed a murder, a cold-blooded, premeditated murder, and that you want to escape. There are no extenuating circumstances. All you want is help. The people who'd stick to you and help you escape without asking any questions would, I believe, qualify as real friends."

"That's a rather tough test, John," I said.

He was serious now.

"I know," he said, "I know it's tough, but it's a *real* test."

"I'd help you," Jeanie said resolutely.

"You know that aiding or abetting a criminal is a crime itself, don't you, dear?"

"I know it. I would become your accomplice if necessary and help you escape."

"I'm sure you would," Wilson said. He patted her back affectionately. "Good old Jeanie. Only you'd probably foul up the details so they'd catch me . . . and that's why I wouldn't come to you."

Miss Wilding got up from the table. "You bastard," she said. "You absolute bastard," and she flew out of the room.

Wilson roared with laughter. He got up from the table and brought the girl back. She was crying. Randsome poured her a stiff drink of neat gin, but she continued to sniffle.

"I was just kidding you, for God's sake," John said to the girl. "Of course I'd come to you for help."

"Who else?" Randsome asked.

"Well, Pete, probably . . . if he wasn't off skiing at the time. . . ."

I felt flattered and happy. "I'd come to you for help, I know, under similar circumstances," I said.

"Well, I think you wouldn't regret it," Wilson replied, "and if I hadn't just committed a murder of my own, I would certainly try to get you out of the country."

"What about Paul?" Randsome asked.

"Any time," Wilson declared. "Paul is a real guy in the clutch. You wouldn't have to worry about going to him. And I'll tell you something else . . . there are a hell of a lot of guys who've already been to him for help."

"Murderers?"

"Well, probably not many murderers, but a lot of other people. He has a loyalty to the underdog that he developed in his youth, and it's a big thing with him. He's been an outcast of society often enough so that he remembers the feeling very vividly, and there's always that suspicion in him that it might just happen again. Anybody who's had to sleep in the gutter has that feeling. Anybody who's been on the lam has the fear that it might happen once more."

He went through the list of all of our friends, and discovered that very few of them would qualify under the rules set up by Wilson. John's "real friends" included a Sunset Boulevard madam, a jockey, a very rich playboy, three women with titles, Landau, myself, two actors of bit parts, and his wife. My list was much less colorful. It included Landau, John, my wife, my mother, my father, and a very nice guy with whom I had served in the OSS. It excluded quite a few of my otherwise close friends.

It was five-thirty by now, and Randsome was going through his list, which was a laborious process as we hardly knew any of his acquaintances. Wilson was already bored with the game, and devoted himself to sketching a caricature of Jeanie Wilding. The doorbell rang, and the butler admitted Anders, Reissar, and Landau. None of them had brought girls. They hesitated in the doorway of the living room and stared with amazement at the scene that confronted them. The room was filled with smoke. We were all in our shirt sleeves. Miss Wilding was having her third neat gin with her feet up on the table on which John was sketching. The ash trays were overflowing.

"Well, hello, guys," Wilson said, and got up to greet them. "Come on in."

"You're still working," Landau said. "Are we early?"

"You invited us for five-thirty cocktails, didn't you, John?" Reissar asked.

"I sure did, and you're not early," Wilson said. "Furthermore, we stopped working about half an hour ago." He motioned to the butler to clean up the mess on the table. Miss Wilding was already on her feet. She prepared to mix a cocktail for the newly arrived guests.

"What'll you have, Sidney?" Wilson asked Reissar.

"Whatever she's mixing," Reissar said. They all sat down.

"We've all had a tough day," Landau said. "I called you this morning, John. Where were you?"

"Pete and I were taking a walk around London," Wilson replied.

"We went to the British Museum and studied the costumes of the period," I said.

"That was awfully clever of you," Anders said. "I wouldn't have thought of that in a hundred years. Really, I wouldn't."

"Oh, sure you would."

"No, honestly."

"Well, to tell you the truth," Wilson said, "it was all Pete's idea. We were getting stale on the script when he suggested going there. It helped us a lot."

"You're certainly earning your money, Pete," Landau said magnanimously.

"What money?" I asked. He gave me a dirty look. Miss Wilding passed out the drinks. She spilled a little of Reissar's on him. Landau gave her hell for it. Wilson seemed not to have noticed the disaster.

"You know what we were just talking about, Jules and Jeanie and Pete and I?" Wilson asked.

"We have no idea. Tell us," Landau replied. He knew that Wilson was in a "charming" mood, and he wanted to show him off.

"We were saying that a test of real friendship would be to have committed a premeditated murder without extenuating circumstances and then to go to your various friends and ask for help to escape the law. It's amazing how few people one knows to whom one could go under such conditions. That is, if you discuss the problem seriously."

"I know no one," Reissar said immediately.

"Oh, come on now, Sidney," Wilson said. "That can't be true."

"Oh well, I suppose I could go to Roger," Reissar said, indicating Anders.

"I'd be much obliged if you didn't, thank you," Anders replied tartly.

Landau was signaling to Wilson. He obviously didn't like the trend of the conversation.

"Do you know a lot of people you could go to?" Reissar asked Wilson.

"Quite a few," John said. "Quite a few." He started out on his list.

"Oh, if you're willing to include relatives," Reissar interrupted him once Wilson had named his wife, "that's quite different."

"The whole discussion is ridiculous," Landau said. "Not one of us here is really liable to get into that kind of situation. John, as usual, has gone too far."

"Not at all, Paul," Wilson said. "I think every one of us is at this moment walking a very narrow plank of false respectability. Every one of us is a good citizen merely by accident, by hook or by crook."

"John, really, you don't mean that?" Anders said.

"I think he does, and I think he's right," Randsome said suddenly. It was the first time he had spoken since the arrival of Landau and the two Englishmen. We all looked over at him. What is this man? I could almost hear the others asking themselves. Murderer? Revolutionary? Dope fiend?

"Would you like to qualify what you just said?" Landau asked irritably. He had a natural instinct that told him when he was confronting someone who could do him no harm, and his manner sharpened whenever this happened.

"I'd like to qualify what Jules said," Wilson interrupted. I knew we were approaching a wild, dangerous curve, but it was too late to try and put on the brakes. "We are all potential outcasts from society," Wilson went on excitedly. "Every one of us, and everyone we know has really only one great personal loyalty, and that loyalty is to himself, his own survival. That's why the loyalty hearings are so ridiculous. Our society makes life so perilous that it is almost like feudal times. We're all little fish struggling to keep from being eaten. We're loyal when it helps us. And we're potential criminals when our safety is threatened. I'll be specific. You, Paul, are a man who has been directly opposed, violently opposed, to one government already in your lifetime. Hitler's Third Reich. You became an outcast there. The same thing might happen to you if America suddenly became anti-Semitic. Furthermore, you might even become opposed to your present government without that. If you made a fortune at the races, let us say, a real fortune, and all the problems of your life seemed to be solved if only you didn't declare your winnings to the Collector of Internal Revenue . . . Now don't interrupt me . . . let's say this happened, and let's say temptation overcame you, and you cheated on your tax return. Let us furthermore say you were about to be discovered and flight was the only alternative to three years in jail. You might well flee, then. If your money was outside the United States, you might be tempted to make your life elsewhere rather than go to jail. And most of us would understand your actions. I know, I know, you have a thousand objections now," he said as Landau started to speak, "but none of them are really valid. A few people we know have already been in this spot, and one specifically who is known to all of us lives outside the United States right now."

"I don't play the races," Landau finally managed to say.

"All right, the stock market. Anything where you might suddenly make a fortune that was hard to trace. What I'm getting at is that when a large enough sum of money becomes involved, your morality might well run directly contrary to the morality of the law. I know that, Paul."

"It just isn't true," Landau said, but Wilson disregarded him.

"Now take Pete," Wilson went on. "Suppose he wrote a great book, and talked too much about it prior to publication, and some one of his friends stole the idea and wrote another version of it. Pete would then be tempted to break the law. He might only commit robbery and try to steal the other man's manuscript. If the other writer resisted this, he might use violence. Murder might result from the struggle over the manuscript . . . and then flight. Take Jules. Suppose he finally got a chance to make some dough in Hollywood, and suppose some malicious bastard who wanted to spoil Jules's chances threatened to bring up Jules's past. I won't be specific about it, but again I feel, Jules might take the law into his own hands. Take Sidney and Roger . . . suppose they saw their personal fortunes threatened by a new Labor government, a government that wanted to socialize the film industry and confiscate the studio they worked so hard to build. Wouldn't they be tempted to use extra-legal methods?"

"What about yourself, John?" Reissar asked.

"The same thing goes for me," Wilson said, "only it's much more complicated. I have no fortune, and I don't write books. It would have to be an extraordinary thing that would force me into illegal action."

"He turns out to be the most respectable one of us all," Landau said with amazement.

"That's right," Wilson said. "I don't care about most things: money, art, my reputation . . . that's why I'm safer."

"We're in business with a rather dangerous character, aren't we?" Reissar said, laughing halfheartedly.

"He's joking," Landau said nervously. "He's trying to make himself intellectually interesting."

"Well, if you care to think so," Wilson said, "that's all right with me, Paul. Actually I haven't been more in earnest for a good many days."

"Anyway we've been warned," Anders laughed.

"Yes, of course," Reissar said. "Thank you for warning us, old boy."

Wilson grinned. He had created the kind of situation he most enjoyed. Landau was tortured because Wilson had undermined everyone's confidence in him. Anders and Reissar felt threatened, but not threatened enough to do anything about it. There was a brief silence.

"Shall we talk about the picture for a change?" Landau asked. "I don't think this last discussion was very profitable."

"I think it was," Wilson said. "Any clarification of what we're all about is valuable. Adventurers should know each other well before setting out on an adventure."

"It's not really an adventure, John, is it?" Anders asked.

"It's the biggest goddam adventure any of us have ever been involved in," Wilson said. "An independent picture always is. It's life and death. And an independent picture to be made in Africa is even more a matter of life and death."

Fortunately the doorbell rang. The butler admitted three new guests. While Wilson greeted them, Landau and the two Englishmen wandered thoughtfully around the dark corners of the room. I moved over near them. I wanted to find out if Wilson's latest torture treatment had had any actual effect.

"Perhaps we should try to make the picture in England," I heard Reissar say to his partner.

"Then he won't do it," Anders said.

Landau took me by the arm. His heavy, warm hand pulled me away from them. "You see," he said. "I wasn't joking. He's a maniac. He's going to wind up in a padded cell."

"Oh, come on, Paul. He's just enjoying himself . . . relaxing a little."

"Fine relaxation," Landau moaned. "I've just been working out the final clauses of the contract with these two guys. They concern our exceeding the budget. Do you realize that they want John and me to be responsible for every cent over two hundred and thirty thousand pounds? You think I've got a chance to beat them off that isea now?"

"What'll you do?" I asked.

"Give in, of course."

"And be liable for a couple of hundred thousand pounds if things go wrong?"

He struggled helplessly. "What can I do?" he said.

"Suppose we have bad luck with the weather? Suppose the camera gets trampled by elephants? Suppose the leading man goes off on a drunk?"

Landau reached for the arm of a chair. He needed support. "Don't even say things like that," he muttered. "Oh, how did I ever get involved with him?"

It was our turn to be introduced. The new arrivals were a strange group. One of them was a young baronet, obviously one of John's social and hunting friends. With him was a fading Broadway actress with bright red hair, probably another remnant of Wilson's past. The third gentleman was a theatrical agent, although he looked more like a baronet than the baronet did.

"Well," said John once they were all seated, "we've just been having a grand time here. It turns out we're all potential murderers or thieves, and we're off on a great adventure together. What'll you guys drink?"

"Anything at all," the fading beauty chirped. "But please do go on with it, with your adventure. It sounds absolutely fascinating."

Well, I said to myself, I guess we'll talk about the script some other day.

8

My suspicions were well founded. The unexpected cocktail party continued until ten o'clock that night. This was due principally to the talkative nature of the actress. Although she had asked to hear more about the adventure, she didn't wait for Wilson's reply. She was off on her own bent, chattering about her life, and the parties she had been to, and the movies she had seen, and the people she knew. She drank endless orange blossoms, which took care of Miss Wilding. The poor girl disappeared into the kitchen and commenced squeezing orange juice; she never returned from this task.

Randsome withdrew to help her, but soon I saw him disappear up the stairs to his own mysterious domain. Feeling that her audience was leaving her, the actress felt obliged to increase the pace of her talk. Very deftly she guided the conversation to her own business activities, and then bluntly disclosed that she was planning to make a movie. She apologized to Reissar and Anders for her planned dilettantic intrusion into their "métier," but explained that she had found such a wonderful story that she felt she just had to see it made. Reissar and Anders were polite. So were all the other guests, unfortunately. Thus aided by all of our company manners, the lady divulged that she intended John to direct her picture.

"That would be nice, wouldn't it . . . after all of these years . . . you and I together, John."

"Be just wonderful, dear," John said. I felt irritated with him. Whenever he wasted time and did it interestingly I didn't mind, but now he was encouraging this fierce bore to waste our entire evening, and he was only doing it because she had been clever enough to bring along her own aristocrat and her most social agent. She had roped Wilson in with his own snobbery, and he was allowing himself to be thrown and tied.

Without any further warning, the lady now began to tell us the story of her film. It was about a dog, a puppy dog. He was the hero, the star. And his adventures were endless. Reel after reel poured out of the woman, complete with setups and dissolves and dialogue. No one dared interrupt for fear of extending the length of the film, and so she went on, following detailed scene with detailed scene, sequence after sequence.

At the end of the first hour Anders and Reissar sneaked out. I heard Reissar mutter something about seeing the last part of it in his projection room at the studio, and then they disappeared into the hall. I followed them. They were both pale with anger.

"Wilson is right," Anders said fiercely. "I could become a murderer overnight. I could become one right now. I'm just not sure of that damn agent. Everybody else in the room would stand by me if I killed that woman."

"I'd drive the getaway car," I said.

They didn't even say good night. They rushed out of the house into the refreshingly damp air of the London night.

I shut the door and found Landau confronting me. He looked pale and used up. He stumbled a little as he came toward me.

"Are you going to buy the lady's story?" I asked him, jerking my thumb in the direction of the room where the torture could be heard continuing.

"Please don't make jokes tonight," he said. "I just can't take it any more."

"Well, it's probably the only way to stop her," I said.

"Pete, Pete," he implored me, "please. I've been with lawyers for six hours today, arguing for our lives, for our futures. And I lost. I assumed a financial burden much larger than anything I've ever dreamed of. Then I came here and we got into that horrible conversation about murderers. And now this!" He sat down on an ancient chair. It cracked and tottered beneath his weight, but by sheer will power he kept it upright and remained seated.

"What can we do?" he moaned. "We're lost. It's hopeless."

"Not at all," I said. "You're just tired."

"No, I'm not," he said. "I'm dead. I'm not alive any more. I know that it goes on like this day and night in this house of horror. You never work. I know that. You talk. People come in and drink, and you go on talking. And in the meantime we're facing a starting date with a script that isn't right. Do you realize in two weeks the principals will arrive from the States? We can't show them what we have. It's not professional."

"We'll start working tomorrow," I lied.

"No, you won't," Landau said. "Tomorrow it'll be the same thing again. Saturday he's supposed to go to Africa on the location trip. He hasn't even met the assistant unit manager he's to go with."

"Send him a few days later," I said. "We'll discuss the changes, and then I'll make a rough draft of them while he's gone."

"No use sending him later," Landau said. "If he stays in England this week end he'll go hunting. You know him by now. If there are women or horses within reach he can't control himself."

"I hope you're not referring to that thing up there as a woman."

"No, that's a horse," Landau said with a sad smile. He sighed deeply. "Oh God, oh God, oh God," he moaned.

Wilson appeared. He looked perturbed. The voice droned on upstairs.

"Intermission, Johnny?" I asked.

He shook his head groggily. "No," he said, "this is the part the censors are going to cut out anyway. The dog's in heat."

"Couldn't be," I said. "His name is Horace."

"Well, as the plot goes on," he said with mock seriousness, "it turns out to be a story of mistaken identity. Horace has a twin. A bitch. She's called Geraldine. Now she's in heat." He looked down at Landau. "What's the matter, Paul?" he asked brightly.

"I don't feel well," Landau said.

"You should pull yourself together, kid. That's our next movie. You should hear it."

"I'm not making any more movies," Landau groaned. "I'm leaving the business."

"Well, that's a shame," Wilson said. He winked at me and started back up the stairs. "If there's as much love in that old gal as there is talk, I'll be dead in the morning."

"I hope both of you are," Landau said, but Wilson didn't hear him. I stood near Paul as he mopped his brow. He shook his head in silence.

"What shall we do, Pete?" he asked plaintively, after a while.

"I don't know, Paul."

"Shall we just give up?"

"It seems a shame. It could be a good movie."

"But it isn't worth it, is it?"

"I don't know."

The baronet came hurrying down the stairs. He rushed past us without noticing our presence.

"Third-act trouble," I said. "It isn't holding them in its spell."

"Please don't make jokes," Landau said as the front door slammed.

"Rude bastard, wasn't he?" I observed. "You were saying what shall we do?"

"What do you think?"

"Well, I know what I would do," I said. "I'd send him to Africa, where he wants to go anyway, and where he has no past, and where there is no fox hunting, and there are no dames."

"What about the script?"

"I suggest I make a first draft of the changes here, and then join John in the jungle for the final draft."

He sat in silence for a while. "Suppose you can't get him to work down there?" he asked.

"He'll work, don't worry. He doesn't want to make a lousy picture either."

"What about the ending?"

"God damn it, Paul, don't make me mad," I said. "You can't win 'em all."

The agent came hurrying down the stairs.

"You're not leaving, are you?" I asked sarcastically.

"Oh, I've heard it twice before," he said, smiling his elegant smile.

"You what?" Landau asked. He got slowly to his feet.

"I've heard it twice before, Paul," the man said in a matter-of-fact voice. "I think it has some awfully good things in it. John seems to like it too."

"If you believe in the material I'll give you John on a loan-out, and you can make it independently," Landau said angrily.

"Well, I don't know, old man," the agent replied lightly. "Let's have lunch tomorrow and talk about it."

"By tomorrow I'll be in a loony bin," Landau shouted. "We'll have lunch there."

"Oh, now really, Paul, don't take it so big, old boy." The agent smiled at me and hurried out of the front door. We watched him get into his custom-made Bentley.

"That son of a bitch," Landau said. "He's the one who brought her here."

"Forget it. Stick to the point," I said.

"Yes, the point," he said in a dazed voice. "I think you're right. I'll send him off on Saturday."

"I don't think you'll regret it."

"I won't regret anything that gets him far away from me," Landau said. "Good night."

He staggered down the front steps and started slowly up the sidewalk. He looked like a beaten man, a stranger in the cold, foggy city. He walked slowly, with his coat hung over his shoulders in the central European manner, its tweed folds flowing behind him in the wind. An elegant, despairing Moses, I thought, starting toward the sea without his people. Poor Paul. What Wilson had said about him was true. He was a desperate man. I saw him pass a prostitute a few hundred yards up the street. The girl spoke to him, but he seemed not to hear her. He went on, slowly and elegantly, into the night.

I closed the door and went up the stairs. For a moment I paused outside the living room. The husky, tireless voice droned on.

"He's alone now, poor Horace," I heard the woman say. "We dolly with him as he trots slowly down a deserted street. He turns into Grosvenor Square. We cut to a long shot as he starts across it. Then we cut to another angle, a long shot. Geraldine can be seen coming down Brook Street. She passes Claridge's. Then she enters the square. Suddenly they see each other, Horace and Geraldine. There is not a human being in sight. They race toward each other. The music swells. We hold the final picture in an extreme long shot, as they meet and turn and go off together. That's the end. They find each other. . . ." I heard a slight sniffle from the lady as she finished.

"Well, honey," I heard John say, "isn't that something? Isn't that something?"

"Do you like it?" she asked faintly.

"I think it's just swell," Wilson said. I went quickly toward my lonely bed. It was a wonderful feeling to be entering a silent room.

9

We had a family breakfast; at least the whole thing had a familiar atmosphere about it. Randsome was in his usual blue suit with dark blue shirt; the redheaded actress was still talking quite volubly although she seemed to feel a little strange in the gloomy, early morning atmosphere of the living room, still dressed in her white, décolleté evening gown, and Wilson was unchanged and unperturbed. I felt rested. I suppose I was getting used to the cold, uncomfortable nights on my couch, as well as to the disorderly life I was living. I knew that it would not last indefinitely, that either Africa or a return to Switzerland would soon put an end to it. Furthermore, as I was not yet seriously involved with either the people or the project, I could sit back and enjoy it all without worrying too much about the outcome.

Actually Wilson had always had that effect on me. He made me feel like a passenger in a wildly careening car, driven by a drunken driver, a passenger who knows that an instant before the crash, an invisible all-powerful master will reach down and lift the driver out of the vehicle. It had always turned out that way and I felt sublimely confident that no matter what might happen this time, Wilson would survive the crash. He had been through so many muddles, through so many wild rides, that he no longer seemed to notice the pace or the howlings of the imaginary tires. He got up slowly and languidly each morning, and stepped out of the strewn wreckage of the night before, showered and shaved, and started the next incredible day.

Now, as we shared this rather fantastic breakfast, he seemed completely changed from what he had been like on the previous evening. He was thoughtful and kind. He seemed to be worrying about something. At first I assumed it was the lady's honor. To drive home through early morning London in that white dress seemed like a terrible fate to wish on anyone, even the author of the dog script.

"John, have you a coat or something I could borrow?" the lady asked.

"What, dear?" His mind was obviously far away.

"A coat. I can't go home wearing this white fur piece."

"Well," he said. "Let me see. Call Jeanie, will you, Pete?"

I went out into the kitchen and produced the very hungover Miss Wilding. She was wearing one of John's silk dressing gowns. It was the final touch that the breakfast needed.

"Yes, Mr. Wilson," she said stiffly, after having said a doubtful good morning to everyone present.

He didn't seem to notice how she was dressed. "Have we a coat this lady could borrow?" he asked. "A coat that's a little less conspicuous than what she has on."

"I'll see, Mr. Wilson."

Jeanie disappeared. John sat on the couch and read the morning paper. Then he looked up at me. "We've got to spend some time together today, kid," he said. "I'll be leaving tomorrow, and we've just got to discuss the changes on the script."

"I'll be available all day," I said.

"All right. I'll come back here for lunch."

"About what time?"

"Oh, one-thirty or so. I've got to go to the studio and look at that color test. Then I'll come back and we'll go through the whole thing, and talk about the ending again."

"I thought that was the one part of it you didn't want to change?" I asked, surprised.

"I don't want to change it, but I think we might discuss

it once more. I've been thinking about it."

Miss Wilding appeared carrying a woman's overcoat. She looked very pleased with herself.

"This is a coat Miss Lawrence left here last week," she said. "Perhaps it would do?"

Wilson gave her a dirty look. "It's just for the car, isn't it?" Miss Wilding asked with false innocence.

"Yes, it's just for the car," Wilson said. Then he turned to me. "I guess Jeanie really wouldn't be much use to us in Africa. The climate would be bad for her."

"I'm not sure I want to go any more," Miss Wilding said. She put the coat down, and left.

"Poor dear," the lady in white said. "She's awfully keen on you, isn't she, John?"

"She's getting over it," Wilson said. He went back to reading his paper. "You know," he observed after a long pause, "I really hate to leave Saturday. It's the last chance I'll get to go hunting. When we come back from Africa it will be too late." He got up. "Well," he shrugged, "you just can't do everything in life, I suppose. Come on, dear. Duty calls."

They departed, leaving me to the early morning mercies of Randsome and Jeanie. The girl was truly upset.

"What an awful evening that was," she said.

"Well, at least we didn't have to go to a night club," I said.

"Did you hear the end of the dog story?" Randsome asked.

"Yes. It all turned out well. Horace got Geraldine."

"She wasn't the only bitch who got what she was after," Miss Wilding said. Randsome and I looked at her with surprise.

"I say, Jeanie," her compatriot rebuked her, "you really must pull yourself together, old girl."

"All of you say things that are much worse than that," Miss Wilding said rebelliously. "I'm damned if I know why I should be the only polite person in this house."

I decided to let them argue it out. I went back to my room and re-read the script. At one-thirty Wilson returned and woke me up.

"Hard at it, eh, Pete?" He grinned.

"I read it again, and then I closed my eyes to think about it a little, and this is what happened."

He laughed. "It has the same effect on me all the time," he said. "Well, I'm your man whenever you can pull yourself together."

We spent a very profitable afternoon. Miss Wilding took notes on the things we decided to change in the script. Obviously Randsome's rebuke had had a good effect on her. She only interrupted us twice, both times to take sides against me in an objection I had against the original version of the manuscript. Wilson listened attentively to what she had to say. I realized that that was another one of his great virtues. He dismissed no one's opinion. He listened and then made up his own mind. We arrived at the ending.

"Well, what do you think, kid?" Wilson asked me. "Do you still feel the way you did when you first read it?"

"I honestly don't know, John," I said. "What makes *you* doubtful now?"

He hesitated. "You'll laugh," he said, "but it's Landau. He's against the ending for all the wrong reasons, just as he was *for* color because he saw a few more dollars coming into the till. Well, I saw the test this morning, and he's absolutely right. Color is very important for this picture. It will make the audience come out of the theatre feeling they've really been to Africa. They'll have suffered heat, and malaria, they'll have been drenched by the tropical rainstorms. And color will create a large part of this illusion. They'll remember the shining black skins of the natives, and the unrelieved green of the jungle, and the bright, blinding sun."

"You want to do all this for those eighty million popcorn-eating idiots?"

He grinned sheepishly. "You know," he said, "you occasionally have a horrible feminine quality of remembering the wrong thing at the wrong time."

"It's not necessarily feminine," I said.

"It is with you. You know that's part of your great success. You don't realize it. You think the world is your oyster because you're occasionally attractive to women. You're wrong. If you rise in this world you will owe it all to the fact that men like you."

"Can we discuss this without bringing in our various personalities?" I asked.

"We could," he said. "But we won't."

"O.K.," I said. "You know what your success is based on?"

"No, kid, tell me."

"Your deep-seated sadism. You love to torture people, the audience included. You love to put them through hell and reward them with futility and disappointment. Your cruelty is your biggest box-office quality."

"Then you think the trader and his wife should die?"

"If you make the picture, sure."

"All right, I'll tell Paul I was willing to change the ending, but that you persisted in sticking to what we have."

"I don't give a damn. Go ahead." I could sense that we had already spent a little too much time together.

"Well," he said, "I'm glad you're working with me on this venture. You'll help keep my integrity intact, if you do nothing else."

"Kill everybody," I said. "The hero, the heroine, the crew, the backers. Have all the fun you can."

"That's why we're going to Africa, kid," Wilson said.

The discussion continued in an even less friendly tone. I told him that I probably wouldn't join him in Africa, and he shrugged and said that that wouldn't matter too much to anyone except Landau. Then he fell silent. Miss Wilding transcribed the notes we had given her, and he read them carefully. It was evening by that time.

"Well," he said finally, rising slowly from the armchair where he had been sitting for hours, "shall we have a drink, kid?"

"I don't want one," I said. "You go ahead."

He laughed, his strange mirthless laugh. "Good God," he said, "I've never been attached to a dame who's as difficult as you are." He shook his head. "You and Jeanie . . . my two helpers. I certainly like to make things difficult for myself."

"You can get rid of both of us any time you like."

He looked surprised. "Are you really sore, kid?" he asked.

"Hell, no. What would be the use?"

He clapped me on the back. "You had me worried, kid," he said. He went over to the small table and started mixing himself a drink. "You know, Pete, I've never told you this, but I think ultimately you and I are going to

wind up together. When we're old that is, and when no
dame wants to look at us any more. We'll wind up in a
little cabin up in the Sierras, with a couple of plugs we
can ride to town once a week to buy beans. We'll pan for
gold, and shoot rabbits, and sit around at night with an
oil lamp burning in our shack, and lie to each other about
all the things we've done, and the first guy who dies will
bury the other one. Not too deep, of course, because we
won't have too much strength left, and then when the
coyotes come around at night, the guy who's left will sit
up with a flashlight and a rifle and guard the other guy's
grave, and that's how we'll end. It doesn't sound bad, does
it?"

My irritation left me. "Maybe we'll strike it rich someday, and have a big spread, John," I answered. "Then
we'll hire somebody else to guard our graves."

"Yes, maybe," he said. "But I don't really think that
will happen. We'd better get dressed now."

"What's on for tonight?" I asked.

"Some friends of ours are giving us a little party," he
said.

"Not Anders and Reissar?"

"Who else?" he grinned.

The pattern of our London life repeated itself once
again. We ate quite well, and went to a night club. There
were a few toasts and a good many hopeful statements as
to the possible success of the venture. The British producers paid the check.

In the morning I took Wilson to the airport. The assistant unit manager and the art director were waiting for
him. He greeted them warmly.

"Well, I'm certainly delighted to be going with you
guys."

"We're very happy to be going with you, sir," Harrison,
the wiry little art director, said solemnly.

John smiled his most paternal smile. "I'll be with you
in a minute," he said, taking me by the arm. We walked
out in front of the customs hut and leaned against the
wire fence that separated the passengers from the taxi
lanes. A huge BOAC Hermes was warming up its motors.

"I certainly wish you were coming along, kid," he said.

"I'll be there soon," I replied. "It's just as well that I'm
staying. I'll do a rough draft of the changes."

"Not too rough," he said.

The loudspeaker called his name. He straightened, and grinned at me. "I'll be waiting for you down there, kid," he said. "Hurry up now, and get the work done."

"You can count on me," I said. We shook hands. I felt fonder of him than I had ever before. He pulled his ludicrous small cap down over his eyes.

"Oh, you animals of the wild," he said, "take to your lairs. The great white hunter is on his way."

"Good luck, Johnny."

"Thanks, kid. I'll need it."

He walked hurriedly toward the customs shacks. The backwash of a propeller lifted his coat. I could see that he was wearing boots and leggings. His thin figure seemed to be blown forward by the wind.

He turned and waved, holding onto his cap. Then he disappeared. A few minutes later I saw him climb up the gangway into the belly of the plane. Only then did it occur to me that he had forgotten to take a copy of the script.

10

London was lonely without Wilson. Although the people I had met with him continued to invite me, it was not at all the same thing. Reissar and Anders were nice, but somehow without Wilson prodding them into revelations and confessions they became strangers once more, correct and polite: a different breed of animal. They had their well-regulated lives which consisted of office, and dress-for-dinner and going away for the week end, and although they often asked me to share these functions with them, I didn't get much out of it. Aside from pictures, their interests were absolutely foreign to mine. They enjoyed theatrical gossip, went to austere cocktail parties, and conferred with their bankers. They had none of the abnormal

passions that I had acquired over the years and that connected me to Wilson and everyone else I knew. They
cared nothing for horses, or shooting, or skiing. Literature
was only important to them when it could be applied to
the movies.

Life with Landau was equally unsatisfactory. He had a
large group of prewar acquaintances, and after Wilson's
departure he returned happily to their non-torturing company. I became aware of this almost immediately. Waves
of refugee Hungarians started washing onto his shores
less than an hour after his partner's plane had started
south. I had stopped by his suite to give him the bad news
of the forgotten script. I must say he took it quite calmly.

"Harrison, the art director, probably has a copy, or
Lockhart, the assistant unit manager." He was lying in his
broad bed, trying to get his eyes open. He had stayed on
in the night club to celebrate Wilson's departure, and he
was worn out.

"I don't think so, Paul," I said. "I've checked with
Jeanie and she says they weren't issued scripts." He picked
up the phone beside his bed and called the office. One of
his most irritating qualities was that he never believed
what he was told. He always checked for himself.

"Well, I'm not surprised," he said, after what I had told
him had been verified by the office. "You know when we
came over from New York he swore to me that he had
no room for the script or a copy of the book. Later I
found out why. He was carrying his hunting saddle, three
pairs of boots, and his pink coat. So of course one copy
of the script was the straw that would have broken the
elephant's back."

"Camel's back, Paul."

"What's the difference?" That was a bit of animal lore
he was ultimately going to learn the hard way.

"Can we air-mail a copy?"

"Yes, I suppose so."

Someone knocked on his bedroom door and two men
in tight overcoats entered. There was the happy babble
of Hungarian, several exchanged kisses, and his world engulfed him. It was a world from which he did not really
emerge for more than a week. Every time I saw him after that the Hungarians were with him. They usually
played three-handed gin rummy with a beautiful girl sit-

ting in a corner of the room leafing through the pages of a movie magazine or the *Hollywood Reporter*. Sometimes there was a Hungarian or two left over, and he was always detailed to conversing with the beauty, whoever she happened to be. After two such evenings I gave them up as hopelessly foreign.

I spent the next week working on the script. Occasionally Randsome and I would have dinner together in a little pub in Belgrave Mews, but as I always had to pay, even this social contact was ultimately abandoned. I had very little money to spend. Landau and I had closed our dubious deal, but no cash had been forthcoming, and so I was forced to exist on whatever small handouts I could get from him. And once the Hungarians forced me to abandon Claridge's, I found myself rather short on funds. Randsome became a luxury I could ill afford. Then followed a lonely "movie" period. I saw all the films that were playing the West End. I could venture no farther because I invariably got lost coming home whenever my sense of adventure lured me deeper into the city.

After the movie period came the sleep period. I worked in the mornings and visited the automobile showrooms in the afternoons. Then I had dinner at home and read a little and went to bed. I averaged ten hours a night, and finally became so sated with sleep that I began to feel quite ill. I was just contemplating a return to the sunny slopes of Switzerland when Landau called me.

"Where have you been keeping yourself, Pete?" he asked solicitously.

"Oh, I've been in London," I said. "Just got back to Budapest tonight. How're things?"

"Why didn't you call?" he asked, disregarding my attempt at humor.

"I have trouble understanding Hungarian on the phone."

"Pete, are you going to act like John now that he's not here?"

"No, of course not, Paul. Where's my dough?"

"I told you you'd get it as soon as our deal is signed," he said, raising his voice.

"When will that be?"

"Very soon. Probably tomorrow. Have you finished the changes?"

"Yes, I have, Paul."

"Well, why haven't you brought them to me? I want to read what you've done."

"No tickee, no washee, as we say back home."

There was a long silence. I thought I could hear Landau breathing hard on the other end. When he spoke again his voice was controlled and polite.

"The principals are arriving this afternoon from New York," he said. "I'm giving a party for them. Would you like to come?"

I knew both of our stars from Hollywood, and although I rarely saw them at home, I felt very eager to meet them here in London. Compatriots have a strange way of clinging to each other abroad.

"I'd love to come," I said.

I was not disappointed by the reunion. Although they had only been away from home a few hours, our stars were as happy to see a familiar face as I was. Phillip Duncan, our leading man, was a fairly typical Hollywood actor. He had lived most of his adult life in Southern California. An early New York success in a gangster melodrama had caused him to be transplanted to the West Coast while still quite young, and for one reason or another he had stayed there until the year after the war, at which time, in his full glory, he had tried the New York theatre again. Unfortunately, the vehicle he had chosen became the easiest target that the New York critics were offered that season, and so he escaped home to his yacht and his third wife. He was a nice, insecure man, given to aggressiveness when not entirely sober, a not uncommon Hollywood trait.

Kay Gibson, his co-star, was quite a different proposition. She was a fine actress, a domineering personality, and one of the few actresses I knew who still made me behave like a self-conscious idiot whenever I encountered her. Her fame seemed to surround her as the atmosphere surrounds the world. I always caught myself looking at her face, and then I would see her in one of her unforgettable closeups, the perfect, unusual features appearing twice in my field of vision, as they were in life, and as I remembered them from a dark theatre.

I had been in love with her at the ages of fourteen, eighteen and twenty-one. I met her first when I was twenty-six, and discovered that love had left its mark.

Now, years later, being greeted by her with true enthusiasm, I felt as awkward as ever.

"Are you coming to Africa with us?" she beamed.

"I sure am."

"Oh, thank God." She turned and called out to Duncan across the room. "Pete's coming with us, you know. At least we'll have one sane, reasonable person along."

"He's going first," Duncan called back in his rasping voice. "Paul says he is, anyway."

"And he's going to find a real comfortable place for us to live," Mrs. Duncan added. "None of this camping-out crap for us kids."

Miss Gibson put her long arms around her knees and beamed up at me. "Won't it be exciting?" she said. "I've never looked forward to anything as much in my whole life."

Landau came over to our group. "We're getting an enormous river boat for the company to live on. I've just received a cable from Entebbe. It's a ship that was built quite recently and it has baths, and games rooms; all the comforts of the *Ile de France*."

"I hope it won't be too comfortable," Kay Gibson said. "I should like to rough it a little."

"Listen to her," Mrs. Duncan shouted. "Oh, God, Kay . . . don't say that, even in jest. It'll be horrible even if it's the *Ile de France*."

"The food better be good," Duncan said in his most menacing manner. "I've been on a lot of locations, and nothing can ruin the morale of a company quicker than lousy chow."

"I'm going to Paris next week end to hire a chef," Landau replied.

"You are, eh?" Mrs. Duncan said. "Well, I'll go with you to make sure."

"You have to stay here, dear, for publicity stills," Landau said. "You'll have two busy weeks ahead of you."

"Not too much of that now," Miss Gibson said. "I'll do my share, but not too much."

"You love it, for Christ's sake, Kay," Duncan said. "Why put on that act?"

"Don't always judge others by yourself," she answered. "I don't love it, and I never have."

"Where's the ogre now?" Duncan asked, turning to Landau. "Why wasn't he here to meet us?"

"He's in Africa, choosing locations."

"You should be with him, Paul," Mrs. Duncan said. "He'll select some god-awful place for all of us to die in. Just like he did in Cuba, remember?"

The British producers arrived. They seemed as impressed by the Hollywood personalities as the crowd of autograph hunters that was waiting outside the hotel.

"Is all that luggage yours, Miss Gibson?" Anders asked, blushing like a schoolboy.

"No, it's Mrs. Duncan's," Kay Gibson said sweetly.

"I've come prepared for Paris, and not Addis Ababa," Mrs. Duncan said. She was a very beautiful young woman, and she was obviously going to make sure that she remained one throughout the trek.

We went to dinner and a night club. The crowds of autograph hunters followed our caravan of Rolls-Royces in taxis and private cars. They were quite nice and well behaved, even when they surrounded us in the street.

"Welcome to England, Miss Gibson," they said over and over again.

"Hullo, Phil," they shouted to Duncan as he emerged from his car. He raised his clasped hands over his head like a fighter acknowledging an ovation. They loved him for it.

The headwaiter, who had rejected me a few nights ago, now led us to a ringside table. The house sent over two bottles of champagne. Anders and Reissar were beaming.

"They're both amazingly popular, aren't they?" Anders whispered to me.

"They'd better be," I replied. "Or else why are you paying them all that dough?"

Mrs. Duncan sat beside me. "I'm sure that bastard John is thinking up some horrible gag for us," she said. "He wants us to get off in some horrible hole, and then just stay and stay and watch us all suffer."

"I don't think so," I said. "He's got a lot to do down there."

"How is the script, Peter?" Kay Gibson asked, leaning across the table.

"I think it's going to be fine," I answered. Landau kicked me under the table.

"It's wonderful, Kay," he said. "Pete's a perfectionist,

that's why he says it's going to be fine."

"I am too, Paul," Miss Gibson said. There was an uncomfortable lull in the conversation.

"As long as we can all come back healthy and alive," Suzy Duncan said. "That's all I'm hoping for."

I was much less worried about that now than I had been. The familiar faces, the familiar fuss, made me feel safe. These people would look after themselves, and no matter what happened they would make sure that we were not too uncomfortable.

Anders rose. He was fast becoming a British Grover Whalen. "I'd like to welcome our American stars," he said, raising his glass. As we drank, Miss Wilding appeared. I saw at once that she looked worried and upset.

"Hello, Jeanie," Reissar greeted her. "Did you want to see me?"

"I'd like to see Mr. Landau for a moment," the girl said hesitantly.

"Can't it wait?" Landau asked irritably.

"Obviously not, Paul," Anders said. "What is it? Has something gone wrong?"

"Well, perhaps I'd better wait until you're finished," the unhappy girl murmured.

"You're here now," Reissar said. Both of the British producers seemed unwilling to let the matter rest. I suspected they wanted to hear the bad news immediately. Someone pulled up a chair and introduced the girl.

"Would you like a glass of champagne, Jeanie?" Landau asked pleasantly. I knew that he wanted to kill her, and I admired him for his restraint.

"Thank you very much." Jeanie never refused liquor of any kind, I observed.

"Well, what is it?" Reissar asked impatiently, after the girl had been served. She hesitated, making the most of her small moment.

"I've just received a call from Harrison, the art director," she said.

"From where?" Landau asked, amazed.

"Nairobi. It seems that Mr. Wilson is on his way back."

There was a stunned silence. "Oh, oh. John no likee Africa," Mrs. Duncan said in an aside to me.

"On his way back?" Landau repeated excitedly. "Well, have they found all the locations?"

"No, I don't think so. It seems he wants to shoot the picture in the Belgian Congo, and he feels he wants to talk to you about arranging the finances."

"But that's not a sterling area," Reissar said at once. "We can't do that, Paul."

"Is he coming back all that way just to talk to us?" Anders said with horror.

"Yes, I'm afraid so."

"Can't we stop him?" Reissar asked.

"He left this morning," Miss Wilding said. "He'll arrive sometime tomorrow."

"Oh, God," Landau moaned.

"I don't think it's as bad as all that," Kay Gibson said in her sane, quiet voice. "I think it's all to the good. I want to discuss my costumes with him, and furthermore he can tell us all what to expect."

No one answered her. "I think he has a fitting at his tailor's the day after tomorrow," I said to relieve the tension. Landau turned angrily on me.

"How can you say a thing like that?" he exploded. "Pete, sometimes you amaze me. This is no time to make wisecracks. This is a terribly serious moment."

Kay Gibson came to my rescue. "We must never lose our sense of humor, Paul," she reproved him. "If we do that, then we'll all be at each other's throats long before the picture is finished."

It was a sentiment that many of us echoed again and again in the time ahead.

The party continued halfheartedly. Landau and the two Englishmen gathered at one end of the table and began speaking excitedly among themselves. The words "Belgian Congo" and "sterling area" could be heard repeated occasionally in agonized voices in their many accents.

"Well," I said, turning to the others, "what's the dirt from home? I've been away for a long, long time."

11

Wilson arrived at noon the next day. As he stepped from the plane I sensed that a change had come over him. He looked thin and used up. When he smiled at me it was like a man smiling because he was arriving, that was all. I noticed that he still wore his breeches and his leggings. His beautiful jodhpur boots were caked with mud. His shirt looked stained, and it seemed to me that it was the same shirt he had worn the day he left.

"Hello, John," I said. "I was just coming down to join you. Lucky I didn't, eh?"

He nodded vaguely. The chauffeur took his bag. It, too, looked battered and muddy.

"The menagerie has arrived," I said cheerfully. "Phil and his wife and Kay."

"They have, eh?" he answered. He seemed not at all interested in that important event. We got into the car.

"Well," I said, "how was Africa?"

He shook his head. "Boy, oh, boy," he answered in a low, mysterious voice, "have I got a lot to tell you."

"You like it?"

He shook his head again. "It's quite a place," he said. "Quite a place."

"Are you eager to get back there?"

"I would never have left if it weren't for Paul."

"What do you mean?"

He seemed to be collecting his thoughts. "Well to answer your first question, you don't like Africa," he said, with a slight overtone of irritation creeping into his voice. "It's bigger than that. It's just the goddamnedest place you've ever seen. It's the most fascinating place in the world. You could spend ten years down there and know nothing about it. It's just . . . well, wait till you get there, kid."

"Then we're going back together?"

"Just as soon as we can. I'll tell you something, Pete:
I wouldn't mind spending a couple of years down there.
Or if I couldn't do that, I'd like to go back every year for
a few months. Not to make a picture, or anything like
that, but just to be there and find out all about it. It's a
part of the world I can't imagine living without from now
on. As if someone were to say to you you could never put
on skis again, or climb on a horse. You know what I
mean. It's a thing that gets under your skin, Africa. . . ."

"What is it about it that makes you feel that way?" I
asked. "The country, or the people, or what?" I was trying to catch a glimpse of my future, for whatever had
affected him so deeply was certainly going to affect us all
very soon.

"The people are interesting, yes, and the country's nice.
A lot of it's like northern California, Kenya especially. But
that's not it. And it's not the jungle, either, or the life the
white settlers lead."

"What is it then?" I asked impatiently.

"Well, this will probably sound silly," he said, "but
there's one thing down there that has a fascination for me
that's bigger than anything I've ever encountered, bigger
than horses, bigger than fox hunting . . . bigger than any
sport or passion. It's the shooting."

"The shooting?" I was amazed. Some years ago I had
introduced Wilson to duck hunting, and he had been enthusiastic about it, but as far as all the other forms of
hunting were concerned, he had never seemed very interested. I knew he had shot deer a few times before the
war, but killing harmless animals had become distasteful
to him since his discharge from the service, as it had to so
many of us. He had once told me that since the crossing of
the Rapido, which he had witnessed, he had never really
wanted to have a gun in his hands again.

"You know I lost my taste for killing things in the war.
I remember that we talked about that. But this is different. This is big game. It's something I can't explain. I flew
with a guy down there over a herd of buffalo, and I had
the damnedest reaction, when I looked down at them.
They'd run when the plane came down low over them,
and then they'd turn and look sore, as if they were saying,
'Come down here, you bastards, and fight like men.' Then

I saw elephant, and rhino, and it was like seeing our world thousands of years ago, and asking yourself, How the hell would I have stood up then, with just a piece of hide hanging around my loins and a spear, facing some huge animal, and testing my strength and my wits against him?"

"What about lion?" I asked.

"I didn't see any. But in the Nairobi national park I saw leopard. They'd just killed a zebra, and a whole family of them were having supper. The hyenas were hanging around about fifty yards away, waiting for what was left, and every once in a while one of the leopard cubs would get up and chase them away."

"Just like home," I said. He disregarded my irreverent flippancy.

"It was the damnedest thing you've ever seen. Then we flew over the Congo, and boy, that was even more impressive. Five thousand square miles of forest, an area almost as large as the United States, one huge belt of impenetrable jungle, and you look down and you just know everything evil is going on down there, animals eating each other, or eating natives; snakes, and swamps, plants that devour flesh; Pygmies with poisoned arrows, lepers, the black pit of the world just lying in wait down there."

"Paul says that's where you want to shoot the picture," I said casually, as if that were a ridiculous notion.

"Oh, we're going to," he said.

"But it's not a sterling area, John. We can't operate in the Congo. We have no money."

"That'll be arranged, kid," he said. "That's the main reason I came back, to stir Paul off his ass. We're going to make a lot of the picture there."

"Well, I'm not so sure you'll manage," I said.

"You'll see, kid. We'll be in the Congo in a month from now."

"What are the other reasons why you came back?" I asked.

"Well, the money is one. I got some more cables from home while I was in Uganda."

"Situation desperate."

"That's right."

"That'll be taken care of, don't you think so?"

"I know it will. If I have to wring Paul's neck in order to do so . . . it'll be taken care of. And the other thing, kid, is that we've got to get equipped. We need guns and ammunition."

"To shoot the picture?" I asked facetiously.

He remained serious; gaunt and serious. "Of course," he replied. "We'll have to have quite a few guns on hand all of the time, to protect the company. Then before they get down there we're going to have a couple of weeks of hunting . . . you and me."

"What about the script?"

"Oh, we'll finish that first," he said casually. All of the uncertain time-wasting quality seemed to have been baked out of him by the African sun. He was tense and nervous, and eager to get going on everything.

"Wait till I tell you about some of the guys down there. There's an Englishman, a hunter, who's given up his whole life just for shooting. He's built himself a house near the Ruwenzori, the Mountains of the Moon, a house that's hundreds of miles from the nearest native outpost, and in the early morning he can sit in his living room and look out at the plains and see the elephant moving off to their grazing grounds, an old man smoking his early morning pipe and sitting there watching, spying on eternity. Oh, boy . . . I tell you kid, it's something you'll never forget . . . Africa."

"It seems to have left its mark on you already," I said.

"It sure has," Wilson said. "I'm a changed man."

I could see that. I could see also that no one would ever be able to change him back until he'd done what he wanted to do.

"I know I want to get a buffalo," he said intensely, "and maybe a lion, and if we run into a big tusker, I'm going after him. You'll be there with me, kid, backing me up, and shooting whatever you want. We're going to have a real time for ourselves, a real time."

12

Exactly five days after Wilson's arrival we were at the airport again. The change that Africa had brought about in him was felt by everyone in London during those five days, for he crowded three weeks' work into one hundred and twenty hours. Even Landau was impressed with him, despite the fact that most of Wilson's energy broke like a wave on top of his partner. They had countless fights, but their battles were different from the ones they had had before. Wilson no longer tortured Landau. His arguments were very much to the point; he was in a hurry to get back to Africa and he fought everything that stood in his way.

The first fight was about the Congo. In half an hour Wilson proved that it was possible to convert some of the sterling currency allocated to the making of the film into Belgian francs. Then he telephoned a friend in Brussels and proved that permission to shoot the picture would also be forthcoming. The governor of the Belgian Congo controlled the making of motion pictures in that area, and the authorities in Brussels felt that as long as the film was not derogatory there was no reason why it could not be filmed there.

The next battle was about money. The sum Landau had promised Wilson's family in California had not arrived as yet, as the American backers were still insisting on war clauses and completion guarantees. They also seemed to be worried that if one of our leading actors became ill, or perished, the picture would not be finished. To my amazement Wilson found a solution. He agreed to waive half of the money he was to receive for directing the picture in case any one of the principals fell by the wayside. He also arranged a conference that included Duncan and Kay Gibson, and at that meeting he convinced them that they should agree to similar settlements in case one of them fell ill. Although I did not attend this last gathering, I was told later by Duncan that John cut through the legal chatter of the lawyers and arrived at a conclusion in less than twenty minutes. Everyone agreed that he was in great form, and the spirits of the company rose.

The next serious dispute concerned itself with the equipment Wilson wanted to purchase. He asked for a thousand pounds with which to buy guns for the expedition. The three producers opposed him unanimously. He paid no attention to them; at Wilson's request I spent a day visiting the leading gunmakers of London. I found out that we could resell all the guns we bought, and that the final cost to the company would not exceed two hundred pounds. Landau and his British partners were forced to agree to the purchase of a small armory, especially as the money would go toward protecting the lives of the expedition.

We spent the following afternoon selecting our weapons. In this we were slightly handicapped by our lack of knowledge and by the fact that neither one of us had ever shot at anything larger than an Idaho mule deer, although Wilson seemed to know more about what was required than I did. He knew that he wanted a couple of big guns, weapons capable of killing an elephant or a buffalo. Unfortunately we could find only one .475 magnum in all of the stores we visited, and one .375. Wilson decided to buy the .475 and gamble on picking up another big rifle in Nairobi. It was then that I discovered that the usual range at which one killed buffalo was well under a hundred yards. The bony little West End gunsmith who gave us this bit of information seemed to assume that this was common knowledge.

"A hundred yards doesn't seem like very much, I said dubiously.

"Oh, you never zero in one of the big rifles for more than that. They wouldn't be accurate at a greater range."

"Of course," Wilson said irritably. "No one ever tries to kill a buffalo at a greater range than that."

"About seventy-five yards is an average shot," the gunsmith said, rubbing his palms together.

"Suppose the thing's coming at you?" I asked. "I understand they travel about sixty miles an hour. You don't have much time to aim, do you?"

"Well, that's why you have a white hunter along," the gunsmith said.

"Have you arranged for a white hunter, John?" I asked.

"We'll see, kid, we'll see," he replied. "We can't do anything about that now."

He bought two smaller rifles and a 12-gauge shotgun for the close-in shots on leopards. The smaller rifles, two .256 Mannlichers, were to be used for the pot. The gunsmith assured us that they were excellent weapons for antelope and waterbuck. Unfortunately it was too late to fit them with telescope sights.

"We really need one more big gun," Wilson said. He looked concerned. There wasn't much time left, as we had to go to Scotland Yard to get licenses for all of the weapons in order to take them out of the shop. "Well, we'll just have to do something about this in Nairobi," he decided. He told the gunsmith that he would have someone call for the weapons, and we went off to Scotland Yard.

It was a clear spring afternoon, and we drove past the ancient flags that were flying everywhere to celebrate the Exposition. The park was green, and a company of horse guards passed us. How much easier it is to stay at home and guard the Crown, I thought to myself, than to go out among the head-hunters and tribesmen to establish the power of the Empire. I was no Drake, I knew that. A Bacon perhaps, intriguing in the antechambers of the queen, but not an adventurer setting out for worlds unknown.

The next day we had our shots. It was a painful, embarrassing procedure, as most of them were aimed at our behinds. I looked again for another .475 magnum, while Wilson said his extensive farewells. I didn't find one. Early the next morning Miss Wilding picked us up in a Rolls-Royce. The floor of the limousine was covered with crates of ammunition. Our baggage had to be strapped onto the back of the car. Miss Wilding stood on the sidewalk checking items off a long list she had made.

"You've said good-by to Mr. Duncan and Miss Gibson, haven't you?"

"Yes, dear." He was fiddling with the magnum, squinting down its double barrels.

"You've got the scripts?"

"Pete has."

"Have you picked up the rest of the things at Tautz's?"

"They're in my bag."

"Mr. Anders and Mr. Reissar wish you good luck and good hunting."

"Fine. I'll dictate a thank-you note to them on our way out to the airport."

"Mr. Landau said he'd be there to see you off."

Wilson nodded. He closed the breech of the gun, just as Randsome came out of the house.

"Sorry I couldn't be of more help, Jules," Wilson smiled.

"You've been most kind. I only wish I were going along."

"We wish you were too," he lied. We got in the car. Miss Wilding sat next to the chauffeur, her dictation pad in her hand, and we started off toward the airport.

"John, old man," I said solemnly, "this is a great moment. We are leaving the constant, babbling voices of women behind us. Aren't you glad?"

"I certainly am," he said. "I think that's one of the chief causes for the expansion of Western civilization . . . women's voices. They filled Magellan's sails, and started Cortez on his way, and they practically blew poor old Raleigh halfway across the world. But you'll be glad to hear them again in a couple of months, Pete. Don't kid yourself about that."

He dictated half a dozen tender farewell notes as we drove through the early morning streets. I sat in silence, listening to his persistent voice.

What the hell am I doing this for? I asked myself. I'm not an explorer or a big-game hunter. I don't like heat and flies and camping out. I like Paris and London and New York, and when I feel sporting I like a good tennis court, or a long, packed slope. I don't like to fly halfway around the globe in order to shoot at a wild animal who's never even heard of me.

And then I remembered the preface to Bolitho's wonderful book. Adventurers must begin by running away from home, he had written, and I remembered that years ago I had been impressed by that phrase. Cagliostro and Columbus had turned my head. *Twelve Against the Gods,* the book was called, and now here were two of us, leaving peaceful London in a Rolls-Royce full of weapons and ammunition. Two against the gods, I thought, and I looked at the passing city with a superior air.

We arrived at Heath Row. The plane was waiting for us and so was Landau. He looked sleepy and tender.

"Please be careful, will you, boys?" he said. "Work hard on the script and don't do any shooting with all those guns you bought."

"All right, Paul," Wilson said gently. "You look after this end."

"I'll be down once everything is settled. I'd like to get in a little hunting too, you know."

No man ever told a bigger lie. Two BOAC attendants were lugging our guns and ammunition onto the scales. Miss Wilding had tears in her eyes.

"You promised to send for me, you know," she said.

"Well, I will," Wilson said. He kissed her fondly. Then he turned to me. "Go ahead, Pete," he said. "Probably the last white woman you'll get your hands on for quite a while."

I did as I was told. Then I shook hands with Landau. He pulled me toward him unexpectedly and gave me a quick bearlike hug. I'm sure he never expected to see me alive again.

"God bless you both," he said.

We were shunted off into a waiting room. Wilson bought an armful of magazines and a couple of paperbacked books. I purchased two soggy tomato sandwiches.

"How do you feel, kid, setting out on this great adventure?"

"My behind is sore."

He grinned happily. "So is mine."

"I'm sure that doctor could have found a better place if he had wanted to."

"It's too late to worry about that now."

Our fellow passengers were an unimpressive lot, pale-faced Britishers in cheap suits, with their homely wives, and enough infants to promise a not altogether noiseless trip. There was one man, a large bony fellow with a leathery skin, who looked as if he might be a frontiersman or hunter, but all the rest of them were pasty-faced white-collar workers, the stay-at-homes Bolitho had not written about. Because they were going to Africa they were all wearing absurd hats; their wives were shouting at their children, calling them back whenever one of the small monsters strayed.

A rather pretty stewardess called our flight. We got into a bus and were driven a hundred yards to the waiting plane. All seats were reserved. We discovered with relief that most of the children had been placed in the tail of the plane. We were near the front. A steward told us that our destination was Rome, and that we would fly at an altitude of so many thousand feet, and that we were due to arrive at three o'clock in the afternoon, Roman time. We strapped ourselves in, and a few minutes later we were airborne.

We rose quickly through thick layers of dirty clouds, and found our rightful place in the pure atmosphere. The sun was reflected on our silver wing tips. The endless blue of the clean area outside the world was above us. Wilson loosened his necktie and tilted his seat back.

"Well," he said comfortably. "We're on our way."

"Are you at all sorry to leave London?" I asked him.

He shook his head. "No, are you?"

"Europe, yes, but not London. It's always sad to think that it's spring in Paris and I'm not there."

He shrugged. "You'll be there often enough before you're finished. This is something you won't get another chance to do."

"I know. That's why I'm here."

He half closed his eyes. His last night in England had ended very early this morning. "You know, Pete," he said hazily, his voice barely audible above the roar of the motors, "I've come to the realization that all city life is pretty much the same sort of thing. Paris, New York, Hollywood, London. You see the same people and you do the same things. Restaurants, offices, hotel rooms . . . cocktail parties where you hear nothing but nonsense, and where you spend your time chasing some dame. It's an endless cycle of wanting things and getting them, and wanting something else . . . and finally you discover that the mundane life is a great, crashing bore." He seemed to be in one of his contemplative moods.

"Life in the country repeats itself too," I said.

"Yes, it does," he answered, "but there's kind of a nobility about that repetition. I remember when I had that small farm in the San Fernando Valley. There was something to it, you know. The dew on the grass every morning, and that clean wonderful smell that you get out there at the beginning of each day; and then the horses being fed, and the chickens and the cows, and the work starting, the men going out in the clothes that will get sweaty and soiled by the earth they dig in. Then it gets hot, and the flies start to hum, and the horses move slowly in the corral and kick up dust. At lunchtime you drink ice-cold beer, and afterwards you go out into the blazing sun. The afternoons are always long and kind of endless in the country, and then the evening starts, the cool evening, and the sage gives off that special perfume that it has, and the sky turns a darker blue. Sometimes the desert wind comes up and blows the dry grass, and everyone starts the evening chores. Even when I've been getting nowhere with a script all day long, that's a wonderful hour, and I get myself a drink and sit out on the porch, and they turn the sprinklers on, and you can just almost hear the grass drinking, and then it's nighttime, and black and quiet, and once in a while a car passes down the road, and the frogs begin to croak, and a coyote howls, and the stars are out. God damn, that's a better life than what we've just been living."

I sat in silence. It was astonishing how clearly things occasionally registered with him, and how he could make them sound ideal. In reality his farm had been in a region that was much too hot for comfort, and the animals had often been sick, and there had been dust and wind on most summer days.

"A city boy could make the same kind of a speech, John," I said. "Have you ever gotten up early on a summer morning in Paris, and watched the water wagons sprinkling the empty cobblestones and then the streets filling up with cars and people . . . everybody going to work?"

"Oh sure," he said. "I know there's something to that, too, but it's just not for me. I know it's wonderful in the afternoon in the summer when the cafés are crowded, and the 'blue hour' is great, especially if you're having a drink with a beautiful girl you know you're going to wind up in the hay with, and then the lights go on, and the hustling starts, and then later it all empties itself again, and the streets are black and shiny, and the whores begin to parade. I know, a city boy is just nuts about that sort of thing, but I was brought up in the country."

"So was I," I answered.

"That's why you'll like Africa," he said. "It's just made for a country boy, what with hunting, and living outdoors. You'll see."

The plane rose abruptly and then fell quickly back to its normal altitude again. "You know," I said, "I'm a little worried about the hunting."

He looked at me with surprise. "What do you mean, Pete?" he asked.

"Well, I'll tell you a story," I said. "Nobody in my family ever went hunting. My father was in the theatre all his life, and so was my mother. They liked the country, but in a different way, the way intellectuals like nature. I guess I went shooting for the first time out of protest. I was fourteen, and some of the neighborhood kids who were a little older than I was took me along. I got all the excitement out of it, right away. We went up into the hills near Oxnard, after quail. It was wonderful, walking along with a shotgun in my hands. I didn't even know what a quail looked like. They told me it made a hell of a noise when it took off. Well, I walked along by myself, clutching a loaded shotgun, thinking I had to get a quail, because the other fellows were going to get some. Still, I was worried. I didn't quite know why. All of a sudden a bird started up out of a bush near my feet. I turned and blazed away at him, and as I was a beginner, I had beginner's luck. One of my pellets hit it in the wing and knocked it down. It took refuge in a mesquite bush. Are you listening?"

"Yes, sure, kid, go on."

"Well, I was stunned. The other guys heard me fire, and they started yelling. Had I gotten one? Was it a quail? I yelled back that it was. Then I moved closer to the bush, and I saw that it was a small brownish bird, and that it had no plume. I knew that it was much too small to be a quail, and I knew that I had wounded it for no reason at all. It looked at me with a terrible fear in its eye. I remember it as if it were yesterday. It clung to a branch, twitching its wounded wing, and stared at me with fear. 'Why did you shoot me?' it seemed to be asking. 'Why? I'm not a quail. I'm a helpless small bird you can't eat, and you've broken my wing.' I started to sweat. My heart was pumping inside my chest. I felt like a murderer, John. I moved closer to the bush, hoping the bird would be able to fly and therefore prove that it was not too gravely wounded. But it couldn't. It just sat and stared at me, its eyes full of fear and the knowledge that it would have to die. I knew that the merciful thing to do was to kill it, and I wanted to shoot it, so that it wouldn't look at me any more. But if I fired again the others would want to see what I had shot. To tell them that I had missed twice would be an unpleasant confession to have to make. The bird squeaked, a kind of desperate cry for help. I couldn't stand it any more. I stepped back a yard or two and fired, and at that close range there was nothing left of the bird once the smoke had cleared. The others yelled again, of course. I knew I would have to tell them that I had missed. Still I felt a little better. The bird was dead. The small, reproachful face didn't exist any more. I didn't load my gun again, but started back toward the car. Everything had changed. I felt terrible. I didn't know what the hell had made me come out hunting in the first place. I had killed a living creature wantonly, for no reason at all. I felt guilty about it. I felt I would ultimately have to pay for my crime, and all I could remmber were those frightened, wild eyes looking at me, and the frightened squeak that it had uttered as its last comment on life was all I could hear. I sat down on the running board of the car and felt like crying. Of course the others made fun of me when they returned and I told them that I had fired twice at a quail and had missed. But even that didn't bother me. I felt so disgusted with myself that I hardly heard them. I kept wishing that it was all a dream and hadn't really happened. Then we drove home. I didn't go out hunting again for years and years, and when I finally did it was after the war. I went duck shooting with a guy who'd been in my outfit. . . ."

"Is that right?" Wilson said. "Well, what made you go then?"

"Oh, I learned to reason that killing game yourself was no worse than eating meat that had been butchered, and I learned to enjoy the sensation of reaching out into the sky and knocking down a duck in full flight."

"It is quite a feeling, isn't it?" Wilson said.

"Sure. It's a kind of vice, I guess. Anyway, that's not the point I was trying to make. The point of the story is that since killing that first bird I've never really shot at anything I couldn't eat, and I've always made damn sure of what I was shooting at."

"I don't think that's the point of the story at all," Wilson said. "I think the point is that you killed your innocence with that first swallow or blue jay you murdered. It took you a couple of years to realize it, but that's what happened."

"Maybe. I know I was a pretty straight kid, and I'm not that straight a guy now."

"Well, that's what I mean. That's all there is to the story. That was your first step toward growing up. You became a man and you learned to do worse things and accept the guilt."

"Not exactly a wonderful development."

"An inevitable process."

"Are you sure?"

"Positive. You see, if you had told me this story and had concluded it by saying that you never went hunting again, and that you have never eaten meat since, then I'd say, 'Get off in Rome, Pete, and visit the museums.' But that isn't what you told me, and that's not what I know about you. You're just saying you only want to hunt to eat, that trophies don't interest you. Well, that's all right. You should still make this trip. Because first of all, if you want to, you can just shoot for the pot when we go out on safari. And secondly, maybe you'll change again. Maybe when you're confronted with an animal that is likely to kill you, if you don't kill it, you'll forget about the first bird you shot."

"None of them want to kill you, unless you threaten to harm them."

"Don't be too sure of that, Pete," he said. "There are rogue elephants, and old hungry lions that are too slow for anything except man, and very often there are buffalo that are just as mean as anything you'll ever meet."

"Well, maybe I'll change again," I said. "Maybe I'll take one more step toward becoming a real monster, but I rather doubt it."

He sat in silence for a while. "That's not quite true, kid," Wilson said. "It isn't necessarily monstrous to kill just for the sake of killing, or to kill for trophies. It's a way of finding out about yourself, finding out a lot more than you did up in Oxnard when you were just a kid."

"Is that a good thing to do?"

"Why, sure it is. You should find out as much as you possibly can about yourself, and you should even try to find out about others, if that's possible."

"It's not a very pleasant prospect."

"Well, I don't know about that," Wilson said. I think he was beginning to sense that there was a great difference between our two characters, and I think his fondness for me had decreased somewhat. He took out a couple of books and opened one of them. I saw that it was a book on African hunting.

I sat not doing anything for a long time. You can learn from him, I told myself. He is ready to investigate everything in the world. You're not. That's a failing. That's a soft side of your nature that will prevent your growth. But is that really true? I asked myself. Maybe in the end he will feel nothing at all, and you'll still be able to remember the eyes of that wounded bird in the mesquite bush.

The clouds had vanished under us, and we were flying over blue sea. Adventurers begin by running away from home, I reminded myself.

13

We landed in Rome. As we made our approach I was struck by the soft green countryside over which we were passing, and the brown earth. It looked softer and less crowded than England. Wilson pointed out some of the ruins along the Appian Way which we could see briefly from the plane, and then a moment later we were on the ground.

"Have you ever been in Rome?" Wilson asked me. We had found two empty chairs outside the terminal building in the sun.

"No, I've only been to northern Italy."

"Well, we can stop here for a week or so on the way back," he said. "I'd like to spend a little time in Italy myself."

"You sure I shouldn't get off now and stay?" I asked.

"Don't be silly." He turned back to his book on big-game rifles and hunting. "You know, you ought to read this book," he said presently. "It's very instructive."

"I'll learn by doing," I said.

He shrugged, and continued reading. He was obviously tired of talking, and I began to suspect that he had had enough of personal revelations for the time being. He looked up once more. "You know, I'm worried about the guns we bought," he said. "This guy seems to feel that the .256 Mannlichers are useless on a trip of this kind. They're all right for deer stalking in Scotland, and that kind of thing, but he says that in Africa they're just excess baggage."

"This is a hell of a time to find that out, isn't it?"

"It sure is. Well, we'll probably have to get another rifle or two when we get to Nairobi."

"But we're going to Entebbe now, aren't we?" I asked.

"Yes, but we'll get to Kenya before we go out on safari."

Our plane was called and we resumed our journey. The air was clear as we flew along the Italian coast, passing over Capri, on our way down to Sicily. We flew a little too high to see anything but the contours of the peninsula below us. The plane droned on. I tried to read, but my eyes felt tired, and so I went to sleep.

They woke me for the inevitable meal, the unappetizing little lumps of food that all airlines so delightfully serve their customers. I ate very little of what was given me. Wilson ate everything, continuing his reading throughout the meal. I didn't try to talk to him. After a while I dozed off. The stewardess woke me with the news that we were approaching Cairo.

The electric sign over the crew compartment door had been flashed on and we fastened our safety belts. Wilson closed his book.

"You know, there's something I forgot to tell you," he

said as the plane began slanting down toward the earth. "This'll amuse you. Remember Sylvia Lawrence?"

"Sure. The advice to the lovelorn girl."

"That's right. Well, she called me just before we left the hotel."

"From jail?"

"No, from bed. I asked her if she'd gotten her husband back, and she sounded surprised as hell, and said no, that was all over. She's found a major in a Guards regiment, and she's mad for him. Of course her husband wants *her* back now, and she won't have any part of him."

"Did she ever try out what you told her to do?"

"No, she never got a chance. She met this new guy on the street outside our house."

"Well, we wasted a lot of time on her, didn't we?"

"We sure did," Wilson said. "But she wasn't the only one."

The lights along the landing strip flashed past our window, and the plane settled with a bump.

"Egypt," Wilson said. He looked vague. "Feel the mystery, kid?"

"I sure do."

We were herded out into the warm, evening air. There wasn't a cloud in the sky. Men in fezzes were riding red and yellow Shell gasoline trucks out toward the plane. I could see our pilot and his crew out on the wings, getting ready to supervise the refueling.

We were herded into a bus and driven a few hundred yards to a low building with a terrace, where there were tables and umbrellas. The black waiters who moved among them were dressed in white flowing robes with wide red bands at the waist. The night air was mild and pleasant.

Wilson and I walked through the restaurant. At the far end was a half-finished porch with a low crumbling wall that seemed ultimately to dissolve into the sand of the desert. To our left the lights of Cairo set up a rose-colored glow. In the shadows not fifty yards away from us a mangy hyenalike dog was digging in the sand. An old Chevrolet coupé drove by, filled with airport officials in their sloppy tunics.

"Feel the mystery?" Wilson said in a tired voice, repeat-

ing his joke. He looked old and tired in his brown suit
and large-brimmed hat. He had taken off his collar and
tie, and now he had the look of a railroad bum from
somewhere in the West. "Night on the desert," he went
on. "An Arab with a long gleaming knife creeps through
the darkness, the sahib's tent his ultimate destination."

"I'm thirsty," I said.

We went back to the porch of the restaurant and sat
down in the green folding chairs that stood under the
parasols. A huge, barefoot Negro came over to us.

"Coca-Cola?" he asked.

Wilson nodded his head. *"Sí, amigo,"* he said, holding
up two fingers. *"Duo."*

"Coca-Cola?" The Negro asked again. He felt instinc-
tively that Wilson was making fun of him.

"Yes, my friend," Wilson said in a burlesque-show Mexican accent. "Go to the reevar and get Coca-Cola."

The Negro shuffled off grumpily.

A moment later another Negro waiter was looking down
at us.

"Coca-Cola?" the new waiter asked.

"Muchas gracias, amigo," Wilson said, nodding his head.
"Por favor."

"You speak English?" the Negro asked aggressively.

"A little," I said. "We want two Coca-Colas."

He nodded curtly and went away. Wilson shook his
head. "You won't get anything out of traveling that way,
Pete. You've got to speak the language of the country."

"I'll let you handle it, from now on."

"Good." He opened his book on African hunting, and
stretched his feet out on the canvas chair opposite him.
He asked me once more if I felt the mystery, and then
was lost in his book. The waiter served us our drinks,
staring down at Wilson with curious contempt. A few minutes later a fat Egyptian in a BOAC tunic announced that
our plane was ready to leave. Wilson rose, sighing. He
bowed politely to all of the waiters, smiling a strange and
superior smile he seemed to have invented for the occasion. *"Hasta luego, amigos,"* he said.

We took our seats in the plane and fastened our safety belts. A few minutes later Wilson was asleep. I sat in
the darkness for a long time listening to the steady roar
of the motors. Wilson stirred in his sleep and turned to-

ward me. His strange, almost handsome face was smiling. I had known him for such a long time, and yet his moods and his thoughts were unpredictable to me. He behaved like a kind, fatherly fellow so much of the time, and then he would suddenly change and become a torturer, a man bored with himself and bored with his fellows. At other times he became a clown, a bum who allowed himself to drift along uselessly, who seemed to want everyone around him to take advantage of him. Still, he was really never fooled by anyone. But the thing that puzzled me most was the huge gulf that seemed to separate what he had experienced personally and what he wanted to produce as a writer. His stories were always about tough men of action, lost in fruitless adventures, when actually he was a complete stranger to that life. He was a bum and a snob, an intellectual and a frustrated country boy, and he seemed never to be interested in the reality that surrounded him. Perhaps that was the source of his talent, the fact that he only saw the life he wanted to see, the strange romantic existence that did not exist around him, that he brought along himself, and used to color what he ran into.

I went to sleep with my back toward him. When I awoke it was light. The motors were running at a different pitch. I looked down at the earth. It was brown and dry. There was no vegetation at all, and no sign of life. Wilson stirred and opened his eyes.

"Feel the mystery, John?"

He moaned. "Yeah, I feel it. God, my tail hurts. Doesn't yours?"

"It's numb."

He glanced out of the window. "That fellow Livingstone walked a long way, didn't he?"

"So did Stanley."

"I never would have gone after the son of a bitch. Would you?"

"Certainly not."

We landed in Khartoum. There were a number of wooden barracks built near the three or four local trees, and that was all there was. That and the heat. We drank bitter coffee while the sun rose higher in the cloudless sky and the heat increased. The fans inside the passenger reception shack started to turn indolently. The flies multiplied before our eyes on the plates of sandwiches which were spread out on a table near the door. A rather pretty Arab girl in a starched khaki dress served coffee.

"We ought to do a play about this place," Wilson said. He seemed to be waking up out of his "feel the mystery" stupor. "An English poet turns up here in Khartoum on a walking tour, and meets our girl friend over there. He has a book of Elizabethan sonnets with him, and his dinner clothes, that's all. He's traveling light. He realizes that this girl is what he's been looking for all of his life, but she's the mistress of the local base wallah. A dust storm starts, and a desperado arrives in a stolen Cadillac convertible."

"A part for Duncan."

"That's right. He can make the picture for Warner Brothers on his way back."

"Shall we cut Bob Sherwood in on the profits?"

"No, he'll never recognize our plot." He waved to the girl to bring him more coffee. "Has Kitchener been around lately?" he asked.

"Pardon me?" she said.

He beamed his false smile. "I'd like some more coffee," he said charmingly. Then he lit one of his long, dark brown cigarettes. "You know," he said to me, "I've been thinking about the story you told me on the plane. I don't believe it, Pete. I think you made it up."

"I did like hell," I said.

"Come on. Don't give me that. That's one of the stories you use on whatever girl you're trying to make. I just don't believe it, that's all. You want to appear as a sensitive soul, and so you tell this fairy tale. Oh, it's a good story, all right, but you just can't sell it to me. I know you, just as I know myself. You're a conscienceless bastard. Whatever you do that's bad, you forget. You're just like I am. You have no soul. To take the place of one, you invent whatever will make the biggest impression at the time. But down deep you're hollow. There's no hurt in you, no old wounds. That's probably why you can't write any more. You have to make everything up, and then when you reread it, you realize how phony it all is. So now I'll tell you what actually you ought to do . . . devote yourself to the movies."

The long journey was beginning to enervate him. I didn't argue. "You're quite right," I said. "I'm an empty

shell, just like you are. I don't care what I do to people
or animals. I'm a spoiler too, only I'm a little more careful
about hiding it than you are."

"You think I'm a spoiler?" he asked, looking up quickly. I saw that my reply had struck a nerve.

"Everybody knows that," I said. "You ruin whatever
you come into contact with. Look at the women you've
had. They never look the same once you're finished with
them. And that goes for your horses and your friends."

"You think so, eh?"

"Sure. I know you as I know myself."

We were called back to the plane. "Well," he said as
we settled back into our seats, "we've got to talk about
this." He opened his book and started reading.

We took off and flew south. Slowly vegetation began to
appear on the ground below us. Then there were masses
of clouds, hiding the earth. We flew through rain, through
layers of white nothing, the plane dropping suddenly every
once in a while, and the motors changing their tune as
they held us up against the thermals. Then we came down
lower, and the earth was green, covered with trees and
jungle. The rivers we passed over were brown, brackish
and the color of earth, as were the occasional grass hut
villages. Wilson closed his book and began staring out of
the window over my shoulder.

"Might see game any time now," he said. His mood had
changed again. He seemed wide awake, eager to arrive.

"Is this country something like the Congo?" I asked.

"No, nothing like it at all. This is small-time jungle.
This is like Cuba. In the Congo the trees are hundreds of
feet high, and you can't see the ground beneath them at
all."

"What's that down there?" I asked, pointing.

"Cows," he answered. "Native cattle."

We saw no game. Only endless green forest and brown,
rain-soaked land; and banana trees and grass huts and
muddy roads with water standing in the ruts. The plane
flew lower and then banked sharply to the left. I caught
a glimpse of an enormous body of water and a small
green peninsula that jutted out into it. The water was
grayish blue, almost indistinguishable from the sky. The
other passengers began pulling their raincoats off the
racks over their heads.

"We're arriving," Wilson said.

The stewardess warned us to fasten our seat belts, for the last time, and we started to approach the field. We were flying over well-kept lawns stretching out in every direction, dotted with clumps of trees and neat white bungalows. It was not at all what I had expected. We had flown a long way around the curve of the earth, into the heart of Africa, and I felt that very little had happened to me. Even after they had opened the doors of the plane, and the motors had stopped, and the humid air had come rushing into the cabin, I didn't feel that we had traveled very far.

Wilson stood in front of me and waved to a man in a khaki tunic and shorts. I followed him out into the warm rain, grateful that our time alone together was over.

"Well, kid," he said, "we're here. Another one of your boyhood dreams has been realized. Another great adventure has begun." He stumbled, on purpose, and then went slowly down the gangway on his skinny legs.

14

I think there are three basic reasons why love ends between people. The first is boredom, which is usually the result of spending too much time together alone. The second is disenchantment, which is usually caused by some basic revelation of character that one or the other parties did not know existed. The third is the appearance on the scene of some new object of love. In Wilson's and my case all three reasons came along almost simultaneously, walking into our lives hand in hand. Our trip provided mutual boredom; my qualms about hunting had served as the unpleasant revelation of character; and the third, the appearance of a new object of love, was the man who was waiting for us at the Entebbe airport. The moment Wilson greeted him, I knew that my relief had arrived, and I couldn't help thinking that he had come just in the nick of time.

He was a man of medium height, with a handsome face, marred only by features that were a little too small. He had straight blond hair, carefully combed and parted above a sunburned forehead. Over the left pocket of his khaki tunic he wore RAF wings, above three solid rows of ribbons. I recognized the Distinguished Flying Cross among them. He walked slowly out across the muddy field and stood at the foot of the gangway, smiling quietly, a black cigarette holder jutting out of his mouth at just the right angle. Wilson put his long arm affectionately around the pilot's shoulders.

"Well, Alec," he said, "it's good to see you."

"Good to see you, John." They turned their backs on me and moved off toward the entrance of the airport building. I followed them, taking in my new surroundings as we moved through the mud. Low green hills bordered the field, their ridge lines covered with thick vegetation. At the end of one of the taxi lanes an RAF bomber with a smashed nose lay helplessly on its side, its landing gear folded up under its belly, one wing pointing like an accusing finger at the brown plaster control tower, which was perched on the flat roof of the air terminal building. A dozen or more native boys in khaki shorts and shirts were standing by to unload the baggage. They were all barefoot, their flat feet splayed out on the wet ground.

"Well, how have you been, Alec?" Wilson was asking the pilot in his "truly concerned" voice.

"Not too bad. Had a touch of malaria last week, but that's all. Probably picked it up on our trip to the Congo."

"You did, eh? Well what do you know about that? Isn't that a shame. How do you feel now, Alec?"

"H'mmm, all right." The pilot turned, hesitantly. "You didn't come down alone, did you, John?"

"No, Pete came with me," Wilson said. "You haven't met Pete, have you?"

They stopped and waited for me to catch up with them. "This is Alec Laing," Wilson said. "Our chief counsel and guide without whom this whole endeavor would fall flat on its face."

We shook hands. "John's told me an awful lot about you," Laing said pleasantly. "You're another big-game enthusiast, aren't you?"

"Well, more or less," I answered.

"Turns out he's just a conscience-stricken duck shooter, Alec." Wilson grinned. "We're going to have to convert him."

"I like duck hunting best myself," Laing said. "Unfortunately the season's over."

We went inside the airport office. Laing turned to one of the natives who was standing inside and spoke to him in Swahili. The native nodded and went out to the plane. Others began to appear, heavily laden with baggage. Laing noticed that one of them stood by empty-handed.

"Boy," he said imperiously, "take this." He gave the Negro Wilson's small bag. An airline official in a starched white uniform, wearing a dark blue cap, came over to Wilson and shook hands.

"Bring any photographic equipment down with you this time, Mr. Wilson?" he asked.

"No, just a few guns and some ammunition."

The official looked doubtful. "That'll have to be cleared through customs, I'm afraid, sir. And I'm afraid you can't have any of your guns until you've been issued licenses."

"Can we do that right now?" Wilson asked.

"Afraid not, sir. That has to be done in Kampala. The provost marshal's office issues the licenses."

"Well, we can do it this afternoon, then?"

"I rather doubt that, sir. Probably have to wait until tomorrow. Of course you can make out your applications today."

"You don't intend to use them immediately, do you, John?" Laing asked.

"No," Wilson said absently, "but I'd like to get it done as soon as possible."

"Well, we'll get on it," Laing said. "I've got a car and driver standing by to take us to the hotel."

"That's fine, Alec." He was still staring longingly at our weapons. "Well, we might as well go," he said finally.

"What about our passports?" I asked.

"That'll all be taken care of, kid," Wilson said a little irritably. "Don't worry about it."

I followed them out through the building, and we all squeezed into a small black sedan. Wilson and Laing sat in front with the driver. I found a place in the back of the car with the luggage, and we were off, splashing down a muddy road at full speed. On both sides of us there was thick green grass, and occasionally a tall, conelike mound of reddish mud that rose up out of the fields. Natives in brightly colored robes were walking along both shoulders of the road, quite a few of them balancing large bundles on their heads. Their black arms and faces shone brightly. The sun had come out, and it was hot and damp. Wilson turned briefly toward the rear of the car and pointed to one of the reddish mounds of earth.

"Anthills," he said. "There are thousands of them in every field."

"Your first time in this part of the country?" Laing asked.

"Yes. My first time in Africa."

"Well, you'll have a lot to see. Does he have his equipment, John?"

"No, we'll have to get that for him. Safari clothes, mosquito boots, and the rest of the stuff. Say, there's something else, while I think of it. We need another big gun. I only brought one with me from London."

"What sort of thing do you have in mind?" Laing asked.

"A big rifle. A .475 preferably. Can we get that in Kampala?"

"Afraid not. We'll have to pick one up in Nairobi, next time one of the chaps goes."

"Good. But don't let me forget it."

"Aren't we going to Nairobi, John?" I asked.

"We'll see, kid. We'll see. Is everybody else all right, Alec? Lockhart and the other boys?"

"Yes, they're all right. They're all in Kampala this morning clearing equipment. Some of the camera gear has come down from London, and all of the stuff you bought in Nairobi has arrived."

"That's fine. We're making some progress, then?"

"Well, a bit," Laing replied. "Actually we're holding up a lot of the shipments from Nairobi until you decide where you want to start. If we go to the Congo, there's no use making two moves when one will do."

"We'll have a meeting on that this afternoon," Wilson said.

"Good. The sooner the better. You fellows want a bath now, don't you, after your long trip?"

"I don't know about that," Wilson said jovially. "First I think we should have a little drink."

The muddy road ended abruptly at an intersection, and we drove more quickly down a paved street. The huge body of water I had seen from the plane was to our left, a smooth gray stretch of sea rising to the edge of the horizon. We drove past a well-kept golf course, three or four clay tennis courts, and turned into the driveway of a hotel. It was a large brown plaster structure with a flat roof, built in the same ugly style as the airport building.

"The Lake Victoria Hotel," Laing announced. "Uganda's finest."

There were red stone floors, and half a dozen native boys in khaki. They leaped forward at Laing's command and began unloading the car. A flat-chested young English girl asked us to sign the register and showed us to our rooms. Wilson's room was on the first floor, mine was on the second. I was pleasantly surprised to find clean, recently painted walls and solid-looking mosquito screens. There was a private bathroom, and it was cool even at this time of the day.

"If you want anything, just call for the boy," the young Englishwoman said, and disappeared.

I stripped off my clothes and took a bath. Then I unpacked my things and put on the lightest trousers and shirt I had brought with me. It was a relief to be alone for an hour. After a while I went downstairs to the bar. It was one o'clock and the place was crowded. A few of the men there were in uniform, but most of them wore slacks and were in shirt sleeves.

Wilson, Laing, and another Englishman were seated at a small corner table. Wilson introduced me. The man's name was Lockhart, and he was the assistant unit manager. He was a stocky man with a sunburned face and horn-rimmed glasses. I noticed at once that he had a habit of chewing his nails.

"Sorry I couldn't be there to meet you this morning," he said pleasantly. "Had some business to take care of in Kampala."

"What'll you have to drink, Pete?" Wilson asked me.

"I don't think I want anything, John," I said.

"Oh, come on now, for Christ's sake. Have a drink."

"No, thanks."

He shrugged irritably. "Difficult bastard, aren't you?"

I began to sense that I was really going to take Landau's place in every way possible.

"You're doing the script, isn't that right?" Lockhart said, turning to me. "We're awfully anxious to get it, you know."

"I'm working with John."

"He's supposed to be my companion," Wilson said, "and the son of a bitch is already laying down on the job."

"I've just realized that it's a pretty tough assignment."

Wilson was showing off for the benefit of the others, playing the part of the manly leader. "That's gratitude for you," he said. "I bring the guy down here to Africa, and what do I get in return? A lot of complaints. Petty gripes. He doesn't want a drink. He doesn't want to eat. Christ Almighty, I wish I'd left him home."

"When's the next plane back?" I asked.

"You see? Just like I said."

"Screw you, John," I said. I could tell that he didn't like my open rebellion in front of the others. He turned away from me. Laing coughed uncomfortably.

"Shall we take our drinks in to lunch?" he asked.

"Sure, let's do that," Wilson said. We got up and started toward the dining room. "Will Harrison be coming back for lunch today?" he asked Lockhart.

"I'm not sure," the assistant unit manager replied. "It rather depends on if he gets through with his work in time."

We went through the lobby toward the dining room. I took Wilson by the arm and pulled him off to one side.

"Look," I said, "let's get something straight. I'm not your whipping boy. I'm supposed to help you with the script, that's all. If you need a stooge, you'd better send for one."

He looked perturbed. "Now why do you say that, kid?" he asked with feigned surprise.

"Because I can sense the way the wind is blowing," I replied. "You like to have one guy around to take all the ribbing and the punishment. Well, I didn't hire out for that."

"You're not serious, are you, Pete?"

"I'm serious as all hell," I said. "Lay off me, or we'll be at each other's throats from here on in."

He shook his head. "Well, for God's sake," he said. "You amaze me. I thought you could take a little kidding. What's the matter? Has the sun affected you already?"

"Maybe. In any case, knock it off. I'd like us to have a good time, and not end up this junket in a brawl."

O.K.," he said, sounding injured. "You're a lot more sensitive than I thought."

"I am."

We sat down. A tall, wiry man with a thick shock of blond hair came over to the table and took our room numbers. He was obviously the headwaiter. Then he turned and snapped out a single word: "Boy!"

Three Negroes in long white robes, tied at the waist with red sashes, came running across the room. The wooden floor resounded with the pounding of their bare feet. The headwaiter turned angrily on two of them and pushed them away. Then he spoke in snarling Swahili to the third. The small Negro listened, trembling visibly. He was a man in his late fifties to judge by his gray, kinky hair and the dry skin on the back of his hands. When the headwaiter had finished with his instructions, he clapped his hands, and the Negro ran wildly toward the kitchen, almost colliding with another waiter who was hurrying across the room with a tray.

"He'll look after you now," the headwaiter said very politely to Wilson.

"Thank you very much," Wilson said, endeavoring to smile.

"He knows how to handle these boys, Harry does," Lockhart said, biting the extreme corner of his thumbnail. "Gets a lot of work out of them."

"The service is really quite good," Laing added.

Wilson and I exchanged brief glances. Despite the enmity that had broken out between us, we found that we were being driven together again.

"He's a charming guy," I said. "Why doesn't he get himself a whip?"

Laing laughed quietly. "He does seem a bit rough on the boys, but I think you'll find there's just no other way to handle these people."

"They're not like the Masai," Lockhart said, "or the natives you find in Kenya. They're a lazy lot. You've got to keep after them or they just won't do anything."

The floor was throbbing under our feet as the waiters raced back and forth around the various tables. Occasionally they almost collided with each other in their great haste. It was like Paris traffic, only instead of the frantic cars, there were human beings racing around, trying to avoid each other.

"Tell us about the Masai, Ralph," Wilson said, trying to find a more pleasant topic of conversation.

"They're the best niggers in Africa," Lockhart said. "Isn't that true, Alec?"

"H'mm, quite true," the pilot replied.

"I've lived out here over five years," Lockhart went on, "and I've been everywhere. Tanganyika, Somaliland, Kenya, the Congo, and Uganda of course, and I've never found natives like the Masai. They're all big fellows, over six feet, and they own cattle for the most part. They still hunt lion with spears by surrounding the beasts and letting the lion charge them. One or two of them always get mauled or killed before they get the cat. They're damn brave chaps, the Masai, and tough. And don't think the other niggers don't know it. If you're ever out in Masai country and one of your boys gives you trouble, you just threaten to toss him off the back of the truck and leave him there, and you should see the buggers snap out of it. They're more afraid of the Masai than they are of lion or buffalo." He turned in his chair. "Boy," he shouted, to our waiter, who was just approaching, *"mimi nataka moto."*

"Now what does that mean?" Wilson asked.

"He's forgotten the water."

The Negro looked stunned. His hands were loaded down with the first course of our luncheon, and he was obviously in doubt whether he should serve us first and then get the water, or obey the most recent command immediately. He decided to put down the plates of hot rice and curried lamb and go for the water. Now Laing shouted at him, in Swahili. The Negro seemed to be even more frightened of the pilot, for he started to serve us.

"Food'll get cold if he leaves it there," Laing said. "Now get the water, quick smart," he said angrily once we each had a plate in front of us. The waiter raced off toward the kitchen.

"Stupid bugger," Lockhart said.

"You know, in some of the best restaurants in New York, like Twenty-one, a waiter is apt to forget the water once in a while," I said.

"I know," Lockhart said, "but they shouldn't forget here."

"Have you been out in the Masai country a lot?" Wilson asked Laing. He was obviously anxious to avoid an argument on the racial issue.

"Quite a bit," the pilot replied. "Never have seen them on a hunt, though. It's rare now."

"H'mm, is that right?" Wilson said thoughtfully. "I'd love to see one, wouldn't you, Pete?"

I nodded. Although the lamb curry was quite good, I really didn't feel hungry. Lockhart seemed to sense the reason for my lost appetite.

"When you first arrive out here," he said to me, "you think the white men overdo it a bit. You think they're too hard on the blacks. But you soon discover that it's the only way. Of course the government we have now seems to be bent on ruining it all. Why, there's even talk about giving the people in Kenya their independence. But they'll find they have a battle on their hands if they try that. The white man made this blooming country, and he's not about to turn it over to the nigger again."

"You haven't read the script, have you?" I asked Lockhart.

"No, I haven't," he said. "I'm keen to, though."

"You'll love the ending," I said.

"I'm sure I will," he replied.

"As soon as Pete and I finish our work we're going to take off on our safari, Alec," Wilson said to Laing, "so we've got to get it all laid on now."

"That shouldn't be too difficult," Laing replied.

"It's got to be just right," Wilson said. "It'll be the only chance we'll have to do any hunting."

There was a commotion at the far end of the room. Harry, the headwaiter, was screaming at two of the boys. He swung at one of them with his open hand and missed. The waiter ran through the swinging door into the kitchen. Now Harry turned his wrath on the two Negroes nearest him. No one in the dining room paid any attention to the scene.

"It's really a very pleasant place, Entebbe," Lockhart said to me. He bit viciously at the cuticle on his index finger. "Probably the nicest place you'll find anywhere in all Africa."

"I'm sure of that," I said. A large group of Negroes stripped to the waist was starting out across the lawn in front of the hotel. I watched them through the window.

They spread out in a long line across the grass, and began swinging little steel clubs with sharp, curved ends.

"What are they doing out there?" I asked.

"Just trimming the grass," Lockhart said. "They get almost a shilling a day for doing that, too. That's the government for you. Overpays them, and spoils them . . ."

The black, shining bodies moved rhythmically, swinging their clubs. The sun beat down on the lake. A gentle breeze stirred the trees outside the veranda.

"What a beautiful country it is," I said to Wilson.

He nodded vaguely, and produced the book on hunting out of his jacket pocket.

"Have you read this, Alec?" he asked, holding it up.

Laing glanced at the picture of the buffalo on the cover. "Tells you how to shoot a buffalo, does it?" he smiled. "Well, I suppose if I'm going with you I'd better study it a bit.

15

The little car raced over the hilly asphalt road, swinging around frequent columns of natives in their brightly colored robes, women and children and old men moving steadily in both directions. Lockhart gave them about three feet of lebensraum, and a lot of horn. The tall, black women with their ramrod-straight backs grabbed their children as we approached and dragged them off into the mud of the soft shoulders. A few of the men jabbered excitedly as we rushed past, but Lockhart merely pressed his disfigured hand down on the button in the center of the steering wheel.

"Get out of the way, you stupid buggers," he said tensely under his breath. He turned to Wilson: "They will walk out in the street, these people. They knock off about ten a month along this road, but that seems to make not the slightest impression on them."

"Is that right?" Wilson said disinterestedly. I could tell Lockhart was beginning to get on his nerves, for he was agreeing too often with him and not listening. He turned to me. "What do you think of Alec Laing?" he asked.

"He seems very nice. I haven't had a chance to talk with him. His racial theories leave something to be desired."

"H'mmm," Wilson said. It was obviously a topic he wanted to avoid at the present time. "He's quite a guy, Alec, you know. He was an ace during the war; one of the best, I understand, and now he operates the most successful charter service in this part of the country."

"He's known everywhere," Lockhart said. "The Congo, Mombasa, Tanganyika, any place you go they recognize him the minute he steps out of his plane. He's an awfully pleasant bloke to hang around with."

"Did you notice his eyes?" Wilson said. "Those cold, hard eyes. He'd got the look of a killer, hasn't he? A real killer." There was an overtone of admiration in his voice.

"He does look like a man who's very good at something," I said. "That special look. I don't know if the ribbons help but it's there."

"That's right. That special look of a man who is awfully, awfully good at something."

"Is he our pilot?"

"He's doing everything for us," Wilson said. "Helping us find locations, working out the transport problem, and of course we charter his planes. But we could never hope to pay him for the help he's been giving us."

"Look at that stupid *bibi*," Lockhart shouted. He slowed the car down and leaned out of the window and screamed something in Swahili. A wonderful-looking Negro woman leading two small black children looked up at us, startled and frightened.

"Bloody fool," Lockhart grumbled.

"What'd you say to her?" Wilson asked. He was looking back at the woman.

"Just told her off," Lockhart replied. "Walking out in the middle of the road like a bloody queen."

"She was beautiful," Wilson said. "Did you see her, Pete? Oh boy, she was something."

"Wonderful figure," I said, looking back.

"Just beautiful," Wilson repeated.

Lockhart shook his head. "How can you say that?" he asked. "Beautiful? She was black as the ace of spades. And you fellows have only been here a few hours. I've been here for years and they look no whiter to me."

"Because she *was* beautiful," Wilson said dogmatically. "Just as you said, she had something queenly about her. Somthing straight and solemn."

Lockhart shook his head, and laughed suggestively. "Not for me," he said. "Not if I have to cut it off first."

Wilson disregarded him. "You know that fellow I told you about who lives out near the Ruwenzori, the hunter I met? Well, he says he can't even look at white women any more. They all look pale and sick to him. The pale, white skin, he told me, disgusts him."

"He must be off his rocker," Lockhart said.

"No, I don't think so, Ralph. I can see what he means. That black, wonderful skin they have, and those long smooth bodies."

"What about the bloody smell?" Lockhart asked.

"I don't know about that," Wilson replied. "If there is a bad smell it's the smell of poverty, and you can get that in a bus on Piccadilly."

"It's not just that," Lockhart said, outraged by Wilson's insinuation. "I know chaps who've washed these bloody women, and perfumed them, and the smell stayed right on them. It's in their skin. And all the stuff they eat. Why, they hardly know what meat tastes like. Bananas is all they ever want, and some pasty kind of meal."

"That's probably all they can afford to buy," I said.

"Nonsense. Even if they could buy meat, they wouldn't do it," Lockhart argued. "They're animals. Why, it's common knowledge that their brains are about a quarter the size of ours."

Wilson lit a cigarette. The dust rose inside the car as it bounced over the uneven road. Outside there were grass huts without floors hidden among the banana trees, and on the green hills that rose beyond, there were more huts, and small reddish patches of land which had been cleared and cultivated.

"They're the most wonderful thing about Africa, as far as I'm concerned," Wilson said. "The animals and the natives. They're poor, and sad, but they're also beautiful and gentle, and the fact that they're black seems just right to me. Any other color somehow doesn't belong. Those black shining skins moving in the hot sunlight. They look clean somehow, even when they're filthy dirty, and they look healthy even when they're sick. I don't think it would be much of a place if they weren't here."

"Well," Lockhart said, "you're right there. Couldn't do any work in this country without them. But the part about them being beautiful . . . I guess I just know them too well."

We were approaching the town. There were swarms of natives now, gathered around crude wooden shops. I noticed that there were a good many Indian names painted in white letters on the store fronts. Lockhart came forward with an unwanted explanation.

"They own the place, the bloody Indians," he said. "And if anything they're worse than the blacks. Filthy people, all of them. They're rich as hell, of course. If we're not careful they'll take over this part of Africa. They own most of Kampala as it is. Of course we don't let them in our clubs, and the Lake Victoria's the only hotel that'll have them. Government-owned, you see, so they can't turn them away."

"Why are they barred from the clubs?" Wilson asked patiently.

"Because if you let them in they don't know how to behave. They won't bring *their* women, and they'll come over and ask a white woman to dance, just as soon as not. A filthy lot, with their black greasy hair wrapped up in their turbans. And they're harder on the blacks than any white man would ever be. They're trying to stop them from coming into the country, now that it's too late."

We drove down the main street of Kampala. The afternoon sun beat down on the muddy pavement. Under the arcades an endless crowd of multicolored people moved slowly past the shops. Lockhart found a place to park the car. He was sweating profusely as he backed in toward the curb.

"Any of the nigger girls you see with short skirts are whores," he explained. "And they're polluted with syphilis and gonorrhea."

"It seems to be a lovely place, Kampala," I said.

Lockhart grinned. "Oh, it's not so bad, but I'm always glad to get back to Entebbe." He turned off the motor.

The heat inside the car was insufferable. "I've got a few chores to do and then I'll meet you over in the main store. You can start getting your kit." He got out of the car and left us. Wilson took a deep breath, and opened the door on his side.

"I can see where a little of Mr. Lockhart will go a long way," he said.

I got out of the car and followed him across the street. I was wringing wet. "I'm sorry I got sore a while ago," I said.

He grinned happily. "Forget it."

"I can see now where us poor white folks will have to stick together."

"Yes, I can see that too," he said.

There were swarms of beggers in the shade of the arcades, most of them disabled Negroes. They sat holding tattered hats out to the passing throng, the flies gathering on their crippled limbs. I followed Wilson into the general store Lockhart had pointed out to us, and together we bought several suits of safari clothes. Wilson bought himself another hat. He selected a large, brown felt hat with a wide brim. The British manager of the shop directed us to the provost marshal's office and we went there for our licenses.

Each gun required five long application blanks to be filled out for it, and we worked for more than three quarters of an hour with scratching pens in the humid darkness of the office. Then we returned to the store where Lockhart had said he would meet us. He wasn't there, and so we stood on the sidewalk waiting for him.

"Feel the mystery?" I asked Wilson. The grimy, poverty-ridden dregs of mankind seemed to be moving past us in a steady stream. Wilson stared at them all with fascination.

"You forget the abyss of civilization that we all live above," he said. "Just think of this town, what goes on here at night behind those rickety shutters. And think of India and China, all filled with towns and villages a hundred times worse than this one." He shook his head. "God damn, what a mess it would be if they all ever got together," he mumbled.

"Travel broadens, doesn't it?"

"Travel can occasionally scare the hell out of you," he replied.

Lockhart appeared, bathed in sweat. "First shipment of electrical equipment gets in tomorrow," he said. "Have to get cracking on it in the morning."

We got back into the car and drove through the hot evening air. A rainstorm came up and cooled the night. When we arrived in Entebbe the sky was clear. The breeze off the lake was cool and dry.

"How about a swim?" I asked.

"Where?" Lockhart asked.

"In the lake."

"Can't do that. Water's full of little bugs that get into your body, and the shore's teeming with crocs."

Wilson beamed happily. "Makes you feel good, living beside a poisoned body of water the size of the British Isles," he said. "Come on, let's have a drink at the bar."

We sat out on the veranda in folding chairs and drank cool beer. Laing and Harrison joined us. The little art director had changed greatly since I had seen him off two weeks ago at Heath Row airport. His face was bright red, and his short white arms were covered with mosquito bites. He was excitable and given to sudden hopeless gestures with his hands.

"Awful place, isn't it, Mr. Verrill?" he said to me.

"Entebbe?"

"No, Africa. When I think I turned down a job in the south of France to come here."

"Well," Wilson said, "let's talk about our problems. First of all the equipment."

"It's coming along nicely, John," Lockhart said. "Only we must decide where we're going to start working."

"That's difficult, isn't it?" Wilson asked. "We have to find all of our locations first."

"Are you still set on the Congo, sir?" Harrison asked.

"I am if it can be done," Wilson said.

"Well, I think we'd better send someone over there to find out," Lockhart said. He rubbed his shining face with his shirt sleeve.

"Would you mind going, Alec?" Wilson asked. "You know the country, and you know what I'm after."

"Wouldn't mind at all," Laing replied. "Will you be coming along, John?"

Wilson considered the question briefly. He was quiet, and seemed to be well organized in his own mind. "Not this time, Alec. I think you and Harrison should go and scout things out. I'll stay and work with Pete. Basil Owen will be down in a week or so with a few more fellows to help get things organized. Then we can leave him here, and I'll come over to the Congo with you."

"It'll create quite a transportation problem if we start over there," Lockhart warned. "The roads into the Congo are frightful, and we'll have two moves to make. One going over there, and then coming back, of course, as your village is already half built up at Masindi."

The conversation branched off into the complexities of working in both the Congo and Uganda. It was like a staff officer's discussion of a difficult operation.

"You're quite decided to go to the Congo, are you, John?" Laing asked.

"I'd like to try doing some of the river stuff there," Wilson said.

"It complicates things, you know," Lockhart said. "You wouldn't like to consider the original plan and shoot everything here?"

"I don't think so, Ralph," Wilson said gently.

"Save a lot of money and time."

"Not your money, though, Ralph." His gentle voice sounded ominous to me.

"No, but the money I've been hired to look after," Lockhart said foolishly. I felt sorry for him as he went on. "We could shoot everything up at Masindi, and have just one move to worry about. Get all the stuff from London to Entebbe direct, and then move it all from here right to the location. Wrap it all up in six weeks and go home." Wilson nodded pensively. "Seems like the Congo is just one more foolish complication," the little man went on.

Wilson sat up rather suddenly. "It's all foolish, Ralph," he said. "The whole damn thing. We could have made the picture on a river in England and in the studio. That would have been the sanest thing to do."

"I quite agree," Lockhart said with an insecure little smile. He bit at his non-existent thumbnail.

"That's why we might as well go on with the foolishness," Wilson said. "You see, Ralph, movies are all foolish. They're an exercise in insanity, until you get them shot and cut together, and then very often they're worse than insane. But especially while you're making them, they're pure madness. To set out the way we're doing and go thousands of miles away into a wilderness, and try to create a story which never happened, about people who never existed, in a time that is long past . . . well, there's madness in that, real madness. And to risk your health, and maybe your life, doing it, makes it even greater folly. But we're stuck with that. We're not building a road or subduing a native tribe. We're not even looking for Dr. Livingstone. We're just making a movie, and we're going to be as caught up in it as if we were conquering the great wilderness for the queen. That's why I say it's crazy, and so are we, all of us, who've chosen to do this. But as we're in this thing, why, we might as well bluff our way through to the bitter end. And that's what we're going to do." He looked compassionately at Lockhart, before continuing, as if he really felt sorry for him. "You see, Ralph, there are always little guys like you who are sane who get caught up in a thing like this, and they always advance a lot of logical hurdles. All the way down the line there are practical little guys like you putting jumps up, and barricades, and objections. All the way down the line there are Ralph Lockharts resisting the great madness. And I have to beat my way through them. I've had to do it for years. Usually in the end they see things my way. Sometimes they fall by the road, and I have to go on without them. But I always win against them, even when they're right. Because I'm the boss, Ralph, you see. My name's on it. I'm responsible. I don't mind your quibbling and fighting as long as you get this one thing straight, and that's that I'm in command, crazy and illogical as I may be. I'm the boss, and I like to have things my way."

There was a long silence. A huge moth fluttered against the screen door behind us.

"I suppose I've just been told off," Lockhart said with a nervous laugh.

"No," Wilson said sweetly, "that was not my point. I was just explaining the fix you're in. I don't care what you say or what you think from now on, as long as you remember that. To save time you might even pass on this lecture to whoever arrives from London to help you out." He smiled benignly. "Now how about another drink, fellows?" he asked.

The storm was over. The soldiers looked doubtfully at their captain. "You know what we must do after dinner, Alec?" Wilson said pleasantly. "We must have a poker game."

Laing nodded. "Sounds fine," he said. I could see that he was pleased to be in the charter business, and not involved too deeply in the making of movies.

"Just one more question," Harrison asked in his high-pitched voice. "Laing and I are going to the Congo tomorrow or the day after? Is that right?"

"Whenever Alec feels he wants to take off. I leave it all up to him," Wilson replied smoothly.

We all drank another beer, and then went in to dinner. The waiters scurried around us as usual, their naked feet pounding the wooden floor, and Lockhart was fiercer than ever with the boy who was assigned to wait on our table. Wilson looked up angrily at him occasionally, but he said nothing. He talked about elephant hunting with Laing throughout the meal. I discussed the south of France with Harrison. After dinner we went up into the lounge and started playing poker. The manager of the hotel joined us, as did Harry, the headwaiter.

Wilson decided that it should be table stakes. That kept it from being a pleasant evening, for Lockhart played recklessly, bluffing wildly without ever having the cards. I made one stupid mistake which pleased Wilson immensely. I failed to call Laing when I obviously had his three of a kind beat with a flush. At two-thirty in the morning it was all over. Laing and Harry were the winners. Wilson and Harrison had broken even. I had lost five pounds and Lockhart had lost twenty-eight. He rose flushed and excited from the table.

"Afraid this just wasn't my day," he said. He had lost more than two weeks' salary in five sweaty hours.

"You'll get another chance," Wilson smiled. "We'll pay off our debts when we leave here. Come on, Pete, let's take a little walk."

"Mind you don't run across a python out on the road," Laing warned happily.

We walked slowly across the lawn in front of the hotel. Small, harmless flies swarmed around our heads. We stopped and looked up at the strange constellations in the black sky.

"Quite a place, isn't it?" Wilson said. "Quite a place."

I didn't answer him. I was silently counting up how much time it would take us to get our work done. I had decided that I wouldn't stay on much longer after that.

16

As usual there was something basically true in what Wilson had said. There was an insane quality about the life we led in the following weeks, and our work was partly the cause of it. It was an exercise in insanity. Probably all creative work appears to be a mania after a certain period of time, because in order to do it one is forced to create an unreal world quite apart from the one which exists. That world has to be complete, and believable, or else the script, or the novel, or the story suffers. It has to be as strong as one's actual environment, stronger really, for every day it has to overcome the interests of that environment, and the reality of it. That is where the required insanity comes in.

We were living in a hotel in British East Africa. The life around us was the life of rural England. The officials and employees of the government who lived in Entebbe had worked hard and had ultimately been able to reproduce exactly what they might have had at home. They went to work in the mornings in their small British cars, and spent their days in offices very much like the offices in England, only warmer and better lit. At four-thirty or five the work stopped and everyone had tea. Then there was the long, warm evening in which most everyone turned to sport. There were tennis courts and a nine-hole golf course and a soccer field. The young, violent types played soccer and rugby. The older group played golf or mixed doubles. All the games were fairly well played, with the proper equipment, and were intensely discussed in the various club bars afterwards. Then everyone went home to bathe and dress for dinner.

On Friday night there was usually a dance at the

hotel. A small, discordant band played fox trots and most of the men dressed and everyone danced in that strange distant way which makes you wonder how the race has avoided extinction. It was considered to be quite a pleasant life. Still, everyone talked about going home, and leaving Entebbe, where they said people gossiped too much, and there was very little to do besides the "sports" and chasing someone else's wife. The plane from England arrived twice a week with mail, which was an event in Entebbe. All the people who worked at the airport changed into their best uniforms and everyone else was very excited about the prospect of news from home. Even Wilson and I began to look forward to the plane.

Our life was even more temporary, more suspended. We knew that we would only stay in Entebbe until we had finished the script. Therefore we had no desire to get involved in the things that went on around us. We were recluses, doomed to each other's company. We rose early and had breakfast alone. Then I would report to Wilson's rooms for work. We usually wasted an hour or two talking about some irrelevant subject, and then slowly we would begin our task. After lunch we would resume work until it became too hot to bear.

Wilson's rooms caught the afternoon sun, and at about five we were usually forced out into the fresh air. Laing and Harrison had left for the Congo two days after our arrival in Entebbe, and Lockhart was busy in Kampala until suppertime, so we were left to our own devices after five. Wilson suggested that we buy a couple of rackets and play tennis. That settled the problem of what to do with our late afternoons. Wilson played badly, but as he felt it was good for him he insisted we play every day. After tennis we sat out on the veranda of the hotel and watched it get dark. We drank a good deal of beer, and spoke very little to each other, and then we bathed and dressed for dinner. After dinner we usually worked. Once in a while we played poker.

There were always the same faces around the poker table: Harry, the headwaiter, Lockhart, Wilson, myself, and the hotel manager, a cadaverous fellow with an RAF mustache, who had been a pilot during the battle of Britain. His name was Dickie. We never found out what his last name was, and it didn't seem to matter very much

to him what he was called. Dickie played fairly good
poker, and, except for the fact that he was terribly pukka,
and still full of RAF slang, seemed to be quite a nice
man. Wilson was as charming to Dickie as he usually was
with people he did not know well. He was polite and distant with Harry, and he made an effort to be nice to
Lockhart. The assistant unit manager had changed quite
a lot. He played very conservative poker, and never
bluffed, as he was trying hard to win back what he had
lost on the first night. He also asked for Wilson's opinion
on everything that came up, and agreed vehemently with
whatever Wilson had to offer.

In so far as this routine was concerned, our lives were
sane and normal. What went on inside Wilson's rooms was
what made it insane, for there among the bare furnish-
ings we lived our other life: the script.

At first, everything went smoothly. We rewrote most
of the opening together. It played in New England, and
was all fairly simple. The trader and the young woman
met at a ball in Boston, and fell in love. Wilson added a
lot of comedy to this part of the script.

He emphasized the vanity of the trader, and played
endless scenes for me, taking the part of a young man
who is smitten by a girl. He primped in front of the mirror, and posed endlessly. He was delighted when I found
his act amusing.

"God, the things we go through when we're chasing
some gal," he laughed. "We pose, and strut, and act heroic, and tell all kinds of lies about ourselves. Isn't it awful?" He laughed delightedly.

"What about the woman?" I asked. "How does she re-
act to this guy's making a fool of himself?"

"Oh, she loves it," Wilson says. "She sees right through
him, of course, because she's much more intelligent than
he is, but she's also intelligent enough to realize that
there's something beyond his foolishness. She knows he's
a real guy, underneath all the fancy-Dan routine, and
she's attracted to him. We never fool anyone, you know.
Even the dumbest broads we get involved with are way
ahead of us while we're trying to make them. They just
decide at some point, usually early in the game, whether
they're going to give in or not. All the rest is just waste
motion. Interesting, but meaningless."

After three days we were both more or less satisfied with the beginning. I felt it was a little too long and too slow, but this didn't seem to bother Wilson. "I'm scared to death of a movie that really starts with a bang," he said. "That's the easiest thing to invent, a good beginning. A car races along a road, and turns over and burns. Or there's a robbery, and the fellows who do it don't quite manage to get away. That's all fine, but suddenly reel one is over and your pace slows down and there you are, left with eight more reels to go. Almost every movie you see has a wonderful beginning. And then they die. I'd rather have a lousy beginning and a wonderful end."

"I think ours is a little better than lousy," I said.

"Sure, sure, but it's not wonderful. I think it's about right."

He lit a cigarette and went over to the window. He seemed to be in a fairly good mood, and I felt relaxed and satisfied.

"Now, let's see about the rest of it," he said. I straightened in my chair, and picked up the new scenes I had written in London. "Now just a minute, Pete," he said. "Don't look at the stuff you've written for a little while. Just let's think about it."

"I've thought about it a good deal, John," I said.

"Well, have you really, kid? I doubt it, you know." He began to pace the room very slowly, stopping occasionally to inspect some piece of his safari equipment that lay around on the spare bed and on the chest of drawers. Then he sat down opposite me and took a piece of paper and began to draw a horse. "You haven't really," he said. I began to sense that the torture was starting. "You haven't thought about it enough, anyway, otherwise you'd see all the holes I see. The one big hole, anyway."

"What's that, John?"

"You mean you give up? You just want me to tell you, is that it?"

"Well, it might save time."

"Uh-huh. And it'll save you thinking. All right, if you're such a lazy bastard, I'll tell you. What you've written is all wrong. As wrong as what there was before."

"Why didn't you say so yesterday?"

"I didn't know yesterday. I hadn't thought about it enough. You see, the whole basis of their relationship is

cockeyed. Just let me go on, now, Pete. You asked me."
He rubbed his thin calf, reflectively. "You see, this is a
story about a dame who meets a guy and falls in love
with him and goes off to Africa. The way we have it
now, she's pro-slavery, just the way he is. Then when
she gets to Africa she sees what the 'trade' really means,
and she's revolted by it. She begins to hate him, because
he's in the trade. In the end she convinces him to her
point of view. Well, I say she's a stupid bitch. What the
hell did she expect? But let's say that's all right too; it
still won't do what we want it to. Because both of them
really go through the same development. That's wrong.
I don't see why we have her in the picture at all. Why not
just tell his story? A guy with his point of view goes to
Africa and learns that his point of view is horrible. Then
he has to back out of what he has agreed to do. He has
to quit his job. It's cleaner and simpler that way. Why
bother with her at all?"

"Kay Gibson is already in London, John," I said. "We
can't take her out of the story now."

"That's no argument," he said angrily. "Stick to the
logic of the thing. You're telling two identical stories. It's
going to be a goddam bore. Either her character is just
along for the ride, or his is. They feel the same things,
only they do it in turns. That's lousy."

"No, it isn't. It's complex. It gives them something to
discuss. It provides conflict."

"Balls," he said. I could sense that he was arguing for
the argument's sake. "Things are only good if they're simple," he said.

"Not always."

"Always. That's what creates really important literature, really important art. Simplicity."

"There are no rules, John."

"There are hundreds of rules. Now you admire Hemingway. I agree with you. He stands out among all the others. Why? Because he was the first one to dispose of all
the crap, the artificial trimmings. He gave the simple
words their old honorable meanings again. He reinstated
them in the language. All the other writers had been
burying these same words, had been piling the dead bodies
of words on top of them, choking their true meaning.
All right, he got it from Stein and Joyce. What differ-

ence does that make? He influenced us all by scraping the crap off the language. He made it basic and clean again."

"The language, yes, but God knows his attitudes are complex, and what he says is many-sided."

"You're wrong again, kid. What he said was simple too. He reduced all life to simple terms again. Courage, fear, impotence, death . . . all those things stand out singly in his books. And his stories are simple. They don't have plots. Take *Farewell to Arms,* or *The Sun Also Rises.* There's no plot. People's lives are simply exposed. One thing happens after another and there are no subplots or any of the nonsense everyone else sweated over in the past. Stendhal is like that. Flaubert. Tolstoy. Melville. Their simplicity makes them great."

"O.K.," I said, "you win. We'll make it simple. The woman is not for slavery in the beginning. She has no attitude at all."

"She must have an attitude, damn it. Everyone did in those days."

"All right, she's against it in the beginning."

"Then why the hell does she marry the guy? Because he's so wonderful in the hay? Come on now, kid. Work a little. And if she's against it in the beginning, there's no development in her character. She's against it in the beginning and she's against it in the end. Why waste all that film on her?"

"She's a simple character. Simplicity is great. He's simple too. He's like Laing and Lockhart. He thinks Negroes are animals, and whatever you do to them, they don't really feel it."

"Laing isn't like that. He just goes along with that attitude because he lives down here."

"All right, he's like Lockhart."

"Well, who the hell wants to make a picture about a jerk like that?" Wilson asked. "Come on, now, think a little. Don't just talk."

I fell silent. I could see that if Wilson allowed this objection of his to grow, it would cripple our work. We would have to redo the beginning of the script as well as everything else. I knew that he was probably sincere but his objections were based on prejudices. He resented the repair work I had done. He resented my facility and he was suspicious of it. He said so a moment later.

"Nothing that comes easily is any good," he pronounced. "I've worked for years and years on stories and scripts, and the things I invented easily, I've always had to get rid of."

I didn't answer him. This is your picture, I said to myself. If you want to complicate it, go ahead. We'll sit here and argue for a week or two and that'll just prevent you from going hunting and perhaps killing both of us.

"What are you thinking about?" he asked me.

"I was thinking that I was a god, and that what I invented had automatic life. I was thinking that all that talk about dramatic progression and identical character development was the talk of a mortal, of a movie producer who was worried about the box office."

He didn't answer me. He went into his bedroom. I waited a few minutes and then followed him. He was lying on his bed, reading his hunting book.

"Are we finished for the day, John?" I asked.

"We are, if you don't feel like thinking."

I shrugged and went back to the workroom, and started reading Graham Greene. I read for half an hour, and Wilson appeared again.

"What are you reading?" he asked.

"A very simple book without plot. It's called *The Heart of the Matter*."

"Are you being paid to further your literary knowledge here?"

"I'm being paid to be your companion," I said. "You're reading and so I didn't want to disturb you. I'd be a lousy companion if I did that."

He shook his head. "You're a difficult bastard, aren't you? You're like a sensitive queen who's had his feelings hurt."

"And you're like a mean prima donna. You know what somebody at home said about you? They said you were a director with iron whims."

"Who said that? Landau?"

"No, somebody else."

"Who?"

"What difference does that make? If the shoe fits, wear it."

"Oh, balls," he said, and went back into the bedroom. I read until one o'clock and then went down into the bar.

Dickie was there, having his morning beer.

"Get a lot done?" he asked.

"Not much."

"How's John?"

"Charming this morning. Absolutely charming."

"I'm sure he can be quite difficult when he wants to be."

"You're right there, Dickie, old man," I said.

A short, redheaded Englishman in the uniform of the East African Constabulary was standing next to us at the bar. Dickie introduced us.

"Lieutenant Marlowe can tell you a lot about hunting," he said.

"Going out on safari?" Lieutenant Marlowe asked me.

"Maybe . . . if we get our work done."

"You want to go to Kenya," Marlowe said. "This country's worthless. Kenya's a little better. Not much, but a little."

"Marlowe's an India man," Dickie said.

"That's the country all right. I'd still be up in old Kashmir if we hadn't given it all back to the buggers."

"You didn't exactly give it back, did you?" I smiled.

"Well, really, old man," Lieutenant Marlowe said, through his beery mustache, "if you have a houseful of rabbits and they're kicking up an awful fuss, what do you do? Well, you simply make yourself a rabbit stew, that's what, a rabbit stew!"

Dickie laughed uproariously. "Have a beer, Mr. Verrill?" Marlowe asked me.

"Thank you."

We drank to our safari. Lieutenant Marlowe started to reminisce about India.

"Did you do much tiger hunting while you were out there, Lieutenant?" Dickie asked him.

"H'mmm, rather. Killed about twenty-two tigers in my time. My father did a lot better than that, of course, in the old days. That is, before one of the buggers got him."

I found myself wishing Wilson was there. To stand at the bar and look out at the tropical sun beating down on the lake and discuss tiger hunting would undoubtedly have improved his mood. It would also have made him feel more in a hurry to break the mental deadlock that he had created over the script.

"Your father was killed by a tiger?" I asked politely.

"H'mm, he was that. I was just a lad at the time, out on my first tiger hunt. We came on this tiger up in a tree, rather suddenly, you might say, and my father fired at him. Shot too quickly, for he only wounded the beast. The tiger came right for him. He fired again and missed. His gun-bearer dropped his gun and took to a tree, the black bastard. My father grabbed my rifle but it was too late. He never got a chance to fire it."

"Good God. What did you do?"

"Well without a gun I was fairly useless. Took to a tree myself, and sat up there crying for a couple of hours. The tiger mauled the old man and then dragged him off into the brush. I sat there listening to him roar while he worked over the carcass of my old man." Lieutenant Marlowe pressed the cold beer glass against his hot, bronzed forehead. "Ghastly show."

"How the hell did you ever get over that?" I asked.

He shrugged. "I was just a lad. Fourteen at the time. But I never forgot it." He took a black leather wallet out of the breast pocket of his starched tunic and produced a tattered clipping. I read the fading print. The local Indian paper described the incident rather curtly.

Wilson appeared. I could tell that he had been sleeping. His shirt was crumpled and his eyes were still thick with sleep.

"What the hell happened to you?" he asked.

"I got thirsty. This is Lieutenant Marlowe, John Wilson. The lieutenant was just telling us about tiger hunting in India."

"He was, eh?" Wilson smiled at the constabulary officer. His irritation with me vanished. "Well," he said in his charming, interested voice, "I'd better hear about this."

Lieutenant Marlowe repeated the story. I realized that he had been dining out on the story of his first tiger hunt for years. Wilson was fascinated. He invited Marlowe for lunch and they discussed African hunting until three o'clock in the afternoon. Marlowe's disgust with Uganda was exactly what Wilson needed to cement his point of view.

"I know," he said. "This is nothing. Kenya's the place."

"Mind you, they have leopard here and elephant, and some buffalo, but it's not the same sort of thing. The big tuskers are in Kenya. And, of course, there's a lot of other game there, too, that you won't find as plentiful here."

"What about the Congo?" Wilson asked.

"Can't say. Never been there," Marlowe replied.

"Well, what have you heard about it, Lieutenant?"

"Not too much, actually. Plenty of game there, though, I believe. Elephant and buffalo, principally. Up along Lake Albert where the Semliki and the Nile feed into the lake there are supposed to be a lot of big tuskers."

"You don't say. That's where we were planning to go."

"As soon as we finish our job here," I put in.

Wilson looked over at me and smiled falsely. "If I can get this guy to work," he said, "we'll take off for there in a week or two. You wouldn't like to come along, would you, Lieutenant?"

"Like to, but I can't. Have to be getting back to the outpost. My leave's about over."

"You couldn't put in for another one, eh?"

Lieutenant Marlowe smiled. "I doubt that," he said. All the other chaps are waiting for their turn to come back for a little civilization."

"You're staying for the dance tonight, aren't you, Marlowe?" Dickie asked.

"Rather," the lieutenant replied. "Wouldn't miss that. You'll be there, won't you, Mr. Wilson?"

"Oh sure," John replied.

We returned to our hot little prison.

"Now, that's quite a guy, isn't it?" Wilson observed. He had been impressed by the stocky little lieutenant.

"Sensitive soul."

"Quite a guy," Wilson murmured.

"You wish someone in your family had been killed by a tiger?"

He pretended he hadn't heard me. "A real man," he said.

"The fact that he's so keen on tonight's dance kind of worries me."

"Well, I guess these bony old gals would look pretty good to you too, if you'd just spent six months out in the brush. As a matter of fact, I find myself looking at them with rather new eyes."

"Are we going to this dance?"

"I guess we'll have to," he said. "Now let's get to work. No tennis today."

Throughout the long hot hours of the afternoon we continued to argue our problem. Wilson refused to give way. Finally just as it was getting dark he relented somewhat.

"Isn't it amazing," he said, "that you run into this kind of thing with every script: a momentary deadlock, a problem that seems insoluble. After a while you find yourself in a mental hell. Nothing makes any sense any more. Nothing is real."

"Maybe we should stop thinking about it for a while?"

"Probably. Let's take a walk."

The courtyard of the hotel was filled with hundreds of the small flies we had noticed on our first evening in Entebbe. As we walked along the covered passageways we could see the boys on the lawn below us working spray guns.

"Awful little beasts, aren't they?" Wilson said, slapping the air in front of him. The tiny flies had a tendency to lodge themselves in your nose and mouth as you moved through their swarms.

We crossed the golf course and walked down toward the shore. There were fewer flies as we approached the water. The sun was down and large gray stacks of clouds were piled up in the light blue sky over the lake.

"That's Hippo Bay down there," I said.

"What do you mean, kid?"

"Haven't you heard about Hippo Bay? It's a cove down here a little way where a family of hippos hangs out."

"Is that right? Well, let's go down and look at them."

"O.K. But better not get too near the water. It's lousy with crocs."

"Maybe one of them can help us with the script."

We crossed a pasture and went on toward the lake. A few mosquitoes passed us in the night air. There was a thick band of reeds along the edge of the lake and the smooth, futile waves of the sick water rose among them. I kept my eyes on the bank to the right of us. Dickie had warned me that the crocodiles often slept high up on the shore and that to walk between them and the water might prove dangerous. Suddenly Wilson grabbed my arm.

"There they are," he said excitedly. "Jesus Christ, are you blind?"

"No, I see them now." Fifty yards or so to my left I could see the nose of a hippo and its small clipped-looking ears. Other hippos rose near it and blew out spumes of water. I stumbled over a rock. The hippos dove deep and disappeared.

"You made too damn much noise," Wilson said angrily. "I saw them way back there and you just went on walking, kicking the grass with those big feet of yours. Don't you ever look ahead of you?"

"I was looking up toward the shore."

"Well, that was intelligent, after you told me the hippos were in the water. Good God." He shook his head irritably.

"Why didn't you say something?" I asked.

"Hell, I thought you'd seen them. How could I guess you'd be looking the wrong way."

I controlled my temper. "I was looking up at the bank because Dickie told me to watch out for crocs. They often sleep up there in the evening and if you get between them and water it can be damned unpleasant."

"Dickie," he said disdainfully. "For Christ's sake, what the hell does he know?"

"He's lived here for over two years."

"In the bar, sure. But that's about the only place he's ever been. Come on, let's go back."

We turned and started back along the edge of the water. It was almost dark now. Suddenly a hundred yards or so ahead of us something began to move. I stopped and grabbed Wilson's arm. We stood motionless. A small crocodile, looking evil and fat, slid forward across the clipped grass into the reeds. It happened so quickly that neither one of us had time to be frightened.

"I think I'll join Dickie in the bar from here on in," I said.

Wilson stood staring at the reeds in front of us. I could tell that he was not at all frightened, not even in retrospect.

"Well, for God's sake," he said, grinning. "What do you know?"

"Maybe it was just an optical illusion," I said. "Like a mirage."

"He wasn't very big," Wilson said.

"No. Just a mite. Probably would have been satisfied just to bite one of our legs off."

"Well, you were supposed to be watching for them.

And you walked right past the son of a bitch."

"He wasn't there when we went by or I would have seen him. He probably was higher up on the bank."

"Balls. You just walked right by him. Hell of a country boy you are."

"What about you?"

"I was looking at the hippos."

"So if he'd nipped one of us it would have been my fault?"

"Sure. Dickie didn't warn me."

We turned off to our left and walked inland until we hit the road. Thick swarms of flies began circling our heads as we began to approach the hotel.

"One thing is definite," Wilson said expertly. "It's foolish to walk around out here at night without a rifle of some kind."

"You're not allowed to shoot close to the hotel," I said. "I suggest we don't walk around at night. That's a simpler solution."

"God Almighty, what a yellow bastard you are," Wilson said.

I didn't answer him. I had decided that that was exactly the part I would play from then on. I would be the yellow bastard, and wait for him at home, and listen appreciatively to his stories as long as he managed to return.

"It would be no fun if we were all brave," I said. He started to trot toward the lighted buildings ahead of us.

"Come on," he said, "for God's sake. These damn flies . . ."

I watched him run down the road ahead of me, his tall figure silhouetted against the brightly lit buildings. From the dining room I could hear the faint wail of an orchestra. They were playing "La Vie en Rose," and I thought nostalgically about Switzerland, and the clean, snow-covered mountains, which were only dangerous when you were on them, and which were wonderfully safe when you looked up at them from the valley floor at night.

17

The heat came with the flies. Paradise was invaded twice and still it continued to resist. The dining room was brightly decorated with flags and bunting, and the fans twirled languorously. The dancers moved rhythmically through the heavy air, the fans blowing the tiny swarms of flies into the butter and into whatever thick sauce was left uncovered on anyone's plate. Still the party continued. Dickie and Lieutenant Marlowe sat at our table, both in black tie. Wilson and I had put on dark suits.

No one ate any dinner; but the waiters suffered most because of the flies. That was as it should be. Although the scourge victimized both black and white, the blacks still bore the brunt of the burden, for they were held responsible for what happened to the food.

"Boy," Dickie screamed. Our poor, frightened waiter rushed over to our table. Dickie held up a pitcher of cream. "Can't drink this. It's filthy with the beasts. Get us more cream. Hurry."

Our boy raced off, dodging electric fans and dancers, trailing a small piece of green paper streamer that had become entangled in one of his toes. Dickie shook his head.

"Good job they don't bite," he said. More than a dozen lake flies were lodged in his RAF mustache, their bodies moving among the stiff hair.

"H'mm, rather," Marlowe said. He turned back to Wilson. "The elephant is dangerous only because he's such a hardy bugger," he said. "You can kill him only if you hit him in one of two places."

"Yes, I know," Wilson said. "The shot right between the eyes, and the heart shot."

"Not right between the eyes," Marlowe corrected. "The place to aim is between the eyes and down about six inches. Otherwise your bullet will merely bounce off his thick skull."

"They're easy to track, aren't they?" Wilson asked.

"H'mmm, rather. You can get up to within thirty yards of them without any trouble at all. But if you miss your shot, well, then you're for it, old man. And you're shooting up, at an absurd angle, you know. Pointing way up at the bugger. I prefer the heart shot."

"From what I've heard, that's the one to try for," Wilson replied.

Dickie winked at me. "Where would you shoot a croc, Pete?" he asked.

"I wouldn't," I said. "Live and let live is my motto."

"Quite right you are, too," Dickie observed. Wilson and Marlowe were now discussing the best place to aim on a charging buffalo.

"The head shot's practically impossible, you know, when they're coming at you. Still, it's the only target you're offered."

"Some of my best friends are buffalo," I said to Dickie.

Wilson grinned faintly. "You ought to listen to this, kid," he said. "If you won't read the book, you better listen."

"I'm listening," I said. "What's the best shot to try for on a lake fly, Lieutenant?"

"The after end." The lieutenant smiled.

"Wait until they're on the butter, I always say," Dickie put in, "and the stab the buggers with a knife." He rose, suddenly. "I'm awfully sorry, I didn't see you coming, Mrs. MacGregor."

A rather fat, plain-looking girl in a pink tulle dress had arrived at our table. She smiled, oblivious of the thin beads of perspiration that were trickling down her plump jaw.

"May I present," Dickie said formally, "Mrs. Mac-Gregor, Mr. Wilson, Lieutenant Marlowe, and Mr. Verrill."

We got to our feet. "How do you do, dear," I heard Wilson say in his most mellow voice above the wail of the band. They were playing "La Vie en Rose" again. Mrs. MacGregor, who looked like *la vie en rose* personified, sat down between Marlowe and Wilson.

"Awfully warm, isn't it," she said, offering her dimpled

face first to Wilson and then to the lieutenant. "And these flies. Good thing they don't bite."

"What will you have to drink, dear?" Wilson asked her. "A little champagne or some whisky?"

"I'll have a gin fizz," Mrs. MacGregor said daringly. "I like that best when it's warm."

"Boy," Wilson said. "A gin fizz." The waiter beamed at him. Since our arrival at Entebbe, Wilson and I had been trying to make up to the waiters for the conduct of the others at our table. We both overtipped them, never leaving less than a shilling on the table. We were also careful to wrap every one of our demands in huge smiles. The service we received in exchange was unbelievable.

"You know you spoil these chaps, John," Dickie said.

"Oh, you mustn't," Mrs. MacGregor added immediately. "You go away after a while but we stay on and have to make do with them."

Wilson smiled. I could tell one of his favorite stories was coming. "The other day," he said, leaning across the table toward me, as if I hadn't heard the story already, "I left a tip for the boy, but he was out in the kitchen getting coffee when I put it down, and so the other boy took it, the one who serves the drinks. Well, our boy came back and put down the coffee, and while I sat drinking it I could hear strange noises coming from behind me —muffled groans and great straining sounds—and I looked around quickly and there were these two darkies in mortal combat with each other. Oh . . . they were really struggling for that shilling. Well, I sat there, not knowing what to do for quite a while. And the struggle went on. Finally I just threw another shilling on the table and that ended it." He grinned. "It was really something," he said, "these two boys just trying to kill each other without making any noise."

"Isn't that just like them," Mrs. MacGregor said, making a horrified face. John grinned sweetly at her.

"It was really funny," he said. "Our little fellow is just as nice a little guy as he could be, you know."

"How can you say that?" Mrs. MacGregor asked, outraged.

"You see," Dickie said triumphantly. "We all feel the same way about them out here."

"They're just horrid," the lady said. Dickie winked at

me. He was obviously delighted that beauty had declared itself to be on the side of intolerance. I got up.

"I think I'll go to bed," I said.

"All right, kid," Wilson replied. I could tell that he was relieved to see me leave the racial-discussion group. "See you in the morning, Pete."

I made my way across the crowded dance floor. The band was playing a samba and all the couples were moving doggedly through the insect-infested room, never quite getting the beat. Harry, the headwaiter, pushed one of the boys out of the way with his usual violence and opened the door for me.

"Turning in already, Mr. Verrill?" he asked pleasantly.

"Yes, I'm tired."

"Sleep well." The glass door fell shut behind me. I could see Harry turning and shouting at another boy. I went up the exterior stairway and followed the second-floor passageway to my room. The flies were thick everywhere in the courtyard. The red cement floor was covered with millions of brown bodies that crunched underfoot. I went into my room and shut both the hall door and the door that led to the bathroom. Then, without turning on the light, I got into bed.

The light being turned on in my room woke me. Wilson stood at the foot of my bed, fully dressed. He looked upset.

"Holy God, have you ever seen anything like it," he said.

"Turn the light out or the room will be full of them."

He flicked the switch and then sat down in the darkness opposite me. "My room is just full of them," he said. "I can't sleep there."

"Did you leave the light on while you were downstairs?"

"No, I just put it on for a minute to read a cable that arrived this afternoon. The woman at the desk forgot to give it to me, I guess."

"Was the cable from home?"

"Yes, I wanted to show it to you." He lit a match and started to read from the blue slip of paper in his hand. " 'Situation desperate,' he read. 'Have received no funds. Becker suggests you return immediately and accept assignment MGM. Doubts trader financing will be completed. Love, et cetera.' . . . What do you think, kid?"

"God, I don't know, John. It doesn't seem possible."

"God damn Landau," he said angrily. "Son of a bitch. I knew this would happen if I left London."

"He probably can't help it. The American backers are still scared of a war."

"But he should have told me. I never would have left, had I known. This is just awful, Pete."

"What are you going to do?"

"I'm going to tell him I'm coming back." He paused. "What I'd really like to do is get him out of the deal, get someone else to take his place. This is just impossible."

"You can't bow out now, John. Think of Anders and Reissar."

"That's what Paul's counting on. He knows I won't do anything rash because it would ruin them." He sat quietly for a few minutes. "God damn it," he said finally. "That's really what I should do. Go back, make a picture for someone else."

"You'd have to start all over again, John, looking for a story, writing a new script . . ."

"Oh, I've got a story," he said. "One I've been wanting to do for years. That would be no problem."

"What about Duncan and Kay?"

"That's just it. That's why I can't bow out now, although I have every right to. I can't let everyone else down. What I should do is just take two weeks and go hunting and then start home."

"Poor Paul," I said. "I bet he's sweating."

"I hope he is." Wilson lit a cigarette and peered down at the cable again, using the light of the match. "This is just awful. I can imagine what's going on at home with all the creditors descending on the house. God damn it!"

He was really upset. "Well, we're stuck on this one, anyway," I said, to make him feel better. "Maybe working on a new story would be a relief."

"It certainly would be," he said. "You know I don't think I've ever told you about this story," he went on. "It's one I've wanted to do for years. It's not like anything I've ever done. It's about a kid in a small Midwestern town right after the turn of the century. Would you like to hear it?"

"Sure. I'm awake now."

He leaned back in the darkness and drew thoughtfully

on his cigarette. "Well, this kid is about fifteen," he started. His debts were already forgotten, as were the heat and the flies. "His father's dead, and he lives in a cheap boardinghouse with his mother. She's a woman in her late thirities, still kind of beautiful, with a great manner about her. They have just a little money, barely enough to live on. Their life is drab, colorless. They have only one thing to make them happy, and that's their love of horses. They save on food all week long, just to be able to go to the livery stable on Sunday and hire a couple of hacks and go riding for an hour. Every Sunday they do that. They each have their favorite horse. That's what they live for, this one hour of happiness a week, when they can ride out into the country together. Well, a guy comes into their life, a kind of flashy guy, who's passing through the town, a salesman. He's there on a business deal that will keep him in town for a couple of months, and so he goes on the make for the widow. Of course she has to work all week long, and she doesn't get a chance to go out with the guy on any day except Sunday. At first she fights it, and goes riding with the boy anyway. But she's been lonely too many years. Nobody has made love to her. And so finally she gives in and makes a date with this guy who's been after her. And the kid goes out alone. Well, it happens once and then the next week again, and then their whole life together collapses. The kid doesn't say anything. He doesn't complain. He's too proud to. He just goes out by himself every Sunday morning on his horse, and when he gets way out in the country he gets off, and sits down and cries. The horse stands there and waits for him to finish, and then he gets on again. Then one day while he's sitting there on the ground, a trap drives by with a team, and he can see his mother with this guy, sitting there on the seat very close together, and he realizes that she's left him for this character, and everything that he ever felt about her changes. At first he plans to kill the guy, but then he realizes that he can't do that, so the next Sunday he decides to run off. Well, the rest of the picture is his flight, about how he starts across country, toward the west on this stolen horse, and he has the goddamnedest adventures, and he grows up. He makes his first money and he falls in love, and finally he comes back. He's an adult now, and he realizes that what his mother did was normal and forgivable, and that she really behaved rather well. She only betrayed him on Sundays. But he can't find her when he gets back to this town where he once lived. He picks up her trail and follows her, and he discovers that she became a lost soul after he ran away, and that she went to hell. The guilt that she felt about him has made her into a drunk and a prostitute. He goes from city to city, searching for her, and finally, when he's about to find her, he discovers that she's dead. A month or so earlier, she's gotten drunk and gone out on a livery hack and the horse has thrown her in the street and she's died in the charity hospital. And that's the end. This guy goes back to the life he's made for himself out West. The last thing you see is him arriving at his ranch. He goes out into the pasture near his house, and he just walks out among the horses, and that's the final shot, this guy walking through his pasture, and you know that he's been marked for life, that he'll never love again, and that he'll always be alone. He stands there, looking at the horses while they gallop away, and he feels like crying, but he can't even do that any more. . . ."

We sat in the dark room, listening to the flies circle around us. I felt suddenly that I didn't know him at all. All my theories about his love of violence were shattered. He was a sad, skinny poet, and the movies had prevented him from declaring himself.

"I think it's a good idea for a story, John," I said. "I'm not sure anyone would want to make it."

"I suppose not," he said. "But that's what I'd really like to do. You see, I care about those people. Not like this made-up, synthetic thing we're working on. I don't really give a damn about this slaver and his wife."

"Well, shall we dump them into Lake Victoria?" I asked.

He sighed. "I'm afraid we can't do that, kid," he said sadly. "Too many people expect to eat off them in these next few months."

"Well, then I guess we'd better make them as palatable as possible."

"O.K., kid. See you in the morning."

"Spray your room with the aerosol bomb and that'll get rid of the beasts."

"I can't find mine."

"Here, take this one."

He took it gratefully. *"Hasta luego, muchacho,"* he said.

"John," I asked him as he reached the door, "is that story a leaf out of your book?"

"Hell no," he replied. "My mother never had enough money at the end of the week to spend it on horseback riding. And she was much too fine a horsewoman to ever want to rent a horse."

But he didn't sound very convincing. "Good night, John," I said. "Good job these buggers don't bite."

18

The deadlock was broken the next day. We found a middle road that led us out of our dispute, and the work went well. That evening the unit manager arrived from London. He brought good news with him; the deal had finally been signed. Not only Landau, but Anders and Reissar as well, had told him that they had seen the papers with the signatures of the American backers attached.

John's mood improved immediately. We played tennis again. The following day Owen left for Nairobi to expedite the sending of the photographic equipment. He was a much better man than Lockhart, and Wilson had confidence in his abilities. Then the permission to shoot in the Congo came through. Lockhart brought it to our workroom, beaming excitedly.

"Everything seems to be going fine, sir," he said. He was like a pompous little sergeant major reporting a victory to the regimental commander. Wilson felt sorry for him.

"Things certainly seem to be improving, Ralph," he agreed. "Now if Laing and Harrison find a couple of good locations for us, we'll be in clover."

"The village up in Masindi is almost complete. The huts have been built, as well as an enormous enclosure for the slaves. It was quite a job, sir."

"Is that right?" Wilson said disinterestedly. He was sketching Lockhart.

"Do you still think we'll be starting in the Congo?"

"That depends on Laing's report. But I think we can start preparing for the Congo, anyway."

"We've got it all staffed out. We're going to truck all the equipment in from here."

"What about the roads?"

"They're not very good, sir, but if we allow five days for the move, we should be all right. During the move back you can shoot all your cover sets at Masindi."

"Suppose you get bad weather and you've used up all your cover sets?" I asked, just so the feeling of good cheer wouldn't get out of hand.

"Then we'll have to sit and wait, I guess," Lockhart said gloomily.

"We can go out hunting if it rains," Wilson said.

The lake flies were now putting in their appearance early in the afternoon. Standing at the windows of Wilson's room, we could see them approaching. They looked like a black waterspout as they came in off the lake. We slammed shut the windows and sat sweating as the heat increased.

"Great place to work, isn't it?" I said to Wilson.

"In London the dames, and here the flies," he groaned. "Incidentally . . . we're having dinner with the beautiful Mrs. MacGregor tonight, so spruce up."

"What for? I don't want anything from her."

"Well, then do it just to keep me company."

"I'll take a bath. That's as far as I'll go."

"A welcome change in any case," Wilson said.

"Where's her husband?" I asked.

"Upcountry," he replied. "Establishing native pro-stations."

"That would be a good job for her."

"You're speaking of the woman I love," he said. "Come on. Let's get to work. These two characters have been nice to each other long enough. Now our heroine discovers what a ruthless, nigger-whipping bastard she's married to."

"Let's get some fresh air first," I said.

Wilson stretched his long arms; then he inserted one hand into his shirt and rubbed himself lovingly.

"Does your skin itch?" I asked.

"No," he beamed. "I'm just crazy about myself."

"What about some tennis, or a short walk?"

"All right, Pete," he said very slowly. "To hell with work." He waved his long, thin hands through the air in front of his face. "Damn these flies."

"Good thing they don't bite."

He made a pained face and we left the room. We walked slowly across the great expanse of lawn in front of the hotel. Clouds of flies passed us, undoubtedly on their way to our rooms. From the soccer field we could hear the faint cries of the players.

"Let's go over and watch them for a while," Wilson suggested. "Seems to be a big game today."

There was a crowd seated along the side lines of the field, which was unusual, and then we saw the cause of all the excitement. The Entebbe Soccer Club was playing an all-African team. Short, barefoot natives were running wildly among the tall, white men in cleats, and along the side lines, a good distance away from the benches of the white spectators, we saw a crowd of Negroes squatting on the grass.

"Well, for God's sake," Wilson said, grinning. "Isn't that the damnedest thing. Isn't that just like the English? They won't admit that these people are human but they will accept them on the soccer field."

"They'd better accept them. These guys are good."

The African centerback was dribbling the ball upfield, his naked black legs flashing in the sun. He avoided a British player with a deft feint and passed the ball forward. Another African player came quickly up to the flying ball, changed its course with the calf of his leg, and charged down toward the white goal.

"Look at the goalie," I said excitedly. "Holy smoke, it's Harry."

"Well I'll be goddamned. So it is."

The tall, sinewy headwaiter was tensely guarding his team's goal. His face was set in an expression of extreme hatred as the three African forwards bore down on him. Like an angry beast he awaited their charge, standing his ground inside the goal. Then with a fierce grunt he rushed forward, just as the ball was kicked toward the goal. He blocked it with his body. I could hear the hard leather ball smack into his stomach and bounce off. Immediately he started to go after it, to kick it out of the danger zone, but one of the other Negro players was racing toward it and Harry realized that he would arrive too late. He stopped and reversed his field, his fierce eyes still on the ball. Then as the next kick for goal came he flung himself to the ground, trying to block it. The ball grazed his thin shoulder and bounced off into the net behind him. There was a loud, joyful cheer from the African section of the crowd. An instant later the ball was in play again.

Wilson and I beamed. It was the most beautiful thing we had seen since our arrival in Africa.

"Oh, this is wonderful," Wilson said. "And just think, we almost missed it."

We squatted down on the ground, near the white section of the crowd. "Come on, Africa," I shouted, "do it again."

An elderly Englishman in white flannels and blue blazer turned toward us. "They're awfully good," he said. "Went to England last year, but of course there they hadn't a chance."

"Why is that?" Wilson asked. The provost marshal was dribbling along the side lines, moving warily forward toward the black goal.

"Well, they're very clever with their feet, but against a really good British team they're just too small. Real blocking and checking just throws them off. They don't go in for that at all, you see."

"They'd probably be lynched if they did," I said.

"Oh, not at all," the Englishman said haughtily. "We're not like you Americans."

"Of course not," I said.

The provost marshall attempted to pass the ball across the field to one of his forwards but the African back cut short the pass and started the ball back toward the white goal again. A few seconds later Harry was again fighting for his life. His face was red with rage and exertion. He blocked two attempts at his goal before a third kick finally scored.

"Oh boy," Wilson said. "Oh boy, oh boy."

Harry was shouting angry instructions to one of his

backs as the play started once more, but obviously none of it was any use. Again and again the Africans swept the ball back down the field. The British players were moving more slowly now, trying to catch their breath, but the Africans gave them no respite. The play got rougher. Very often now, an African player was knocked down by one of his white opponents, but somehow they always managed to propel the ball forward to a point where another African could take it in full flight and move it on toward Harry and the goal. We watched, fascinated, as each violent episode ended the same way, with Harry waiting angrily in his cage, and then sallying forth like a wild, chained dog, only to have the ball sail past him into the silent net behind his back.

"God help the poor waiters at the hotel tonight," I said.

"You better shut up," Wilson told me, "or we'll be asked to leave."

It was an altogether perfect afternoon. There were no lake flies on the soccer field, and we sat in the warm sun and enjoyed the show. The game ended with a score of 15—2 against the Entebbe Soccer Club. We walked slowly back to the hotel and worked in perfect harmony until it was time to dress for dinner.

"Shall we ask Harry if he had a busy afternoon, John?"

"We must do that," Wilson said enthusiastically. "No, we've even got to do something better than that. Let's really think about it."

We met Mrs. MacGregor in the bar. She was dressed in a rather stylish linen dress with a fairly low neckline. Wilson looked pleased.

"Now, isn't this swell, having dinner with a beautiful lady, in the heart of Africa," he said.

She smiled, pleased with the compliment. "Did you have a good day?" she asked.

"Wonderful," Wilson said. "We worked hard, and then we went to the soccer game."

"Wasn't it awful?" she said, as expected. "I only stayed a little while, and then I went sailing."

"I thought it was a wonderful game," Wilson said.

She smiled coquettishly. "You didn't really. You know it was horrid. The boys will be impossible now for five or six days."

"Oh, I don't think so," Wilson said. "They realize that

sport is one thing and life another."

"They don't at all," she said. "They'll be ever so much more impudent just because they've seen some of their own kind win out over us."

"They're not impudent," I said. "At least I've never noticed it."

"You don't know them," she said. "You haven't been out here long enough. They have an impudent way of looking at you which is unmistakable."

I saw Lockhart standing at the other end of the bar. "Excuse me a minute," I said. "I've got to talk to Ralph."

"Tell him all about it, kid," Wilson said, winking at me.

I bought Lockhart a beer and described the game to him. I left nothing out. He listened patiently and then shrugged.

"It's just what I've been telling you," he said. "We're idiots the way we treat the natives here. You wouldn't see that sort of thing down in Johannesburg."

"I think this team played down there."

"Well, even if they did, that proves nothing. It's all foolishness. Like sending them to school."

"Worse," I said. "They're so very good at soccer."

I joined Wilson and Mrs. MacGregor and the lake flies in the dining room. They were already calling each other John and Margot. I ate most of my meal in silence. I had made up my mind that I would not be drawn into their conversation at any price. John talked about England and hunting. It was a subject which was close to his heart and he could lose himself in praise for the class of Englishman the lady most admired.

"I do miss it," she said. Our boy brought us each a portion of partially melted vanilla ice cream.

"We'll have to eat it fast, dear," Wilson said, "or it'll be full of flies."

We did as we were told. Mrs. MacGregor finished first. I felt she did so because she wanted to have a chance to talk.

"You know, I wasn't too happy in England, really," she said. "The war was just awful for us in London."

"Well, I don't know," Wilson said. "The people behaved so magnificently that I rather enjoyed being there, despite the blackout and the rationing and the bombs."

"Oh, they didn't," Mrs. MacGregor said.

"Well, it seemed to me that they did," Wilson said. "It was the only city in the world where everyone really behaved like soldiers at the front. They were kind to each other, and brave, and they never lost hope, even when everything was going to hell all around them."

Mrs. MacGregor paled visibly at the word "hell," but then she composed herself and made an effort to bear up. I think she was reassuring herself that she was among artists, so that that kind of language was permissible.

"You were probably in the West End all of the time," she said to Wilson. "The West End was different."

"No, I was everywhere, dear," Wilson replied. "I made a film about London, and so I saw all sides of it."

"You couldn't have. A foreigner never really sees all sides of a country. You should have been in Soho where I lived. It was just awful."

"Now how do you mean, dear?" Wilson asked. I recognized the gentle, interested voice that I had heard so often when he was on the make.

"Well," Mrs. MacGregor said, straightening her spine and pushing her ample bosom forward over her empty plate, "perhaps I'm telling tales out of school, but where I lived the people were horrid. I don't know how you feel about it," she went on, glancing nervously at both of us, "but I lived in a neighborhood where there were an awful lot of Jews. It was just horrible."

I took a deep breath. "Now, now, Mrs. MacGregor," I said warningly.

"Margot," she corrected me.

"All right, Margot. I think you're going off the deep end. You better stop. Because I'm a Jew."

"You're not," she said, smiling at me. "I know you're not. You don't look like a Jew, and your name's not Jewish. You're pulling my leg."

"I'm not pulling your leg. I'm Jewish," I said. I could feel myself blushing, and getting angry.

"But that's silly," she said. "Of course you're not. Perhaps I shouldn't say this, but that was the one thing about which I thought Hitler was absolutely right."

"Margot," Wilson said. "The man has warned you."

"Well, I don't believe him," she went on. "Anyway, the Jews were awful in London. They ran the black market, and they didn't go into the Army, and whenever they did, they pulled strings to keep from getting sent to the front. Hitler was absolutely right about them."

"Please stop, Mrs. MacGregor," I said. "You'll be sorry in a minute."

"Not at all," she replied. She felt uncomfortable but she didn't know how to get out of it now. "Even if you have Jewish blood, I think you're intelligent enough to be able to realize that these things I'm saying are true. Perhaps there are upper-class Jews but I'm not talking about them. I'm talking about the kikes in Soho. They were all foreigners, too, and they were horrid people."

"I'm a kike," I said. "My father and mother are kikes. My grandparents were kikes . . . kikes and foreigners."

Wilson grinned faintly. "That's right," he said.

She turned to him for help. "Now you're going to tell me you're Jewish too, I suppose," she said.

"No, dear," Wilson said sweetly. "I'm not going to do that. That would be a lie. And I don't want to lie to you . . . ever. But I do want to tell you a little story."

"I wish you would," she said. She was blushing, and trying to smile. I couldn't look at her.

"Don't interrupt me now," Wilson said in his sweetest voice. "You're much too beautiful to have to interrupt people. Just sit and listen to my story."

"All right," she smiled. She glanced nervously at me.

"You see, I was in London in 1943 and one night I was having dinner at the Savoy with a group of people, some of them very famous and very wellborn. Next to me at dinner was a beautiful lady, just like yourself."

"You're pulling my leg again," Mrs. MacGregor said.

"No, I'm not. And you mustn't interrupt me, dear. Well, I think we were at the Savoy. In any case, we were dining at one of the fashionable hotels and the bombs were falling outside, and it was 1943. I repeat that because it's important to the story. The conversation somehow got around to the style of architecture of the room we were in, and someone said it was Empire, and that started everyone talking about Napoleon and comparing him to Hitler. Are you listening, dear?"

She nodded, and put her finger across her lips. "Mustn't interrupt Daddy," she said.

"That's right. You're too beautiful to have to interrupt," Wilson repeated. I felt embarrassed but there was no stopping him now. I knew that.

"Well, everyone was rather brilliant, the way we've been tonight, and suddenly the lady next to me, and she was a beautiful lady, said that the one thing she didn't mind about Hitler was what he'd done to the Jews. That was the one thing she agreed with Hitler on. She said that if she had her way she would put all the Jews in the world in a camp too, and then kill them in gas chambers, just the way Hitler had done. Everyone started to argue with her, although no one there was Jewish, mind you, but she persisted. She said that was the way she felt. Well, dear, I turned to her, and everyone was silent, and I said, 'Madam, I have dined with some ugly, goddam bitches in my time. I've dined with some of the goddamnedest, ugliest bitches in the world, but you, dear, are the ugliest bitch of them all.' "

There was a silence in the room. Our boy grinned happily to himself. His favorite master was speaking, and everyone was listening to him. All was as it should be. Wilson paused and then went on, his voice soft and gentle, his face beaming at Mrs. MacGregor.

"Well, this lady got up very suddenly, and she tripped over her chair and fell down on the floor. And we all just sat there. She looked around for help but no one came to her rescue. Even the waiters stood rooted in their places. Then she picked herself up. And then I repeated what I had said, very slowly and clearly, so that everyone should hear it. I said: 'You are the ugliest bitch I have ever dined with,' I said, and she didn't answer. She didn't know what to say. Finally she just turned and left. A couple of days later she went to the American Embassy and reported me. She told the ambassador, or someone there, that an American major named John Wilson had insulted her in public. Well, they investigated the case, and I was called up, and then they discovered something truly amazing. They discovered that she was a paid German agent, and they locked her up."

Mrs. MacGregor looked stunned. "Why did you tell that story?" she asked after a long pause.

"Oh, I didn't tell it because I thought you were a German agent," Wilson said, unruffled. "It's just that I wanted to say the same thing to you tonight, and I didn't want you to think I had never said it before. I don't want you to feel too lonely, but you are the ugliest, goddam . . ." He stopped and grinned. "Well, you know the rest, don't you? No use repeating myself. Won't you have coffee, dear?"

"No, thank you," Mrs. MacGregor said. She was bright red. Her face glistened with perspiration.

"What about you, Pete?"

"No, thank you, John." I stared at him with amazement and fascination. I could never have done what he had just accomplished. I could never have remained precise and friendly and clear. I could never have been as fatally destructive, even if it had been demanded of me. It was like everything else about him. He dared go further than anyone else. And he always found the exact, deadly spot at which to strike.

"I think it's rather late," Mrs. MacGregor said. "I'd better go back to my room."

"We'll take you there," Wilson said gallantly.

"Oh, you needn't bother."

"No bother at all, is it, Pete?"

"Certainly not."

We followed her out of the dining room. She lived in an adjoining building and we walked slowly through the cool night air.

"If you'd like to go sailing sometime," she said faintly to me, "I go almost every afternoon at five o'clock."

"Thank you very much." I felt terribly sorry for her. She seemed to be moving in a trance, no longer fully alive. We stopped at the foot of the open stairway that led up to her room.

"Good night, Margot," Wilson said sweetly. "Good night, dear."

"Good night," she mumbled. "Thank you very much for dinner."

"We'll do it again real soon," Wilson said.

I managed to smile at her. "Good night, Mrs. Mac-Gregor."

She waved and climbed slowly up the stairs. Wilson and I turned back toward the main building of the hotel.

"Well," he said, "the evening didn't turn out exactly as planned, did it?"

"It's all my fault."

"Sure." He grinned. "Because you're a kike." He laughed happily and slapped me on the back. "I'll tell you one thing . . . if you go sailing with her she's sure to push you out of the boat."

"An African Tragedy." We started back toward the bar. I was still upset. "I don't know why those things always bother me, but they do. Damn good lesson, isn't it. We go on for weeks listening to all the horrible things everyone says about the natives and it never really strikes home."

"Well, as I always say, the Jews are no worse than the Negroes as long as they keep their mouth shut." It was obvious that he was finished with the subject. He didn't want to discuss what had happened. "Hell, Pete," he said, opening the screen door that led into the bar, "what do you expect from a dame like that?"

"Nothing. It just never fails to bother me."

He shrugged. "Just like you say, kid. It's a damn good lesson. We had it coming to us."

19

It was no use trying to work after that. We sat in the bar and drank beer. After a while Wilson switched to scotch. I didn't think he was getting drunk. His voice remained unchanged, and he moved steadily enough whenever he got up to go to the bathroom. Only when he started talking about hunting did I begin to suspect that he was not altogether sober.

"Listen, kid," he said. "We've got to finish our work this week. The company will be down in less than a month, and then we won't be able to go on safari."

"With a little luck we ought to be able to get through most of it in eight more days."

Lockhart came over to the table. "Have a good dinner, John?" he asked solicitously.

"Excellent, Ralph. I'm only sorry you weren't there. It was most instructive. A most instructive evening was had by all. Have a drink, Ralph?"

"Thank you, I will."

"Scotch, or beer?"

"Scotch, if I may."

"Boy!" Wilson called.

The bar boy came over to our table. He was an extremely tall Negro with huge shoulders and a very slight waist. He had a gentle, girlish face, and whenever Wilson called him he smiled happily.

"Another scotch, *por favor*," Wilson said.

"Yes, bwana." He turned and started off toward the bar at high speed.

"What a sweet guy he is," Wilson said. Lockhart sat in silence. He had learned by now that it was best not to discuss racial problems with any of us. "Don't you think he's a sweet guy, Ralph?" Wilson asked.

"He's one of the best boys here," Lockhart said grudgingly.

"They're all good boys," Wilson said. "You should have been at the soccer game this afternoon, Ralph. The small frontal lobes of their brains were not at all in evidence. Hard skulls, yes. But plenty of savvy underneath, too. Played the pants off the local supermen. The breeches, excuse me."

"Pete told me about it," Lockhart said. "Is the work coming along well, sir?"

"Just fine, Ralph," Wilson said. "But don't change the subject. We were discussing our black brothers."

Lockhart smiled falsely. "Sorry, sir. Didn't mean to stray." He bit at one of his cuticles.

"You know I'm getting to be rather fond of Ralph," Wilson said loudly to me. "If he didn't have such damned white skin, I might even get to like him."

"Well, I'll black up, if you like," Lockhart said weakly.

"Do that, Ralph," Wilson replied. His words were not coming out any too clearly. Just then there was a terrible commotion at the far end of the bar. The tall, good-looking boy had dropped a tray. He stooped hastily to pick up the small whisky glass that was rolling on the floor. All around him voices were raised in protest. Behind him, more outraged than anyone else, stood Harry. He gave the boy a violent push while he was bent over, and the boy's white cap fell to the floor. Harry kicked at it with the same viciousness that he had so often used on the soccer ball that afternoon. His knee caught the Negro in the side of the head. He rose quickly, putting his hand to his face. I could see a red cut in the brown skin.

"Pick up your hat," Harry shouted furiously. "Damn it, boy pick it up."

The Negro stood holding his cheek. He looked terribly frightened. One of the other boys retrieved his hat for him.

"I didn't touch you," Harry shouted. "Take your bloody hand away, damn you. Get out into the kitchen." He grabbed the unfortunate Negro by the shoulders and started him on his way out of the bar.

"Black buggers," he said angrily. "I'll teach all of you to be more careful around here."

Wilson was staring at Harry. He had witnessed the entire scene, just as I had.

"Well," he said very softly, "what do you know about that?"

"That boy will probably put in a complaint," Lockhart said. "We're not allowed to touch them, you know. It's against the regulations."

"What'll happen then?" I asked.

"Oh, probably nothing. Everyone will testify that the boy cut his head on the bar. Was a bit rough, though, wasn't it?"

Wilson had gotten to his feet and was slowly making his way past my chair. I got up quickly.

"John. Where are you going?" I asked.

"No place, kid," he said, very quietly. "Just going over to talk to Harry."

I followed him. Harry was complaining bitterly about the boys to the other men at that end of the bar.

"What happened, Harry?" Wilson asked.

"Oh, the clumsy black bastard spilled a drink all over this gentleman."

"On purpose, Harry?" The quiet, gentle, questioning voice sounded ominous above the hum of British talk.

"Who knows?" Harry said with righteous anger. "The black bastards."

The other Negro waiters stood around in angry silence.

"Harry," Wilson said, "I think you're sore because you took a beating this afternoon."

The headwaiter looked at him with contempt and hatred, the two expressions that usually inhabited his thin, homely face. "Not at all," he said.

"Harry, I think you're a yellow, rotten, sadistic son of a bitch," Wilson continued, very slowly and clearly. The entire bar grew still.

"Now, Mr. Wilson," the headwaiter said angrily, "I don't have to take that kind of talk from anyone. I don't care if you're a guest here or what you are."

"Don't call me Mr. Wilson," John said. "You don't call me that when we're playing poker upstairs. Call me John. Call me just what you'd call me upstairs. You see, Harry, this is a kind of poker too. I'm asking to see your cards, Harry. I think you're a big bluff. A yellow, sadistic son of a bitch, who loves to kick people around who can't fight back."

"I don't have to take that kind of guff." Harry began to shout.

"No, you don't," Wilson said. "That's why you can come outside right now and prove that you're not a yellow, sadistic son of a bitch."

"John," I said, "for God's sake. Not tonight."

"Tonight's a good night for poker, kid," Wilson said. "Table stakes. What about it, Harry? Want to try kicking me around?"

The headwaiter's face was bright red. He was watching all the men around him, trying to find out what he should do.

"You're drunk, John," he said. "Sit down."

"Yes, I'm drunk," Wilson said. "But that doesn't change anything about you. You're yellow, Harry. Bright yellow. You're a coward. Oh, you're great when it comes to kicking the boys around. But you're yellow when you're facing someone like me."

I grabbed Wilson's arm but he pulled away from me. His face was intense, his head slightly lowered.

"I'm not supposed to fight with the guests, Mr. Wilson," Harry said. He looked worried. Someone ran out of the bar to get Dickie.

"I'm not a guest tonight, you yellow bastard," Wilson said. "I'm an intruder."

Harry closed his eyes for an instant. Then he turned and started out through the screen door. Wilson followed him. I grabbed him by the coat, trying to hold him back.

"Let go," he said. "We've fought one bout for the kikes. This is the main event . . . for the niggers."

"There's no sense in it, John."

"Isn't there?" He turned with a look of surprise to face me. "Suppose Mrs. MacGregor had been a man? Wouldn't you have belted her?"

"Sure, but that was different."

"This is worse, kid," he said. "Believe me, this is really bad. Let go of me."

I knew that he was right. Still, I couldn't let him fight; he was too drunk. But I knew also that there was no stopping him now. Lockhart took my arm. "Shouldn't we do something?" he asked.

"It's no use." I thought I could detect a faint smile crossing Lockhart's face.

"Harry's quite fit, you know," he said.

Those were the last coherent words I heard. The headwaiter had turned and taken off his white jacket. Wilson stepped up to him and swung. The first blow caught the man on the side of the head, exactly the same place where he had kicked the Negro. I saw a thin line of blood easing out of his cheek. Then I saw him lunge at Wilson.

It wasn't really a fight. Nor was it a brawl. It was a kind of ludicrous dance that Wilson and the headwaiter performed out on the lawn of the hotel. At first they circled each other, their fists clenched. Then they backed away. Wilson cursed him in a steady stream of obscenity. Then he swung and hit him hard in the face. Blood spurted out of the waiter's nose and then all at once he came to life. His hands began to work like pistons. He moved in close and jarred Wilson's frame with short, quick punches. Wilson bent his thin body forward as if in great pain. Then all at once he sat down. But a moment later he had leaped up. The waiter knocked him down again. He got up, swinging wildly, cutting holes in the African night. Again and again Harry knocked him down, and again and again Wilson got to his feet. I started forward. Lockhart and Dickie grabbed me.

"Let me go, you stupid jerks," I shouted. "He'll kill him."

"Steady, old man," Dickie said.

Wilson was getting to his feet very slowly now. He brushed his sleeve across his bleeding face. His hair was matted down with sweat and blood. Harry was standing back, confused. Wilson stumbled and fell down by himself.

"Please don't get up, John," Harry said in a pitiful,

helpless voice. Then he turned to us: "Aren't you going to stop it?" he asked. No one moved. Wilson got up slowly and started toward the headwaiter.

"Yellow bastard," he mumbled, and swung. His fist landed on the side of Harry's head, and the Englishman tripped and fell back on the grass. Then immediately he leaped up again. He hit Wilson twice, once with a straight left and then again with a looping roundhouse punch. Wilson tottered, and went after him again. I turned a little, and kicked hard at Dickie's shins. Then I jumped forward and grabbed John. I clung to him, holding his thin arms to his side.

"Stop it," I said. "Stop it, for Christ's sake."

We wrestled with each other, but all of his strength had been used up. He reeled and tripped over my legs and we both fell to the grass.

"You've proved your point, John. Stop, for God's sake, stop."

"Let me go," he murmured. "I'll kill him." Dickie and Lockhart came to my rescue. We held Wilson, pulling him up to his feet. His face was covered with blood. Beyond his head I could see a group of four or five Englishmen standing around Harry. They were talking quietly and convincingly to him. Finally he turned and started back toward the bar. I could see the Negro waiters hurry inside through the screen door as he approached. Well, at least they've seen that someone was willing to fight for them, I thought.

"Where is he?" Wilson asked drunkenly. "Where is the yellow bastard?"

"He's called it quits, John," Dickie said. He was trying to keep his white linen suit from getting bloody.

"He has, eh?" Wilson said, spitting weakly. "I told you he was yellow."

We half carried him through the main entrance of the hotel. A frightened crowd of women stood staring at us. We went past them down the hallway to Wilson's room. Lockhart and I put him down on his bed. I dropped a towel in the bathtub and turned on the tap. Then I wrung it out. I was covered with blood, and my pants were soaking wet. I went into Wilson's room and put the towel over his face.

"What the hell are you doing, kid?" he asked angrily. "You want to smother me?"

Dickie started out of the room. "I'm going to get the doctor," he said.

"Is he as badly hurt as that?" Wilson murmured. I sat down on the bed and laughed helplessly. Lockhart was bathing Wilson's face.

"Holy God," I said. "He almost killed you, John."

Wilson glared at me. "You're full of crap," he said. "I was just getting ready to finish him off when you grabbed me. Didn't you hear him pleading with me not to get up?"

"Are you badly hurt, sir?" Lockhart asked. Wilson pushed him away violently, and sat up on the bed.

"I'm fine," he said. "Where is the son of a bitch?"

"It's all over, John. You're back in your room. It's all over."

He grinned suddenly. "It is, eh?" he said. "Well, what do you know about that?" He was like a drunk waking up. "I feel pretty good," he went on. "You see, like I always told you, as long as you get in there and fight you feel good. You feel lousy and your stomach feels full of pus if you don't fight, but if you go in there and get the hell beaten out of you, you feel great."

The bedroom door opened, and Dickie came in, followed by the doctor and Harry. The headwaiter had put on his clean white coat again. His face was covered with small cuts.

"I'm all right," Wilson said as the doctor put his bag down on the bed. He was a gray-haired Englishman with a mustache. I recognized the same man we had sat next to at the soccer game. Wilson looked up at Harry and grinned.

"Well," he said, "you yellow bastard. I guess that's the last black boy you'll kick while I'm in Entebbe."

Harry swallowed hard. Then he put out his hand. "I'm awfully sorry this happened, Mr. Wilson," he said, "but you just wouldn't listen to reason."

Wilson shook his hand. He looked suddenly very tired. "Get the son of a bitch out of here, will you," he said. Then he lay back on the bed and closed his battered eyes. "You know we've got to work tomorrow, kid," he said to me.

Someone turned out the light. The bed was already covered with thousands of tiny flies. Wilson lifted his hand to brush some of them off his face, but he didn't quite make it. He didn't have enough strength to complete the movement, and his arm dropped by his side. Then he grinned at me. "Feel the mystery, kid?" he said.

20

The fight was not immediately forgotten; in the week that followed, it was the favorite topic of conversation in Entebbe. Most of the temporary government employees who lived in the settlement were solidly against Wilson. Only a few of the permanent residents dared to take his side. They felt that it was high time someone called the headwaiter on his excessive brutality, and despite the fact that John had lost the fight, they were pleased with the stand he had taken. As a result we found ourselves moving into a new group, making new friends.

Among them was a man called Phillip Morehead. He had been a professional soldier most of his life, and had only recently retired as a lieutenant colonel in the Royal Engineers. He was still a fairly young man, and in order to augment his retirement pay he had come to Africa to work for the government. He taught at the native school in Kampala, instructing the Africans in the use of surveying instruments.

I met him at tea in the upstairs lobby of the hotel. He was hot and dusty, dressed in khakis and Wellington boots, a thin, sunburned man with watery blue eyes.

"I say," he called across the room, immediately after I had placed my order for tea, "are you the American chap who had the fight the other night?"

"No, that was my friend," I replied wearily. I had already had a few disagreeable arguments on the subject and I wanted to have my cup of tea in peace and quiet.

"Well, jolly good for him," the stranger said. "It was time someone gave old Harry a hiding."

"It didn't quite turn out that way," I said.

"Oh really?" The man looked alarmed. "Well, jolly

good for your friend in any case." He turned to the native
boy and spoke rapidly in a strange singsong language that
sounded like fake Chinese. The boy scurried off and returned with more hot water.

"What language was that?" I asked curiously. "That
wasn't Swahili, was it?"

"No, that's Luganda, the real language of the country.
As you probably know, Swahili is just a get-around dialect
that the whites invented." He smiled. "The country is
called Uganda and the language is Luganda, and the
people are Bugandans. It's all rather strange."

I moved over to the couch where Morehead was sitting and we introduced ourselves. I could tell immediately
that he was quite different from the other people who
lived in our hotel. He spoke with real fondness of the natives and the country and his work. He taught in a native
school where they trained surveyors, and he declared that
he intended to stay in Uganda for the rest of his life.
"I like the people," he said. "They're friendly and gentle,
and there's really an awful lot to be done." Wilson appeared, his face still somewhat battered-looking. I introduced them.

"You don't look so bad, old boy," Morehead said, inspecting John's bruised face. "Harry's one eye is still
closed, you know, and you can see out of both of yours."

"I would have really fixed him if they hadn't stopped
it," Wilson said, airing his favorite theory.

"He only knocked John down fifteen times," I said,
"and he was getting visibly tired."

"I was just getting onto his style," Wilson said. "Another ten minutes and I would have killed him."

Morehead smiled. "In any case it was worth doing," he
said.

Wilson nodded. "It certainly was," he said.

"Mr. Morehead was telling me about the game he has
seen out in the country where he works," I said. I had
heard enough of the fight. I wanted to forget the picture
of the blood-soaked scarecrow, picking itself up again and
again.

Wilson tried to make his face look interested, but he
couldn't quite manage it. He was not yet the master of his
new features. "Game?" he asked. "What kind of game?"

"Well, I was saying that it's rather funny sometimes.

You look through the finder of your surveying instrument and there is your line, with the native boys strung out along it, cutting an avenue through the tall grass, and all at once they disappear. Then you just have to grab your instrument and jump off into the grass and pretty soon a buffalo will come charging down the neat path you've cleared, and will go by you like a huge, snorting truck. They don't like to make their way through the thick cover any more than we do."

"You carry a rifle, of course?" Wilson said.

"Well, just a .22 for guinea hen," Morehead said with a smile. "I wouldn't like to shoot a buffalo with one of those, although I have killed leopard with the .22 long-rifle bullet."

"Leopard? You don't say!" Wilson managed to look amazed. This was something he had not read in his book.

"It's not a good idea as a rule, but when you come across one of them in a tree, there isn't much else you can do. The natives expect you to kill them, and so you just have to hit them in the right place."

"You don't say. Well, I've never heard of that."

"Mr. Morehead will take us out on a guinea fowl hunt, if you'd like to go," I said.

"Well, I certainly would," Wilson replied. We made a date for the following afternoon.

The pace of our work on the script increased immediately with the prospect of hunting. We finished two sequences that night, and another one the following morning. At two in the afternoon we met Morehead outside the hotel, dressed in our safari clothes and armed with our shotguns. Morehead carried his .22. We climbed into his station wagon and drove out into the countryside. A few miles from Entebbe the scenery changed abruptly. There were large patches of jungle, and the dirt road ran through thick walls of underbrush. Every few miles we came across a native village on a cleared plot of ground, and Morehead would speak to the old men and children loitering near the road. They always stared with amazement at him after his initial greeting.

"*Jambo*," he would call from his car. It was the Swahili word for "greetings."

"*Jambo, bwana*," would come the nervous reply. Then Morehead would start speaking Luganda, and immediately a fantastic change would come over the Africans. They would smile delightedly, and flock around the car, jabbering away in their strange singsong voices.

"Did you ever see anything like that?" Wilson beamed. "Their faces just light up when they hear you speak to them."

"Well, it's their language, and they're naturally pleased when a white man speaks it. They know he's taken the trouble to learn it." He turned back to the crowd of small, half-naked boys that were standing outside his window and asked them if there were any guinea fowl about.

"*Mingi, mingi, Kanga,*" they replied. Morehead translated that in the opinion of the crowd there were a great many guinea fowl in the region, and that they had answered in Swahili in order not to be rude to us.

"You've got to be careful, of course," Morehead said. "They want to please you, and so they always say there's a lot of game around. Often it isn't so." He spoke to the tallest of the boys, and with a look of excitement on his dark face, the boy got into the car. He sat next to Wilson and took over as the guide for our expedition. We turned off the dirt road and bounced through thick brush. At last the car ran into impenetrable brush and we stopped. The boy was talking a steady stream of Luganda and pointing up at the hills to our right.

"They're up in the high country," Morehead said. "We'll have to go after them."

We got out of the car and loaded our shotguns.

"What's the drill if we see a leopard?" I asked Morehead.

"Just don't pay attention to him," he answered. "If he's very close, ten or twenty yards away, and we're all together, we might risk a shot. But we're actually after guinea fowl today."

"I am, anyway," I said. Wilson gave me a hopeless look, and we started out through the thick grass.

It was hard work. Insects of all kinds buzzed around our heads, and the sun beat down on our shoulders. It seemed to burn right through our bush jackets. A few minutes after we had started I was bathed in sweat. My feet clung to the slippery, uneven ground. My hands were cut by reeds and brambles. The barefoot Negro boy moved steadily on ahead of us. I looked back at Wilson.

His battered face was bright red under his huge brown hat. He panted, dragging his shotgun through the vines and the thickets which seemed intent on pulling it out of his hands. We went on, climbing steadily, until the vegetation around us decreased.

"Holy God," Wilson said. He had stopped, and was squatting on his heels. "This is work."

"I'm for hunting on the plains," I said. "From now on."

Morehead was waving for us to come on. He was sweating too, but his face had not changed color.

"This'll get us in shape," Wilson said. We climbed one hill, and went down into a thick valley beyond it, and then climbed up toward the next ridge line. Wilson stopped. He looked worse than when Harry had finished with him.

"I think the little black bastard is lying," he said with a faint grin. "No guinea fowl could live in this stuff."

"They fly, remember," I said.

"I wish I could," Wilson replied.

My months of skiing had hardened my legs and feet, and I was getting used to the heat. I followed Morehead up to the summit of the next hill.

"John's feeling the strain," I said. Morehead nodded. He took out a canteen and went down to meet Wilson. John took a salt pill and a few swallows of the warm water. Then we went on. He was more than fifty years behind us when the first birds broke out of their cover.

"Yours, John," Morehead shouted. The large gray hens moved slowly through the air in front of Wilson. He raised his shotgun and fired twice. The birds flew on unharmed. We waited for him to reach us.

"Couldn't shoot," he said apologetically. "My hands were shaking as if I had the D.T.s."

"Doesn't matter," Morehead said. "There'll be plenty more."

He proved to be right, for we had not gone more than fifty yards when two birds broke cover in front of us. Wilson fired twice and missed. I fired once with the same effect. We started toward the next slope. Wilson stopped abruptly.

"I'll wait here for a while," he said. "You guys go on ahead."

In the next valley two more hens rose up in front of us.

I shot the first one and missed the next. The boy scurried off into the brush and retrieved the dead hen. He looked very pleased.

"Well, at least we won't go hungry tonight," Morehead said.

"I think I winged the second one," I said. "He went down in that patch of jungle over there." The fever had started; I could feel it burning, that strange, excited feeling that wipes out discomfort and makes you stop thinking about how far you've gone and how far you'll have to go back. I forgot about Wilson. It didn't even occur to me that he was waiting for us. We moved on at a rapid pace, scrambling through the thick brush, down into the valley where I had seen the second bird light, and up the next hill on the other side. Suddenly Morehead stopped and fired. A large hen fell out of a tree some fifty yards away.

"Great shot," I said.

"It's all you can do with rifle," Morehead said. "You've got to shoot them while they're sitting on a tree or on the ground."

The boy retrieved the bird. We stood on the ridge and looked back. Wilson was nowhere to be seen. A cool evening breeze had come up. In the valley below us we could see a few grass huts and a small cultivated field. Two natives were climbing up toward us.

"Where's your friend?" Morehead asked.

"Back over that way, I think," I said. Morehead looked worried.

"Has he got a good sense of direction?" he asked.

"I hope he has." Every hill behind us looked very much like all of the others over which we had passed. There was no road in view, only endless rolling country with thick jungle growth in the valley bottoms.

"We'd better start back," Morehead said. "It's bad country to get lost in."

"I can see that," I said. "I couldn't get back to the car now, if I had to."

The two other natives who had been climbing toward us arrived. They spoke excitedly to Morehead, their faces bright with smiles. There were *mingi mingi, Kanga* just across the next rise. They would take us there. Morehead explained that we had to go back and find the other bwana and they looked disappointed. Still, they decided they would come along.

It was cooler now. The sun was almost down. We worked our way back over the country which we had covered so rapidly an hour before. Morehead grew more and more worried about Wilson.

"He's got his gun, hasn't he?" he asked. "He'll know to fire it a couple of times in case he's lost, won't he?"

"I hope so."

We reached the summit of the next hill. One of the boys found an empty shell casing.

"This is where you killed your bird," Morehead said. "He shouldn't be too far off now."

But Wilson was nowhere to be seen. We stopped and I fired twice into the air. There was no reply. The country lay quiet all around us. Only the needle-sharp hum of the mosquitoes could be heard buzzing around our naked heads and hands.

"Damn it," Morehead said. "This is bad."

We separated and combed the ridge lines to our right and left. Then we climbed back to the top of the hill where the boy had found my cartridge. It was getting dark.

"What'll we do?" I asked.

"I don't quite know." He turned to the natives who stood behind us, their bare feet and legs marked with white scratches from sharp vines through which we had traveled. Morehead spoke rapidly in Luganda but the natives looked as dumfounded as we were.

"We better start back toward the car and get help," Morehead said.

I followed him in silence. Was this the way it would end? Had we lost Wilson the first time out? It didn't seem possible. We were not more than thirty miles away from the hotel and the civilized life of Entebbe, and already we were in trouble.

"What would happen if he were forced to spend the night out here?" I asked.

Morehead shrugged. "Well, he might be all right, but then again he might not be. It's really our fault, you know."

"The fever gets hold of you," I said. "It turns you every way but loose."

"We've got to get back to the car," Morehead said.

We went through the increasing darkness until we came out onto the road. Then I saw the car.

Wilson was sitting on the front fender smoking a cigarette. On the ground around him squatted half a dozen natives, all smoking cigarettes as well. He grinned at us.

"I've had quite a time," he said happily. "We've discussed Proust, and life, and the superiority of the American cigarette."

"Christ, you had us worried," I said.

Wilson seemed not to have heard me. "These are sure swell guys," he said to Morehead. "The old fellow over there has been trying to tell me something. Will you ask him what it is, Phillip?"

Morehead shook his head and smiled. He spoke quickly to the native John had pointed out to him.

"He wants to take you to a place where there's a leopard," Morehead said.

Wilson grinned. "He does, eh? Well, tell him I'll be back in a few days with a bulldozer and a big rifle."

"John," I said, "I think this country is too tough for us. Let's face it. We're a couple of Vine Street characters. Let's take the warning while there's still time."

Wilson looked annoyed. "What are you talking about, kid?" he said. "We just have to get in shape, that's all."

"And we have to get two brand-new compasses and learn how to shoot."

"Don't you worry," Wilson said. "When we start using rifles it'll be a different story."

"Oh sure," I said. "But remember . . . the nice thing about guinea fowl is that they don't fight back."

"That's what's wrong with them," Wilson said.

We distributed the rest of our cigarettes and got stiffly back into the station wagon. Wilson sat in front with Morehead.

"Well now, Phillip," he said. "That was a wonderful afternoon. We'll have to take you out elephant hunting just to pay you back."

"I'd love to go."

"We'll have to arrange it then." He waved to the natives out on the road. "What swell people they are, Phillip. I don't blame you for wanting to make your life out here." He rambled on about Africa, and how much he liked it. I tried not to listen.

I sat in silence, holding onto the sides of the car as we

bounced along the jungle road. I could remember the darkness closing in around us on the endless hills, could remember the sudden silent threat of nature and wilderness. We stopped for an instant in order to find our way around a muddy crater in the middle of the road. There was a wild cry from somewhere in the distance.

"What's that?" Wilson asked.

Morehead listened attentively. The cry was repeated. "Just a hyena," he said with a smile. "Did you think it was your leopard?"

"It sounded like Harry speaking to one of the boys," Wilson said. "We'd better get back to the bar."

21

I had hoped that Wilson's first encounter with the jungle might diminish his eagerness to come to grips with big game, but that was a foolish hope. Although he was stiff and sore the next morning he was not the least bit discouraged. He seemed to have forgotten all about the hardships of the guinea fowl hunt. He was already concerned with the next thing. I found him in his room, his feet soaking in a tub of hot water, the good book propped up on his skinny knees. He looked up briefly as I entered.

"Good morning, Pete. How do you feel?"

"All right. My legs are a little stiff, but that's about all."

"You're in pretty good shape, aren't you?"

"Not bad."

He leafed back through his book. "Just listen to this," he said. "I marked it last night. I want to read it to you." He found the place he had marked, and began. " 'A wounded buffalo is the only beast which, when charging, I have never known to be turned. An elephant, a rhino, a lion . . . they can all be turned. A charging elephant, even if he is not knocked down, provided that a reasonably heavy bullet is used, will certainly be turned.' Then it goes on, and then he says: 'A charging lion, if knocked down, may or may not attempt to press home the charge. It depends to a very great extent on how close he is to you: he may do so, but on the other hand, he may attempt to slink away. But in my experience, and in that of every other hunter with whom I have ever discussed them, there is only one thing that will stop a charging buffalo: and that is death . . . either his or yours.' "[1] He looked up, smiling happily.

"Very encouraging," I said.

"You've got to read this book, kid," he said.

"I will as soon as you stop memorizing it."

He didn't reply. He continued reading. "John," I said, "I want to ask you something. Are we going to be hunting in the same kind of country we were in yesterday?"

"I don't know, Pete." He shrugged. "All depends on where we go." He closed his book. "Well, shall we attack the ending?"

"Sure. In a minute. I just wanted to say that maybe we ought to try and find a place that isn't quite as rugged. I don't think either one of us is in good enough shape to go on for hours through brush of the kind we ran into yesterday."

"The country will be the least of our worries," he said brightly. "Now come on. Let's get to work."

I realized again that the worst thing I could do was to press the issue. If I insisted on discussing the dangers that might confront us, I would only goad him into taking greater risks. I let the matter rest, and we started going over the various scenes that led up to the end of the script. For once he was amazingly agreeable. Nothing I said brought forth an argument from him. The discussion ended and we started working on the actual dialogue of each one of the scenes. Suddenly he looked up from his copy of the script.

"Tell me, are you worried, Pete?" he asked.

"About the ending? No. I think after what I've seen here in Africa it's the only logical conclusion."

"No, not the ending," he replied. "I know you're not worried about that, you bastard. You just want to get it done. Are you worried about our safari?"

"I'm a little worried," I said.

[1] John Taylor, *Big Game and Big Game Rifles.*

"Why, kid?"

"Well, I know something about game fever. I felt a little of it yesterday after I shot the first hen. It's like every passion: unreasonable and destructive. It's like gambling, or sex, or skiing even. It suddenly overpowers you, and you get into things that you would normally shy away from. You stop thinking rationally. The thing you're after is all that matters. In gambling, money loses its value. In sex, you suddenly throw away your natural critical judgment of people. And hunting I think is even worse. You disregard risk. You no longer think about what might happen to you. Just like yesterday. We were rushing through dense grass. We didn't think about poisonous snakes, or insects, or leopards, or anything at all except those damn guinea fowl. We could have walked right into the middle of a herd of buffalo, or lions. It's silly. It's unreasonable. And that worries me. Both of us might get the same kind of fever when we're after bigger game."

"We undoubtedly will," Wilson said. "But that's what makes it worth while. The fever is exactly what we're after, just as the ultimate nirvana that comes after you've killed the beast is exactly what we crave and want. Read your idol on the same subject. Francis Macomber experiences the greatest sensation of his life after he has killed his first buffalo. He has overcome fear. I don't think that's anything to play down. We're after those same sensations. They're big things. When you stand facing a charging elephant . . . well, you're doing something that's the opposite of your daily routine. You're saying to hell with everything . . . to hell with the world, with life . . . and when you survive it, then you experience the great emotion of remembering your defiance, your conquest of life."

"John," I said. "There's one very important thing in the Hemingway story that you've forgotten."

"What's that, kid?"

"The white hunter tells Macomber that it isn't done to talk about that wonderful sensation of having overcome fear. Remember?"

Wilson grinned sheepishly. "Well, we're different," he said. "We think it's O.K. to talk about everything. come on, let's stop wasting time and get to work."

"Just one more thing, John," I said. "Bear with me. I've glanced at your book and one of the other things that bothers me is still the death of the animal. Even when I read about it, I feel displeased, and slightly nauseated. I can see the endless carcasses of elephant and God knows what littering the plains of Africa and there doesn't seem to be any reason for it all. It's such a wasteful way to establish your ego."

He shook his head. "That damn bird you killed in Oxnard is squeaking again. Forget it."

We went back to the script. Shortly before one o'clock we heard the noise of a plane passing low over the hotel. Wilson rushed to the window.

"Alec," he said. "Come on. We'll go down to the airfield to pick him up."

We met Laing and Harrison in front of the airport building. They looked tired and thin. Laing's once immaculate tunic was crumpled and caked with mud. His eyes were bloodshot. Harrison stood with his shoulders drooping, staring listlessly at us.

"Well, how did it go, guys?" Wilson asked them cheerfully. "You look pretty bushed, I'd say."

"We've got what you wanted," Laing said slowly. "We've found a location."

"Where?" Wilson asked excitedly.

"In the Congo," Laing said. "Let's go get a drink and I'll tell you about it."

I fell back a little and walked beside Harrison. Wilson and Laing were out of earshot, ahead of us.

"What's it like, Dick?" I asked him. "Antibes or Beauvallon?"

He tried to smile. "It's bloody awful, Pete," he said. "The Congo, all of it, is just no place for a man to live."

"What's the location like?"

"It's jungle," he said, "the thickest jungle you've ever seen. There's a black-water river, exactly as John wanted, and a few huts. At night there are mosquitoes and in the daytime it rains. The trees are all over a hundred and fifty feet high. I hope I don't ever have to go back there."

Laing's description was a little more cheerful. We sat on the terrace of the hotel talking about it.

"It's quite an amazing place, you know," the pilot said. "The flowers and vegetation are nothing like any you've ever seen. I've been around Africa quite a lot, and even I was quite amazed."

"Will it be possible for a company to live down there?" Wilson asked. It was the first time he had ever expressed any doubts about the hardships that we would have to face.

"Oh yes," Laing said. "That's all laid on now too. There's a railroad that runs to within thirty miles of the place from Pontiaville. We've found a contractor who's willing to build a camp, and we can get a boat or two down to the river. All we need now is your O.K., John."

"Well, I'll be ready to go down and take a look at it any time you say."

Laing nodded. "Tomorrow maybe, or the day after. We've got to get this aircraft back to Nairobi for a checkup, that's all, and then we can leave."

"That sounds fine."

"How's the script coming along?" Harrison asked.

"Fine, just fine," Wilson said. He turned to Laing. "Don't forget the other big rifle when you go to Nairobi, Alec. If you can, get two of them."

Laing nodded. "There's a lot of work to do, you know," he said. "Wonder if you'll have time for your safari?"

"Oh, we'll have time for that, Alec," Wilson said. "We'll make time if we have to. Tell you what, on the way to the Congo we'll stop in at the Masindi location and inspect the native village they've been building there. That way I'll gain a day or two."

Laing nodded. "That's easy enough to do. Fly in there for two hours and then move on. If we get an early start, that is."

"It'll all work out," Wilson said. "You'll see."

That evening Basil Owen returned from Nairobi. He brought a young man with him, a tall, dark-haired man in an enormous hat and very bleached safari clothes. His name was Victor Paget, and we learned that he was to serve as both white hunter and draftsman.

It was not love at first sight between Paget and Wilson. Paget was a casual young man who looked rather skeptically at us all. I had often encountered the same kind of look in Switzerland when a mountain guide was first introduced to the party of climbers he was supposed to lead. "So these are the fools who will be hanging onto the same rope with me," the look always said. "What a lousy business I'm in." Paget glanced at Wilson in the same manner.

"Done quite a bit of shooting?" he asked.

Wilson straightened slowly at his place at the bar. "Quite a bit," he said hesitantly. "Not an awful lot. That's why we'll want a couple of days' shooting at antelope or waterbuck before we start after the big stuff."

"How long do you expect to be gone on safari?" Paget asked.

"A couple of weeks," Wilson said. "Ten days at the minimum."

"That's hardly enough to get started," Paget replied. "We never go out for less than a month."

"Well, we just haven't got that much time," Wilson said.

Paget shrugged. "No use going then, I'd say."

Wilson scowled. "Well, we *are* going," he said. "With or without you, we're going."

Paget flushed. "What do you expect to get on your safari, Mr. Wilson?" he asked.

"A buffalo, and a big tusker maybe. And anything else we have time for."

Paget nodded. He turned to Owen. "I'll have to think about this, Basil," he said.

"No, you won't," Wilson said aggressively. "You can stay here and work on the blueprints of the sets with Harrison. We'll get someone else."

Paget nodded. "That's all right with me," he said. Wilson turned away from the bar and sat down at his usual table. I followed him.

"I don't like the son of a bitch," he murmured. "First of all I don't think he's a white hunter. Why would he work at being a draftsman if that's his trade?"

"I don't know, John. I just met the guy."

"Well, I just met him too, but I don't like him." Laing and Harrison had joined Paget at the bar. Wilson motioned for Owen to come to our table.

"Is that the best you could do?" he asked him.

"What do you mean, John?" Owen was a slight man with very white skin and a permanently startled look on his face.

"The guy with the big hat, who thinks he's Gary Cooper."

Owen looked worried. "He's a very good draftsman and he's supposed to be a first-rate white hunter. We're saving money by hiring him."

"I thought there was something at the bottom of it."

"Don't you think he'll do?" Owen asked.

"I don't like him," Wilson said. "I don't like his superior manner."

"He's just a kid."

Wilson nodded. "All right," he said briefly. "We'll see. Now let's get this thing organized. I'm taking off with Alec tomorrow for the Congo to look at the location. You'll take over here. Get all the equipment checked in and started on its way. The company will be down in a couple of weeks and so we don't have too much time."

Owen nodded. "I think we may be starting a little later than we planned to," he said cautiously. "But I'll get it all going. Then I'd better join you down there, don't you think, or would you rather have Lockhart?"

"Leave Lockhart here," Wilson said. "He and Paget and Harrison can make up the rear echelon once we're established in the Congo."

"Just as you like, John," Owen said. "What about Pete? We have to arrange his transportation."

"Pete will come down later," Wilson said. "He'll finish our work here first." He straightened in his chair. "Well, shall we have dinner, guys? We have a lot of work to do tonight."

Wilson and Laing left the following day. I walked out to the plane with them, helping carry our small arsenal. Wilson was in breeches and puttees. Laing wore a fresh uniform, complete with ribbons.

"What kind of a ship is this, Alec?" I asked.

"A Rapide," Laing replied. "Not the latest thing out but I like to have two motors in front of me when I'm flying over all that forest."

"Two motors suit me fine," Wilson said. I could see that he was not giving the plane any thought. Airplanes were like taxis to him; he got in and out without looking at them. I watched him climb into the cabin, pulling himself up by the struts that seemed to hold the fragile wings in place. Laing followed him.

I stepped back and the motors coughed and started. The fabric along the wings and fuselage trembled nervously, and the fine, reddish dust of Uganda swirled up behind the tail. Laing waved from the pointed tip of the cabin. I could see that Wilson had already opened his book. The plane wheeled slowly and started clumsily down the runway. I stood watching it as it turned and the motors increased their speed, and then, very slowly, like a fat, grayish bird, it bounced past me and rose slowly into the clear air.

Everything was proceeding as planned. There was no excitement about any of it. Perhaps all your worries are foolish and unfounded, I told myself. I went back to the car and drove past the anthills and the natives and the lush green fields. At the hotel I sent a cable to Landau, telling him that we were almost finished with the script. Then I went in to lunch. Harrison and Paget had already started and Paget was abusing the waiters.

"What a bloody stupid boy," the white hunter said disgustedly. "Why doesn't he go on and serve our meal?"

"He's probably waiting for me to catch up with you," I said.

"But we didn't tell him we wanted to wait," Paget said. "You know what we'd do with a boy like that out on safari? We'd give him ten smart lashes to wake him up. That's what we'd do."

I turned to Harrison. "Let's talk about the south of France, Dick. What's the weather like now in Juan-les-Pins, you think?"

Harrison smiled. "I should think it would be just about perfect," he said. "Warm enough to swim and cool at night. Not too many people as yet, but still a few lovely creatures on the *plage*, and of course wonderful food. Just think, what would you give now for a *salade Niçoise* and a nice, cold bottle of white wine?"

"I'd give you Uganda and Tanganyika," I said, "and fifteen points."

We sat for a long time on the veranda of the hotel, waiting for it to get cooler. Harrison was the only one in the crew who was allowed to rest after lunch, as he had just come back from the Congo.

"Wouldn't it be lovely if this were over and done with," he said, opening his third bottle of cold beer, "especially if we were all still alive and healthy."

"It would be nice," I said.

22

The following day I received a long letter from Landau. It had obviously been dictated in haste and mailed without his having reread it, for it was full of errors. He was very worried about the script and Wilson. The word had gotten back to London that John was drinking a lot, and that his mean streak had come to the fore. This had caused him to beat up on the local headwaiter. Landau stated that such exhibitions were in terribly bad taste, and might jeopardize our work in Africa. Wilson must immediately be made to realize this, so that there would be no repeat performance. Of course this was a difficult job, but he, Landau, felt that as I was Wilson's oldest friend, I was the only one who could quiet him down a little. Landau was still very busy in London and could therefore not come down to handle the matter himself. But he was counting on me. The last paragraph repeated all of his previous pleas. "I beg you to do everything you can to bring John to his senses. Of all the wild beasts in Africa he is the most dangerous. The next time he picks a fight with a helpless employee of the hotel or the company, you have my permission to hit him from behind." Then followed greetings and love of all kinds, and a brief reminder of what good friends we had been throughout the years. The secretary had signed it in Paul's absence. He was leaving for the Continent that morning with Miss Gibson and Mr. and Mrs. Duncan.

I tore up the letter and went looking for Lockhart. He was working on a budget report in his room.

"Good morning," he said cheerfully, as I appeared.

"Morning, Ralph."

"What can I do for you, Pete?"

"You can't do anything for me, Ralph," I said quietly, "but you can do something for yourself."

He looked startled. "What's that?"

"Stick to your job," I said. "Don't spy on Wilson and send back false reports."

"Spy on Wilson?" He rose, his face getting pale beneath his heavy tan. "What do you mean?"

"Exactly what I said. If you write Landau about what goes on here you can at least be accurate."

"Have I written anything that wasn't true?"

"You have. You said Wilson provoked the fight with Harry. That isn't exactly true. He only challenged Harry after the son of a bitch had behaved outrageously. Somebody should have hit him years ago."

"I only referred to the matter very briefly," Lockhart said. "I didn't think it was important enough for me to give all of the details."

"Then you shouldn't have mentioned it at all. In any case, you're backing a losing horse. No matter what happens, Wilson is the boss here and there isn't a damn thing Landau can do about it. He's more scared of him than you are. So if I were you, I'd just keep my mouth shut."

I left him chewing his nails nervously. Then I went back to work on the script. It was typical that the one decent thing Wilson had done should be misrepresented. Now the news would spread quickly. The ogre was on the warpath, hitting headwaiters and abusing the natives. The wise guys at Romanoff's would be grinning, laying all kinds of bets that the picture would never be completed.

At dinnertime I sensed that Lockhart and Paget had made a pact between them. Paget was the spokesman for the rebel element.

"When the tall chap coming back?" he asked insolently.

"Who do you mean?"

"You know . . . the one who's gotten all of his hunting out of a book."

"Mr. Wilson?"

"I suppose so. That's his name, is it?"

"Yeah. I think you'd better write it down and memorize it, seeing as you're working for him."

"I'm not working for him," Paget said. "I'm working for Owen and the company . . . as a draftsman."

"You given up being a white hunter?"

"Here I have," Paget said aggressively. "I'm not going

on any damn fool Hollywood safari."

"I guess he'll hire a real white hunter then," I said.

Paget flushed. "I'm real enough for anything he wants to kill."

"How long have you had your license?"

"Six months. But I was raised out here. I was shooting lion when I was fifteen years old. And I never had to consult a bloody book to find out how to do it."

Lockhart grinned, delighted with his partner. "Whyn't you tell all this to Wilson when he comes back?" I asked Paget. "Why bend my ear?"

"I will tell him if I see him again."

"Oh, you'll see him again all right."

"Might not," Paget said, smiling at Lockhart. "One of those blooming Pygmies might get him in the Congo. Shoot a poisoned arrow through that big hat of his. That would fix him, wouldn't it?"

We were like schoolboys arguing about a teacher after school. I left the table and had coffee with Morehead and his wife.

The days passed very slowly. I finished proofreading the script and sent my copy back to London to be mimeographed, as I knew they were waiting eagerly for a final draft.

I was on the golf course when I saw the Rapide coming in over the hills surrounding the lake. I hurried back to the hotel.

Wilson and Laing were already there when I arrived. Owen, Lockhart, and Harrison were seated in the bar with them. Wilson got up and came over to me.

"It's all set, kid," he said with a strange intensity in his voice. "I've really got us fixed up. We're going to have the damnedest safari anyone ever had."

"Where, John?" I asked warily.

"In the Congo. The game warden of the whole area is laying it on for us."

"We're not going to hunt in the forest, are we?" I asked.

"Well, wherever this fellow takes us. He's quite a guy, Pete. We'll leave here the first thing Monday morning."

"Why did you come back?"

"Well, there was no use waiting down there. There's nothing for me to do in Stanleyville. They're getting our camp ready at the location, and everything else is in order, so I thought I'd come back here with Alec, in case there are any more foul-ups."

"How are the locations, John?" I asked.

"Fine," he said. "Just fine, kid. The village at Masindi is finished and ready to go. The boys did a swell job. It's exactly as we described it in the script. Took two hundred natives to build it."

"What about the Congo location?"

"The Congo. Oh boy. You've never seen such a place. Right in the middle of the forest. Black and green mambas everywhere and enough crocs to make Paul a happy man."

I smiled. It was one of the things Landau had included in the letter. He had always wanted a scene with a crocodile in the picture and Wilson and I had always resisted him.

Laing looked up. "Have you told him about all of the existing diseases?" he asked.

"No, I was coming to that. We inquired down there what there was to look out for. Well, it seems that the syphillis rate is one hundred per cent among the natives and the leprosy rate about seventy per cent. You can't drink or bathe in the water, and there was a leopard killed a mile from the campsite the night before we arrived."

"No elephants, John?" I asked.

"Oh sure. The forest is full of all kinds of game but it's so thick you can't see them. You hear them at night, though. The damnedest things are the monkeys. You can hear them arguing all day long." He screwed up his face. " 'Gimme that goddam banana,' you hear one say. And then the other one will yell: 'It's mine, I saw it first. It's my banana,' and then they argue. Boy, wait till you get down there, kid." He turned to the others. "I'm going to take a bath, guys, and then I'll be back and we'll really plunge into everything."

Laing came over to me, once Wilson had gone. He looked worried. "We've got a little job on our hands, Pete," he said.

"What's that?"

He leaned thoughtfully against the bar. "Well, while we were down in the Congo, John met the local game warden. Of course he asked him about the hunting, and this fellow promised to take him out."

"He told me that it was all arranged."

Laing shook his head. "It's foolishness to go all that way," he said. "We'll have to fly all day to get down there and pick this Belgian fellow up, and then I'm sure we'll have to fly halfway back to get to any place where there's hunting. You can't just go out into the forest and shoot, you know."

"Well, what do you want me to do?"

"Just back me up tonight when I bring up the problem. The safari will tie up a plane for a week, and the Rapide's the only two-engine job I have available. And Owen says he needs *it* to haul personnel and supplies."

"If you talk to him, Alec, he'll listen," I said. "He doesn't trust anyone else."

"Doubt if he trusts me," Laing said. "You see, there's perfectly good hunting a hundred miles from here, near Masindi. All the elephant and buffalo a chap could want. Going all the way over to the Congo is just waste motion."

"Is that why you brought him back?"

Laing nodded. "He wanted to come too, of course. But that was part of my scheme. Get him back here where both of us can argue with him."

"It's no good making a plot of it," I said. "He'll catch on that we're ganging up on him, and he'll be more stubborn than ever."

Laing shrugged. "We'll have to do the best we can."

After dinner, Laing and I took Wilson upstairs into the empty lounge. The lake flies had not started their invasion as yet.

"What's this all about, Alec?" Wilson asked suspiciously. I knew things would not go well with our cause right then and there.

"This hunting trip, John," Laing said.

Wilson looked troubled. "You're not backing out, are you, Alec? I've got it all arranged for the three of us."

Laing coughed. "Well, it's not as simple as you think, John," he said. "If I have to fly you and Pete down to the Congo to pick up this guy, and then fly you back somewhere for your hunting trip, I'm going to have to tie up the Rapide, and I'm not sure I can do that."

"Why not, Alec?" Wilson asked quietly.

"Well, Owen needs it for equipment."

"That can wait."

Laing hesitated. "And I need it at the end of the week for a charter job I've promised some chaps in Nairobi."

"We'll get another plane then," Wilson said. It all seemed perfectly simple to him.

"We only have one Rapide," Laing said. "A Lodestar isn't allowed in on any of the small fields, and that's the only other twin-engine aircraft I have."

Wilson rubbed his large hands along the upper part of his legs. "Why didn't you say all this earlier, Alec?" he asked. His voice was still friendly but I could see that he was making an effort to control himself.

"I didn't know you were serious when you mentioned this Belgian chap taking you out. Seemed like foolishness to fly all that way, when you can hunt right here with Paget."

"I wouldn't go cootie hunting with Paget," Wilson said. "Furthermore, I told this guy we'd be there. You knew that, Alec. You heard me."

"But why fly all that way for nothing?" Laing complained. "Tie up an aircraft for more than a week when you can leave with a hunting car right from Kampala."

"Because this guy is arranging everything for us. There's nothing arranged here now and it'll take time. I have this one period to do my hunting in and I'm not going to leave anything to chance. That's what I came to Africa for, Alec."

"You're going to have to fly a thousand miles for nothing."

"Why do you say that?"

"Because no one hunts in that forest. It isn't possible."

"This Belgian fellow does."

"I don't believe that, John. You're going to have to fly back to open country, and that's six hundred miles wasted right there."

"Then we have to have a hunting car, and that has to be sent ahead," I said. "That's another bit of waste motion, John."

Wilson straightened in his chair. "I don't know about any of that," he said, anger creeping into his voice. "Maybe they don't use hunting cars in the Congo. Maybe they hunt right there in the forest. In any case, I told this man

I would be there, and I'm going to keep my word. Now if you have no plane, Alec, we'll hire one somewhere else. Or we'll take the Beechcraft and make two trips."

"That would be a solution," I said. "You and Alec take the Beechcraft and pick up this fellow in the Congo, and I'll stay here."

Wilson turned on me. "You're going," he said menacingly. "That's one thing I know. I planned that from the very beginning. You're going and so am I, and we're not going to let this fellow in Stanleyville down."

"I'm not looking forward to it," I said.

"Well, that's all right. You're going anyway," Wilson repeated. He was pale with anger.

"But it's impractical," Laing said. "It'll cost you a fortune, and you won't get what you're after."

"The hell we won't," Wilson said, clenching his fists.

"John, Alec lives in this country. He knows what he's talking about. Listen to him."

"I have your interests at heart," Laing said. "I want you to do this thing right."

"Balls," Wilson said. "You want me to go out with that phony character Owen hired, off on some wild-goose chase that we still have to arrange. You want me to drop something that's all laid on for that? I tell you I won't do it. We're going to the Congo if we have to drive there in a Hillman Minx. If we have to walk. Y'understand?"

"I need the Rapide," Laing said in a low voice. "The company needs it. What's more important to you? To get the equipment down to the location or to go off on your safari?"

"The safari," Wilson said unhesitantly. "It's the most important thing in my life right now. More important than the movie, or your goddam planes, or anything. It's top priority. Double A. Even if we have to start the picture a week late."

"You don't mean that, John?" I said.

"The hell I don't," he said angrily. "This is it, for me. It's why I came down here. I would have stayed in Hollywood if it was only a picture and I would have made twice as much money. I came down here for one thing, the hunting. It's something I've wanted to do all of my life. Ever since I was a kid. And I'm not going to let a goddam plane or anything else stand in my way. I'm going to the Congo, which is where I've always wanted to go, and I'm going to hunt down there, and then when I've gotten what I was after we'll worry about the movie. Is that clear, Alec?"

"Well, I suppose so," Laing said quietly.

"I'll repeat it if you like," Wilson said, rising. "This is what I've been after for years, see. And now I'm close to it, I'm not going to let anything stop me. Not you or a plane or anything. I'll write it down for you if you like. Now, do I get the Rapide next week, or shall I take my charter business somewhere else?"

Laing tapped the low table in front of him with his small, wiry hands, "All right," he said. "If that's what you want, John."

Wilson turned and left the room. The screen door slammed behind him.

I sighed. I had known that it would end that way. "He's a hard man to argue with, Alec," I said.

"It's crazy," Laing said. "I could prove to him that it's crazy. They don't know anything about hunting in the Congo. It's a new business there. *We've* done it for years. Nairobi has been the port of departure for thousands of safaris."

"I'm on your side, Alec," I said. "I don't want to hunt elephants in the forest any more than I want to swim across that poisoned lake out there."

Laing shrugged. "There'll be a lot of trees to climb, anyway. There'll be that on your side."

"I'll always be three branches higher up than you, old man," I said.

Laing shook his head. "No, you won't be," he answered, "because I'm not going. I'm bowing out."

"You're going to send me into the jungle alone with him?"

"I've got a wife and two kids to consider," he said. "They worry enough about me as it is." He got up. "You think it's really true that he's been waiting for years to hunt elephant in the Congo?"

"I doubt it. I think it just seems that way to him tonight."

Laing shook his head. "I'll buy you a drink," he said with a sad smile. "We both need one."

23

Wilson's rupture with Laing changed our lives. There were no long lunches now, no late poker games, no more exchanging of endless anecdotes about the war. Wilson withdrew from the company of his crew and devoted himself entirely to finishing the script. He was like a disenchanted lover who suddenly feels he must escape the society of his friends and avoid those faces that might remind him of his former, unworthy passion. I was the only one Wilson was willing to put up with now, and this was because I was somehow necessary for the job at hand. Unless he spent a large part of each day with me he would never be liberated from the script in time to go to the Congo.

Three days before our planned departure to the hunting country, we went to visit the location at Masindi. I had never seen the native village that had been built there for our purposes, and I was very impressed. It was the first concrete evidence that the picture was an actual reality, not just a jumbled bunch of pages up in our hot workroom.

The village was also a living tribute to the efficiency of our crew. It was real from every angle. It had even been properly aged. The grass huts that covered the immense cleared area in the middle of the jungle looked as if they had been there for a long time, and they seemed actually to have been lived in. For the first time I was able to visualize the entire film. The trader and his wife belonged there, in that village, and the slaves belonged in the enormous wooden stockade that had been a few hundred yards farther down the river.

But that was not all that had been accomplished. Six huge bungalows had been built for the use of the company not more than half a mile from the village. There were showers, and screens on the windows, and even a small bar and clubroom. Wilson beamed as he inspected it all.

"Isn't this something," he repeated over and over again. Basil Owen smiled proudly.

"Have a drink, John," he said, and produced a bottle from inside a cupboard.

"By God, I sure will have a drink," Wilson said.

"Do you think you should?" I asked. He had not been feeling well during the last days.

"No doubt about it," he said.

In the afternoon the small plane took us back to Entebbe, and we continued our work. But it was much easier now. I had seen the village, and I could visualize the destruction of it as a great physical sequence, something an audience would long remember.

Wilson was feeling a little worse the next day. He decided not to go down to lunch, but to take a nap instead. I found him sprawled out on the couch when I returned from my meal, his hunting book spread out on his stomach. He awoke with a start, and then seemed to have considerable trouble recognizing me. He shook his head, as if to clear it.

"Say, Pete, have you been taking your paludrine?" he asked me once he was fully awake.

"Not regularly. Have you?"

"No, but I guess we'd better do so. I've been feeling kind of funny lately, kind of weak and shaky."

"Probably the food," I said. "Shall we get going on this?"

"No, I don't think it's the food. I would have felt that before now."

"Maybe it's a result of your fight with Laing. Your soul's been bruised."

He scowled. "I'm not a fag, you know. Alec was wrong, and believe me, I felt no ill effects because I told him so."

"Well, then maybe it's malaria."

"Don't look so happy. That won't get you out of going on this safari. I'd go hunting even if I had chills. Anyway, this paludrine will pull me through." He sat up. "Well, let's finish this goddam script. I'm tired of looking at it."

The work went well that afternoon. As the last two sequences were almost entirely action there was very little to do except change a few sentences for the benefit of the art department and the prop shop. The last ten pages went into the new script exactly as they had originally been written. I underlined the words "FADE OUT," and stretched.

"Great feeling, isn't it, to finish the damn thing?"

"It certainly is," Wilson said. He went back to the couch. "Usually you feel kind of empty after you've done a job like this. Like a woman who's just given birth. I feel that way after every picture is finished. Once the last shot is in the can, I feel lost. The same thing is true of the last words you write. But it's different this time. Now our life really begins."

"You think the script's any good, John?" I asked.

"Yes, I think so," he said slowly. "It's certainly much better than it was. It'll never be a great, profound masterpiece. I told you why a few weeks ago. But I think it'll be interesting." He rubbed his forehead. "God, I feel lousy," he said. "Probably picked up some bug in the Congo. You know, I tried out the small rifles while we were waiting for the plane to pick us up the other day. Shot at a few monkeys."

"Did you kill any?"

"A couple. The natives love to eat them. Probably got stung by an anopheles mosquito while we were out in the jungle at that." He closed his eyes. "What did you do with your copy of the first hundred pages?" he asked faintly.

"I sent them back to London to be mimeographed."

"Good. You might send the rest of this stuff, then."

"I hope it'll get there before the company leaves."

"Oh, it will. Anyway, we don't shoot the last sequences for another month or six weeks." He shook his head as if trying to clear it of pain. "Damn it, I feel lousy. Should have taken my paludrine a little more regularly, I guess." Then suddenly he sat up. "Say, get the two small rifles out of the closet, will you? I just remembered that we forgot to clean them."

I found the rifles. They were in their waterproof canvas cases. "We'd better not start on this junket if you're not feeling well, John," I said.

"Oh, I'll be all right. I told you I'm not going to let a little fever stop me."

I pulled the bolts out of the guns and looked down the barrels. They were both covered solidly with rust. As soon as I told him the bad news Wilson sat up. He seemed to be immediately cured.

"Good God, this is awful, Pete. Get the oil out right away, and the ramrods."

"Hot water and soap is the best cure. At least that's what they used to tell us in the Marine Corps."

The room was soon transformed from an office into an armory. We worked feverishly on the barrels of both rifles. Wilson took the shotguns and the magnum out of their cases, and we cleaned them as well. But the small rifles were not such a simple proposition. Small islands of rust remained in the bore, no matter how often we ran the ramrods through them.

"This is just awful, kid," Wilson said again and again. He was more upset than I had seen him in years. He seemed to have forgotten about his sickness altogether. At least he seemed to be temporarily cured.

"Sometimes firing a round through the bore helps loosen the rust," I said.

"That's the lazy way," he reprimanded me. "The barrels will be permanently pitted if we do that." He was working frantically now, his hands covered with grease and rust. I had never seen him apply himself to physical labor with such intensity. I suppose he felt that he had fallen down in the eyes of his silent mentor, the author of his favorite book on game and rifles.

We worked until dinnertime, in the choking heat of the room. The floor was covered with oily rags and gun patches, and there were small cans of soapy water standing everywhere on the floor. At seven o'clock Lockhart appeared. "We're supposed to be having a meeting, aren't we, John?" he asked.

"Yes. We'll be right down," Wilson said.

Owen, Paget, and Harrison were waiting for us in the lobby.

"Where's Laing?" Wilson asked, once we were all seated.

"He's gone to Nairobi with the Rapide. I think he wanted the plane checked once more before you took it to the Congo."

"That's funny," Wilson said. "He didn't even say good-by. Well, it doesn't matter. We'll have to brief him when he gets back tomorrow."

But Laing didn't return the next day. Instead he sent the

Beechcraft, piloted by a young Englishman. There was a
note for Wilson, and a second big rifle which Laing had
rented in Nairobi. We were sitting in the bar when Wilson
received it. He shook his head and handed me the letter.

> Dear John [I read], Sorry that I can't make your
> safari, but I have rather pressing business here. I've
> been neglecting my job too long, and I think I'd
> better stay home and get my work done.
> Mike Looschen, who is the bearer of these sad tid-
> ings, will fly you to Tatsumu in the Beechcraft to-
> morrow morning. You'll have to stay there overnight,
> as the weather over the Congo is usually bad in the
> late afternoons and the emergency landing strips are
> few and far between. The Rapide will pick you up
> there the following morning. Have a good trip, and
> good hunting.

I folded the letter and handed it back to Wilson.

"From this and other missions one of our pilots is missing," I said.

Wilson shook his head. "I'll be damned," he said. "I
thought Alec was eager to come along."

"Will you still be going tomorrow?" Owen asked, concerned.

"We certainly will," Wilson said. He turned and smiled
at the young Englishman who was standing next to our
table. "Won't you have a drink with us?" he asked in his
snake charmer's voice.

"Thank you very much," the new pilot said. "My name's
Mike Looschen."

"Glad to know you, Mike." We were all introduced.
"Have you been working very long for Alec?"

"Only a few months. I used to be out in Burma, and
came over here looking for a job when that folded up."

"Done any hunting?" Wilson asked.

Looschen smiled cannily. He had obviously been well
briefed. "No, I'm afraid I haven't," he said. "Never had
much time. But I know the way to Tatsumu, if you're worried about that."

"Oh, we're very worried," Wilson said. "Never fly with
anyone unless I've seen their complete credentials." A
new conquest was beginning. Looschen was the most re-

cent arrival, and so it was only natural that he should receive the full blast of Wilson's charm. I pulled him off to one side, as we went in to dinner.

"Did Alec have a message for me?" I asked him.

He grinned. "Well, not really. He wanted to send you a set of those hooks telephone linemen use to climb poles, but they were hard to come by in Nairobi on such short notice, and so he just said to say hello."

"It was damn thoughtful of him to try," I said. "If you see him before I do, tell him I'm sending his white feather to him through the mail."

The lake flies were thicker than ever that night. It was impossible to eat anything that was brought to us. In the morning there was a solid carpet of tiny dead bodies everywhere in the hotel. Wilson looked haggard as he followed his boy out of the main entrance to the car. He was dressed in a bush jacket, breeches, and puttees; his high, beautifully made English shoes were well shined. Over his shoulder was slung his BOAC bag, filled to overflowing with yellow boxes of rifle ammunition.

"How do you feel, John?" I asked him.

He shook his head groggily. "Not too good, kid," he said, "but boy, am I glad to get out of this place. The damn flies are just ruining me. Can't sleep at night, and can't read because of the light. Just have to get out of here, that's all."

Mike looked anxiously at his watch and then at the sky. There were low black clouds everywhere, and a slight onshore wind. "Better get going," he said. "Weather doesn't look too promising."

We crawled into the car. There were guns in one corner of the back seat and two large wooden crates filled with ammunition were on the floor.

"There's no room for the driver," I said.

"Mike'll drive," Wilson said.

Lockhart had come out of the hotel. As a farewell gesture he started biting the nails on his left hand. "What about the car?" he moaned. "We need it this morning."

"Well, someone will have to drive you out to the airport to get it, that's all," Wilson said. "And if that doesn't work, you'll just have to walk." He waved cheerfully. " 'By, Ralph," he said.

Mike ground the gears against each other and cursed

softly. "Not too good at handling engines, is he?" Wilson grinned. His mood was improving. We were finally on our way. The car jerked forward, stalled, and then started again. Lockhart waved sadly as we pulled away from him.

"Good-by, you worthless, no-good son of a bitch," Wilson said in a low voice, smiling back at Lockhart. "Goodby, you pearl of Central East Africa. Good-by, you flies, and you bucktoothed, flat-chested ladies. Good-by forever."

As we drove out onto the field, it started to rain. The hard-packed ground turned to mud as we loaded our gear into the small, all-metal fuselage of the Beechcraft. Wilson crawled into the right rear seat of the small cabin. I got in next to Mike, and buckled the safety belt across my stomach. Two native boys pulled the blocks clear and the engine started, the propeller cutting through the rain directly in front of us.

Looschen was very businesslike as he revved the engine and started to taxi to the end of the runway. It was raining hard now, torrents of water splattering against the glass in front of us. Then as we waited for the green light from the tower, I slipped on the earphones and listened to the instructions that were coming through the static. Mike pushed the throttle in and we started bounding forward through a flood of water. The rain sounded like a thousand bullets spattering against the nose of our plane. Very quickly the speed of the plane increased and Looschen pulled back on the controls. We rose quickly and effortlessly through the storm. Entebbe lay below us to our left as we circled and climbed. The green grass and the neat houses that bordered the lake slipped out of view, and we were flying over the thick hilly countryside of Uganda.

Suddenly we were in the sun. Great stacks of black and white clouds rose on all sides of us. Looschen's hand was moving along the tabs on the dashboard in front of me, adjusting the mixture, trimming for level flight. Then he took off his earphones and laid them on the ledge of the cowling in front of him.

"That's the end of the radio," he said quietly. "Can't ever pick up the frequency they operate on in the Congo."

"What happens if we're forced down?" I asked.

"Well, I've sent an ETA to Tatsumu, and if we're very late, and if there's a plane available, they come out and look for us."

We continued on between walls of clouds. The rain stopped very suddenly, and then started again.

"We always fly very high when we're off to a place like the Congo. Gives you a lot of time to choose a field or a river in case your engine conks out."

I looked down at the endless, furry hills. Looschen unfolded a map and put it down on his lap. I turned back to look at Wilson. He was asleep.

We flew on for a couple of hours. The sky cleared and we saw that we were flying over grassland.

"Masindi and Butiaba are off to our right now," Looschen said. "That's where you were the other day, visiting the village."

I nodded. The country looked green and harmless, lying below us.

"That's Lake Albert over there. We fly across the southern tip of it. The Congo starts on the other side."

We were flying across blue water. The bright sunlight reflected in the surface of the lake. The plane cast a small, meaningless shadow over the rippled surface of the water. Then there was endless grassland marked with small islands of trees in the bottoms of the gulleys. Mike leaned forward, and then quickly turned the plane over on its side, banking sharply.

"Antelope," he said.

They were like tiny brown statues standing on the green floor of the earth and as we banked down toward them they suddenly broke and ran, racing off in all directions.

"God, they're beautiful," Wilson said. "Isn't it a wonderful country?" He was like a small boy showing off some miraculous possession of his own. Looschen righted the plane and we flew on. After a while he picked up the map again, and pointed off to the right. Very far off in the distance I could see a brownish-red rectangle of earth.

"Tatsumu," Looschen said. We circled the field. There was a shack built of bamboo shoots, and a few houses scattered among the green grass underneath us. A tattered wind sock was barely visible, flying from a long curving pole.

"Cross wind," Looschen said. We tightened our belts as we approached the field. Then just before the wheels touched the ground we were caught in a sudden gust which threatened to push us off our course, but Looschen throttled a little, and we came back toward the brown strip of land. The plane settled smoothly, and the turning of the propeller ceased. The sun beat down on the plastic roof over our heads.

"Well," Wilson said, "this is the place where we'll try out our guns. Are you staying with us, Mike?"

"I wish I could," Looschen answered, "but I've got to get back to Masindi tonight and pick up some of your crew."

We stopped near the hut and unloaded the plane. A young Negro in coveralls asked us in fairly good French if we wanted fuel. A few minutes later the Belgian customs officer arrived in a pickup truck. He was a youngish man in white shorts and shirt, wearing a tropical helmet. I served as an interpreter for Mike, and in a very few minutes he was ready to go again. I watched rather sadly as the small silver plane soared off the end of the runway. We were alone once more, the two of us, on the border of the Congo. Wilson sat down in the shade of the hut, sorting out the ammunition in his blue flight bag.

"You wish to go to the hotel?" the Belgian asked me.

"Yes, if you'll take us?"

He looked dubious and explained that he wouldn't be able to leave the field for an hour because another plane was due in. But he would telephone. Perhaps Monsieur Lebeau would come out to get us in his car.

"Tell him he's got to come and get us," Wilson said. "We can't sit out here all day."

The Belgian cranked the phone. The sun beat down on the flimsy roof of the shack; the noise of Looschen's plane had long ago faded away. We were in the middle of the wilderness, and again I found myself wondering why.

24

There was the sound of howling tires, and then the bamboo hut was engulfed in a cloud of dust. Wilson started to cough, his head hanging down below his thin shoulders, his body doubled up as if he were in extreme pain. I watched him with concern. Finally he managed to get to his feet and stumble toward the door.

A horn blared as the dust settled around us, and we stood facing a man in a dust-covered De Soto. At first glance it was obvious that the relationship between the vehicle and its driver was not a superficial one, for the man seemed intent on remaining inside the car, no matter what might ensue. He looked as if he belonged inside the machine, very much the way a horseman occasionally looks as if he existed only on top of his horse. His face was covered with a wrinkled, tanned skin that grew reddish white near the base of his throat. His hair was dust-colored. His fat arms looked solid and hot as they came out of his short sleeves. He squinted quizzically at Wilson, as the tall, bony man in leggings and breeches came slowly toward the car.

"Monsieur Lebeau?" We had waited half an hour for the car to arrive, and Wilson no longer felt the need to turn on the charm.

The huge man nodded. He made no move to get out of the car or even to open one of its doors. He sat with his hands firmly holding the steering wheel. This car is mine, he seemed to be saying. It's my favorite possession. It's the only thing that works well within a radius of a thousand square miles.

Wilson put out his hand. The Belgian stirred slowly and grasped Wilson's fingers. Still he didn't speak. He mumbled some incoherent French phrase and tried to smile.

"How do you do, monsieur," Wilson said slowly. "I'm

John Wilson. Do you remember me? I came through here with Alec Laing less than a week ago."

The Belgian smiled suddenly. "*Ah oui, Monsieur Laing, le pilote.*"

"Yes, I was with him. Do you remember?"

Monsieu Lebeau nodded. "You telephone?" he asked. "You want go hotel?"

Wilson grinned crookedly. "*Si, amigo,*" he said. "That's the general idea."

Lebeau was still nodding as I approached, and then, turning very quickly, he asked me not to slam the door too hard. Wilson was already in the front seat. "Pete, tell him that we want to stay the night. He doesn't seem to understand my English."

I explained in French what we wanted. Monsieur Lebeau grunted assent, and pulled the gear lever down into the driving position. We started with an excess of power. He drove straight out onto the landing strip and made a U-turn, the tires howling. Wilson and I clung to the straps on the side of the car as we raced past the customs hut and turned down a reddish dirt road. Monsieur Lebeau obviously belonged to that school of dirt-road drivers who believe that fifty miles an hour makes for the smoothest ride. We roared through puddles, sending sheets of brown water out toward the clumps of grass that lined the road. Natives stopped on both sides of us, and took off their hats as we passed, bowing reverently. We passed a few houses built of red brick. There were neat yards surrounding them, and large screened-in porches that gave out onto the road. Then suddenly we turned off to the left down a long, palm-lined drive. Monsieur Lebeau's huge hands caressed the steering wheel. Occasionally his left hand would slide lazily toward its center and press down on the horn. The natives stood quite still with the dust swirling around their naked legs. Halfway down the long, stately drive we turned to the right, hardly decreasing our speed. There was a short, winding path, and then we slid to an abrupt stop in front of a large white house. With great care, Lebeau turned off the ignition and put the keys into his shirt pocket.

"This is it," Wilson said. "This is the hotel."

Monsieur Lebeau nodded mutely, and led the way through a screen door into a large room. There was a bar, the front of which was decorated with a stretched snakeskin, and several low wooden chairs. To the right was the dining alcove. There were five tables, two of them occupied by diners. At one there was a man and his wife, with two small children and a baby. They were round, ball-shaped, all of them including the infant, and they ate systematically, their utensils clattering noisily in the general silence. They looked up briefly as we entered, but no one spoke. At the other table there were two Belgian government officials in white shorts and shirts, with high boots, which were laced across their fat legs. One of them glanced vaguely in our direction.

A huge woman appeared behind the bar, obviously the mate of our driver, for she was made in the same shape that he was, and covered with an identical hide. She watched us cross the room toward her in silence and only when John shook her hand did she venture to say, *"Bon jour."*

Wilson smiled winningly and asked what there was to drink. There was beer, the woman said aggressively, Belgian beer, and Coca-Cola. I decided on Coca-Cola. Wilson chose to investigate the beer. While the woman was occupied with opening the bottles we turned to look at the rest of the room. Two native boys in soiled shirts and denim shorts were serving the diners, who looked at them with hatred as they moved slowly around the silent tables in their bare feet.

"The joint's jumping, isn't it?" I remarked.

Wilson nodded and filled his glass with the strange-smelling beer. He drank a little of it, and made a face.

"Ask her for another Coke, will you, kid?" he said.

"Doesn't he like the beer?" the woman asked unpleasantly.

"He's not used to it," I explained. "He was expecting something different."

The woman took the bottle by the throat, her slow, massive right hand grasping the neck. "The bottle is open now," she said to me.

"We'll pay for it," I said. "It doesn't matter. Just bring us another Coke."

She shrugged and produced another bottle. Then she asked me if we wanted to have lunch. Wilson shook his head.

"Just a sandwich or two. You know, last time I came through with Alec we met a guy who has a farm near here and he invited me to come out and shoot at his place, and so if you'll ask the old gal here how to get out there, we'll take off."

"What's the man's name?"

Wilson closed his eyes. Names were always escaping him. Now he was making a great effort to remember. "Berg or Berger, or something like that. He has a farm right near here. Madame will know."

She shook her head and shrugged. There was no Monsieur Berg or Berger in the neighborhood.

"I know he lives near here," Wilson said irritably. "Ask her what the name of the man is who was having lunch here the last time I came through."

She shrugged. Lebeau arrived with a plate of sandwiches on white bread and she put the problem up to him.

"Bergère," he said with a curious smile. "Charles Bergère. But it is a long way to his farm."

"Ask him how far," Wilson said eagerly.

"Eight kilometers, for those few who have occasion to go there."

"Well, that's not far, if he'll take us there in his car."

Monsieur Lebeau shook his head. It was impossible to get to the farm by car, he explained. There was a river to cross and there was no road.

"Well, how does Bergère get into town?"

Monsieur Lebeau smiled gleefully. "He walks," he explained. But he did not come often, and anyway, now it was too hot to try to go there.

"It's not as hot as all that," Wilson said. "Ask him if he can send someone along to show us the way."

Monsieur Lebeau was obviously not delighted with the idea. He could perhaps give us two boys, he said doubtfully, but he didn't think we could make it in the heat of the day. Wilson insisted that we could. The Belgian shrugged. If we were foolish enough to try, well, he wouldn't stop us. He sighed hopelessly and withdrew.

We finished our sandwiches and took our belongings up to our room. Wilson took both the Mannlicher and his magnum, as well as his flight bag filled with ammunition.

"You really think you can make it, John?" I asked. "You weren't feeling so well yesterday."

"I feel fine now, kid," Wilson said. "This is what we came here for, you know."

"Eight kilometers is about five miles," I said. "That's ten miles there and back."

Wilson looked annoyed. "Come on, quit stalling, Pete," he said. "If you don't want to go, I'll go alone."

"Then there'll be nobody to carry you back."

"We've got to have a chance to try out these guns," he said testily. "In a couple of days we'll be facing elephant and buffalo. You don't seem to realize that."

The Belgians at the two tables were just finishing their cheese course. I called for Monsieur Lebeau, but he was nowhere to be found; neither was Madame. Wilson made me ask one of the native servants if we couldn't be driven part of the way but this boy explained that Monsieur Lebeau had left, taking the keys of the car and the pickup truck with him.

"The son of a bitch wants us to stay here and eat the lunch," Wilson said. "God damn it, we'll show him." We went out into the blazing sun. Two natives were squatting on the gravel driveway in front of the house. The De Soto stood at the foot of the steps, its windows rolled up and its doors locked.

"Shall we let the air out of the tires?" Wilson asked. "Just to teach him a lesson?"

"Let's wait until the plane arrives tomorrow to pick us up. I'd hate to get stuck here, and be at his mercy."

"Tomorrow we'll burn the damn place down," Wilson said. The natives rose. One of them took the flight bag and the other one took the magnum. Wilson and I carried the .256 Mannlichers. We went down the drive, and then turned off and followed the palm-lined road. There was a long row of red brick houses on both sides of the street but there was no sign of life. We passed a few native children.

"Jambo," Wilson said.

They stood staring at us, and then faintly they replied in their high, frightened voices: *"Jambo, bwana."*

Sweat was pouring down my back; my face was hot and wet. Wilson dropped back and walked next to me.

"What the hell's wrong with this road?" he asked angrily. "It's smooth as Wilshire Boulevard."

"I don't know," I replied. "Maybe it's mined. Or maybe

there's a law against helping tourists out here."

Wilson shook his head. His face was bright red under his huge hat. "The son of a bitch," he muttered. "We could have driven all this way."

We went on for almost an hour, down the broad palm-lined road. There were a few banana orchards among the houses and then finally there was only green brush on both sides of us. The road climbed a little and then fell off again. We passed a huge brick stockade. Through the heavy iron gate I could see natives in torn blue denim shorts, sorting bricks inside the yard. A native guard, carrying a long, antiquated-looking rifle, saluted us as we went by.

"The local lockup," I said, pointing it out to Wilson, "and the source of all building material. I wonder what a guy has to do to get thrown in the jug in this part of the world."

Wilson looked sullenly out from under the brim of his hat. "Well, if he forgets to bow as the De Soto goes by, he gets two months on the brick pile. If he gets drunk, he has to do two years. If he talks back to a white man he gets life."

"We've got to build these brick houses," I said. "You don't understand the problems we have in our country. We've got to keep these people in hand. They're savages, you know. Their average brain size is only a square millimeter larger than that of an orangutan."

"Quite right, old boy. Wonder if the black buggers know how to play soccer."

The road ended abruptly, and now we followed a narrow dirt path leading through thick grass. Wilson plodded on. His bush jacket clung to his narrow back. We wound our way up onto a clay plateau. There was another prison with a double stockade built on both sides of the road. Fifty or sixty natives were manning a furnace in which the bricks were obviously being baked. I noticed that several of them wore chains on their ankles. They stared at us with unconcealed hatred.

"This would be a wonderful location for us, wouldn't it, John?"

"Just swell," he said. "The spirit of the place is perfect."

He nodded pleasantly to a group of prisoners on our

left, and said, *"Jambo,"* but no one answered him. They expected no greeting from a white man, and they were not prepared to give one.

"The white man in Africa faces tremendous odds," Wilson said. "Of course you people who come here for a few weeks couldn't be expected to understand. You feel sorry for the blacks. Well, you might as well feel sorry for cattle out on a range."

"I quite understand, Colonel," I said. "The barbed-wire fences and the brands on their hips may seem inhumane at first glance, but the place would be an awful mess without them."

He nodded. "You are beginning to understand the country and its problems," he said. "Usually this takes more time."

The path led down a steep incline, and we were flanked by high grass and bushes once more. There was the thick smell of stagnant water, and the heat increased. Then all at once the brush fell away in front of us and we stood on the banks of an orange river. There was a landing fashioned out of logs, and next to it, in the water, there was a dugout canoe. Two natives squatted on the landing, one of them in a khaki shirt, and the other dressed in a heavy G.I. sweater, which bulged around his huge arms and shoulders. We exchanged *"Jambos"* and Wilson got into the pirogue. I slipped on the muddy bank of the stream, but the native paddler caught my arm and held me up.

"He should have asked permission before he touched you," Wilson said.

The two natives stepped gently into the canoe, and the paddler pushed us off. There was more current than had been evident at first glance but he timed it perfectly, first poling upstream, and then letting the canoe glide down until it bumped gently against the landing on the other side. We crawled out, and Wilson gave each native two cigarettes.

"Well, this is where the pavement ends," Wilson said.

The vegetation was even thicker than on the other side of the stream. The grass was shoulder-high, and there were clumps of bushes that cut off the view of the surrounding country. We went on through the intense heat of the day. There was no breeze, no movement of air of any kind.

We went on. The sun dropped lower in the sky, striking our faces. Then all at once there were tall black trees that cast a dense shade, and it was a little cooler. The path turned and in the distance we could see a large brick house set off to the right of the path.

"This must be it," Wilson said, increasing his pace. I glanced at the house. There was no sign of life. Vines covered most of the walls, branching up over the green tin roof. In the front of the dwelling there was a large covered porch, with rusted screens that were torn in a good many places, and on the knee-high grass that ran up to the stone steps there were a dozen or more rotting skins, covered with flies. Wilson stopped and stared at them.

"Buffalo," he said. "Big ones." He went slowly up the steps and knocked on the decayed wood of the screen door. It was a cartoon by Charles Addams, the tall, thin man in the breeches and leggings knocking politely on the rotting door of the abandoned house in the middle of the wilderness. But a loud voice replied from within, and an instant later a white man appeared inside the porch.

He was gaunt, of medium height, dressed in a soiled pair of white shorts. His body and his legs were bare, and his naked feet were thrust into low black oxfords, the laces of which had been torn and knotted a dozen times. I noticed that his legs were covered with welts and there were small black holes where the blood of bite wounds had dried on the skin. His face was unshaven, a thin mad face, with tousled black hair falling across its forehead.

"Oui," he said. *"Qui est là?"*

Wilson opened the screen door and stepped inside. Our two native boys were already squatting in the shade next to the house, while I stood near the rotting buffalo hides and waited.

"Monsieur Bergère?" Wilson said.

"Oui?" There was suspicion in the man's voice.

"I'm John Wilson. Do you remember me? We met in Tatsumu last week."

There was a sudden mad cry of recognition and the man leaped forward to grasp Wilson's hand. "Of course, of course," he said. "You are of the cinema. I remember you. And now you have come to see me. Well, that is wonderful." He pushed open the screen door. "Do not stand out there, in the hot sun," he called. "Come into the house."

There was a strange musty smell as I entered the house, a smell obviously caused by lack of ventilation. I shook hands with Monsiur Bergère, and then he was off again, moving excitedly around the porch, scratching the wounds on his legs, running his hands through his hair. "Things are not arranged," he said. "You must excuse me. I didn't know you were coming."

"That's perfectly all right. I only hope we're not bothering you," Wilson said.

"Of course not, my dear Mr. Wilson. I am delighted that you have come."

We went into the main room of the house. There was a rough wooden table and a cot with graying sheets out of which someone seemed to have recently risen. There was no other furniture.

"You are hot and thirsty, no doubt," Bergère said excitedly. "I will have some organge juice made for you . . . from my own trees." He called out in Swahili. A small black woman appeared in the doorway across the room. She looked frightened. She was dressed in faded rags and she wore an old piece of soiled scarf around her head.

Bergère clapped his hands and spoke rapidly in Swahili, and the woman withdrew. "I have only one servant," he explained. "The others all run away. There is a rumor that I eat native women." He laughed loudly; I felt uneasy as I listened to his laughter. It sounded as if it might never stop. "That is what they are trying to do now, to drive me out of here with rumors. The blacks are afraid to come to work for me, and so everything is left like this, like you see it here. We live like bachelors, alone, my friend and I." He turned to the back of the house. "Raoul!" he called. There were footsteps and another white man appeared. He was a good deal younger than Bergère, with powerful legs and arms, and a rather handsome face.

"This is my friend Lescelle, who lives with me. He is a painter. Unfortunately he speaks no English." We shook hands with the painter. He bowed politely, his black, silent eyes appraising us.

"You paint, do you?" Wilson asked interestedly.

"Yes, yes," Bergère answered for the other. "You will see some of his things later. Now he must go and collect oranges for your drink."

"Don't bother," I said. "We can drink water."

"No, no, no, he will go." The silent painter left the room. Bergère beamed at Wilson. "So you have come all this way as you said you would, Mr. Wilson. Now, that is nice of you."

Wilson smiled, and walked slowly around the room. "This is quite a place you have here, Monsieur Bergère, quite a place."

"It was, it was," the Belgian said in his ringing voice. "But they have stolen everything from me, all the furniture, even the glass in the windows. I went home for two months to look after my affairs and rented the house to a widow, and of course she stole everything and went off. And now there is nothing I can do, because they will not help me. They want to force me to sell, to get me out of the country, but the price will not even pay my debts, and so I must hang on. They do everything against me. They spread rumors among the natives, they send the police to question me. Everything. Last month the elephants came and destroyed most of my orchard, and when I asked for the army to come and help me they sent ten men, ten recruits with rifles they did not know how to shoot. They did not kill one elephant. They looked at the orchard and shrugged, that is all. Oh, I will show you, and you will see that it was a wonderful place before."

"Who's 'they,' Monsieur Bergère?" Wilson asked.

"The government," Bergère said. He lowered his voice. "They want to get me out of the country. And I want to go, but I cannot leave everything I possess, just like that. I want my price for the farm and then I'll go."

"Why do they want to get you out?"

He shook his head. "Politics. I will explain to you later. They think I spy on them. They think I know too much. I came here during the war, you see, and in '45 I sent my report to Brussels about what they are doing here, and so now they want to punish me, to drive me out." He laughed insanely. "But I will stay. I have my rifle. I hunt to eat. I have a few orange trees, and I will wait." He scratched his bleeding legs. "I am a hard one, you know," he said. "Not fat, like the rest of them. I can live like a native. With a little ammunition now and then I can live here for years." He smiled self-consciously. "But you did not come here for my stories, my dear Wilson. You came to see the place. Perhaps you can use it in your film, eh?"

Wilson smiled. "What we really came out for was to

do a little shooting. We're going on safari and we wanted to try out our guns."

Bergère looked surprised. "Ah," he said, "you came to shoot. But that is fine. We will go in an hour when it is a little cooler. You will drink the orange juice, and then we will go."

"Is it much of a walk, Monsieur Bergère?" I asked. "You don't shoot near the house, do you?"

"Oh, it is nothing, monsieur, nothing at all. Ten minutes, twenty, maybe. And you have everything. Antelope, elephant, buffalo, leopard, if you like. Ten minutes from here. Why, it is a paradise. For a hunter, that is. There is nothing a man could want that is not here. In the evening you take your gun, and you walk into the garden, and there is game everywhere. Ten minutes from here."

"You don't say!" Wilson said excitedly.

"You have brought your guns?" Bergère asked.

"Everything," Wilson said. "Guns, and ammunition. Plenty of it."

"Good. Marvelous," Bergère shouted. He went quickly out to the porch and returned with a rifle. "I have only this, and a .22. And I have three shells left. That is all. And one little box of shells for the .22." He laughed uproariously.

"Well, we can leave some for you," Wilson said.

"You will not have the right size," Bergère said sadly. "You have British rifles. But it does not matter," he added brightly. "You have enough for yourselves, that is all that counts. If you leave a little meat in the house when you go, well, *tant mieux,* as we say."

"I wouldn't count on it," I said. "We've never fired our rifles."

"We may be a little rusty," Wilson added. "Now what will we be going after? I want to know which guns to take."

"Take them all," Bergère said. "In Africa you must always be ready for everything. You may be shooting an antelope and run into buff or lion. Last night I was in the orchard and I saw two bulls. Enormous fellows. I had only the .22, and that is not a gun for them."

"It certainly isn't." Wilson smiled.

"What are the hides doing out in front of the house?" I asked.

"They are there to attract *les hyènes* at night. Hyena,

you say, or jackal. Raoul likes to shoot them with a light. It is his sport." He laughed again. The painter came into the room carrying a tray with two tall glasses full of green liquid. Although it was sour, it was cool and refreshing.

"This is just wonderful," Wilson said enthusiastically.

"What about our boys?" I asked. "Shouldn't we get them some water?"

"Oh, they will look after themselves," Bergère said. "Never worry about the natives. My old woman will have taken care of them long ago." He went over to Wilson, who was examining the dried horns of a buffalo that hung from the wall. He slapped him jovially on the back. "You like it here, eh, Mr. Wilson?"

"It's just a wonderful place, Monsieur Bergère," Wilson said. I think he meant it.

"Well, this is nothing, this house," Bergère said. "You will see in a little while. In half an hour. Out there on the plains. You will see. You will kill your game tonight, Mr. Wilson. You will kill your game."

He turned back to me. "Would you like another orange juice?" he asked. "There is much, much more hanging on the trees."

25

The sun lost some of its strength as we sat on the porch of the empty house, in the homemade wooden chairs. Wilson and Bergère talked of guns and hunting. The Belgian sat facing us, his rifle across his knees, stroking it with his scarred fingers. There was no varnish left on the stock, and the bluing was worn off the barrel, but he seemed to love it tenderly. He worked the bolt back and forth, and the clicking of the smooth steel punctuated his speech. Lescelle moved restlessly about the porch. The conversation was in English, and he felt excluded; he smoked Wilson's cigarettes and looked out at the wild garden. After a while he came over to Bergère.

"It's time to go," he said in French. "There will be less than two hours of light if we leave now."

Bergère nodded and rose. "Take only your guns and ammunition. Leave everything else here."

Our two boys were waiting for us near the rotting buffalo hides. They accepted their burdens in silence. Bergère had put on a khaki shirt, but on his feet he still wore the battered city shoes. He led us past the rear of the house, through the tangled garden. I caught a glimpse of the native woman standing at the back door, watching us go. One of the boys called out to her, and she answered him with a short high-pitched jabber.

We crossed a dried-up vegetable garden, and then immediately the vegetation closed in around us. The path was even narrower than it had been before, covered with broken vines that clung to our clothing and whipped at our legs. The brush was well over our heads. Bergère had an old pipe clamped in his stained teeth, and he carried a rough wooden stick. His rifle was slung over his shoulder.

Lescelle brought up the rear with the .22. He moved warily, his face flushed with excitement. Every once in a while he would stop and move off the path to the left to find a small piece of high ground from which he could look out at the plains beyond. Then he would hurry after us.

We went on for half an hour. It was cooler than it had been before, but the air was still heavy, and I started to sweat again. I was wondering about the unarmed members of our party, the native boys; what would happen to them if we came across a buffalo or a leopard? If Wilson wounded a dangerous animal they would be completely at its mercy. It was a disquieting thought.

The path rose slightly. The bushes decreased in number. It was all grassland on both sides of us now, a deep green sea, with hills like enormous waves. Bergère stopped and raised his hand. He bent down slightly, put his finger over his mouth, and then turned and went on. We imitated him, and crept forward.

I looked back and saw that Lescelle had stopped and was making his way through the grass on our left again. He reached a small hill and rose to peer out. Bergère had not noticed what the painter was doing. He was moving forward very slowly and cautiously. Suddenly Lescelle came running after us.

"Charles," he whispered, *"ils sont là, juste là."*

Bergère nodded, and put his finger across his lips again. I saw him take his pipe out of his mouth and then start off through the grass on our left. Wilson followed him, thin and eager. He waved for me to join them. I crept up to where they were, and rose very slowly to peer out over the tips of the grass. There was a slight breeze and the green sea moved restlessly, and I could see out to where Wilson was pointing. There, standing deathly still, was a herd of antelope, their graceful brown bodies motionless against the sky. One of them, a large buck, had climbed an anthill and was staring in our direction. They looked to be about a hundred and fifty yards away. There was no sound. Only the grass rustled slightly in the wind.

"Come on," Wilson whispered. The wind was blowing toward us.

"You go ahead."

He shook his head adamantly. "No, come on."

We crept forward. I noticed that the two boys remained behind. We went another twenty yards, and then straightened again. As we did so the herd came to life. They turned and started to gallop off.

"They have seen you," Bergère whispered.

Wilson looked upset. "Take off your goddam shirt, Pete," he said to me. "It's too light."

I took off my shirt and tied it around my waist. The ground was uneven and I stumbled. Wilson looked back angrily, and then turned and hurried on. He no longer seemed tired. His thin body seemed to have found new strength. He had crumpled up his hat and tucked it inside his shirt. His long thin legs reached out through the thick grass as he endeavored to cover more ground with each step.

The herd came to an abrupt halt. I watched Wilson as he made his way toward the antelope, using a huge anthill as cover. He reached it and stopped. I could see him fiddling with the safety on his rifle. Then he raised it and aimed. I held my breath. It seemed like a very long time, and there was the flat, loud report of the Mannlicher. The herd had started to run an instant before I had heard it, and Wilson fired again at the antelope as they galloped through the thick grass, bounding high with sudden, powerful leaps.

"They're gone," Bergère shouted. "Come along. We go after them."

We hurried forward over the uneven ground. We went for a few hundred yards, almost running. Then Bergère stopped again and pointed off to the right. There was another herd in front of us. Wilson waved for me to join him. Bergère nodded excitedly.

"You go too. Hurry. Two guns are always better."

Wilson watched me approach. "Keep lower," he whispered. "They can see you."

"They can see you too, for Christ's sake."

We crawled forward again, keeping an anthill between us and the antelope. Wilson stopped, twenty yards to my right. I could see him fiddling with his rifle again. At least he has sense enough to put it on safe while he's running, I thought. I picked out an animal to my right and aimed. I wanted to wait until he had fired, but he took too long, and finally I squeezed the trigger. The instant I did, I realized that I had not aimed carefully enough. Wilson fired a second later, and the herd was off again.

"Damn it," he said. "They were too far away."

"There are more," Bergère shouted. "There are more."

We were cautious no longer. We ran ahead as fast as we could go. There was another herd on my right, and I turned off toward them. Bergère followed me.

Suddenly I saw a huge buck standing less than a hundred yards to my front. The Belgian pointed to an anthill and I nodded. My heart was pounding inside my chest. I got to the anthill and pushed the safety tab over. Then I aimed very carefully and squeezed the trigger. Nothing happened. I cursed myself. I had forgotten to pump another round into the chamber. Buck fever of the worst kind. I slid the bolt back. My hands were wet and slippery as I pushed it forward. A live round slid into place inside the chamber. I raised my rifle but before I had gotten it set in my shoulder it went off. I had touched the hair trigger. The bullet smacked into an anthill a hundred yards beyond the horns of an antelope. He turned and was off. I pumped another round into the rifle, and fired again, but it was no use. Bergère came up to me.

"What happened?" he asked.

I shook my head. "It wasn't loaded and then it went off before I was ready."

He laughed. "The first time it is often like that," he said. "But it is a shame. He was a good head. A trophy."

I felt like a fool. I handed him the rifle. "Take it. You need the meat."

He shook his head good-naturedly and pushed the rifle away. "No, it is you who must kill the game today. You are the guest."

"You'll go hungry," I said.

We went back toward Wilson. Once we reached the high ground we caught sight of him off to the left. There was another herd in front of him, and as we watched, he fired. Bergère shook his head. *"Raté,"* he said.

"Lucky we didn't run into buffalo the way we're shooting."

He shrugged. "We may still, you know," he said. "You can never tell. At this hour . . ."

"Well, if we do, it'll be just too bad. The boys are about two miles back with the big rifle."

He looked perturbed. "Ah, that is true," he said. "They should not be there. Still, I have my rifle."

We went on, but no more antelope appeared in front of us. We heard Wilson fire once again, but we couldn't see him. He was lost behind a line of hills.

"I only hope Mr. Wilson will be successful," Bergère said. "It is important to him. He must kill something today."

I was becoming conscious of time and distance again. The sun was down and the wind had increased. I had no idea where we had left the boys, or in which direction the house was. Suddenly Bergère stopped again. A small herd stood grazing to our front. I shook my head. "We can't fire at them," I said. "John's off in that direction."

Bergère shrugged. "I do not think so," he said.

"It's a risk."

He hesitated. "Perhaps you are right," he said. "But you must make yourself ready. Sometimes when they run they will circle back, and you can shoot them then."

But the antelope did nothing of the kind. They bounded off, straight to our front. I ran up onto the hard-baked earth of an anthill and watched them; they were running toward the light border along the sky, bounding through the grass, swerving back and forth.

"I hope John will be able to find his way back," I said.

Bergère shrugged confidently. "He will have no difficulty," he said. "We are still on the land of my farm, you know," he continued after a pause. "All of this, this paradise, belongs to the house. I have shot four different kinds of game in an evening without leaving my land."

"It's a shame you have to sell it," I said.

He shrugged. *"Que voulez-vous?* Life is like that. You go after one thing for years and years, and you get it, and you say to yourself, Ah, now I am satisfied, now I have a place to grow old in and die. And then suddenly, pouf . . . everything blows up. It turns to nothing in your hands, and you must go on and start again." He slapped his leg, and gestured hopelessly. "Well, it does not matter. Have you fire? My old pipe is out."

I cupped my hands against the wind, and helped him light his pipe. The outlying hills were dark blue now, and the sky was bright red. A few hundred yards ahead of us we saw a series of dark brown rocks that loomed up out of the grass.

"There are the boys," Bergère said, pointing.

They were seated on one of the rocks, smoking and watching us approach. We chose a rock near them and sat looking out at the country around us. It was almost dark now. Only a narrow strip of yellow sky gave light to the plain.

"I'm worried about John," I said.

Bergère shook his head. "He is a hunter, Mr. Wilson, one can see that. A real hunter. He has the passion for it. He will be all right."

It grew dark. There was a cool wind now. We sat and waited. Suddenly one of the natives pointed excitedly at something in front of us. I heard the word "Bwana," and a few minutes later I caught sight of Wilson's bedraggled figure moving toward us. Each step seemed to be an extreme effort for him. His thin shoulders sagged. His right hand, carrying the rifle, hung limply at his side, while the barrel dragged through the grass.

"Hello, guys," he said in a weak voice.

"Did you get one?" Bergère asked eagerly.

Wilson shook his head. "Nope. Never got a really good shot after the first two." He looked sad. "We really made a hash of it, didn't we, kid?"

"Well, it was the first day."

"You never shoot as well in Africa as you do at home." Bergère said. "The climate, the exertion of the hunt . . . you miss shots you would never dream of missing."

Wilson stood leaning on his rifle, trying to catch his breath.

"Are you beat, John?" I asked.

"Not so bad," he said cheerfully. "Disgusted, though."

Bergère got up abruptly. "Well, we must go home," he said.

"What about Raoul?" I asked.

"Oh, he has gone back to cook," Bergère said. "He has been home for hours."

Lescelle was seated on the porch of the house when we arrived. He had made another pitcher of orange juice. Our glasses were there waiting for us.

"Now isn't this just swell?" Wilson said. He settled down on the floor of the porch, his back against the side of the house. I remained standing. I knew that if I once sat down I would have a hard time getting up again.

"Raoul will take you back with his light," Bergère said.

"That's not necessary."

"Oh, it is nothing. A little walk in the evening is good for him. Perhaps he will have a chance to shoot a jackal." He laughed happily. "It is his favorite game, you know."

"It's just been a wonderful afternoon," Wilson said gratefully.

"I am sorry that you killed nothing," Bergère said. "But that is the pleasant thing about hunting . . . even if you come back empty-handed, you feel you have had a good time. It is often like that. That is why it is the only sport in the world for me. The only thing that matters in life. Everything else . . ." He shrugged and spread his hands. "One is always *déçu*. Disappointed. All of the other passions are worthless, once they are spent. Women, drink, gambling . . . they leave you with nothing . . . emptiness. Even when you are a success, when the wine is very, very good, or the woman surrenders, or the cards come just right. It is over and you have nothing. The money you spend. The wine wears off, and you cannot remember the taste. The woman betrays you. But hunting . . . it is good when it is about to begin, good when it is going on, good when it is over. That is why I have given up everything for it. Everything. My life. My friends. I live like an animal here. All for that, my dear Mr. Wilson. But it is worth it, I think when I sit here in the evening. It is the only thing. Perhaps what you do, Mr. Wilson, is also worth it. Art. But that is all. The only two things that matter. The sport, and the art."

"I agree with you," Wilson said, "only I wouldn't include what I do. It was worth it once but it isn't any more."

Bergère laughed. "I do not believe that. A great master like you . . ."

"Well, the kick just isn't there any more, I'm afraid," Wilson said. "Nothing like this anyway." He sounded serious. I wasn't sure that he wasn't just trying to flatter Bergère, or if perhaps he was lying to himself.

"Work has its moments, John," I said.

"Not like this," Wilson said. "And we got nothing today. Like having a useless conference with a producer. But still, as Monsieur Bergère says, we have had a wonderful experience. To see those elusive animals running through the grass . . . well, there's just nothing like it. And then walking back, with it getting dark." He shook his head. "I tell you, kid, I've never felt the same kind of thing."

"I have," I said.

"You are young," Bergère observed gravely, "and everything is not used up, and you think you will go on forever with all of your passions. But it is not so. They will fall by the way, one after another. You will do them too often. You will abuse yourself. And suddenly one day you will be like us, like Mr. Wilson and me. Not old, but not young any more. And the one passion that will remain will be the sport. For the game is always young, always on good, strong legs, always very alive until you kill it. And that will be the passion that you will never lose, the fever that will never burn out."

"I hope I never really get it," I said.

"Ah, but you will," Bergère said. "You are in Africa now, going on safari, and you will be infected. For everyone carries the fever. The hunter who will take you, the native boy who carries your gun, the cook back at the camp. Everyone. You will catch it, and you will have it always, all of your life, and you will not want to be cured."

"I think you're absolutely right, Monsieur Bergère," Wilson said.

Bergère smiled at him. "We know," he said. "We are both old and sick with it. That is why we know." He rose. "I get more orange juice."

"He's quite a guy, isn't he?" Wilson said softly.

"Yeah, quite a guy. Crazy as a loon."

"Well, I don't know," Wilson said. "Maybe he's not so crazy. His life is no worse than ours. At least he doesn't have to go through all the crap we do. The parties we go to, the conferences we attend, the endless talk of money and success."

"Let's discuss it at the Tatsumu Palace," I said.

Wilson didn't answer. He got up slowly, using his rifle as a cane. "Maybe I'll spend the night here," he said. "We could hunt a couple of hours early in the morning and still walk back in time to meet the plane."

"I'm going back," I said firmly.

"Well, that's up to you. You can walk out in the morning and pick us up. I'll ask Monsieur Bergère if there's room for me." He went into the house.

He returned a moment later with a satisfied look on his face. "It's all set," he said. "Raoul will take you to the river, and I'll stay. Then you'll come back for me at five-thirty tomorrow morning."

"Where are you going to sleep?" I asked.

"They've got a cot for me. You just be sure you're here at five-thirty. Later than that the hunting is no good."

Raoul appeared. He was strapping a black flashlight to his forehead. Wilson fastened the band for him.

"On part tout de suite?" he asked me.

"Any time," I answered.

"I'll see you at five-thirty, then," Wilson said. "Be sure to bring the boys. And tell Lebeau to have the truck waiting for us at the river at ten."

"He will do it, if you pay," Bergère said. "He is not a bad fellow."

I shook hands with Bergère and went out through the screen door. Our two boys rose out of the shadows and we started through the burnt grass in front of the house, past the buffalo hides. Raoul's light pierced the darkness ahead of us.

"It's really swell of you to let me stay, Monsieur Bergère," I heard Wilson say.

"A pleasure," the Belgian answered. "To have a sportsman like you in the house is always a pleasure."

We went slowly through the darkness. The vines that grew along the trees on both sides of us appeared to be huge snakes, and the small phosphorescent bugs that swarmed through the night looked like countless eyes, coming at us through the thick brush.

26

Raoul led the way, moving through the darkness with long steady strides, the light flickering high over the path as he walked along. It was cool now and the birds were silent. The only sound was the breaking of dried branches under our feet. We left the broad, overgrown road and started down the narrow path. There was just room for one person to move forward at a time. An owl screeched over our heads, and beat its wings recklessly through the tangle of vines and branches.

Suddenly Raoul stopped. He brought the rifle quickly up to his shoulder, and then very slowly he lowered it. The light flickered slightly, and I saw two gleaming dots, the eyes of some animal. We waited on the trail and then to my amazement I realized that the eyes belong to a young Negro who was making his way slowly toward us. He moved steadily forward on sturdy legs, his tattered shirt tight across his broad shoulders.

Lescelle said nothing. Ten paces in front of the painter the boy stopped. Neither of them spoke. Then very deliberately Raoul took him firmly by the wrist and began to twist his arm. The light shone directly into the boy's face as they stood there, the tall Belgian towering over the native, torturing him while neither one of them uttered a sound. Then very abruptly Raoul released him, throwing the arm down with a grunt of disgust, as if it were used, dirty. They had still not exchanged a word, but the boy seemed to have understood whatever threat was intended. He stepped into the thick grass at the side of the path, while our column moved past him. As he stood there in the darkness with his head bent forward, and his arm hanging limp at his side, I saw that he had tears running down his cheeks.

It was a threat. Despite the fact that the boy was returning to Bergère's establishment from an errand on which he had been sent, the painter seemed to be reminding him that any thought of running away that he might have had was dangerous and evil.

We went on. After an hour, the damp smell of the river was evident again. The country had changed. There were no trees, only thick brush and grass on both sides of the path. Raoul stopped and turned off his light.

"You are a few hundred meters from the river now," he said to me in French. "I'll start back."

I thanked him. He bowed politely, and we shook hands. "It was nothing," he said. "I was glad to have been of service to you. *Au revoir.*" Then he turned to our boys and spoke in Swahili. They listened attentively, nodding all the while he was speaking to them.

"Ndio, ndio, bwana." They hurried past me through the grass and took their places on the path. The painter and his light turned and started back. A few seconds later he had disappeared.

Now only the shirts of the natives were visible ahead of me. The rest was darkness. We arrived at the river. The canoes lay in silence on the calm surface of the water. The only sound was the hum of mosquitoes. One of the boys walked slowly to the muddy edge of the bank, cupped his hands against his mouth, and called out. His partner squatted in the mud and lit one of the cigarettes I had given him. A few minutes later the canoe arrived, and I got into it, crouching on the moist wood as it slid across the smooth, earth-colored river.

The rest of the walk was easier. The road had an even surface, and I felt that there were no more dangers now, as if the river were a boundary line, a Styx that ran along the outskirts of that hell. We passed the prison. From inside the high brick walls came a constant sound of low wailing, a faint continuous moaning of tortured voices. But it was not a wail. The prisoners were talking to each other, exchanging stories of their plight, asking each other why they were there, and as I stood listening to them I began to feel that all Africa was like that crowded, walled-in place; a continent full of black prisoners, murmuring to each other in the heat and the darkness, asking for an explanation that only time could supply, and only God could give them.

Dinner was over at the hotel when I arrived. It didn't matter to me. I went up to my room and stripped off my clothes. Then I ran water into the rusty bathtub. It was a thick, brown liquid, lukewarm. I held my hand an inch under the surface, and the water hid it from view. What difference did it make? I asked myself. From now on the water would always be that color.

I dried myself and put on a clean pair of shorts and an undershirt. Then I crawled in under the mosquito netting. It was hot, and there seemed not to be enough air in the room to keep me alive, but I fell asleep despite it all.

I awoke in the sweltering darkness. It was raining outside, and there was a slight wind rattling one of the shutters. It was five o'clock. My legs felt stiff and my feet were bruised, but I knew that if I didn't go after Wilson he would not arrive in time for the plane.

Madame Lebeau was having breakfast alone in the dining room downstairs. She nodded to me, her mouth full of bread and hot coffee.

"I'm going out to Bergère's," I told her. "I'll need the truck to take me to the river and to meet us at ten o'clock when we come back."

"You will have to ask my husband."

"Where is he?"

"He's asleep."

"All right," I said, "I'll wake him."

She looked distressed. It was obvious to her that I meant what I said.

"You cannot do that," she whined. "He works hard, and he is not well. You cannot wake him in the middle of the night."

"I can't walk out to the river either."

"But the keys of the truck are in his room."

"I'm sorry. I'm not going to walk," I told her. "I'll wake the whole neighborhood before I'll do that."

She looked at me with unconcealed hatred over the

rim of her coffee cup, as she finished drinking and chewing. "I'll get the keys," she said. She turned and spoke in Swahili to one of the boys.

A few minutes later he brought the key to the truck, and we went outside. The two natives who had been with us the previous day were already waiting, crouched in the drive. They nodded gravely as I appeared, and crawled into the back of the truck, their toes gripping the top of the steel tail gate. The houseboy got behind the wheel and we started out.

The drive was brief. The warm air felt good as it came in through the open windows. I went down to the river and crawled into one of the pirogues. The water lay dead still in the cool, damp morning air, quietly awaiting the heat of another tedious day. I lit a cigarette and watched the faint lines of light blue that were forming along the horizon to my left. From the huts near the path I could hear the chatter of the natives. One of the boys had gone to wake the ferryman, and I could hear them talking as they approached. He was obviously not too happy about starting his day at such an early hour, but he gave no hint of his feelings once he saw me.

It was getting light quickly now. Only in the most overgrown passages of the path was it still night. Wherever the plains on both sides of the road were visible I could see the sky changing color and the green beginning to stand out against the distant blue. Africa is a country for early morning, I thought. Mornings and evenings, whenever the light is dim and the air is cool.

I found Wilson and the two Belgians waiting for me on the screened-in porch. They looked rested and clean. Wilson came over to me, looking pleased and mysterious.

"Boy, you missed something, kid," he said in a low voice. "You really missed something."

"What? Did you have barbecued Negro for dinner?"

"No, I'm not kidding. It was just the goddamnedest night I've ever spent in my life. Boy! The stories I heard! God damn. You wouldn't believe it. I'll tell you all about it later."

Bergère stretched and yawned. "You are ready?" he asked me.

"Don't you want to rest for a minute?" Lescelle asked me.

"No, I'm all set. The walk was just a good warm-up. Let's go."

We picked up our weapons and went out past the house along the same path we had taken the previous evening. Wilson dropped back and walked next to me. "It's just the damnedest story you ever heard," he said in a low, intense voice. "Whew. What goes on here. It's a dictatorship, the Congo. A black kingdom. Brussels sits back and nods its head, because they want to go on making money, but they don't run this place. The guys out here run it, and they can do just as they like. Not just with the natives, either. With all of us. And the things that have gone on! This guy really knows, too. He worked in leper colonies, and in prisons, and in the mines, writing reports for the government, and that's what ruined him. That's why they're all after him now. They've even threatened to have him thrown in the booby hatch just to get rid of him. But he won't budge."

"Maybe we shouldn't shoot our picture here after all," I said.

"No, we'll be all right. Just have to keep our mouths shut and our eyes open."

Bergère stopped on the trail ahead of us, and put his hand up to his lips. Wilson nodded, and trotted forward. The Belgian pointed out through the brush. In an instant Wilson was a changed man. The hunt was on.

We turned out into the open country. It was light now everywhere. In the distance herds of antelope stood out against the deep color of the grass. We hurried forward, against the wind, the smell of the game passing over us quite suddenly. But it was no good. We had shot at them too much the evening before, and now they were wild. They bounded off, always keeping more than two hundred yards of prairie between us and them.

Bergère was unhappy. "I have never seen it like this," he said. "Every day I have come out here, and have killed game. I have shot one, and the others have run around me like Indians, and I could have shot twenty. I cannot understand it."

Wilson stood leaning on the barrel of his rifle. His face was bright red under his wide hat.

"It doesn't matter," he said, panting. "I don't care about the antelope."

"You wish us to try other game?" Bergère asked. "There is a place near here where there are always buffalo. If you want . . . ?"

"Sure," Wilson said. "Let's go."

"Are you positive that we're ready for that, John?" I asked doubtfully.

"You're damned right we are." He waved to the natives, who were still a few hundred yards behind us. "We'll take the big rifles."

Bergère nodded. "It is better," he said.

"We haven't really had much of a chance to shoot, John," I warned.

"For Christ's sake stop worrying," he said.

"There are no trees to climb. I've got to worry."

He paid no attention to me. The boys arrived and we exchanged rifles with them. Bergère led the way, turning south through the thick grass that was dry now, and that rustled in the faint wind. There were a few clouds in the sky, but the light of the day was glaringly bright. We went down into a gully, and there was a sudden patch of jungle ahead of us. Bergère stopped.

"They are often here," he said, "in the shade of the trees. I have walked by and they have given no sign, and suddenly they have come out."

Wilson's face was intense with excitement. His long fingers clutched the stock of his rifle. His glasses were clouded with moisture. His lips were dry and covered with a faint white crust that was thickest along the corners of his mouth. We went deeper into the gulley. The grass rose on both sides of us, shutting out the view. I could feel the sun burning the back of my neck. Wilson and the Belgian stopped and whispered to each other again, and then they went on more slowly. The trees were quite near now, and the ground under our feet was wet and marshy. It pulled at my boots, trying to hold me back. Suddenly there was a thrashing noise directly in front of me, the sound of breaking branches and hoofs. Wilson froze, and crouched low. And then suddenly an animal came out of the thicket. It was a cow, a brown and white cow with wide horns set above frightened eyes.

"Well, for God's sake," Wilson said. He started to laugh. Bergère was cursing in French, the mild curses that that language has to offer. He picked up a stone and flung it after the beast. It struck the cow in the flank, as it galloped up toward the grassy tableland on our left.

"You sure you don't want it?" Wilson said. He raised his rifle to his shoulder. "It's meat."

"It will only cause trouble if we kill her," Bergère said disgustedly.

Raoul shook his head and grunted. It was obvious that he thought it was still our fault that we had killed no game. I looked at my watch.

"The plane will be waiting for us in an hour and so will Lebeau," I told Wilson. "If we get to the airfield late we won't be able to start for Stanleyville tonight."

"There are still other places to hunt," Bergère said defensively. "This is not all that we have to offer you."

"I guess we'd better start back," Wilson said.

The Belgian shrugged. "If you must go there is nothing to do," he said. He spread his thin arms in a gesture of helplessness. Then he went over to where Raoul was standing, watching us contemptuously. "They must return," he said in French. The painter nodded, and together the two Belgians started back in the direction of the house.

We followed them. Wilson looked tired, but he was not nearly as disgusted as I had expected him to be.

"We'll get plenty of shooting where we're going, kid," he said. "All we want."

"I hope so. For your sake."

He bent over as he walked up the slight incline that led out of the gully. "We should try the big rifles, you know," he said. "Shoot at a target. Anything. But we've just got to try them."

"I'll ask Bergère to take us to a good place," I said. The Belgian nodded when I spoke to him about it. A mile or two from the house there was a perfect spot for target practice, he assured me. I noticed that Wilson had dropped back quite a way. The sun was directly over our heads now, and there was no wind. I waited for him to catch up.

"You all right, John?" I asked.

"Fine." He smiled. "Just fine, kid." His face was bright red again. "What lousy luck we've had, haven't we?"

"Well, that happens," I said. "I've gone out a lot of times and come back without any game to show for a

hard day's work. In Idaho and Nevada . . . in some of
the best hunting country we have at home, I've come back
skunked. The funny thing is that there's usually some pattern to it . . . that you understand later."

'What do you mean, kid?"

"Oh, some days you're overconfident, and the game
starts too suddenly, with a whole bunch of ducks rising
up in front of you out of a stubble field long before
you've even loaded your shotgun, or you've just gotten
into your boat, and you get a perfect double, and you
miss your shot, and you say to yourself there'll be plenty
more and of course there aren't. That's happened to me
a lot of times. Somehow somebody always makes you
pay for having been a boob or a wise guy."

"You're a superstitious bastard, aren't you?" he said,
smiling.

"I try not to be, but when I run into something outside
my control I often give way. I start looking for moral
patterns, and symbols, any kind of explanation. Stupid,
isn't it?"

"I'm not so sure. *I* believe in the signs, you know. I've
met them too often in my life to doubt them. In everything
I've ever done. Work, or women, or gambling. Everything."

"How do you mean?"

"Well, when I broke up with my first wife for instance.
I knew I'd lost the best dame I was ever likely to meet,
and I'd lost her because I'd acted like a horse's ass. And
it turned out that way. I'd done something wrong and I
had to pay for it, and so every time I fell in love again
after that, I knew the disenchantment would ultimately
turn up. And it did. Never failed. Because you get one
good chance at everything in life, and that's all."

"I don't believe *that*."

"Well, you'll see. I learned the hard way and you will
too. Remember that filly I had, Swan Song?"

"Sure, I paid for the memory."

"So did I." He paused significantly, walking more slowly. "I knew that that filly had class, and that I could clean
up with her, make a killing. But that wasn't enough for
me. I wanted to own a real stakes-winning mare. She was
a nice little twenty-thousand-dollar filly, but that was all.
Everybody warned me, but I wouldn't listen. Because she

was mine I wanted her to be better than she was, and so I overmatched her. She could beat any two-year-old filly in California running six furlongs, but I insisted on putting her in a mile race with some real good colts. Well, for six furlongs she beat them all, and then at the three-quarter post she stopped as if someone had shot her through the chest with a six-inch gun, and the field went by her, and she lost. It broke her heart and she never won again, and I went home and lay down on my bed, and I saw my life absolutely clearly, for what it was worth. I knew why it had all happened. I caught the sign, as they say." He looked over at me; his face intense. "I was that filly, Pete," he said. "I was Swan Song, and I knew I was good for six furlongs and nothing more, in a race restricted to horses of my class and value. A seven-thousand-dollar claiming race, that's what you can win, I told myself, and my career stopped dead for two years after that race, because I knew just how far I could go, and that's the biggest brake a man can carry with him. I couldn't write any more. I couldn't make money. I couldn't do anything. I was like that broken-down filly out in the corral, limping around, eating feed that was too rich for the work I was doing."

"But you came out of it, John."

"Sure, I forgot after a while, and things broke right, and I made a little melodrama with a guy who'd always played heavies, and I made him play a hero, and it all started again: a new season, with legs that had been fired, after a long summer in pasture."

"So the signs didn't mean a goddamn thing."

"The hell they didn't. They meant something to me. I never owned a good horse again, and I never had a chance to bet on a sure thing. And as far as my work went, the sign was better than right. I never wrote anything out of my class, and whenever I tried, the field went by me, just as they romped past poor old Swan Song."

"Then you've stopped trying? Is that it?"

"No. I still stick my neck out. I've got to. That's the way I'm built." He stopped and pushed his hat back on his head. "Boy, it's hot," he said.

I stood watching him. The flies gathered around us. "I don't really believe in all that," I said. "I think we know our own limitations without mystic aids. And I think it's better to face them, and work inside their boundaries. But if you want to call it a sign, that's O.K. too. All I say now is, let's accept the sign on this hunting business, and not tempt the gods, because we know how it will end."

"What are you talking about?"

"The antelopes have beaten us, so why go on to the elephants?"

He stared at me, amazed. "Becaus that's the only reason to go on living," he said. "It's no fun if you don't thumb your nose at the gods. It's all crappy and stale if you play the form. Hell, I thought you knew that much."

"I know we're overmatched, John."

"Well, that's the only kind of race worth running," he said. "That's what your mystic aids are for. To show you the boundaries, and to dare you to go on. Everest is there just for that, and the horizon on the edge of the sea, and death is there for that reason, to tempt you, to mock you, and dare you to proceed. And if you're not a clerk with a small heart, you read the signs and you press on. Like Mallory, or Columbus, or Einstein . . ." He shook his head. "I thought you knew that," he repeated, amazed.

"I know it now."

Bergère called out to us: "A little more, Monsieur Wilson. A kilometer more. A thousand yards. Then we can try out your guns."

Wilson went on, wearily. After a while he looked over at me, and shook his head. "God damn," he mumbled. "You only want to enter races where you know you can win? Is that it? Well, why bother living, then? Why waste all that food you're going to eat, when food's so short in the world? Why waste all that time existing if you know the outcome?"

"John," I said, "curb that sadistic urge." He didn't answer. He walked along very slowly, his rifle resting across his bony shoulders. I noticed that every once in a while the two black holes of its muzzle swung around to stare at me.

"Is that thing on safe?" I asked.

He stopped and stared at me. "What do *you* think? You think I carry a loaded .475 around without putting it on safe?"

"I'm not sure. I just don't like looking into those two deadly black eyes."

He shook his head again, disgustedly.

"If you're so sure it's on safe," I said, "why don't you point it at your foot and pull the trigger?"

"O.K." He swung the rifle off his shoulder and put out his foot, pointing the two barrels down at his boot. "*You* want to pull the trigger?" he asked.

"No. I'm not certain it's on safe. You are."

"In other words you're too yellow to pull the trigger."

"It's not my gun, John. And I didn't make a big point of it being on safe. So why the hell should I?"

"Oh balls," he said. He reached down inside the trigger guard and pulled on one of the triggers. There was a click as the hammer fell on an empty chamber. "You happy now?" he asked defiantly.

A cold chill passed along my spine. I stared at him with my mouth open. "For Christ's sake. It *wasn't* on safe. There was no round in the chamber, that's all."

"Shall I try the other barrel?"

"Hell, no! What's the matter with you?"

He broke the gun at the breech. There was an unexploded round in the right barrel.

"Good God Almighty," I said.

He looked superior. "I knew there was a live round in the right barrel," he said, "but I also knew that I was pulling the trigger on the other side."

"You did like hell."

"Of course I did."

"But anyway, it wasn't on safe."

He laughed dryly. "Don't kid yourself. It was. I pushed the safety with my thumb when I took the gun off my shoulder."

"You're a liar," I said angrily. "You thought it was on safe, and you thought both barrels were loaded. Only luck saved you from blowing off your foot. Dumb, unaccountable luck."

"You're nuts."

"John," I said, "for God's sake come out of it. You've just come as close as you ever have to crippling yourself, or killing me."

I could see Bergère and Raoul a hundred yards ahead of us, waiting patiently in the tall grass. The two native boys were behind us, puzzled by what was going on. "Well, if I had to make a choice I'd choose the latter," Wilson said. "Wouldn't be such a great loss." He turned abruptly, and walked off in the direction of the Belgians. The natives circled around me and followed him. I stood there trying to figure what had happened. I couldn't believe that he would risk his foot just to torture me. Still, I knew that his knowledge of rifles was not exact enough to make him sure of which trigger fired each of the two barrels. Very slowly I unloaded my rifle and started out after the others.

I joined them on a small hill. There was a gully behind it with a tall ant heap sticking out of the grass not a hundred yards away. Raoul had placed a white boulder on its very tip. Wilson didn't look at me. He was aiming the big rifle at the boulder, and as I arrived he fired. The stone disappeared. Bergère laughed cheerfully.

"Excellent! Excellent, Monsieur Wilson!"

"Go ahead, Pete," Wilson said.

Raoul ran over to the anthill and replaced the stone. Then he hurried back. I put the heavy rifle against my shoulder. It was badly balanced. The tip of the barrel seemed to have a heavy weight tied to it. I tightened my grip on the stock, lined up the sights, and fired. There was a cloud of yellow dust, and when it cleared I could see the stone still safely perched on top of the anthill.

"You flinched," Wilson said.

"I don't think I did."

"Perhaps the rifle shoots low," Bergère said.

"I doubt that," Wilson said. "We rented it from one of the best gunsmiths in Nairobi. I think Pete flinched." He put out his hand without looking at me. "Let me try it," he said.

I handed him the gun. He adjusted his glasses before he raised it to his shoulder. Then he aimed very carefully and fired. The dust cleared and the stone was gone. Wilson looked at me for a long time, still holding the weapon against his shoulder.

"I suppose there is some lesson to be drawn from all this," he said slowly, "but I guess you'd prefer not to really investigate the affair."

"Not at all. You're a better rifle shot than I am. But that's the only lesson I can see right at this moment."

Bergère scratched his legs nervously. "They shoot straight, your rifles. It is important to know."

"If we don't kill a few buffalo and an elephant we won't

have an excuse," Wilson said, smiling.

"Ah, but you will not be able to make excuses," Bergère laughed. "If you shoot badly at dangerous game there is usually nothing to be said by anyone except prayers."

"Dear God, please admit into your realm this badly mauled screen writer," Wilson said solemnly. "He didn't know enough to stay home."

"P.S. Dear God," I said. "Don't make a man suffer just because he doesn't know how to choose his friends."

"I'm not your friend," Wilson said. "I'm your employer. You employer and your idol. You're the kind of plant that can only grow in the shade of enormously strong trees. Direct sunlight withers you, dries you up."

"Go to hell," I said. "Find someone else to spoil, spoiler."

Bergère looked perturbed. "You are joking," he said, "and that is all right for friends, but you must be careful. On safari jokes do not digest well. You keep them going too long, and finally there is only the bad joke with you all the time instead of the friendship."

"That's what our friendship is," Wilson said. "A bad joke."

"No, it isn't," I told him, "not even that."

He nodded. "You're right. It's a fairy tale. A fairy tale for he-men." He was enjoying himself. "It's the Kinsey report. Dramatized."

"You must go back, no?" Bergére asked.

"We must go back, yes." Wilson grinned.

We went down across the green, sun-baked plain. In the extreme distance the clouds were climbing over each other toward the thinner air. Mysteriously we found our way to the orchard that the elephants had destroyed, and Bergère repeated his story of that disaster again, and then continued on to the other calamities that he had experienced. Although we had heard them all before, Wilson nodded, and shook his head sympathetically. We made our way past the rotting buffalo hides into the house.

The room had been swept and cleared. It was cool now that we were out of the sun. Very slowly my eyes became accustomed to the dim light, and then I saw that there was someone seated in the far corner of the room waiting for us. Bergère saw him too. He was a stocky young man in white shorts and a white shirt, and he wore green naval shoulder boards marked with some kind of insignia.

"Ah, Lieutenant," Bergère said in his high, excited voice, "you have been here long waiting for me?"

The young man rose and was introduced to us.

"Orange juice, Raoul," Bergère said with the fussy tone of a surprised housewife who believes she can indicate her hospitality by snapping at her maid. Raoul trudged slowly out of the room. Bergère and the lieutenant stood with their heads close together, speaking in low voices. Then Bergère straightened. He came over to us.

"Jacques is our policeman," he said, indicating the young man. "One of the few honest ones in the whole of the Congo."

"Is that right?" Wilson said in his interested voice. "You must have quite a beat."

"He doesn't speak English," Bergère said. He took us both by the arm and led us slowly toward the veranda. "You see," he said, his face intense and pleased-looking, "after all, life has its moments of compensation, as the Scotchman said when he saw his wife going over the waterfall." He laughed very suddenly, a crazy, uncontrolled laugh.

"Just what do you mean, Charles?" Wilson asked.

The laugh was repeated. "You do not understand?" the Belgian said, raising his voice. "Compensation is not right?"

"Yes, sure, but . . . ?"

"Well, the Scotchman has left his boat to make pee-pee on the shore, and his wife is alone in it, and the stream takes it, and when he looks up from doing his business, there she is going over the waterfall, and he knows then that life has its moments of compensation."

We shook our heads, thoroughly mystified. "I'm afraid I don't understand," Wilson said.

Bergère pointed at the young man standing behind us. "He has come to arrest Raoul," he said in a stage whisper. "To take him away. And Raoul thinks they have come for me." He laughed uproariously once more.

Wilson managed to grin. I admired him for it. "Well," he said, "I guess then we'd better go."

"Oh, do not let it disturb you," Bergère chuckled.

"We really must," Wilson said. He shook hands very cordially with Bergère. "Thank you so much, Charles, I just had a wonderful time."

"I am sorry about the hunting."

"It doesn't matter. We'll make up for it next time."

Raoul came into the room carrying a tray with glasses and a pitcher of orange juice. We shook hands with him and the lieutenant, and because there was no polite way out, we each had a glass of orange juice. I watched the others as I drank. They had their faces buried in their glasses, each happy with his own cruel thoughts.

"Well, good-by again," Wilson said hurriedly.

We went out of the room, through the veranda, and out of the house. Raoul started to go with us, but Bergère detained him. "They know the way," he said. "Never take a guest to the door if you want him to come back."

Our two boys were waiting for us. They fell in behind us on the path. Millions of flies were on the buffalo hides, clustered on the crusty dried blood. Wilson turned and stopped for an instant. He glanced back at the house, huddled there with its torn screens among the heavy, clutching vines.

"Wouldn't that be just a swell place to own, Pete?" he observed. "Just as a place to come to whenever you had the time."

"Sure," I replied. "It's so handy, too. Be a cinch to come up for a week end between pictures."

"I'm not kidding," Wilson said. "I'd like to be able to buy a place like that."

"I think you'd better talk to your wife before you make the man an offer."

He shrugged and turned away from the house. "You're getting to be more and more amusing," he said dryly. I didn't give it a second thought. From behind as I could hear the sound of raised voices. Wilson increased his pace. Then as we reached the path a man suddenly stepped out of the bushes and stood blocking our way. He was dressed in the same uniform as the policeman back at the house, and he wore a pistol in a holster. His right hand was un-buttoning the flap as we approached.

"Bergère?"

"No, it's not Bergère," I said quickly in French. They were obviously making sure that our Belgain friend would not escape. The man's hand fell away from his belt and he stepped toward us, peering closely at our faces.

"We're Americans," I explained. "We've been hunting with Monsieur Bergère."

"Ah," the policeman said, "hunting. It is the cause of it all."

"What is he talking about?" Wilson asked.

"I don't know. I'm trying to find out." I turned back to the man in the pith helmet and the white shorts. "What's it all about?" I asked. "We don't know Mr. Bergère very well, and . . ."

He lifted his hand and pointed to his forehead. "It is quite simple. Nothing too grave. They are both a little, you know . . . And hunting was the beginning of it. It developed their madness. They did it too much. But there will be no trouble for you gentlemen."

"Then we can go on?"

"Yes, certainly. *Et bonne route.*"

He stepped to one side, and we hurried past him. Once we were out of earshot I translated what had been said to Wilson.

"It's a frame-up," he muttered. "We ought to go back and help them."

"What about shooting the picture here, after that?"

"That's it. We'd be sunk."

"And of course it might be all true. They might both be crazy as a set of green teeth."

"Don't you believe it." He bit his lip. "We should really go back and help them," he said again. But he continued walking toward the river.

"I don't know," I said, hurrying after him. "Hunting *can* become a mania, you know, if you let it get out of hand."

"Nonsense. Bergère is no crazier than you or me."

"Maybe not. But what about that strange remark he made about the Scotchman? What about that?"

He shrugged. "Oh, that was nothing. He'd just had enough of the other guy's company, that's all. It's a feeling I can understand."

"So can I," I replied. "Well, I suppose we'll never know for sure."

"We should have gone back to help them in any case," Wilson said. "They were damn nice to us."

Lebeau was waiting for us on the other side of the brown river, seated at the wheel of his beloved De Soto. We were over half an hour late, and he had been forced to wait out in the hot sun, which was obviously bad for his blood pressure and for the paint of the car. He grunted as we got in, a noise which served the double purpose of greeting and complaint.

"Well, if it isn't our old friend," Wilson said, beaming. He patted Lebeau affectionately on one of his fat shoulders. "How are you, *amigo? Cóm' ustá?*"

The two natives stood waiting outside the car, watching us with questioning eyes. Lebeau turned his massive head toward them and grunted a few words in Swahili. The natives nodded sadly. Then Lebeau put the car in gear and we were off at the usual pace. Wilson looked amazed.

"Hey," he said, "you've forgotten the boys."

Lebeau grunted questioningly, and looked briefly and unlovingly at Wilson.

"Tell him for Christ's sake, Pete."

"He knows it."

"Well, ask him why he didn't take them along."

Lebeau explained that there was no room for the boys in the trunk compartment, and that they stank too much to let them ride with us. Wilson looked amazed as I translated.

"Oh, for God's sake. Well, tell him that he stinks too. And that I do, and that you do."

"What's the use, John?"

"Tell him, God damn it. All right, I will." He tapped Lebeau sharply on the shoulder, and then, pointing to him, he held his nose. "You stink too, *amigo*. And he stinks, back there in the back seat. And I stink." The sign language was unmistakable.

Lebeau stared at him, not knowing whether to take offense or to accept the speech as a joke. He decided on the latter course, and laughed. It was like a hippo's morning yawn. There were rows of yellow teeth set in an abyss of rose-colored flesh.

"*Il est drôle*," Lebeau said, and we slid into the entrance of the hotel. Wilson jumped out of the car and continued his pantomime. He pointed at Lebeau and held his nose, moving hurriedly away from him as he did so. Lebeau laughed a little less genuinely, and went up the steps of his hotel. Wilson continued his act until the man had disappeared behind the screen door.

"For God's sake," Wilson said with astonishment. "He didn't get mad."

"He chose to accept your insult as a joke."

Wilson shook his head. "I can't believe it. I guess I'll have to go on with it for a while." I followed him into the main room of the hotel. The same people we had seen the previous day were having lunch. "Lebeau," Wilson bellowed, but the hotel proprietor had fled. "Son of a bitch has disappeared."

"Are you looking for me?" an English voice said from one of the huge leather chairs. A small man in wilted khakis rose to greet us. He had a narrow, sunburned face, with mild watery eyes, that looked out over his huge mustache. "My name's Hodkins. I'm your new airplane driver."

Wilson's manner changed immediately. He walked over to the small man with his most gentle smile and extended his hand. "Well, I'm certainly glad to meet you, Mr. Hodkins. You work for Alec Laing, don't you?"

"That's right." The small eyes beamed. This was obviously a man who was not used to having a fuss made over him. "If you're all ready, sir, I think we'd better get going. Don't like to start out too late for the Congo."

"We're ready any time," Wilson said.

"I'll go upstairs and get our things," I said.

Wilson and the pilot were seated at the bar when I returned. Wilson was drinking a brandy while the pilot was finishing a Coca-Cola.

"We all ready to go, Pete?" he asked. He looked mysterious. I knew something was afoot, but I didn't feel like questioning him.

"All set, John," I said.

"Have you met Hodkins?"

"Yes, we've met."

Hodkins stood beaming at us. "Call me Hod," he said. He had a hesitant way of speaking, as if he wanted to apologize for taking our time with anything he had to say.

Wilson put one of his long arms affectionately around the man's slight shoulders. "Hod's never been into the Congo," he said with a happy smile.

"Oh, but I'll find the way all right," the pilot said cheerfully. "And if I can't find the way, why we'll just put down in one of those big trees and spend the night."

"Only difficult thing will be getting up in the air again the next morning," Wilson said.

"Well, as a famous pilot once said," Hodkins beamed,

"it's all worth it, all of it, including the final crash."

"That's your philosophy too, isn't it, Pete?" Wilson laughed. "You're just a devil-may-care character, aren't you? The adventurer without regrets. The carefree globe-trotter. Puts his life at stake for the fun of risking it. Lives for the moment."

"That's right, that's my character in a corny nutshell."

"I think we'd better go, chaps," Hodkins said. He searched briefly among the armchairs and found a bleached fishing hat with a floppy brim. Then he picked up a leather map case and started toward the door. Madame Lebeau appeared, and she and Wilson bent their heads over the bill. Hodkins and I went out into the hot sunlight; a native boy in dungarees stood beside the pick-up truck, waiting to take us out to the field. We climbed up over the tail gate. Wilson took his place next to the driver. Madame Lebeau had come out of the hotel to see us off.

"See you again, honey, real soon," Wilson called out to her from the cab of the truck. The woman didn't wave. She stood there calmly in the withering heat, and watched us drive away.

Everything was in readiness at the field. Wilson crawled into the plane while Hodkins and I loaded the gear.

"Is this really your first flight into the Congo, Hod?" I asked.

"Oh yes, quite," the little man answered. "Been all over this bloody continent, but never into the Congo. Well, there's got to be a first time for everything, as the fellow said who ate the oyster." He swung himself up into the fuselage. I followed him. Together we pulled shut the flimsy door. "Now then," he said, "let's get her balanced as well as we can, Mr. Wilson over there, and Pete on the other side to sort of even it out."

The interior of the plane was extremely narrow. Seven leather seats were bolted to the floor along both sides of the fuselage. Our gear was stacked in the tail. The pilot's compartment was well forward in the nose of the plane, open on the right side, and partitioned off by a thin wall on the left. I sat down in the first seat on the right so that I could look into the cockpit. Wilson was stretched out on the other side of the plane.

Hodkins started the small motors, then he turned and

beamed back at me, his eyes hidden by dark glasses, his floppy fishing hat perched well back on his head.

"Self-starters," he called out to me. "Jolly good, what?"

"Jolly amazing."

He grinned happily, and waved to the native boy standing on the ground. "Abyssinia," he called out. The native waved timidly and smiled. We bumped out across the red clay of the runway, the small motors vibrating in their moorings, the ill-shaped wings flopping up and down despite their metal stays. Hodkins' manner became more serious as we turned and faced the sloping runway. His eye swept the red earth in front of us; his hands tightened on the controls. He looked exactly like a gentleman driver of twenty-five years ago, perched high up on the beast he was driving, busy with a vast variety of antiquated controls. He seemed surprised and pleased when the machine responded to his masterful touch and did what it was supposed to do.

The small motors seemed to be making their utmost effort, and then I saw Hodkins pull back on the taped handles of the controls and we were airborne. It was not really a take-off. It was more like a desperate leap, a last attempt of the old machine to obey the laws of aerodynamics after which it had been designed and in which it now no longer believed.

We rose steadily. Tatsumu was already far behind us, when suddenly Hodkins put the plane into a steep bank, and we turned and flew back over the airfield and the town.

"Just like the airlines." Hodkins grinned. "Smooth flying to suit the customer's stomach."

He took a box of cigarettes off the shelf directly above the instrument panel, and twisting his body around the partition, offered it to us.

"Cigarette?" He beamed. The plane dipped a little to the right. Wilson and I declined the offer. Hodkins produced a lighter and lit his own. Then he began fumbling around trying to find his map case. He located it finally, and selected a large map which he spread out across his knees. A corner of the map scraped the tip of his cigarette and he stamped out the various sparks that floated down past his knees. Then he studied the markings on the paper, shook his head, and folded the map up again. The next one seemed to be a better selection. He nodded happily, and smiled back at me.

"This is the map all right," he said. He glanced at the horizon, and then throttled down slightly. We leveled out. I looked down at the ground. We seemed to be flying at about fifteen hundred feet, a fifth of what Laing had told me *he* would fly at. Already the grasslands were becoming sprinkled by larger and larger patches of jungle, and then suddenly the great forest lay in front of us.

It was like a first glance at the open sea on a stormy day. The corner of a cloud mass passed over the sun, and the jungle was bathed in a strange filtered light, gold and gray. It seemed endless, especially at that altitude. There were a few small hills, but they were rare. All we could see were hundreds and hundreds of miles of huge trees growing so close together that only the tallest ones of them were distinguishable. The rest of it was a tumult of growth of all kinds, a dense mass of vegetation, and it seemed that most of the world was covered with it. I glanced back at Wilson. He had lit a cigarette and was staring excitedly out of the window.

"Isn't this something?" he shouted. "This is the part of the world God got bored with, said, 'Aw hell,' and threw in a lot of trees and vines, and all the animals he had left over, and all the people he was too busy to worry about because Adam and Eve were already making trouble in paradise."

We passed over a brown river, and went on. The plane seemed to be descending slowly toward the forest.

"Can you imagine what goes on down there?" Wilson shouted. He screwed up his face to make it look evil. "The goddamnedest things. Murder and rape, and torture of all kinds. Pygmies and buffalo and elephant and every variety of poisonous snake. Hell, if you were stranded down there you could never get out. That's why Laing always flies very high and stays near a road or a river."

The plane was slanting down even more now. Hodkins was sitting very erect over the controls, searching for something on the ground. I sat watching him, with alarm. When the plane was about fifty feet over the tops of the tallest trees, he leveled out. My stomach was contracted into a tight knot. I looked down at the blur of treetops and vines flashing past the right landing gear. Hodkins dropped one wing and looked down at the trees. Then he tilted the plane slowly to the left and stared out at the forest on the other side of the cabin.

"Awful lot of trees," he observed. "Never seen so many."

I nodded in agonized silence. He faced the front again. In the extreme distance a single, tree-covered hill rose out of the horizon. We were flying in a straight line toward it. Hodkins unfolded his map again, and sat looking down at it. The single hilltop came closer and closer. Wilson's face wore a false smile.

"A real character, isn't he?"

"Do you think he sees that hill?" I asked.

Wilson shrugged. A very tense argument was going on inside me. If it were all a gag and I pointed out the approaching hill, Hodkins would know that I was frightened, and he might be prompted into an even more dangerous procedure. But if he actually did not see the hill, I was an idiot and deserved to die there. I grew more and more nervous as the seconds passed.

The hill was only a few miles away now, and even at the slow speed at which we were flying it seemed to be rushing toward us. I leaned forward and tapped Hodkins on the shoulder.

"You see that hill, don't you?" I said, trying to sound vaguely humorous.

He looked up with feigned surprise. "Oh, dear me," he said. "Thanks awfully, old boy." We chandelled up to the left, our wing tip missing the tops of the trees by a few feet. The motors labored to keep us up above the forest, and then quite suddenly we had passed the crest of the small mountain. On the other side, the jungle lay flat and dense. We were a few hundred feet above it now, when to my horror I saw Hodkins push the controls forward again. The speed of the plane increased, and we dove toward the flatlands once more. Near tree top level Hodkins pulled back on the controls, and we resumed our usual altitude.

"We're really charging along, aren't we?" he said proudly.

I nodded. There was nothing I could do. He was the captain of the ship. The fact that he cared very little for his life was something I would have to accept for the next three hours. I noticed that Wilson was already asleep. He was the only one who could have reprimanded our pilot, but it was obvious that he was unwilling to do so.

We passed over a clearing. The giant trees of the forest had been felled, and stripped bare; they lay like huge scattered matchsticks on the burnt earth. I saw a native village at the far edge of the clearing, and then we were past it, flying low over the jungle once more. I stared down at my boots for a very long time, until I felt the plane rise again. Then I looked out. Ahead of us, to the left, I could see a wide, brown river. I felt better. Hodkins was obviously tired of his little game. He was climbing up over the river where he would resume a more normal course. But a minute later the plane slanted down toward the earth once more and we were flying not more than twenty feet above the brown water. The forest rose high on both sides of us. The shadow of the plane seemed to race past us as I looked out at the empty banks. There was no sign of life, no crocodiles or hippos, only brown water into which the vines grew on both banks. The plane banked, and we followed a turn of the river, and then it straightened out over the water again. Wilson was breathing heavily, his mouth open, his head bent forward with his chin resting on his chest. I touched his shoulder. He awoke with a start. The trees were rushing past his window, very much as if he were a passenger on a train passing through the jungle. He stared with amazement at the banks of the river. Then abruptly he regained his poise.

"He's crazy," he said in a hushed voice, pointing forward. "Absolutely nuts. But please don't wake me unless you're sure we're going to crash. I wouldn't want to miss that."

Hodkins turned to look back at us. "Not much of anything here, is there?" he remarked cheerfully. I shook my head. The river turned abruptly to the left. Hodkins banked steeply, and sideslipped past the trees.

"Tight squeeze," he said, grinning. "Awfully narrow bit, that."

I didn't hate him. I felt too frightened to think of anyone except myself. My hands were gripping the metal sides of my seat, and we straightened out again. Then very slowly we rose above the river and the forest. At an altitude of about a thousand feet we leveled off.

"Show's over, folks," Hodkins said happily. "Now we've got to try and find out where we are."

Huge dark gray mountains of clouds were rising up on all sides of us. We passed through a storm; the rain sounded like a thousand pebbles as it smacked against the fabric wings and fuselage. Hodkins sat very erect, holding the controls, as we fought for altitude. It went on for what seemed like an eternity, the rising and falling, the feeling of being suspended like a small kite in a gale. Finally Hodkins turned back to speak to me.

"Heard about a chap flying a Cub out here. Got into one of these thermals at twelve thousand, and the next thing he knew he was up above thirty. Nearly froze to death before he could get his plane down again."

I nodded.

He smiled in a most friendly manner. "You know, Alec told me about you," he said. "You're the chap that's keen on flying, aren't you?"

"I was."

He laughed. "It's jolly good fun once in a while, isn't it?" he said. "Especially when you can come down and take a looksee at the country. Otherwise it tends to get a bit monotonous." He abandoned the map that he had unfolded earlier and searched for a new one. Then he put his finger pensively into his mouth and pretended to bite his nail.

"Now then," he said, "if I've got the right sheet, the Congo River should be down on our right somewhere. Let's take a look."

We rose higher. Fate was kind to us. In the distance, among the black treetops of the forest, we could see a flat, snakelike surface, shining golden black against the gray sky. It looked immense, and swollen, a snake that had eaten much too much. Hodkins banked the plane and we flew toward it.

"Simple as can be, now," he said. "Just follow old man river home."

We turned and flew parallel to the wide belt of water. I could see a pirogue fighting its way upstream, two tiny paddlers standing in each end of the canoe.

"Mighty slow way to travel," Hodkins said.

"Slow but sure."

We could see an air strip ahead of us, a long treeless rectangle cut out of the middle of the forest.

"Well, we found it," Hodkins said contentedly. We passed over a town. Yellow buildings lined one side of the river. There were a few paved streets. A good many large American cars seemed to be moving about below us. Wilson awoke and stretched.

"Stanleyville?" he asked, like a commuter waking up in his train.

I nodded. We flew past the town, and turned back. The sun came out as we approached the field. Very gently Hodkins sat the plane down on the concrete runway, and we taxied over to a group of hangars. Two native boys in dungarees showed Hodkins where to park.

The heat was stifling inside the cabin now, and it grew even hotter once the engines stopped. I went back through the cabin, opened the door, and jumped down onto the grass on which we were parked. A few hundred yards behind the hangars, I could see a large white structure, which looked like an overgrown filling station that had been converted into a hotel. There was a large covered veranda from which the noise of dance music could be heard blaring out through the adjoining jungle. Wilson and Hodkins crawled out of the plane. The natives began unloading our mountain of baggage. We stood motionless in the sudden heat.

"Why, there's René," Wilson said suddenly.

"Who?" I asked.

"The guy who's going to take us out hunting. The local game warden."

I could see a fat figure moving toward us from the direction of the veranda. Wilson hurried off toward his friend.

"I do believe that man's wearing a leather jacket," I said to Hodkins. "It looks rather strange on a hippo."

He laughed curtly. "Does at that," he said. "Well, if you'll all stay here for a bit and guard the luggage, I'll find out what the gen is for tomorrow." He pulled at his rumpled trousers and followed Wilson. I watched them from a distance, feeling weak, but grateful to be alive. The huge man in the leather jacket doffed his fiber helmet and shook hands with the pilot. Then he took Wilson by the arm and they moved off toward the veranda. Hodkins scratched his head and started back toward the plane. He was grinning happily as he approached, a cigarette stuck in his thick mustache. He rubbed his hands together.

"Well," he said, "guess where we're going tomorrow?"

"Down the river in one of those little boats."

"Not at all," Hodkins beamed. "We are flying back to Tatsumu first thing in the morning."

"What?" It seemed incredible, and yet was exactly what Alec Laing had prophesied. "But why, Hod? What the hell for?"

"Can't hunt in the jungle," Hodkins said. "Can't even take a bloody walk, don't you know . . . so we're flying back to the grasslands."

"All that way, over those trees again."

"Afraid so, old boy. Fat fellow's coming with us of course."

"What about tonight?" I asked. "Are we going to sleep in the plane?"

"No, they're sending a car out for us and the gear. The Sabena Hotel's right over there, across the street." He looked quizzically at me. "You feeling all right, Pete?" he asked.

"Yes, why?"

"All that fancy flying back there? Did it bother you?"'

"No, not at all," I lied. I knew that there was another day of flying ahead of me.

Hodkins grinned shamefacedly. "It was your boss' idea," he confessed. "He thought it would be a good joke, a rib, don't you know."

I stared at him. "What if one of the engines had conked out?" I asked him. "That would have been an even better joke, wouldn't it?"

Hodkins nodded. "I worried a bit about that," he said. "But the old boy was awfully keen on his rib."

"Of course he was. Naturally. Such an amusing rib, too."

"You're not sore, are you?"

"No, not at all," I lied.

"I just thought I'd tell you."

"Thanks. Now I know how to spoil it for him," I said. "Just never mention it."

Hodkins smiled appreciatively. "That's the way to handle it, all right," he said.

A large sedan was coming across the runway toward

us. I was thinking of all the things I could do to even the score. But I knew the best thing to do was to disregard it. Otherwise there would be no end to the mutual tortures.

"There's the car," Hodkins said. "Of course there's no one about to help load the gear. That's what a pilot is, out here. A glorified wet nurse. A bloody valet; with wings."

"Ranks with and above a writer," I said.

"Is that what you do? I was wondering what your part in this business was. Well, I've got some fine stories I'll have to tell you. Make a whale of a book. Actual things that have happened to me. Things you wouldn't believe. Like the time the squadron dog bit me in Khartoum, and they thought he had the rabies."

"Tell me later. After we load the gear."

"I will," Hodkins said. The sedan stopped in front of us. A man in immaculately starched khakis got out.

"Are these Monsieur Wilson's things?" he asked in French.

"Yes, all of us," I replied. Hodkins and I started to load the car, while the Belgian went off to find native labor.

It was all a nightmare, a nightmare in a steam bath. I crawled into the back seat of the car, banging my shins against Wilson's elephant gun. "Well, now if this chap ever comes back," Hodkins said, "we'll have a chance to get in out of this hot sun."

27

"At least it's cool in the plane," I said. I hadn't been listening to Hodkins for the past few minutes.

"While we're up high, it's cool," Wilson said, grinning. His joke had been recognized as a great success.

"Do let me finish my story, boys," Hodkins said.

We were seated in the main dining room of a small hotel called the Sans Souci, which looked out over the Congo River. The lights were dim. From the bar the tedi-

ous music of a small band drifted in to us. Wilson and the
game warden, René Delville, were at the far end of the
table with Basil Owen, who had arrived in the Beechcraft
an hour after us, and Hodkins was finally telling us the
story about the dog that bit him at Khartoum in 1944.

"Go-ahead, Hod," Owen said. "You got out of your
aircraft and this little black dog ran over and bit you."

"He wasn't so little, mind you," Hodkins said. "He was
a bloody great thing with lots of fur, and quick as the
devil. He took me by the leg, and bit all the way through
my flight boot . . . just enough to pierce the skin. I gave
him one hell of a kick, and sent him crashing into the
landing gear of a Beaufighter parked next to my ship, and
he just shook himself and ran off. That was the bad part.
He ran off into the desert, the bloody fool. Well, I went
to the squadron doctor and showed him my leg and of
course he asks which dog it was that had bitten me. I
laughed right in his face. I'd just arrived, and I didn't
even know the C.O.'s name, much less the names of the
local dogs."

He drank some of his beer. Wilson moved his long
body forward, listening attentively. It was one of his most
winning characteristics, his ability to listen with interest to
other people's stories. "Go on, Hod, what happened then?"
he prompted.

"Well, they rounded up all the dogs on the field, and
tried to get me to identify the brute, but of course I
hadn't the foggiest notion which one it was, and so the
squadron says: 'Cairo for you, old boy, and the full treatment.' Well, Cairo wasn't much, but it was paradise next
to Khartoum, and so I dumped my kit into the next aircraft heading north, and turned in at the hospital. Awful
mistake, that. For not an hour later they started the anti-
rabies treatment on me. Twenty-four shots, in
twelve hours, right in the belly. That was the order of
the day for poor old Hodkins. Every half hour, in comes
the nurse with a needle as long as a swagger stick.
After the first six I'd start screaming the minute the door-
knob would start to turn, and when I was up to eighteen
they had three aircraftsmen holding me down all the time.
The most awful night of my life it was, and when it was
over and done with they ordered me back to Khartoum.
Well, I got out of the plane holding my pistol in my right

hand, ready to shoot any dog on sight, and that's the way I walked into the mess. And of course sitting right there, next to the C.O., with his bloody paws on the table was this black dog, the one that bit me, and I started to scream all over again. Well, the chaps quieted me down, and I explained that they were all breaking bread with a murderer, and then they sat back and laughed until they cried, for it seems that dog was as fit as you and me, and I'd gone through the tortures of the damned for nothing."

Everyone at the table was laughing hysterically.

"Oh, that's a wonderful story, Hod," Wilson said. "Much better than our gag."

"Wasn't a gag, at all, although for years I thought it might have been," the pilot replied. He was enjoying his success.

The game warden cleared his throat. "Mr. Hodkins, I wanted to ask about tomorrow. Are you all ready to leave in the morning?" He spoke fluent English, with a slight French accent.

"Ready any time, sir," Hodkins said. "From sunrise on."

"I understand we're going back to Tatsumu, John."

Wilson stared aggressively at me. "That's right," he said.

"They don't hunt in the forest after all."

"They do, but we're not going to."

"Is that right, Monsieur Delville?" I asked. "Are there people who hunt in the forest?"

The game warden smiled. "The Pygmies," he said.

"But white people don't."

"Not any I know," Delville replied.

Wilson pretended not to be listening. "We'll leave at eight," he said slowly. "We've got to clean the guns to-night, before we go to sleep."

"That is very important," Delville said unctuously. "The guns must be clean, and well oiled. You have done much shooting, Mr. Pete?"

"Not much. Mostly bird shooting."

"He's lying," Wilson said. "He's shot a lot more than I have."

Delville smiled with complete understanding. We were all being modest. Great sportsmen are all modest, his smile seemed to be saying. No one but a fool and a green-horn boasts before the hunt starts. "I am not worried," he said.

"Now everything is laid on, isn't it, René?" Wilson asked with concern.

"Everything," Delville replied. "The hunting car, the boys, the camp. Everything."

"I think you'll get what you're after, John," Basil Owen put in.

Wilson looked satisfied. He raised his glass. "To the big game," he announced.

"To the sport," Delville replied.

We drank. "The only thing that's worth while in life," I said. "The only true thing. The greatest, most absorbing passion of them all."

Wilson looked at me with extreme irritation, but he said nothing.

Delville nodded wisely. "The thing that man has done longest on this earth," he observed.

"Well, not quite," I said. Everyone laughed cheerfully.

"Shall we drink to the other too?" Hodkins asked. It was obvious that he already felt very much at home with us.

"By all means," Wilson said. He raised his glass. "Hod, here's to the thing man has done even longer than hunt."

"A most pleasant custom," the pilot said, and blushed. He was such a nice little man that I had already forgiven him for his part in Wilson's joke. The company broke up, and we went outside into the stagnant night. A young Negro in a torn shirt, wearing a chauffeur's cap, was waiting for us. Hodkins and I got into his car. Wilson waved to us from the steps of the restaurant. He was staying at the Sans Souci.

"Good night, guys," he called to us.

It was a strange place, Stanleyville, very much like a small Southern town, complete with neon lights and poverty-stricken Negroes and large department stores on the main street, as well as a district of solid family houses built in neat rows along the side streets. Only the forest which served everywhere as a backdrop gave it an African atmosphere. It seemed to be lurking behind everything, behind the short streets, and along the other side of the Congo River, a mass of thick growth, straining toward the façade of civilization that had somehow been carved out of its side.

"You've got an awfully good crowd," Hod said happily.

"Not what I expected at all. Wilson seems to be such a decent sort."

"He's a dream."

We drove up in front of the veranda of the Sabena Hotel. There was no music now, only a large group of weary passengers in transit to some other hot city in the Congo. The native waiters were standing idly around waiting to close up. A very fat Belgian, the manager of the restaurant, was screaming at them in Swahili.

"Shall we have a nightcap?" Hodkins asked.

"No, I can't face the race problem again this late."

The pilot looked astonished. Then he seemed to understand. "Oh, I quite agree," he said. "Those boys here are awfully poor lot. Worst bunch I've seen in Africa. Impudent, lazy. I wish I had a few of them on my place in Kenya. I'd make them hop."

"Good night, Hod," I said.

He smiled pleasantly. I knew that he was a thoroughly nice little man, gentle, well mannered, decent. His attitude toward the natives was just a natural by-product of living in Africa. There was no use even including it in an evaluation of his character.

I walked down a well-kept gravel path to the bungalow where I had been given a room. I unlocked the door and went inside. There was a fan revolving slowly in the ceiling over the bed, stirring the heavy air. I stripped off my clothes and took a cold shower. In a few minutes I had forgotten Wilson and Africa. I slept in a hot, black void.

A hand reached out of the darkness and shook my shoulder. I sat up, my eyes painfully heavy. Wilson was standing over my bed, fully dressed in bush jacket, breeches, and mosquito boots. It was just getting light outside.

"Wake up, kid," he said in a stern whisper.

"What's the matter, John?"

"The guns," he whispered angrily. "You forgot about them last night."

"Well, so did you."

I could see that he was trying to control his temper. "What the hell difference does that make? At least I woke up and thought about them."

"What do you want to do about it?"

"Clean them, of course."

"Right now?"

"Certainly, right now. I'll start on them. You get dressed and meet me on the porch outside."

There was no use arguing about it. I got out of bed and found the rifles for him. He carried them outside.

"Hurry up," he said menacingly from the door. I dressed and followed him. It was ten minutes past five. The white bungaloes of the hotel looked uninhabited. The chairs were piled up on the tables on the veranda. The only sign of life was Wilson, seated on the low brick wall that ran along the front of the porch. He had rolled up the sleeves of his bush jacket and was working a ramrod through the barrel of one of the magnums.

"What a damn fool thing to do," he said savagely as I approached. "You'd think it was enough to forget once. No, we had to do it twice, so that now all our rifles are pitted and full of rust."

"It was a damn fool thing to fire them in the first place."

He stopped working and glared at me. "You think so, do you? You think it was foolish to try out the rifles when our lives depend on them. Well, in that case why don't you go back to bed? Why don't you forget all about the rifles, and go back to sleep and tomorrow when we go hunting just get yourself a big, heavy stick."

"I'm up now. Why don't you just relax a little, take it easy."

"Oh sure," he said sarcastically. "That would be the clever thing to do. We leave in a couple of hours, so why not just relax. That would be smart. Real smart."

"It would be smart not to go at all," I said. "We haven't got time to do any real hunting. Five days. What the hell is that? Most people take two months to go on safari, and even that's hurrying matters."

"You can stay, God damn it. You don't have to go."

"It's too late now," I said. "I've got to find out the end of the story." I picked up one of the rifles and dismounted the barrels. Wilson was working hard with the ramrod. I watched him, and as I did so a small daydream passed quickly through my mind. We were out among wild beasts, on the plains of Africa. Wilson refused to listen to the warnings of Delville, our mentor and guide. He went after a wounded lion. The animal got him. I killed the lion, just a little too late. The company arrived from England, and I met them with the news. Someone else had to take over the picture. They decided to let me try my hand. The accident started me out on a whole new career.

"Are you just going to sit there and sulk?" Wilson asked. "Come on, kid. For Christ's sake. Control your black, hopeless moods."

"I was just wondering who was going to take over the picture in case something happened to you," I said.

"Not what you're thinking, in any case," Wilson said. "I'm going to see to that. I'm going to leave specific instructions with Landau that whatever happens you will not benefit by my death. That's just to protect myself. I know something about psychopathic personalities. You might suddenly get the idea to become a movie director at my expense, and that's not the kind of thoughts I want you to be thinking while you're standing fifty yards behind me with a rifle in your hand."

"You're charming," I said.

"I suppose the thought never occurred to you?"

"It did, but I wouldn't step into your shoes no matter what."

"What would stop you? Sentiment? Don't make me laugh."

"No, not sentiment. I'd never kill you to get ahead. I'd do it for the good of mankind."

"And if they asked you, I suppose you'd refuse to take over the picture . . ."

"That's right. I don't like the script."

He stopped working and stared at me. Then he smiled in spite of himself. "You have a small soul, Pete. I'm just beginning to realize it after all these years. You're a coward, and you have a small, envious nature. Whatever limitations you have, they are all directly traceable to these two traits. You hope for an accident to do away with me. If you were really the guy I've been thinking you were for all these years, you wouldn't rely on an accident. Either you'd kill me to get my job, or you'd die with me, a victim of whatever fate I chose for myself. But that's not you. You are a correct little guy with dirty thoughts, and the accident never happens, and so you never get where you want to be."

"And you're a monster," I said quietly. "A monster with talent, but not the real talent people generally suppose. Not imagination, or lyricism, or any specific artistic talent. No, you just have the ability to look inside people and find their smallest, meanest thoughts. And that's what comes out in your movies."

"Uh-huh." Wilson nodded. "Now we know each other. A good time for it to happen, too."

"That's what long trips are for," I said. "We came to Africa so that we could get some insight into one another's being."

"That's right. A purely educational trip."

I heard footsteps on the porch behind us. Hodkins appeared. "You chaps having a heart-to-heart chat this morning?" he asked pleasantly.

"We certainly are, Hod," Wilson said. "We are investigating each other's souls. It's the most fascinating thing a man can do at this hour."

Hodkins beamed, and picked up the barrels of the rifle Wilson had been cleaning. He squinted through the bores. "Not bad. Might stand inspection if the C.O. was short-sighted, and had lost his glasses." He rubbed his hands together. "Well, I'm going out and see if our ship's all ready to go. By the time I get back, I hope breakfast will be ready."

"I'll go with you, Hod," I said.

We went across the road to the airport. The Rapide was parked on the grass, just as we had left her. Hodkins crawled inside and stumbled over a native boy asleep on the cabin floor. He cursed and screamed in Swahili, while the native ran off, his bare feet splashing through the puddles next to the runway. Hodkins declared over and over again that if he'd had a rifle he would have shot the boy.

"Why didn't you lock the door last night?" I asked him. "This couldn't have happened if you'd done that."

"Don't have a key," he fumed. "Blast his black hide, anyway. The whole bloody cabin stinks like an Egyptian whorehouse."

We pushed open the windows in the pilot's compartment, and Hodkins ran the motors. Then we propped open the door, and started back toward the hotel.

"Don't worry about it, Hod," I said. "The minute we get up in the air it'll be all right."

"Bloody awful way to run an airport," Hodkins said. He was furious. His eyes gleamed, and his fists were clenched as we walked along. "That's the Belgians for you. A sentry out there is something they just haven't thought of."

"That *was* probably the sentry," I said.

"I wouldn't be a bit surprised."

We found Wilson having breakfast with Basil Owen. They were discussing the living quarters that were being built on the location site. It was obvious that Wilson was not very interested in what the unit manager had to say, and that he listened only out of a vague sense of duty.

"Tell Pete all about it," he said as I sat down at the table. "He'll probably take over the picture anyway." He got up. "I'm going to see that Delville is all ready to go, Hod. We should leave in half an hour."

Owen watched Wilson as he crossed the veranda, carrying both of the big rifles. Then he shook his head. "Is he always like this just before a production starts?" he asked.

"Like what, Basil?"

"Disinterested. He acts as if he couldn't care less."

"That's a passing mood. He'll be all right after he's killed his elephant."

Hodkins and I shared the two slices of pineapple that remained. One of the less grumpy native waiters brought us coffee and rolls and marmalade. After a while Delville appeared, accompanied by his wife. He was dressed very much the way he had been the previous evening. He wore a suede jacket, a pith helmet, and heavy woolen trousers. His wife, a plump, rather pretty woman, looked as if she were ready for a summer day in the city.

"Is Monsieur Wilson ready?" Delville asked once we had all been introduced.

"He's been looking for you," I said. "He'll probably come back here if he can't find you."

Delville mopped his brow. He had a pleasant face despite his corpulence. His wife patted her husband possessively on the arm. "You will be careful with my René?" she asked, her voice rising with typical French inflection.

"Very careful," I said.

"I want him to come back."

Delville looked embarrassed. "She worries," he said with a shrug of his shoulders. "I have gone hunting for fifteen years in the Congo, and still she worries."

Wilson appeared, followed by a native boy, heavily loaded with baggage. "Well, René," he said, evidently delighted to see the Belgian. "And Madame." He bent over and kissed Madame Delville's hand. "You have come to say good-by, no?" There was the usual trace of the Mexican accent, and the sweet, ingratiating smile.

"I have come to ask you to be careful with him," Madame Delville said.

"*Chérie,*" the game warden moaned.

"We'll take good care of him, dear," Wilson said. He looked over at the rest of us, raising his eyebrows slightly. "Well, guys," he said, "shall we do this thing?"

Half an hour later we were rising steadily upward once more, passing through the first layer of gray clouds. Occasionally we caught a glimpse of the jungle below us, a mass of tangled, wet foliage surrounding the high leafy masts that had flicked past our wings the day before. It looked harmless now, and remote, a huge green carpet over which it was quite natural to jump, a part of the world which was simple to conquer.

Delville smiled happily. "He is a good pilot, no?" he asked.

"One of the best."

"And the airplane. It flies well for such an old machine."

"Oh, very well. Especially while the motors are running."

"Pardon me?"

"Nothing. A joke. Tell me, Monsieur Delville . . ."

"René," he corrected me. "On safari everyone has to be friends."

I quite agree, I thought. "René, what exactly is the plan?" I asked.

"We fly to Tatsumu. There is a car waiting for us there. It takes us to a camp on the shore of Lake Albert. There we hunt."

"Near Masindi?" I asked.

"The other side of the lake," he said. "The Congo side."

I nodded. Laing had been right. We would hunt approximately thirty miles from where he had suggested we go in the first place, only we had flown eight hundred useless miles to get there.

"Is there a lot of game?" I asked. "Buffalo? Elephant?"

He thought it over before he replied. "Elephant, yes. Not so much buffalo. They are at the mouth of the Semliki. We can go there another time."

"What else is there beside elephant?"

"Antelope; much antelope."

We've had that, I thought. We've chased as many antelope as I want to chase. Still, the absence of buffalo was good news. It eliminated the most dangerous of our natural enemies.

"Then pig," Delville said, "leopard, lion, hippo . . ."

"Guinea fowl?" I asked.

He smiled, his huge mouth making a black half-moon across his face. "Always guinea fowl," he said. "They are good for the pot."

"For Christ's sake," Wilson's voice interrupted disgustedly. "Are you still running after your youth? Is that the only crime you want to repeat?"

"I didn't know you were listening," I said. "I would never have dared ask the question."

Wilson shook his head and turned away. The book on big-game rifles slid from his lap. I reached out and picked it up. Chapter Three was devoted to rifles for elephant hunting. The first sentence rang like a clear bell inside my head. "Where all dangerous game are concerned," I read, "the beginner should use the most powerful rifle he can handle with comfort and ease."[1] The noise of the motors changed abruptly. We fell a hundred feet toward the wet forest. I tightened my safety belt and continued my studies. "Beginner" was certainly a term that applied to all of us, with the probable exception of Delville. I read on. The plane rose slightly and fell again. Rain battered the flimsy wings. The words I read seemed to stand out with clear, biblical simplicity. I touched Wilson's shoulder.

"I'd like to read you a paragraph," I said.

He looked a little annoyed. "I've read the book," he said.

"I know. There's just one passage here that I'd like you to hear again."

"Go ahead," he said.

I started reading aloud, trying to keep my voice audible above the noise of the motors.

"There is an even more dangerous proposition than

[1]Taylor, *Big Game and Big Game Rifles.*

the stampeding elephant [I read]. When closing with a herd of elephant in thick cover you are supposed to place each and every member of the herd before opening fire. Now this sounds very well on paper, and should always be done where possible. But it all too frequently happens in actual practice that, in dense, matted tangles of thorn bush, it is a physical impossibility to manoeuver round and place the individual beasts. Consequently, there may be a nervous or peevish cow standing so close to you on the other side of a thick bush that you could touch her with an outstretched walking stick, had you known that she was there and felt like doing so. But the first intimation that you have of her existence at all is a shrill, trumpeting blast on the heels of the shot you may have fired at some other member of the herd. You look up and find her tusks and trunk literally right over your head. There is no question of it being a charge; she has not got the necessary room in which to charge. It is just a vicious attack. You will not have the time in which to even throw the rifle to your shoulder, much less in which to aim. It is just a case of blazing off in her face with the butt of your rifle on a level with your waist."[2]

"Yes?" Wilson said.

"You've read it?"

"I have."

"O.K."

He turned away from me, disgusted. I stretched out, loosened the safety belt, and fell asleep.

Bright sunlight glaring in through the windows of the cabin woke me up. It was hot again, and there was grassland under the wings. The plane banked sharply and we started down toward the red runway of Tatsumu airport. We sat in silence as the Rapide slid down over the edge of the field, veered sideways as a gust of cross wind hit us, and then touched the ground. It was a very good landing. No one said anything as we taxied up to the familiar hut. The truck appeared, driven by the Negro in coveralls. The motors stopped. All this has happend before, I thought. Wilson and Delville got out of the plane. We followed them, taking

[2]Ibid.

as much gear as we could carry. The two hunters carried only their ammunition and their weapons. It was as it should be. The bearers did the work for the bwanas.

Delville was on the phone when we arrived in the hut. Wilson was standing near him, looking worried.

"Things are fouled up again," he said in a low, ominous voice. "There's no car to take us to the hunting camp."

Delville shook his head. He looked harassed. "Lebeau has a car," he said. "He will take us."

I smiled. Wilson looked dangerous. "And if he doesn't want to. Then what?" he asked.

"He will take us," the Belgian said. "He knows who I am. We will pay him, and he will take us."

A horn blew outside, signaling the arrival of the De Soto, and there was the familiar cloud of dust. I watched Lebeau as he came toward the hut, his eyes on the plane. It was obvious that he knew at once what was in store for him, and I couldn't help but feel sorry for the man. He stumbled as he stepped inside the hut.

"*Ah, Monsieur Lebeau*," Delville said warmly. He put the phone back into its leather case, and the two men shook hands. "*Bonjour. Ça va, mon vieux?*"

"*Ça va*," Lebeau answered in a toneless voice. He glanced apprehensively at Wilson and the rest of us. Wilson smiled and moved forward, his right hand extended.

"*Bonjour, Monsieur Lebeau*," he said with false friendliness.

"*Côm' ustá, amigo?*" I said. "How are theengs in Tatsumu?"

28

There were five craters in the road, laid out in an unavoidable pattern, and although Lebeau managed to miss the first two, he was not as fortunate with the three that remained. The right front wheel hit hard and then I could hear the frame banging down on the rear axle. Lebeau's hands tightened on the plastic steering wheel and we went on, raising a thick cloud of dust behind us.

"Shocking road, isn't it?" Hodkins said. He was wedged in on my right, while on the other side of me was a small mountain of luggage. The front seat, although a good deal wider, was even more crowded. Wilson was on the outside, his thin arm hanging out of the window; Delville was in the center, next to the silent driver. There had been a long argument about the car back in Tatsumu, and since its conclusion Lebeau had not said a word. He had lost, as I knew he would, and now there was nothing for him to say. He merely drove on, regretting his fate and listening to the rattles that were developing everywhere in the body of the De Soto.

"It would have been a good deal simpler to fly," Hodkins observed. I gave him a dirty look. Wilson grinned and nodded. Despite the cramped quarters of the front seat, Delville managed to turn around.

"You understand my position as an official," he explained for the twentieth time. "If they find out in Stanleyville that I was in an aircraft that violated one of the regulations, I would be the one to blame."

The subject of the argument had been extremely simple. As the car that had or had not been ordered had failed to arrive, two alternatives had presented themselves. One was to get Lebeau to drive us to the hunting camp in his De Soto, and the other was to fly to an air strip that was not more than five miles from the camp. This air strip, because of its size, had been limited to single-engine planes, not exceeding a certain weight, and although the Rapide could easily have landed there, it would still have meant a violation of the government's rules. Hodkins had declared himself willing to take the risk to accommodate John, but Delville had insisted that we go by car. His argument with Lebeau had been a lengthy one, as the hotel proprietor was more than unwilling to take on the journey. Ultimately Delville had prevailed. His connections in the government gave him more power than his actual position of game warden would lead one to suspect. He had taken Lebeau aside and had explained matters to him in French, and not five minutes later we were all crammed into the De Soto and on our way.

"No use even talking about it any more," Wilson said. "Anyway, I believe Monsieur Lebeau is enjoying the trip."

"I don't think he is," Delville said sadly. "It is very hard on the car."

"I don't think so," Wilson said. "Out West the roads are often this bad, and people go for hundreds of miles every day."

"In Kenya they're even worse," Hodkins observed.

Lebeau grunted and looked with hatred at Wilson. We passed through a town, the only civilized settlement we had seen since our arrival in Tatsumu. The road did not improve. There were great gaping holes in its surface, large stones crashed up into the steel insides of the fenders, while a fine, constant cloud of dust seeped up through the sides of the car. Ahead of us there was a low range of green mountains and the road wound upwards. We passed a native settlement, one of the many we had driven through that afternoon. They all looked the same, with dilapidated wooden store fronts facing the road. There was always a tailor, and a cobbler and a general store, owned by an Indian tradesman. Scores of miserable-looking Negroes squatted outside, while their children played dangerously close to the path of our car. Often one or two of them would wave: hopeless, small gestures of friendship that would soon be engulfed in thick clouds of dust. The adults scarcely looked up as we went by.

Higher up in the mountains the vegetation changed. The grass was thick, and there were very few trees, and the native villages looked neater as they clung to the small terraces on which they had been built. We rounded a curve and passed three native women in bright red dresses. They had the flat, projecting lips of the Ubangis.

"Well, for God's sake," Wilson said. It was the first time that he had taken notice of anything we had passed on the road.

"You saw the holes in their ears?" Delville asked. "That and the lips are great signs of beauty."

"I wonder who first got the idea to do that to his wife?" Hodkins pondered. "She must have liked him an awful lot to let him gratify such a strange urge."

"It was not for beauty at first," Delville explained. "It was to make the women ugly, so that the Arab slavers would not take them to sell on the coast."

"That's right," Wilson said. "It only became a fashion with the years." He turned to face the back seat. "Make a hell of a scene for a picture, wouldn't it? The Arabs are in town and this fellow decides that he doesn't want to lose his wife because he's nuts about her, and the only way to keep her is to carve her up. So he looks lovingly at her once more, and then gets out the potato peeler. Well, of course it works. The Arabs won't touch her, but once she's all better, he finds he doesn't care much for her either. He starts prowling around after the dames in his village that are not perforated or stretched, and this leads to a hell of a scene."

He stuck out his lips, and played it for us. " 'You did this to me, you black son of a bitch,' she says to him. 'I'd be a happy woman in some Arab's tent if you hadn't had your bright idea. Now you've got to stick to me.' "

Hodkins was enjoying the show. I smiled vaguely.

"You like it, Pete? Well, I'll give it to you. Use it any place it fits."

"It shows deep, poetic compassion," I said. "A sound dramatization of a very sad idea."

Hodkins giggled happily. Wilson turned back to look at him. "You appreciate my stories, don't you, Hod?" he chuckled.

"Yes, I do, John," the pilot said.

"Well, tell that glum-faced bastard next to you to enjoy himself, will you. He's getting me down."

"I'm having a wonderful time, John," I said. "I find you most amusing."

He grinned falsely. "Thank you, old boy," he said. He slid lower in his seat, forcing Delville to make more room for him. His head dropped forward on his chest and soon he was asleep.

He didn't wake up again until very late that afternoon. We had passed over the final mountain range, and were now winding our way down toward the huge expanse of Lake Albert. The late sunlight colored the green hills in front of us, making their soft contours stand out even more vividly. There were many houses now, perched on the hillsides overlooking the lake. Most of them were well built, with neatly clipped tan-colored grass roofs that clung undisturbed to their rafters despite the brisk wind that was now coming up from the valley below us.

There was a truck parked on the side of the road and Lebeau put on the brakes. A few yards behind it we came across two men in white shorts and high leather boots, carrying rifles. The men exchanged greetings with Lebeau, and told him that they had seen a small group of elephants crossing the road. Wilson sat up sleepily.

"What are they saying, kid?" he asked me.

"Nothing much. It seems there are some elephants roaming around the neighborhood."

Wilson stared blankly out of the window, reality dawning on him slowly. "Where?" he asked. "Where are they?"

Delville seemed less excited by the news. "A little further down," he said. "A half mile from here."

"Shouldn't we get the rifles out of the back of the car?" Wilson asked.

Delville looked troubled. "Perhaps," he replied, "although I think they are gone."

"Well, I think we'd better get the rifles out anyway." Wilson opened the door and jumped out. Lebeau unlocked the trunk of the car for him. "Shall we load them, René?"

Delville looked doubtful. "It is better not in the car. Hold the ammunition in your hand. It is safer."

Now the front seat was even more crowded than before. Wilson had trouble closing the door. The barrel of his rifle was a few inches from Delville's nose. As he slammed the door there was the distant trumpeting of an elephant. It was a weird sound, wild and disturbing, like a primitive bugle call.

"Holy God," Wilson said. "Did you hear that?"

"They are far away," Delville observed. He seemed relieved.

"Well, let's go," Wilson said. "What the hell are we waiting for?"

Hodkins beamed. "Might see a little action tonight, eh, John?"

Delville shook his head. "They are gone now," he said. "They have heard the car."

"The wind is blowing toward us," Wilson argued. "They probably haven't heard a thing. Come on. Let's not waste time."

We started down the steep, winding road. The two Belgians had hurried back to their truck, and were following us, keeping not more than thirty yards behind the De Soto.

"Isn't this something?" Wilson said. His face was alive with excitement. "God damn. Elephants. The first crack out of the bat."

But we heard no more trumpeting, and we saw no elephants. A few minutes before we reached the shore of the lake Hodkins suddenly pointed out of the window. "Look! There!" he shouted. The car slid to a stop. A few hundred yards to our right a small herd of antelope stood watching our progress. Just as their cousins in Tatsumu before them, they turned and ran.

"Boy, this country is really full of game," Wilson said enthusiastically. We continued on our way once more. Then there was a small white house overlooking the lake, and Lebeau stopped. The truck made a wide circle around our car and continued on its way. We all got out and tried to move our cramped legs. The road was white and sandy where it ran along the shore of the lake, passing through dense brushland. The sun was down, but it was hotter than it had been any time during the afternoon.

"What happens now, René?" Wilson asked. Delville and Lebeau were standing in front of the car, arguing in French. The backs of their shirts clung to their bodies. Delville came over to us, leaving Lebeau standing a few yards in front of us on the road.

"He does not want to go on," Delville said. "The road is worse from here to the camp."

"How far is it?" Hodkins asked.

"Ten kilometers."

"What does he expect us to do?" Wilson asked. "Walk?"

"He says we should have gone with the truck that passed us."

"Well, why the hell didn't he think of that sooner? Now they're gone."

Delville shrugged. It was a gesture we were to see quite frequently later on. "I will talk to him," he said, and went off to join his compatriot.

Wilson stood watching the two Belgians, as they disputed the matter. In the distance there was the cry of a jackal. Somehow that decided him. He went over to Lebeau. We could hear his voice floating through the still air. "Look, my friend," he said, "try to get this through your head. You can't leave us here. We've got too much gear to carry, and we're certainly not going back to Tatsumu with you tonight."

Delville translated, and then translated Lebeau's reply to Wilson. "He says there's a hotel a few miles back. Just before the place where we passed the truck."

"To hell with that," Wilson said adamantly. "We've got to start hunting tomorrow morning. I've only got a few days left. Ask him how much more he wants to go on."

Delville tried his luck with Lebeau again, but the huge man shook his head adamantly. I could see that his face twitched nervously as he tried to light a cigarette. He seemed also to have acquired a tic since the beginning of our trip.

"He says he doesn't care about himself," Delville translated. "It's the car. He knows he won't be able to make it all the way to the camp. He waited over eighteen months for delivery and he doesn't want to risk spoiling it."

"I'll guarantee him delivery of another one," Wilson said excitedly. "Hell, I'll do better than that. I'll have them send my Cadillac all the way from California and give it to him if something goes wrong."

But all of these promises failed to move Lebeau. Wilson was losing control of himself. "Look, René," he said, pulling at the game warden's shoulder, "just ask him what he wants. Ask him what he's always dreamed of having. The one thing that his heart desires. Ask him, for God's sake." Wilson's voice was rising as he spoke. He gestured wildly. Lebeau shot him a quick frightened glance, and then suddenly he ground his cigarette into the sand of the road and started back toward the car, sputtering French.

"What's he saying? What's happened?" Wilson asked.

Delville walked back toward the car. "He said all right," he translated in a tired voice. "He says he wants nothing. He's sure he can't make it, but he'll try. Just to prove to you how wrong you are."

"Well, by golly, that's a real manly decision," Wilson said. "Let's get in before he changes his mind."

We scurried back into the car. Lebeau started the motor and we bounced forward, following the tracks in the sandy soil. There was the constant, grinding sound of the crankcase hitting the raised center of the road, and the occasional clash of metal as the rifles in the front seat banged together. No one spoke. We were all too busy clinging onto the sides of the car.

I found myself feeling sorry for Lebeau. I knew that Wilson had no feeling about automobiles. He had demonstrated this fact often enough throughout all of the years I had known him. They were objects to be mistreated, as far as he was concerned. They were dead. They felt no pain and no pleasure, and he had no understanding of what they could mean to someone who liked smoothly functioning machinery. I had once tried to explain to him that people could feel as strongly about their cars as he felt about his horses, but he had scoffed at the idea. It was merely a sign of a retarded development, he had told me. It was clearly what he felt about Lebeau.

"We're doing fine," he said now. "Make it easily."

Just then the road turned, and fell off through a small hollow. I caught a glimpse of gray stagnant water standing in the wheel tracks. I tried to shout a warning but it was too late. Lebeau shifted quickly into second gear, and bore down on the gas pedal. His hands clenched the steel crossbars and he leaned well back like a rider going over a high jump in the Grand National. The car hit hard, and bounced clear of the first hollow, and then landed solidly in the gray water ahead of us. Everything creaked then, the springs of the cushions underneath us, the steel doors, the wheels, the chrome molding that ran along the bottom of the fenders. We moved sideways, sliding in the mud, and then quite suddenly we stopped. The engine was dead. Only the water of the puddle still moved as it sloshed around the thick tires.

"Good Lord," Hodkins said, "he shouldn't have tried that. He should have stopped and made us get out."

"He's a fatalist," I answered. "He knew it was no use trying to avoid his doom. There are fifty even deeper mudholes farther on."

"Shut up," Wilson said, without turning his head. He spoke to Delville. "Ask him what he's waiting for. Tell him to start the engine."

Delville did as he was told. Without saying a word Lebeau reached forward and touched the starter button. There was a strange grinding sound in the motor, and Lebeau cut the ignition. He turned very slowly to look at Wilson. Hs face was tragic. There was no complaint, no anger, only complete despair. *"Voilà,"* he said. That was all. He got out of the car, took a large blue handkerchief out of his trouser pocket and wiped his face. The worst had happened, and he undoubtedly felt relieved. At least the period of dread waiting was over. Wilson got out on the other side. He went over to Lebeau and put his hand on his shoulder.

"I am very sorry, Monsieur Lebeau," he said. "I was wrong."

Lebeau shrugged his hand away and walked in silence up the road. Delville went after him.

"I want to know what's going to happen now," I said. "In half an hour it'll be dark."

Hodkins shook his head. "I haven't the foggiest notion," he said. He stuck a cigarette under his mustache and lit it. "I'm sure there will be some walking to do, however, and I'm fairly certain I know who's going to have to do it."

But he was wrong. Both Delville and Lebeau seemed to feel that this was a Belgian crisis, and their responsibility. They came back to the car, and Delville loaded his rifle. He put six extra rounds into the pocket of his suede jacket, and prepared to set out down the road. I went over to Lebeau to console him.

"I'm very sorry, Monsieur Lebeau. But I don't think it's serious. A slight wound."

He shrugged. "We will see," he said, his eyelids twitching.

"We will go and get the truck," Delville said. "They are at the camp, I believe."

"Suppose they're out hunting. Then we'll have to wait here until they come back."

"It is almost too late for hunting now," Delville answered. "They will have returned." He looked down the road with concern. "Do not walk very far away from the car," he cautioned me in French. "This is a lion country, and there are many leopards about at this hour."

"We'll wait here. Don't take too long."

We watched them as they started down the road, the two fat men in their sweat-soaked shirts going off into the twilight. Wilson yawned and got back into the car to sleep. The sandy road ahead of us lay empty. In the faint-

ly colored sky, buzzards were circling. Hodkins took out
the big rifles and handed one to me.

"Never know what might turn up," he said. It was getting dark very quickly. There was the buzzing of mosquitoes around us in the warm air. "Poor old Lebeau," Hodkins said. "Poor old sod. Oh, each man kills the thing he
loves, and then is satisfied."

"What about his wife?" I asked. "She'll worry if he
doesn't show up tonight."

"There isn't a damn thing we can do about that," Hodkins answered. His small, sharp eyes were constantly
fixed on the road ahead of us. "Look," he said after a
short silence, "a jackal."

"After the corpse of the De Soto, no doubt," I said. We
could see a faint movement on the road ahead of us, and
then the animal was gone. "Not an ideal place to spend
the night, is it?"

"It won't be so cramped now that the two fat boys are
gone."

We got back into the car. As the door closed Wilson
awoke. "Are they here?" he asked.

"No, John," Hodkins replied gently. "We'll call you
when they arrive."

It was more than two hours later when the lights of the
truck finally became visible. Lebeau was seated up in
the cab next to the native driver. He got out and locked
the doors of his car after we had emptied it of all our belongings. Then we all climbed into the back of the truck.
Delville seemed to be happier.

"It will be all right," he said to Wilson as the truck
turned and started back down the road. Its feeble yellow
lights illuminated the country a few yards ahead of us.
"But you must watch now. It is very possible that we find
a leopard at this hour. Then you can shoot him."

Wilson loaded his rifle immediately. We clung to the
dilapidated wooden sides of the truck as it bounced along
the bumpy road. Delville smiled at me, his round, good-
natured face somewhat restored by the relief he felt.

"All's well that ends well," he said.

"It hasn't ended well yet, René."

He laughed falsely.

There was not a leopard or a lion on the road. Not
even a jackal crossed our path. The road crossed a dry

river bed, and then rose once more, and there was the strong smell of water. We were very near the lake now. The driver clashed the gears, and we passed through a native village, lying in utter darkness. A single voice floated through the stillness after we had passed, a long, connected jabbering sound. Then there was a short stretch of road lined by neat rows of white stones, and we were in the hunting camp.

The truck stopped. Ahead of us a faint light shone out of an open doorway. We climbed down, dusty and tired. Delville led the way. There was sand underfoot as we followed him, and an instant later we all found ourselves inside a large grass hut, at the far end of which there was a bar. There were a few crude tables and chairs, but I hardly noticed them as I entered, for the walls and the exposed rafters overhead claimed all of my attention. They were covered with trophies. There was a huge buffalo head, and the half-decayed trunk and ears of an elephant directly over the bar. The supporting timbers on all sides of us were heavily hung with antlers of all kinds, and the grass sides of the hut were decorated with hides and the skins of snakes.

"Well, isn't this something?" Wilson said. He had the look of a man entering paradise. His eyes moved continuously around the ceiling of the room. He hardly noticed the strange bald man in shorts who moved toward him, his hand extended.

"This is Monsieur Zibelinsky," Delville said. "This is his camp."

Wilson shook hands with the man. "I'm very pleased to meet you," he said.

And then I noticed a familiar figure standing at the far end of the bar, almost hidden by the darkness. I recognized the cut of the khaki trousers, the wide leather belt; the big, tattered hat with the snakeskin band was all too familiar. It was Paget, the sour white hunter who had been employed as a draftsman, and it was immediately evident that he had not changed. He laughed sarcastically as he came toward us across the sand floor.

"Well, by God, here they are," he said in his clipped accent. "The hunters from Hollywood." He could hardly have found a more ill-chosen phrase of greeting.

29

Despite the presence of Paget, the place where we had now arrived seemed overwhelmingly pleasant. It was amazing to find a large room with fairly comfortable chairs and a solid roof. We had all believed ourselves to be at the end of the world, and the sudden appearance of a bar with glasses and liquor made us feel better. John, of course, was more carried away than any of the rest of us, and I could understand him momentarily. It was like a skier finding a beautiful, clean chalet at the foot of an enormous mountain, with long, unbroken snow fields reaching down to the front door. For this was a well-prepared starting place for what he most wanted to do at this moment in his life. It was apparently the entrance to a vast country filled with game; it was also a base to which he could return at night and sit among the trophies of other hunters and drink his beer and talk about the day's kill.

I must say that the hut appealed to me that way too. It had a romantic flavor. The people who lived here were undoubtedly special people, and their guests, no matter what happened to them later on, were brave, adventurous men, devoted momentarily to a hazardous life.

Wilson took off his large hat and sat down in one of the deep bamboo chairs. He crossed his legs, so that the puttees rested on each other, and took a sip of his beer.

"Well, Victor," he said in his most fatherly voice, "what brings you here?"

Pagent sauntered over to him and stood leaning against a beam. He, too, sipped his beer in a pointedly relaxed manner. "This is the way all your equipment is routed," he said. "It comes across Lake Albert and enters the Congo not ten miles down the road. I've got truckloads waiting over on the other side now."

"You don't say," Wilson replied. "Well, what are *you* doing over here, if I may ask?"

Paget put a cigarette in his mouth with practiced elegance. I had the feeling that he had rehearsed almost all of his minor gestures in front of a mirror long before he showed them to the rest of the world. He tapped the package of cigarettes, and one leaped out. Then he put the package up to his mouth, and the cigarette was in place. The lighter was another eloquent movement, a flick of his thumb, and then a slow bringing of fire to cigarette, the lighter burning inside his cupped hands. With this he showed that he was a man used to living outdoors on the plains. "What am I doing here?" he repeated arrogantly. "Well, I'm seeing to it that all this stuff is properly shipped. Ironing out the snags, as it were. The Belgians want a bloody great bond posted before we can bring the camera gear in, and we just haven't got the money. I'm trying to clear the way so we can move on without it."

"That's a very important function," Wilson said sarcastically.

"You're damn right it is. And I'm not so sure we'll get your stuff through."

"Where's Lockhart?" Wilson asked. "I thought that was part of his job?"

"He's on the other side," Paget said, with a short wave of his hand, "arranging for the shipping."

"I see. And you're just spending the night here."

"That's right." The cigarette was in a holder now, and Paget spoke with it clamped in his teeth.

"You wouldn't want to go out hunting with us, would you?" Wilson asked softly.

"Wouldn't mind a bit," Paget said, "but this here's more important. Customs bloke's coming over from Tatsumu tomorrow or the next day to log all this stuff in."

"I see," Wilson said. "Well, I certainly hope everything goes well, Vic." His tone was patronizing, but Paget seemed not to notice it. Wilson now turned to Zibelinsky. "Quite a place you have here," he said.

The Pole bowed. He had a wild mustache, that, although it was not as thick as Hodkins', stuck out much farther on both sides of his face.

"It is a pleasure to have you as our guests," he said. A

woman entered through the doorway behind the bar. She was quite handsome, in a weather-beaten way, with a strong bony face covered with leathery skin. As she came out into the room I saw that she was wearing shorts. An instant later I realized why; she had excellent legs, with sturdy brown calves, and well-formed knees and thighs. Zibelinsky introduced her as his wife Dorshka. She welcomed us in a deep Russian voice. "A pleasure to see you all," she said. She sounded like one of those slinky hostesses you find in the Russian night clubs in Paris, and she moved with the studied grace of a lady of quality. Only the tight blue shorts made the whole thing seem incongruous.

I asked where I could wash my hands, and Dorshka took me to my dwelling. As we followed her I noticed that beyond the main hut there were at least eight other smaller huts. These were made of mud, with the same kind of thatched roof that covered the main house. Each one of them had a little porch, and then a windowless interior with two cots in the center of the room. In the back of my hut there was a small alcove equipped for bathing. A crude wooden stand with a tin bowl was on one side, while on the other there was a concrete square over which a big oil drum was held in place by thick bamboo poles. A rotting rubber hose with a shower end came out of the bottom of the drum.

I soon discovered that the water barely trickled out of the shower end, but that didn't matter. I found that I could tip the entire drum forward, and get fairly wet that way. I changed clothes and joined the others in a nightcap. Everyone was feeling much better. Wilson and Lebeau were already on excellent terms. They were both drinking Irish whisky, and the disaster of the De Soto seemed almost to be forgotten.

Only early the next morning did trouble again enter our lives. It was barely light outside when Hodkins woke me, but I could already hear voices arguing in the distance.

"We're in awful trouble," Hodkins said. "There's no truck."

"Where did it go?"

"Back to the fishery where it belongs. Lebeau went with it."

"What about the hunting car?"

"That was it."

"You mean the truck was to serve as that?"

"Exactly. We're stranded again."

I dressed and went down to the main hut. It was getting light over the lake. The small trees in front of the camp were silhouetted against the graying sky. Behind us the green hills rose into the night. The country leading up to the hills was rolling grassland, covered with scrub oak and thick clusters of bushes.

I went into the hut. There was a large coffeepot on the table near the door, and a plate of sliced, buttered bread. Wilson, Delville, and Zibelinsky were deep in debate.

"Look, all I know is one thing," Wilson was saying. "We've got to have a car. We can't hunt on foot."

"There is much game near the camp, Mr. Wilson," Zibelinsky protested, "and this afternoon the truck will be back. The boy promised."

"We're going to waste the morning," Wilson said. "God damn it, I know we are."

"Not at all, sir," the Pole said. "The boys are here to take you out. You will hunt here this morning, and you will see that it is very good hunting indeed. I have killed a lion not half a mile from this hut, and that elephant there . . ." He pointed to the rotting trunk and ears. "My wife shot it a half-hour walk from this camp."

Wilson turned to Delville. "I'm worried about this afternoon," he said. "If the truck doesn't come back for us, we're screwed."

"Pardon me?" Delville said. He was still very polite, slightly worried and polite.

"Coincé," I translated roughly.

"Ah, but no," Delville said with desperation once he had understood. "They have promised me. It will come back after lunch. You will see. Everything is arranged."

"I certainly hope so," Wilson said. He went past me out of the hut. Delville shrugged.

"He is very nervous, Monsieur Wilson."

"He's anxious. This is his only chance to hunt."

"Ah, but it will be all right. You will see. Everything has been arranged. The boys are waiting."

They were indeed waiting for us behind the main hut, seven of them, as oddly dressed a group of natives as I had ever seen. The one who was obviously their leader was gotten up in khaki shorts and a U. S. Navy middy blouse, winter service. On his head he wore a Wac's summer garrison cap; he carried a wooden spear with a steel head. Most of the others were in shorts as well, but they were not wearing blues. Instead they wore heavy sleeveless sweaters, or torn shirts, most of which were U.S. government issue. All were barefoot, armed with long sticks. Only the two chief hunters carried spears. They listened intently, as Zibelinsky addressed them in Swahili.

"It's amazing to see what an influence the Army quartermaster has had on the world," I said to Wilson.

He nodded without looking at me. He seemed to be caught up in Zibelinsky's talk as well, which seemed odd, as I knew that his Swahili was as limited as my own. I glanced over at him. He looked like a skinny hunting dog, waiting mutely for his master to stop wasting time in conversations with his wife, and leave for the morning fields.

"What are they saying, John?" I asked.

"Huh?" He looked blankly at me. "What are they saying? How the hell do I know? I just know something else is screwed up." He touched Zibelinsky on the arm. "What's the matter?" he asked.

"The chief hunter was unable to come this morning," the Pole replied. "He had to help out with some problem in the village."

"Doing what, for Christ's sake?" Wilson asked. The dawn was coming up over the lake. The first rays of the sun slanted across the horizon.

"I don't know," Zibelinsky said. "Some of them say he had to go after some lost cattle, and others say he had to help his wife around the house."

"Around the house!" Wilson exploded. "That can't be!"

It was at this unfortunate moment that Delville arrived on the scene. He was freshly shaved, and his long dark hair was neatly combed and still moist. He looked like a very fat businessman who had had a good night's rest and was ready for a day on the golf course. A small, black boy walked behind him carrying his rifle. Wilson turned on him with excited fury.

"Now the hunter's not here, René. He's helping his wife with the goddam laundry. Or he's taking his youngest son out in the stroller. Holy God. Hasn't anything been organized?"

Delville got bright red. He shouldered his way into the

circle of natives and began speaking painfully slow Swahili to them, but no immediate solution seemed to be forthcoming. Wilson turned and walked away. He began pacing nervously up and down on the road behind us. After a few minutes he called out to Delville once more.

"The sun is coming up. In half an hour it'll be too late to start at all."

The Belgian turned away from the boys. "We'll go," he said. "The chief hunter will be here at two-thirty."

"You better make sure," I said quietly. "John's about ready to blow his top."

René nodded. He looked disturbed and nervous. "He'll be here," he said. He called out to the boys and they rose in a body.

"Do any of these guys know where they're going?" Wilson asked.

"Yes. The boy with the hat. He is the second best hunter in the village."

"O.K.," Wilson said. He looked resigned, and fell in behind the boy with the middy blouse and the Wac hat. We started out across the flat land behind the camp, moving in single file. Delville and Hodkins were directly behind Wilson, while I brought up the rear. The rest of the boys followed us through the wet grass, jabbering among themselves while they adjusted their various burdens.

We went toward the mountains. It was light now and the air was cool. A long white cloud hung directly under the peaks of the hills in front of us. It seemed unlikely that we would find any game in so peaceful a countryside. All at once I saw Hodkins break into a run. He caught up with Wilson, and I could see him pointing to something ahead of the column. The native boy in the middy stopped now, too. Then very slowly Wilson, Hodkins, and the boy started forward, their heads bent low, their feet coming high up out of the grass as they moved forward.

I could see nothing. Finally Wilson stopped behind a bush, and aimed. He seemed to be waiting an awfully long time, and I realized that he was fiddling with the safety lock on his rifle. Hodkins was aiming his rifle too, and then Wilson fired. Hodkins shot an instant later, and to our left now, passing us at a range of about a hundred and fifty yards, I saw an enormous herd of antelope. Hodkins fired again, and the herd continued unharmed on its way.

The hunter moved on; Wilson followed him without looking back. Hodkins waited for me to arrive at the place where he was standing.

"Missed," he said.

I nodded.

"They've stopped a few hundred yards farther on."

"They know when they're safe."

We followed the hunters. All at once one of the native boys behind me started pointing excitedly to a large bush to my left. *"Kanga,"* he shouted. *"Mingi Kanga."*

Those were familiar words. I took the shotgun out of the hands of my bearer and started forward. Two guinea fowl rose up in front of the bush. I knocked down the first one and missed the second as it was circling away.

One of the smaller boys ran out and picked up the dead bird. He grinned happily as he brought it back to us.

"Good shot," Hodkins said.

Delville was grinning. "With a good sauce," he beamed, "they taste better than any chicken."

The caravan proceeded on its way. I felt childishly elated, as if I had accomplished some great feat of marksmanship. Actually the birds were large, slow targets, easier to shoot than pheasant or duck.

"I'm proud of you," Hodkins said. "In your own way you're a fine hunter."

"Anything harmless is my meat."

Wilson was waiting for us a few hundred yards farther on. He looked furious.

"Who the hell fired?" he asked.

"I did. I killed a *Kanga.*"

He looked disgusted. "You think we came all this way to shoot birds?" he said. "For God's sake. I was just moving up on the herd and of course when you shot they ran off."

"I'm sorry. I just didn't want us to go hungry tonight."

"Oh, balls," he said disgustedly. "Come up here with me. That's the only way I can control you, I guess. And give that goddam shotgun back to the boy."

I took the Mannlicher and followed him. We had not gone more than fifty yards before we came on another herd of antelope. They stood like beautiful brown statuettes among the squat trees, watching us approach. I kneeled down in the grass and let Wilson go on alone.

Once more he began stalking the game. The boy in the sailor jacket followed him, using the bushes as cover. They stopped halfway between the herd and where I was kneeling and Wilson fired again. I heard the bullet sing as it ricocheted off into the air. The herd broke and ran.

"There's something wrong with this rifle," Wilson said.

I offered him mine. "Try this one."

"What'll you do?"

"I'll watch. One guy shooting is plenty in this kind of country. The minute more than one starts stalking these beasts the jig's up."

It went on like that for hours. The sun rose, and it grew hot. We moved on and on through the grass, running into herd after herd of antelope. Wilson fired more than half a dozen times. Once I thought I heard the bullet strike flesh, but the antelopes raced on ahead of us.

I dropped back and walked with the others. Delville took my place with Wilson.

"Poor John," Hodkins said, his voice full of pity.

"I thought he hit one of them."

"His rifle's too light. You can't stop those big bucks with that small a slug. And of course if we had the truck we could make a mechanized approach and get a hell of a lot closer."

"You could run over them, kill them that way . . ."

The natives behind us were discussing things among themselves, shaking their heads and jabbering. I could see that they were not very impressed with our shooting. In the distance we heard the report of Wilson's rifle again.

"How long do you suppose this will go on?" Hodkins asked. "I'm getting tired."

"Until we run out of ammunition," I said lightly.

"Well, then I suggest we wait here until that happens."

We found a place in the shade and sat down. More than two hours passed. Every once in a while we could hear the distant report of a rifle.

"It's nice country, isn't it?" Hodkins said.

"Do you suppose there's anything here besides antelope?" I asked him.

He shrugged. "You never know in Africa. Might run into anything when you least expect it."

"I think I've had big-game hunting," I said. "It's overadvertised."

"The early morning scenery was jolly impressive," Hod-

278 WHITE HUNTER, BLACK HEART

kins said. "I'll never forget the lake and the mountains and the first antelope standing out there in the bluish air."

The flies droned on over our heads. The shade of the trees grew smaller. All at once one of the boys rose and pointed off across the open country. I picked up my rifle, but then I saw that it was Wilson coming back with Delville and the boy.

His face was bright red. His thin shoulders sagged forward. His bulging eyes were focused on the ground in front of him. As he came past he nodded and went on. Delville stopped under our tree.

"We are going back for lunch," he announced.

"Any luck?" Hodkins asked.

The Belgian shook his head. "Nothing," he said. He looked sad. He had tied his leather jacket around his bulging waist, and his shirt clung to his soft chest.

"Is Wilson upset?" I asked.

Delville shrugged. "I don't know. He doesn't speak."

"Poor John. This is what he's been looking forward to for months. That's why he came to Africa. And he winds up here, in this tropical shooting range, where they have twenty pasteboard antelopes mounted on rails, for the sucker trade. You shoot at them, and then a motor tows them off, and you didn't even get to win a lousy Mickey Mouse doll."

Delville scowled. "You must not joke," he said. "I ask you please not to joke. Under any condition. You must be serious."

"But it's true, isn't it, René? Admit it to your friends. This place is a practical joker's paradise, built by the local chamber of commerce. There's not a live antelope within fifty miles of here. They're all cardboard, all electrically controlled."

"Please," Delville moaned. "It is all going so badly. If you laugh it will make it worse, and he will blame me. He already does. The truck, the absence of the chief hunter . . . it is all my fault."

"Don't worry about it, old boy," Hodkins said. "The worst that can happen is that he'll shoot you. And they say it's a quick way to die."

Delville turned and went off, dragging his long rifle through the brush. We followed him. Half an hour later we arrived in camp. We hadn't gone nearly as far as I had imagined, and had actually never been more than a mile and a half away from the huts. As we moved down the drive next to the lake I saw Paget, standing in the doorway of his cabin, drinking a bottle of beer.

"Good morning, chaps," he said brightly. "Understand you did not do too well."

"Didn't see a really good head, old man," I said.

"Then what was all that banging about? Sounded like the bloody war."

"Target practice."

He grinned smugly. "Go down and get yourself a bottle of beer."

But there was no beer. Zibelinsky's supply was exhausted, and it was unlikely that he would get any more for at least a week. We sat in the large wooden chairs and stared out at the lake. Wilson had taken off his shirt, and he sat hunched over his knees. His thin body was almost as red as his face, and his ribs heaved steadily as he fought to get his breath. Then he began to cough. It seemed almost that he would choke with coughing, that his lungs would burst, that his throat would ultimately come out of his mouth. Finally he regained control of himself.

"Good God Almighty," he said, shaking his head. "I thought sure I'd cough up a lung that time." Dorshka brought us iced tea and we sat in silence, sipping it. Then as lunch was served everyone's mood improved. Hodkins was the brightest of us all. He was enjoying himself; this was a vacation for him. Wilson ate hurriedly and left the table. Through the open sides of the hut we could see him walking slowly back to his quarters.

I turned to Delville. "What about the truck?"

He looked at his watch. "It will be here," he said. "In just a little while. It is too early to go out now anyway, too hot."

The hours passed. Paget went off on foot to the fishing village six miles down the road. The customs official had not arrived, and he decided to go down and look for him. We lay sprawled in the large wooden chairs and listened to Hodkins, as he told us about his life in Kenya, about the house he was building on the edge of the game reserve. He had caught a ten-foot python in his garden, and he had a photograph with him showing six of his boys holding the huge animal. He told us about his wife and his two children, and about how they worked on the house while he was gone, moving the heavy fieldstones into place, and sealing the cracks with mortar. He had a winning manner and a nice way of recounting his disasters. We discovered that he was underpaid, and in constant fear of not being able to pass his flight physical, but the notion that his was a heroic life never seemed to have entered his mind. For a man in his late forties to be flying around the jungle in old-fashioned airplanes seemed something to be accepted as a matter of course. Twice he had been forced down, once in the forest, and once in the desert, but he seemed to think very little of it. He had been saved, which was all that mattered, and the adventures he had had were hardly worth recounting. Only on the subject of natives was he a hopelessly bigoted man.

"Always carry a pistol with me when I drive about," he explained. "Never know when one of these black boys is going to start some trouble. And if you shoot first and ask questions later you can never go wrong."

I looked at my watch. Delville noticed the movement of my head. He got up nervously and went to the door. But there was no sign of a truck. The country around us lay silent.

"You'd better go and wake him. If we're going to do any shooting this evening, we'd better start now."

"But the truck . . ."

"He'll be even more upset if we just let him sleep."

He sighed, and rubbed his hands slowly down his bulging stomach. "If you think it is the thing to do," he said passively.

"I think it is."

He nodded and went off like a doomed man down the path that led to Wilson's hut.

"Poor René . . ."

"It's his own bloody fault," Hodkins said. "He should never have volunteered to arrange this safari."

Wilson appeared, followed by the Belgian. He looked worse than I had ever remembered seeing him, as if he were finally and completely used up. His beard had grown during the heat of the day. His bush jacket flapped around his bony chest.

"What are you going to do, John?" Hodkins asked.

Wilson stared at all of us. "Walk," he said. "There's no truck, so we'll walk."

"What about the boys?"

"Delville's gone to find out. They've probably all gone home. We don't need them anyway. They're no good."

"Might as well wait and see, John," Hodkins said. He was the only one of us who could still talk to him.

"I suppose," Wilson replied. He went outside and stood in the road, his rifle resting in the crook of his elbow, his thin legs slightly bowed as they stuck out of the folds of his mosquito boots. The sun beat down on his large brown hat, but he didn't move. He seemed to be staring out at the empty expanse of lake in front of him.

"Don't you want another glass of iced tea before we start, John?" I called out to him.

He didn't answer. The fact that we were adjusting to the snarled conditions of the safari seemed to enervate him even more than the desperate state of the expedition.

Delville came through the door behind the bar. As Zibelinsky and Dorshka disappeared between meals, we had come to use the entire place as if it were our home. Occasionally when we wanted more ice we would find one of the boys who waited on the table, but the rest of the time we were by ourselves.

"What's the story, René?" Hodkins asked.

"A little better," Delville said. "The chief hunter is coming. One of the other boys has gone out to get him."

"How long before he'll be here?"

"Any minute."

Wilson turned, a skinny Ahab who had momentarily finished with the sea. "Shall we go?" he asked very quietly. "Or have the rest of you decided to stay here?"

"One moment, John," Delville said apologetically. "The chief hunter is coming."

"I don't believe you," Wilson said sweetly. "I don't believe anything you say, René. Not one word. You lie all the time. You have ever since I first met you. You're a pathological liar. You can't help it. It's a disease you've had since childhood."

The soft insidious voice was horribly familiar to me. It was the strange calm that preceded a storm. Delville blushed.

"Why do you say that, John?" he said, trying to accept the whole thing as a joke.

"Because you arranged nothing. Those were all lies you

told back in Stanleyville, about the hunting car, and the guides, and the rest of the arrangements. You were trying to assume a false importance. It's such a pitiful disease that I can't even get angry with you. But I must call your attention to the symptoms."

Delville bristled. He was frightened of Wilson, frightened of the maniacal calm with which he spoke, but he felt he had to defend himself. "I arranged everything," he whined. "I sent messages to two camps. I thought you were coming with a small plane, and then we could have gone elsewhere. You came with the Rapide, and so we had to go to Tatsumu."

Wilson shook his head, and smiled at the rest of us. "Lies," he said, "nothing but lies. Poor fellow."

Delville took a step forward, and tried to look brave. "You cannot insult me like that," he said. "It is not my fault. Things can always go wrong."

"They always do, René," Wilson said. His voice was still soft and pleasant, and he smiled affably at Delville. I knew that he wasn't serious. He was torturing the Belgian, because he himself felt tortured. Someone knocked on the straw blinds that had been lowered to keep out the afternoon sun.

"Come in," Hodkins shouted.

We all turned to the open doorway, and a black man of medium height came timidly into the hut. That is, he moved exactly one foot past the doorway and then stopped. He carried a spear and wore a small green skullcap with a scalloped edge, very much like the caps we had worn in grade school. Long muscular legs, very straight and well formed, came out of his tattered shorts. His feet were gnarled and callused. But his face was what caught the attention of all of us, for it had a long, round crease running down the center of it, like the face of a chocolate Easter Bunny. His eyes were bloodshot, and he seemed to squint. He muttered an apologetic phrase in Swahili.

"The chief hunter," Delville announced proudly.

"Well, for God's sake. You finally came through," Wilson chuckled. "Ask him to come in."

The chief hunter moved a few more paces forward, and raised his hand in salute. Wilson returned it. "Now then, explain what we're after. Tell him we want to find buffalo or elephant. We've chased enough antelope."

Delville translated, and the native replied with a short guttural snort. "What did he say?" Wilson asked eagerly.

Delville looked terribly embarrassed, and then replied with amazing honesty. "He says that for elephant we must have a truck. They are too far away from camp to walk."

"God damn," Wilson said. "Well, ask him if it's any use to go out on foot this afternoon."

"He says it is if we want meat," Delville translated.

"Well, I guess we do," Wilson replied, giving up.

The expedition started out once more; the formation had changed slightly, that was all. First came the chief hunter, followed by Wilson and the game warden, then the boy in the sailor jacket, and then the rest of us.

But from the very first moment that the chief hunter took charge we knew that we were in the hands of an expert. The procedure changed. He did not walk out expectantly into the brush. He studied the ground, he stopped and looked at tracks and antelope dung, and whenever he started forward his eyes moved restlessly like a radar antenna around the fields that surrounded us. We passed a herd of antelope that we would undoubtedly have run after that morning. But the chief hunter explained that they were too well placed, and that an approach was nearly impossible. A few minutes later he stopped again. Then he led us off in another direction, and circled back. A few minutes later we were in the middle of another herd.

It was much too expert a performance for us. We were not prepared for it. Wilson fired, and then there were targets looming up all around us. We were like a column of pioneers that finds itself suddenly surrounded by Indians, and is forced to blaze away in all directions. We hardly had time to aim, and then as abruptly as they had appeared, they were all gone once more.

"I hit mine," Wilson announced excitedly. "I heard the bullet smack home, but the antelope just turned and went on its way."

"He did, I saw him," Hodkins said.

"There were sure a lot of them."

"I've never seen so many. They were on all sides of us," Wilson shouted. He was full of enthusiasm again. "This guy's terrific," he said. "Just watch him. He reads the country as if it were a guidebook. And he's got eyes like binoculars. They're better than Hod's." He turned to

Delville. "Ask him his name, will you, René?"

Delville obliged. He was pleased that things were going better. "They call him Kivu, because he once went there on a trip," he told us.

"Well, now ask him what he thinks we should do. Tell him he's in charge of the entire expedition."

The chief hunter leaned on his spear. Wilson gave him a cigarette, and lit it for him. "You're the boss, you understand," he said, once Delville had finished speaking in Swahili. The hunter was silent for a long time before he answered. Delville looked a little disturbed.

"He says there are too many of us in the party," he said. "He thinks we should separate."

Wilson nodded approvingly. "All right. We'll do as he says."

I volunteered to go with the native in the sailor jacket. Hodkins joined me. Wilson selected two of the smaller boys to serve as gunbearers under the chief hunter's command, and then we started off in opposite directions.

"Make damn sure of what you're shooting at," I called after them. "Let's not start a small war here."

"Don't you worry, we'll make sure," Wilson replied.

We moved off. Hodkins told our guide to take us to the higher country so that we would not get in the way of any stray bullets, and he nodded. He seemed to be glad to be leaving Wilson too.

We walked for an hour until we were on a small plateau a few hundred feet above the camp. Then we called a halt. I distributed cigarettes, and we sat looking down at the plains and the lake in front of us. The camp was off to our right, and to our left the hills became steeper until they formed a cliff that fell off into the lake. Hodkins had a small pair of binoculars with him, and we spent our time idly surveying the country in front of us. There were more than five herds of antelope grazing among the trees, and it was apparent that they were the herds we had been shooting at all day.

"They don't even bother to take to the hills, the dirty little buggers," Hodkins said.

"Why should they? They're safe right where they are."

Hodkins was staring at one point off to our left. He steadied his glasses, by putting his elbows down on his knees. "Good Lord," he said suddenly, "am I seeing things?"

The boy in the sailor jacket had risen and was staring off in the same direction. "I believe it is," Hodkins said. "I really do."

"*Tembo*," the boy said excitedly. He pointed with a shaking hand.

"*Mingi, mingi, mingi, tembo*," Hodkins shouted, his voice rising.

"What is it?" I asked.

"Elephant. About twenty of them. Good Lord. If John were only here. Take a look at them."

He passed the glasses to me, and I stared down at the place where he had been looking. All of the other natives had risen behind us. In the extreme distance I saw an object that looked like a big gray boulder, and then there was another one next to it, and another and another. They were moving slowly through the low trees.

"Do you see them?"

"I do. They look like huge boulders."

"That's right. Good Lordie. Where's old John?"

"Probably stalking a baby antelope."

I swung the glasses to the right and down. The trees became more distinct. I could see the bushes and the brown grass more clearly, and then all at once I gave a short yell. Not more than three quarters of a mile away from the elephants a small column was moving through the waist-high grass. First I saw a green dot, which was undoubtedly the hunter. A tall man in a brown hat was directly behind him, and then there was a huge squat-shaped brown animal, Delville. Three tiny black dots followed. Every member of the caravan had his eyes focused on the ground directly in front of him, and they moved slowly and warily forward. I swung the glasses a little ahead of them, and picked out a herd of antelope.

"I don't believe it," I said. "Look."

Hodkins took the glasses.

"Go right and down a little," I said. "Then tell me what you see."

Hodkins tracked to the right with his binoculars. "Grass, trees, more grass, more trees . . ." He stopped. "Oh no," he said all at once. "Oh, good Lord, no."

He lowered the glasses, and we stared at each other. It was bizarre, comical, the elephants moving through the brush in one direction and not very far away the weird caravan moving in quite another. The strange silhouette of Wilson's group sticking up out of the tall grass made it even funnier. The black hunter, and the tall thin man, followed by figures of steadily decreasing size, all of them gliding silently through the grass like creatures without legs, like ducks in a shooting gallery, made it look truly absurd.

"Oh, my God," Hodkins said. "Oh, my God. One thing I know. We must never, never tell him."

30

But we had forgotten about Kivu. Wilson and Delville alone might have roamed among the elephants for days, but the native had seen their tracks, and had realized at once that they were not more than half an hour old. He had changed his course, and had warned Wilson. Only the darkness had prevented them from following the herd. They had not fired at any of the antelope they had passed for fear of disturbing the elephants, and so it was quite logical to suppose that the big animals were still roaming around somewhere on the plains near the camp.

Wilson's silent mood of despair was gone. His eyes were eager once more; all throughout dinner he spoke of only one thing: the truck. Without it, finding the herd again was almost impossible. They were capable of moving great distances, and tracking them on foot was much too slow.

"You've got to do something, René," he said, again and again. "Send someone down to the fishery. I'll go if no one else is willing."

"We'll send a boy," Delville said.

"At night it is difficult," Zibelinsky put in. "They are frightened of leopard. They will not leave the village."

"Hod and I'll go," I said.

Wilson seemed not to have heard me. "Someone has

to," he repeated again. "We've got to have the truck here tomorrow morning at five. Call Kivu and let's have a talk with him."

The hunter appeared a few minutes later. "Ask him to sit down," Wilson said. Delville looked embarrassed. Zibelinsky shrugged. "Ask him to sit down, God damn it," Wilson repeated. "He's the only one here who's worth a damn, so treat him like a man."

Delville obeyed. Kivu bowed, and with great dignity explained that he preferred to stand.

"Ask him if he's had a good dinner."

Delville complied. Kivu said he was satisfied. Then Wilson proceeded to lay plans for the following day. He took having the truck for granted. Kivu explained that they should go out to the place where they had seen the tracks, and then follow them.

"Ask him if he's got a good place to sleep," Wilson commanded.

"They'll take care of him," Delville said.

"No, they won't, God damn it. Ask him."

Kivu said that he had found a place in the adjoining native village.

"I want to make sure he's here tomorrow morning. He and the truck are the two most important things in my life right now. Make no mistake about that."

As he spoke there was the distant sound of a motor. It came nearer and then it stopped. We sat very still.

"Speak of the devil," Wilson said in a hushed voice. "The truck. And it's stopped near here." He got up excitedly. "Who's got a light?"

"I will get one," Zibelinsky said quietly. He left the hut. An instant later we heard footsteps outside on the road and Paget appeared. He grinned sarcastically as he took off his hat, and bowed to us.

"What luck, Hollywood?" he asked.

Wilson stared at him. "How did you get here?" he asked.

"The truck brought me," Paget answered. Hodkins leaped up.

"It's still here, then," he shouted. "I'll go out and grab the driver."

Wilson ran over to a corner of the hut and picked up one of the small rifles. "Take this with you," he said to Hodkins. "If the driver tries to leave, shoot him. Don't argue with him, Hod. Just let him have it."

Hodkins grabbed the rifle and ran outside. Paget stared at us. He couldn't believe his eyes.

"What's going on?" he asked.

"We need that truck for tomorrow," Wilson said. "And we're going to see to it that it stays here. No more promises about it coming back for us. We're going to keep it here."

"It's coming back to get me tomorrow, anyway," Paget said. "I have to go back to the fishery to speak to the customs man again."

"It's staying here," Wilson said. "You can walk if you have to get there."

"It's eight bloody miles," Paget protested.

"You're a white hunter, aren't you?" Wilson sneered. "Eight miles can't mean much to you."

"I've got to be there at seven," Paget said aggressively. "Lockhart can't get across the lake with the equipment unless I'm there. I'd have to start out at four o'clock in the morning in order to make it."

"Well, what are you afraid of?" Wilson asked. "A few lions or leopards shouldn't bother a fellow like you."

"It's not my bloody movie," Paget said. He was starting to whine. "I don't give a damn if you have the equipment or if it just stands and rots in Masindi."

"Neither do I," Wilson said. "It's not important to me right now. The truck is. Get that through your head. If you don't want to walk, stay here. I'll take the blame."

Hodkins came back triumphantly. "Caught the bugger," he said. "Took his keys away. Oh, he screamed like a stuck pig, but I've got them."

"Good boy, Hod," Wilson said happily. For the first time since our arrival he was completely in control of the situation. Kivu stared with bewilderment at all of us.

"Now, René, tell Kivu to get a good night's sleep and be ready to move at five. The truck is all set and so we should have no more trouble."

"The truck belongs to the fishery, John," Delville said. He looked very worried.

"I know, I know," Wilson replied absently. "Just tell Kivu good night, will you, René."

The native took off his skullcap, bowed, and left. Delville got up nervously and lit a cigar. "Did Lebeau get off all right?" he asked Paget.

"He's leaving tomorrow," Paget replied. He was turning his hat in his hands, watching Wilson.

"Now, I guess we might as well all turn in," Wilson said triumphantly. He smiled at Hodkins. "You sure they can't start that truck by connecting the ignition wires?"

"That's a thought," Hodkins said. "I'll have them park it in front of my tent when I go to bed. I'm a light sleeper."

"Fine," Wilson said. He turned to Paget once more. "You can go with us tomorrow, if you like, Vic."

Paget shook his head. "No Hollywood safari for me," he said bitterly. Wilson looked at him for a very long time. Then he lit a cigarette, lit it slowly, as if it were a difficult, important operation.

"That phrase," he said, "has crept into the conversation quite a few times."

"What phrase is that, sir?" Paget said. He did well to add the "sir," for Wilson's mood was not improving.

"Hollywood," Wilson said. "I know it's just the name of a town, but the way you use it, it has an added meaning."

"I wasn't aware of that," Paget said.

I felt uncomfortable. Wilson began to pace up and down across the sand floor of the hut. He seemed to be thinking hard. "I think you were," he said, after a long silence. "But I'm not angry with you. You brought the truck after all, and so you're kind of a savior in these parts, an inadvertent savior, let's say. That's why I feel I should be instructive rather than kick your ass."

"I said nothing," Paget objected. He was trying to backtrack, and he looked appealingly at all of us.

"I think we're oversensitive in regard to that word, John," I put in.

"No, I'm not," Wilson said. "You see, the way Vic uses the word 'Hollywood' is as an insult. Now, don't contradict me. I've heard it before. In the Army, in the theatre in New York—hell, everywhere. People say 'Hollywood' when they want to insult you. But it isn't an insult, really, and that's what I want to tell our 'white hunter,' here. Are you listening, Vic? Well, then . . . I'll continue. Hollywood is a place where they make a product; it's the name of a factory town, just like Detroit, or Birmingham, or Schaffhausen. But because the cheap element in that town has been overadvertised, it is insulting to remind a man that he comes from there." He smiled his false smile. "Now actually, Victor, if you think about it there are cheap guys all over the world. There are scared guys, who hang around places because they want to snap up whatever money there is to be stolen without work, scared and cheap, you follow me. Well, unfortunately, in Hollywood they often leave their mark on what the hard-working guys make, and the world points at it with disgust and says, 'Look . . . Hollywood.' Hollywood means cheap and phony and lousy when it's used that way, and that's too broad a meaning for that word. I wouldn't like it to creep into the language on that basis, because it would get worn out with use. Somebody might ultimately even talk about a guy from Kenya that way . . . you get me, Vic?"

"But *I* didn't mean to use it that way," Paget declared.

"Yes, you did," Wilson said gently. "Why, I've meant it that way a hundred times, and so has Pete and nearly all of my friends, but it doesn't bother me so much when they say it, because I know they're talking about the hustlers, and the flesh peddlers, and the pimps who sit in the sun out there, around the swimming pools, and get brown. They mean all the crummy guys who live and breathe dollar bills, who talk grosses and costs until they drive a sane man to drink. They're not talking about the guys who work out there, who try to do something worth while. They mean the whores, when they say Hollywood." He looked quizzically at his victim. "You know what that word means, don't you, Vic?"

"Sure," Paget said. He grinned sheepishly.

"I wonder if you really do," Wilson went on. "Because I don't mean to take a stand against that specific profession alone, you know. Now get this, Victor . . . whores have to sell one of the few things that shouldn't be for sale in this world: love. But there are other things that shouldn't be for sale beside love, you know, and there are other kinds of floosies than the ones you frequent. There are whores who sell words and ideas and melodies, and there are whores who even sell money, who invest it cheaply and not to construct anything worth while and they're maybe the worst whores of all. Now I know what I'm talking about, Victor, because I've hustled a little in my time, a hell of a lot more than I like to admit I have, and what I sold while I was whoring is something I'll never get back. Well, anyway, my point is that it's the whores who put up Hollywood as a big target, and very often they shoot at it themselves just to feel clean again. But when they put Hollywood up as a target they're putting up America, you see, for what's good and bad there is good and bad all over our country in a less noticeable degree."

"John," I said, "for God's sake . . . I think your lecture is being given in the wrong hall."

"No, it isn't, God damn it. You're listening, and so are a lot of other people, and there isn't anything else we could be doing right now. I've digressed a little, I'll grant you, and maybe Vic is losing interest . . ."

"Why don't we finish it off some other day?"

"No, tonight's the night," he insisted, "because we're going out to try to do a big thing tomorrow, and whatever happens, I don't want Vic just to sit in this hut here tomorrow evening, and say 'Hollywood' if it all goes wrong."

"I wouldn't say that," Paget mumbled.

"Yes, you would, you Nairobi white hunter. You'd say, 'That Hollywood director loused up on his elephant,' and I'd rather you say, 'Wilson, that insane son of a bitch, just didn't know how to shoot.' Because when you say 'Hollywood,' you don't know what the hell you're talking about."

"I didn't know you were such a home-town boy." I smiled.

"Well, I am," Wilson said aggressively. "I am when I'm in Africa."

"John, please," I said.

"No, I mean it," he said. "Don't knock it unless you're better than the best that's there. And that goes for any place, brother. For I think Hollywood *is* like any place. That's my point. It's just that the bad elements are over-advertised, are out in the open. Like me, maybe. An extreme example, a radical case, part of the general sickness, but not the germ itself . . . do you follow me?"

Paget nodded.

"Well, I'm glad you do," Wilson said. He lit a cigarette and beamed happily at all of us. "It took Africa to bring all that out of me," he said with a shake of his head. "Africa, and the smell of my first elephant. And it's right that way, Pete. I wouldn't want to say this at Chasen's, where some of those Hollywood characters might be listening to me."

We all rose. Everyone felt happier, because Wilson seemed somewhat restored to a semblance of his former self.

"It's a shame Kivu couldn't have heard you," Hodkins said.

"Oh, Kivu knows," Wilson replied, with his broadest smile, showing us that the storm had really passed. "Kivu knows everything without being told."

"Maybe you should take him back to Hollywood with you," I suggested.

He cocked his head to one side and made his face of serious consideration. "You know, that's not a bad idea, kid," he said. "He could learn to be damn useful around the house.

31

Unfortunately Wilson's good mood did not last, for the possession of the truck did not prove to be a solution to his problems. The following day was as great a day of frustration for him as any that had passed before. We got up early in the morning and drove along the edge of the lake. Kivu sat in the cab with the rebellious driver and guided him to the place where he had seen the elephant tracks. There we turned off and followed the huge footprints across open country. The track led inland over rougher terrain, and we came across countless herds of antelope. Just after sunup we passed a family of bush pigs. We stopped and watched them gallop through the brush, their long, black snouts pushing through the grass. A few minutes later we saw a large group of apes among the scrub oak, and they turned and ran from us. The country seemed to be alive with game, but I felt no desire to shoot. It was enough to stand watching it all move past.

"Shame we couldn't take a shot at the pigs," Hodkins said. "They taste awfully good, if you get a young one."

"We can't risk it," Wilson said. "There might be elephant within a hundred yards of here."

Delville nodded wisely. "It is better not to shoot, unless we find what we are looking for."

We had arrived in the foothills of the mountain that stood behind the camp. The trees grew in dense groves, much too close together to allow the passage of our truck. We continued on foot. The sun rose as we climbed toward the mountains. The grass was thick, with brambles of all kinds that clung to our trousers. Kivu, Wilson, and his gunbearer were soon out of sight. I looked at my watch. It was eleven o'clock. The sky was clear, and the heat was intense. In the extreme distance the clouds were rising, and suddenly we saw the tops of the Ruwenzori, the Mountains of the Moon. Hodkins took out his glasses and we looked at the snow fields, faint white patches along the ridge lines, lying white and clean among the gray rock of the cliffs.

"You're very fortunate, you know," the pilot said. "It's a very rare thing to see those mountains. The natives say that to see them once every six months is often enough for any man."

All of the boys were standing, shielding their eyes, gazing off at the distant peaks. Finally a new layer of clouds hid them from view. We went back to the truck and waited for the others. The driver was bitter about having been kidnapped. The rough country was hard on the truck, and he was frightened of what his master would say. Delville explained to him that he would certainly not be the one to receive the blame, but the native was not convinced. Delville then promised to go back to the fishery with him in the evening and explain what had happened, but the boy didn't believe him. He sat in the cab despite the heat and smoked the cigarettes we gave him without speaking to any of the others, his blue cap pulled down over his eyes so that he wouldn't have to look at any of us.

At one o'clock Wilson's gunbearer returned. Wilson and Kivu had decided to continue their search throughout the heat of the day. The truck took us back to camp. We ate lunch, and in the late afternoon the truck drove us out to the place where we had left the others. We waited for an hour in the shade. Then just as it grew dark Wilson appeared. He looked terrible. He had lost even more weight, and his face was covered with a thick beard. His eyes were glazed.

"They're gone," he said. "They've disappeared into thin air. You sure you saw them yesterday?"

"Positive," Hodkins said. "All of us saw them."

"It wasn't just a gag?"

"Good Lord. Certainly not."

Wilson nodded and tried to climb up on the bed of the truck. He fell back, tripped, and sat down on the ground. He didn't try to get up for a long time.

"You all right, John?" I asked. He looked incredibly weak and thin. Delville helped him to his feet, and Hodkins and I pulled him up onto the truck.

"I'm all right," he said slowly. He sat down among the rifles and held his head in his hands. Then he began to cough. I put my bush jacket across his soaking shoulders. The natives stood around with scared faces, watching him. Kivu crawled into the cab of the truck, and we started back toward camp.

Just before dinner Delville told Wilson that he planned to go back with the truck. Wilson was lying on his cot, the mosquito netting tucked under his mattress, his face barely visible behind the white gauze of the net.

"You won't come back," he said. "I know you won't. And if you do, they won't let you keep the truck."

"I give you my word of honor . . ."

"They may not let you. They'll tell you they need the truck."

"They've got a jeep. They can use that for the next two days."

"How do you know they'll agree? You're taking a chance. If we have no truck tomorrow, we might as well go back to Stanleyville and forget about the elephants."

"It will be here, John," Delville said. He stood very close to the cot. "I promise you."

Wilson fell back on his pillow. "All right, René. There's nothing else I can say." He sounded hurt, defeated.

Paget and Delville left with the driver. They returned at ten that night and were served a cold dinner of Spam and fried eggs. Wilson had eaten his food in his hut and had fallen asleep over his plate. The rest of us sat gloomily at the bar and drank cool tea.

"We have to leave the day after tomorrow, René," I said.

The Belgian nodded. He had changed a lot during the last three days. His kind, jovial manner was gone. He had lost a great deal of weight and it didn't suit him. His face was burned red by the sun, and while he listened, his mouth had a tendency to fall open.

"I know," he said. "I have to be back in my office. I have much work to do."

"And if we don't see anything tomorrow? Then what? John will never consent to leave."

"He'll have to," Delville said. "I've ordered the car."

"Lebeau again?"

"No, another car from Tatsumu. A station wagon. The truck will take us to the fishery, and the car will meet us there."

"What did they say about our keeping the truck?" Hodkins asked.

Delville shrugged. "They expected it," he said.

"But they were not happy, believe me," Paget put in.

"Nobody's happy," Hodkins said.

"Well, Wilson's better off than the rest of us," I said. "At least he's asleep."

"Maybe he's dreaming of elephant," Delville said hopefully. "Maybe he has killed a big tusker in his sleep."

"That won't do," I said. "That's not enough for him."

The sky was overcast the next morning, and it started to rain as we drove out of camp. We stood in the back of the truck with the rain blowing in our faces, and the wooden truck bed getting slippery under our feet. Once again we followed the road but instead of turning off toward the hills, we continued on along the edge of the lake. The ground rose a little, and soon we were climbing up along the cliffs that hung high over the water. The hills looked greener than ever in the rain, with heavy black clouds hanging low over their summits. Nobody spoke. Wilson sat on a wooden box, his back turned toward the mountains, shielding his rifle against the wet.

"Where are we going this morning, John?" Hodkins asked him.

"To a place Kivu knows. The elephants and the buffalo always go there at this time of the year, he says."

"How do you two communicate with each other?" I asked.

"Oh, we get along," Wilson said. "You know I asked him this morning about coming back to the States with me. Zibelinsky acted as my interpreter."

"What did he say?"

"Well, of course he couldn't make a big decision like that right away," Wilson said. "He told me he'd think about it."

"You really did mention it to him?" Hodkins asked.

"Certainly. It wouldn't be nearly as difficult as a lot of other things I've done."

"But what kind of a life would he have out there?"

"Well, he'd live out on my farm," Wilson said, as if it were all reasonable and sane, "and he'd work with Zeke and Nancy, and in the fall I'd take him hunting to Idaho or Montana."

Zeke and Nancy were Wilson's colored servants. They had been with him for years, and were by far the most sensible members of his household.

"He'd freeze in Montana," I said.

Wilson gave me a long, hopeless look. "He's quite a guy, Kivu. He'd get along anywhere."

It was obvious that he was considering the idea quite seriously. He had brought back a monkey from Mexico and a great many pre-Columbian masks. Now he wanted a set of elephant's tusks and a native, to show that he'd been in Africa. I felt it was a little like picking up a stray dog, as far as Wilson was concerned.

"Aren't you afraid of transplanting a human being like that?" Hodkins asked. "Suppose he hates it? Suppose it frightens him and he gets sick?"

"It won't," Wilson said. "After all, *he* won't have to go out to Warner Brothers every day."

The truck stopped, and Kivu jumped out of the cab. His creased, brown face with its sharp little eyes followed our clumsy movements as we joined him in the dried grass.

"When will he let you know?" I asked Wilson.

"Oh, tomorrow or the day after," he said. I caught Delville's eye. It was apparent that Wilson had no intention of leaving the following day. The Belgian said nothing. He shrugged and took his place in the caravan.

The country where we now found ourselves was quite different from the plains surrounding the camp. There were huge trees bordering a deep cleft in the ground, and the bushes grew ten feet above our heads. We moved in single file along the edge of the arroyo, staring down into the wide, moist chasm. The earth was wet and slippery, and in the bottom of the canyon I saw a small stream. We climbed higher along the rim of the canyon. At the far end of it there was a watering hole, its muddy borders marked by countless tracks. The natives grew visibly nervous.

"Buffalo tracks," Delville said.

Kivu found a steep path that led down into the canyon, and Wilson and the gunbearer followed him. Delville stopped and offered me his rifle.

"You want to go down?" he asked.

"No, you better go, John might need some expert help."

Delville looked unhappy, and started down the slippery path. We watched them from above, making their way into the dark valley.

"It'll seem awfully crowded down there if they find a small herd of elephant," Hodkins said.

"Or a lion. We'd better cover their approach."

Hodkins nodded. We moved a little farther along the cliff so that we could see the open spaces on the canyon floor below us.

But the hunters found nothing; only the bones of antelope, and the skull of a buffalo. Wilson looked even more discouraged when he climbed back up toward the truck an hour later.

"This is a place to come in the evening," he said.

"Yeah, the cocktail hour."

He didn't smile. He obviously felt the hopelessness of the expedition once again. He climbed up on the truck and we started back. The rain had stopped. The sun was beating down once more through the receding clouds. The truck swayed dangerously as we made our way back to the road. Suddenly it ground to a stop. There was a herd of antelope to our right. Kivu got out of the cab. He spoke in Swahili to Delville. The Belgian shrugged.

"He says there are no elephant up here, so we might as well shoot for the pot. What do you think, John?"

"Whatever Kivu says." We clambered down to the ground, and the procedure of the past days was repeated. Kivu, Wilson, and Delville began stalking the herd. They moved slowly forward and in a little while they were out of sight. Half an hour later there were two shots, and we could see the herd running off in the direction of the camp. A few minutes later Delville reappeared, followed by the others. They walked slowly, hopelessly, their rifles across their shoulders.

"Maybe they killed a buck and they're coming back to get some of the boys to carry it," Hodkins said.

"Look at their faces, Hod."

The pilot shook his head. "What a shame," he said. "What an awful shame."

Wilson pulled himself up painfully onto the truck. "Our rifles are just no good," he said. "I hit one but I couldn't stop him. It's a lousy thing to do, to wound them like that."

Delville looked even more depressed. "What's the plan, John?" I asked.

"Might as well go back to camp and wait until late afternoon," Wilson said. He slumped down with his back against the cab of the truck.

We drove on. It was almost noon again. The game was settling down in the deep grass, and the flies were coming out by the hundreds, following in the wake of the truck. No one spoke. We clung to the swaying sides of our vehicle. Then all at once it stopped again. Kivu's long, brown arm was pointing out to the right. We gathered along the wooden barrier of the truck. Not more than fifty yards off to the right there was a doe antelope, asleep in the grass. We stared at it. The blond grass was beaten down around the small animal, and it lay basking in the sun.

"Lovely little thing, isn't it?" Hodkins said in a whisper.

The doe whisked its tail. Then it rose slowly, sensing some danger. None of us moved. The thought of shooting it had come to no one's mind. The animal looked much too harmless, too gentle. Its light brown skin shone in the sun.

"Well?" Delville said. No one answered him. Only the flies droned on. Then, very slowly, Wilson raised his rifle. Hodkins and I looked at each other. It seemed impossible, and still it was happening. I thought that perhaps Wilson intended to scare the doe, but even that seemed cruel.

But scaring the animal was not his intention. He leveled the rifle slowly across the steel frame of the truck's side, and took careful aim. The doe stood there, staring up at us, not even frightened any more. We were about to witness a murder. This small beautiful animal in front of us was about to die, killed to relieve a man's frustration. It was clear then, perfectly apparent; Wilson was no longer sane. His ego had finally robbed him of all feeling, of what he was and what he had been; had blotted out all of his natural humanity and compassion. He was a hunter now, a hunter only. All of the influences of his life, of his entire past, were forgotten as he squinted down the rifle barrel at his prey. Finally he wanted to kill, and only to kill. Almost everything I had ever felt about him changed right there.

The report of the rifle was loud in my ears. I was far enough forward to catch the muzzle blast, but I hardly noticed it. I watching the doe, and to my amazement I saw the bullet strike the ground just a few inches behind its front hoof. It turned and rushed off through the thick grass.

There was a long silence. The native driver started the motor.

"I'm very glad you missed, John," Hodkins said quietly.

Wilson scratched his head. "I'm not," he said. "I should be, I know, but I'm not."

Kivu spoke briefly in Swahili to Delville. Then he closed the door of the cab. The Belgian turned to face Wilson.

"The barrel of the rifle," he said in a choked voice. "He says you should not have rested it on the steel side of the truck. The bullet made it swell as it came out and that threw off your aim."

Wilson seemed not to be listening to him. He unloaded the rifle very slowly, and dropped it on the floor. Then he sat down again, in his usual position, his face resting in his cupped hands, his elbows steadied on his knees. He sat that way while we drove back to camp.

He did not appear for lunch. He asked for a pitcher of iced tea to be brought to his hut. The rest of us avoided the subject of the doe. Somehow we didn't want to discuss it in front of Paget and the Zibelinskys; we felt ashamed of having been there, of having witnessed the incident.

At three o'clock in the afternoon, Wilson woke up from his nap and we went out again. The back of the truck had become a prison for all of us, a strained cell from which there was no escape. We drove toward the mountains, mute and disgruntled, holding onto the familiar wooden sides. Wilson had decided to ride in the cab as the driver knew exactly where we were going.

We stopped for a herd of antelope and the hunters followed their usual pattern. But somehow the events of the morning seemed to have changed things. We had reached the low point of our safari, the bottom of hopelessness and frustration. A few minutes after the others had left the truck, there were two shots, and we saw an antelope pitch forward and fall into the grass.

"He's got one," Hodkins shouted. We saw two of the boys running toward the place where the animal had fallen, and a few minutes later Wilson appeared. He looked relieved. He was not happy, but the strained look had gone from his face. Delville was beaming.

"First kill," he announced.

"A good head?" Hodkins asked.

"A doe," Wilson said. "Of course. You think God lets a man off the hook that easily?"

The boys followed a few minutes later, carrying the antelope on a long pole which they held on their shoulders. Its gentle head dragged along the ground, the long graceful ears stained with blood.

"Who got it?" I asked. "I heard two shots."

"John did," Delville said. "I was shooting at another animal in the herd."

Although I didn't believe him at first, it was soon obvious that Wilson's rifle had inflicted the wound. The small hole in the neck could only have been made by one of our useless Mannlichers. The natives dumped the dead antelope onto the back of the truck and we went on. Kivu took his place in the cab, and Wilson joined us once more.

The fever seemed suddenly to have affected the driver as well now, for the next herd we saw, he pursued. The truck bounced recklessly over the ground, twisting and turning as it followed the game. Antelopes were on all sides of us, as close as thirty yards. Delville was shouting excitedly in Swahili, while the rest of us hung on. Finally the truck stopped.

"That's crazy," I said angrily.

"Bloody dangerous, if you ask me," Hodkins complained, "as well as illegal."

Delville reprimanded the driver. "They want meat," he said, once we were on our way again.

"They can have the doe," Wilson told him. "All of it —just let's keep the truck all in one piece."

We stopped twice again, but the game was too wild. No one fired. It grew late. The sun disappeared behind the mountains. The country became blue, and in the distance the trees looked hazy. All at once the truck stopped again. The engine sputtered and died.

"No gas," Hodkins said.

We were miles from camp. The driver got out and opened the hood. Hodkins called out to him in Swahili.

"Silly idiot won't believe me," he said.

Delville clambered down to the ground and began arguing with the native. After a while he prevailed, and the boy dragged a spare gas can out of the cab of the truck. There was no funnel, and so only half of the gas that splashed out of the can found its way into the narrow mouth of the tank. Hodkins told the driver to wait until he could make a funnel out of a folded newspaper. But even after the tank had been replenished the motor refused to start. The starter ground noisily in the quiet of the evening.

"Choke it, you bloody fool, choke it," Hodkins shouted. We stood there, like poverty-stricken maharajahs on the back of our stalled steel elephant. "That boy doesn't know a blessed thing about a motor," Hodkins complained.

"Why don't you get down and help him?" Wilson suggested.

"Believe I will," Hodkins said. He started to climb over the wooden railing near the cab. When he was quite high up he stopped, and stared out into the distance.

"Good Lord," he said suddenly. "Good Lord." Then he dropped quickly back to the place from which he had started and banged on the metal roof of the cab. His voice changed. The gentleness was gone, and the surprise, as he shouted Swahili at the driver. The starter stopped its grinding. Hodkins turned toward Wilson.

"If you will just take a look there, to our front," he said in a whisper, "I believe you will see what I see."

"What is it, Hod?" Wilson asked. He was fiddling with his glasses.

"Well, unless I'm potty, I think I see elephants," Hodkins said. "About a hundred and fifty paces away."

32

The wind blew gently toward us as we stood there straining our eyes, and with it came a strange, musty smell,
reminiscent of the smell of the circus, only wilder, heavier,
and then all at once there was the sound of trumpeting.
The natives stood in back of us, muttering, and staring
out ahead in the direction in which Hodkins had pointed.
Then we all saw them, the huge gray bodies, moving slowly and majestically through the trees. They were going
off to our right, and as we stood there, they seemed to be
passing in front of us in a continous caravan.
They moved very slowly, and yet steadily, and with an
overwhelming security, like battleships moving out of
harbor, more indestructible than anything alive had ever
looked to me.

They were unlike all other game; there was no question of flight, of fear, which was what had always been
immediately apparent with antelope, or bush pig. It would
come, of course, once they saw us, or were fired on, but
there was no question of fear as yet. They looked as if
they belonged on this earth and the earth belonged to
them. They made us look like intruders, like perverse
creatures from another planet, ugly and ill formed and
without dignity.

"Well, for God's sake," Wilson whispered.

For the first time I felt that these, his usual words of
greeting, were well chosen. The elephants had something
to do with God, with the miracle of creation. They made
you feel that you were passing into another age, into a
world that no longer existed. They transmitted, not so
much the idea of jungle and wilderness, as the feeling of
unconquerable time.

"There are more than thirty of them," Hodkins whispered. "Cows and their babies, and a few males."

He gave me his binoculars. Now I could see their huge sagging bodies, which seemed to be draped in long, gray robes, as they ambled slowly among the miniature trees. The big elephants had large black areas around their eyes, like the liverish skin on an old man's face, and they walked with an old man's gait, no longer in a hurry for anything. I lowered the glasses and saw Wilson jumping down from the truck. Delville was already on the ground, standing next to Kivu.

Wilson stared up at me. "You ready, Pete?"

I shook my head. "The three of you are plenty. Go ahead."

He seemed amazed at my answer. "You're not coming?"

"No, John. Go ahead."

He moved closer to the truck. "Listen," he said, "I've never given you much advice, I've never tried to force you to do anything you didn't want to do, but this time it's different. I'm telling you, you should come. I urge you to, as a friend . . ."

"Go ahead, John. I'll wait here." It was neither the time nor the place to tell him that we'd left our friendship back on the road at noon, that although the doe had gotten away alive, our friendship had not been as fortunate.

"You're going to regret this as long as you can remember it," he said calmly.

"I told you before I didn't want to shoot an elephant, John."

He shook his head. "That isn't what I mean. If you don't come along now, it'll be because you want to play it safe, because you're scared and you know it."

"Well, I'll have to live with that, I guess."

Wilson turned and motioned to Kivu to lead the way.

We stood watching them go, the three small figures moving after their enormous prey. They looked evil and inconsequential and undignified, and yet I knew they were brave. Despite the high-powered rifles they carried, they looked to be no match for the vast creatures that they were setting out to kill.

"There's probably a stream up there," Hodkins whispered. "The family's been taking their evening bath."

He gave me the glasses once more. I could see several of the baby elephants hurrying after their parents, and then suddenly an even more enormous shape appeared from behind a large bush. He looked and moved like the pride of the herd. His long, curving tusks reached down to within an inch of the ground. Kivu and the others saw him too, and they rushed forward excitedly. The elephant's ears moved slowly outward and then flapped back along his head again.

"The wind's blowing the right way," Hodkins said. "They should be able to approach quite easily."

"What about us?" I asked. "Shall we follow them on foot?"

Hodkins looked doubtful. "I think unless you've got a big rifle in your hand, it's better to stay here near that big tree."

"It's going to be crowded," I said. Two or three of the boys were already starting to climb it. The driver was hurrying toward it now. He looked back for a moment at his truck, but his sense of self-preservation won out quickly over his sense of duty.

We stood on the abandoned truck, watching the hunters' approach. Kivu moved quickly and steadily, cutting across the path of the elephants. The two white men followed him, kneeling down occasionally in the grass, and peering out at the game.

"They've got to hurry," Hodkins said. "There's about fifteen minutes of daylight left."

Despite the slow gait of the animals, they were covering a lot of ground. Very soon they were barely visible. Wilson and his two companions had completely disappeared.

"We'd better follow after them," Hodkins said. "Don't want to let them get too far away, or we'll lose them."

He climbed down and got into the cab of the truck. The starter ground away more slowly and the engine failed to respond. He got out and walked over to the tree where the boys had taken refuge. I could hear him talking to them. Then he came back over to us.

"They've got to crank the bloody thing," he said. "Never get it started otherwise."

"They don't want to come, do they?"

"We'll give them a few more minutes. They want to wait until someone fires."

But although we waited tensely for it, there was no

sound of a shot. It was dark now. We could still make out the shapes of trees and bushes against the streaked sky, but that was all. Hodkins got the crank out from under the front seat, and together we started the truck. The boys clambered down quickly, and the driver took his place. Hodkins stood on the running board next to the cab. The truck had only one very faint yellow light, and as we started now, we knew at once we were on a perilous journey. The deep ruts and the huge boulders were not visible until we were right on them, and several times Hodkins had to shout a warning in order to make the driver avoid an obstacle. After a while he ordered the boy to stop.

We stood waiting in a clearing, the motor running raggedly under the hood. Hodkins climbed up to the perch from which he had seen the elephants.

"Bad spot, this," he said. "We'll never find them. Just have to hope Kivu sees our light."

"I'm surprised we didn't hear firing," I said.

"Maybe they never got a chance to. It got dark awfully fast, you know."

The driver was grumbling again. Hodkins shouted at him, mustering all the authority he could. "They're scared," he said to me. "They're afraid of getting caught out here." He picked up one of the small rifles. "Might even have a mutiny on our hands."

We sat there until only the sky still contained traces of light. All of the boys were grumbling now. Hodkins took his place on the running board once again, and we moved slowly forward. I could see nothing. It seemed to me that Wilson and the others were hopelessly lost. But then suddenly Hodkins' incredibly sharp eyes picked out a movement in the brush to our right. He shouted a brief command and the truck stopped.

"There they are," he said. "I can see old John's shirt."

A few minutes later we could hear their voices. They came slowly toward us and climbed up on the truck.

"What happened, John?" Hodkins asked.

Wilson shook his head. He didn't answer.

"Did you get up to them?"

Delville nodded. "We were close enough," he said, "but I wouldn't let him shoot. There were too many cows around the big fellow. They would have charged us if we had killed him, and then I would have had to shoot one of them. It's bad business for a game warden to shoot a cow with her young one there."

Wilson lit a cigarette. He seemed very calm, very controlled. "We should have taken that chance, René," he said. It sounded like the end of an argument that had already gone on for a long time.

"I'm sorry, John," Delville replied. "It's a risk I couldn't take."

"Well, all right," Wilson said irritably. "It's no use going over it again. You think one thing, I think another. You had your way, so let's skip it."

We drove back very slowly. Hodkins stayed on the running board until we found the road. No one spoke after that. We drove haltingly through the moist, cool night, following the shore of the lake.

Paget and the Zibelinskys were waiting anxiously for us in the main hut. We trooped in dejectedly. Wilson went to the bar and ordered a whisky.

"No luck again?" Paget asked.

"Not exactly," Delville said. "We ran into a herd of elephant but there were too many cows. I wouldn't allow John to shoot."

Wilson sat down in his customary chair. He had half a beer glass full of whisky. "René's honor as the game warden of the Congo was at stake," he said bitterly.

"It would have been a risk for us all," Delville said heatedly. "For the truck, for the camp, for everyone. A herd of cows can go rogue very quickly if they have their young with them. Then you have trouble on your hands, more trouble than you can imagine."

"He's right," Paget said. "There have been rogue herds in Kenya and Tanganyika that have been created in just that way. Then they have to go out and shoot every bloody one of them."

Wilson pushed the small piece of ice deeper into his whisky. "All right," he said, "we'll forget it. We'll go after them again tomorrow."

Delville gathered up all of his courage. "In the morning," he said pointedly. "Tomorrow afternoon we leave."

Wilson said nothing. He sat looking down at his drink. Then, very slowly, he rose. "You can leave if you want to," he said. "I'm staying."

I looked at him with surprise. "The company gets to Stanleyville the day after tomorrow, John," I said.

"You can go too," he said. "I'm staying."

"John, for Christ's sake, be reasonable."

"I'm reasonable," he said. "I don't care if they get there tomorrow or today. I'm staying here until I get that elephant."

"You need someone with you," Delville said. "You can't hunt alone. Why don't you come back here in a couple of weeks?"

Wilson shook his head. "Don't argue with me," he said. "I'm staying here. Paget can go with me, and if he doesn't want to, well, I'll go alone."

"Really, John," Hodkins said, "it's too dangerous to go out by yourself."

"Kivu will go."

"Come on, John, for God's sake."

"Don't coax me, or wheedle, God damn it. I'm staying here. You can all go to hell. All I want is that truck and Kivu."

There was a long silence. "I'd go," Paget said, "but I've still got my equipment to clear." He turned to Zibelinsky. "What about that old fellow down at the fishery? What's his name? Chap that used to be game warden down in the Zambezi?"

"Ogilvy?" Zibelinsky asked.

"Yes, that's right. He's killed over five hundred elephant in his time and he's still a rough old boy. You could probably hire him."

Wilson shrugged. "Get him down here," he said. "If he wants to go, he's got a job."

"How much longer do you intend to stay?" I asked.

Wilson didn't answer.

"Did you hear what I said?"

He stared at me, his face blank; then he straightened a little in his chair. "How long?" he repeated. "Well, that depends on the elephants, Pete, and on my guides. If this fellow Ogilvy turns out to be just another old lady, I might be here for months, but if he's half the man Kivu is, a professional, well, then it might not be long at all."

"And the picture?"

He shrugged. "Quit nagging me, will you. Good God Almighty. Aren't things bad enough?"

I turned away from him. An hour later the old game warden appeared. He was an enormous man who weighed well over three hundred pounds. He wore only a shirt and a torn pair of khaki shorts. His huge fat legs were tanned and scarred. His naked ankles and calves were honey-combed with thick veins. He had long gray hair that was slicked down across the top of his head where it lay like a moist vegetable, crowning his flabby face. His past life seemed to have left a mark on him, for he looked very much like the game he had most often managed to kill; he resembled an elephant without a trunk. He stood with his legs wide apart in the center of the hut, his huge feet partly buried in the sand.

Wilson's manner changed immediately. His charm came down out of the attic of his being. It was all horribly familiar. The boyish smile and the outstretched hand, the loose, long-legged walk toward the victim, and his head cocked slightly to one side as he said: "Well, Mr. Ogilvy, I'm so pleased to meet you." It sounded sincere and warm, but to me it was like an old chaser leering at a girl and saying, "Where have you been all my life?" I had heard it too often, and had seen it disproved too many times. I was tired of Wilson and all of his routines. The wooing of the elephant hunter was one I wanted to miss.

"Won't you have a drink, Mr. Ogilvy?" Wilson crooned.

I left the hut. When I returned to eat my dinner, the matter had been settled. Ogilvy, Kivu, and Wilson were seated together, making their plans.

"We'll hunt here tomorrow," Wilson announced. "If we have no luck, we'll go up to the mouth of the Semliki. Kivu comes from there. The village where he was born is the best elephant and buffalo country around Lake Albert."

The old hunter nodded. "In the Semliki country it will take us a week to get our elephant, not more," he said. "We'll get a pair of tusks you'll be proud of, Mr. Wilson, and a couple of buffalo skulls to keep them company over your fireplace."

"You sure you don't want to go along, kid?" Wilson taunted. "I hear there's a lot of guinea fowl up there, and maybe even a duck or two."

"I'll go to Stanleyville with the others," I said.

Kivu left us and we sat down to eat our meal. Throughout it Wilson spoke only to Ogilvy, disregarding the rest of us. Only once did he turn to Delville and that was to reprimand him. "We should have gone up to the Semliki country originally. It's only thirty miles from here. We could have gone up by boat and come back the following day."

"I'm sorry I didn't think of it, John," Delville said sadly.

Wilson shook his head; his voice was full of irony and false pity. "You didn't think of it, eh? And you say you're the game garden, René? Well, now how did you ever happen to get that job?"

I left the table and walked slowly down the road out of camp. I felt disgusted: partly with myself, partly with Wilson. I had to get away from as quickly as possible. I couldn't stand to hear his taunting voice any longer, couldn't bear to watch his victims squirm in front of him. I remembered how much I had liked him, and that somehow made it worse. A few minutes later I heard footsteps behind me, and Wilson appeared out of the darkness.

"What's the matter, kid?" he asked aggressively.

"Nothing's the matter. Just taking a walk."

"You're a goddam liar."

"Sure I am," I said. "It's a good way to be."

"Whyn't you speak your piece, for crissake? You're stewing like a dame who's just been kicked out of bed."

"What would be the point?"

"No point. Just be nice to see you behaving like a man for a change."

"All right," I said. "You asked for it. I think you're either nuts, or the most egocentric, irresponsible son of a bitch I've ever met. You're like a spoiled kid who hasn't gotten his piece of candy. A Hollywood brat. You smile and coo at whoever happens to promise you what you want. You kiss their ass, and crawl all over them, and if they can't deliver, you drop them. Your friendships are all the same, all based on the same thing. You either want something from people or you want to show them up by demonstrating that you're better than they are. You'd drop anything and anybody just to get what you most desire at the moment. Well, I'm tired of watching it. I've seen the show once too often."

He was not angry. He seemed vaguely interested, that was all, as if we were discussing a third person whom neither one of us particularly liked.

"There's some truth in what you say, kid," he observed.

"But is that all? Are you finished now? Because I think you should get everything off your chest if you possibly can."

"Well, not quite finished," I replied. He fell into step with me as I continued: "People always said that you were a spoiler, that you left everything dead or beaten up in your wake. Dames, friends, business associates. And I didn't think that was true. I defended you. Now I know that the people who said that were right. That's exactly what you are. A spoiler. A guy whose ego is so big that it has to crush everything around it, and when there's nothing left to ruin, you pick on animals, or on any harmless thing that happens to get in your way."

"That may be so, kid," Wilson observed disinterestedly. "But what makes you say it now? What have I done to you?"

"Nothing, really. Maybe you've shown me that I'm not as brave as you are, and that's all. But that's not the main thing that's griping me. It's watching you operate that's brought this on."

"Well, now," Wilson said, "since you've brought it up, let me ask you this. Did you ever think about it my way?"

"What do you mean?"

"Just this. That all the people I spoil are really guys that are hanging around, waiting to prey off me. Or make some little profit, anyway. They promise me things because they expect dividends, and then when they don't deliver, I turn on them, sure, or I abandon them. Like I'm going to abandon Landau and the picture for a little while, and Delville. But in the end they usually get what they want. Like you got a trip to Africa and Landau's going to *get* his picture, and Laing making a lot of money renting me planes, and Delville got a hunting week end without any cost to him. People use me, so why don't I have a right to use them?"

"What about Kivu?" I asked. "I suppose he's using you to break into the colored-servant circles of Beverly Hills, and so if he dies of homesickness wearing a chauffeur's uniform it serves him right?"

"Not at all," Wilson said. "You're wrong. Kivu is the exception that proves the rule, as he's already turned down my offer. He wants to stay here in the village where he was born, and hunt. Actually that's how I heard about the place. So Kivu's not going to be dropped because he's not corrupt, and he won't be 'spoiled' because he's not willing to hang around. You follow me?"

"Sure I follow you," I said. "I'm even a little ahead of you because I know this is all your justification, nothing more. You have to have that so you can go on from one person to the next. You've got a sick, a roving love for a lot of people, John, that winds up being no love at all."

Wilson nodded slowly. I remembered that one of his most aggravating characteristics was his ability to suddenly agree with any personal attack that was launched against him. "Maybe," he said. "Maybe. Maybe it's all true, what you say. A sick, roving love . . . well, perhaps that so. . . ."

We stood in silence, looking out at the stars over the dark lake.

"You see," he began slowly, "I've thought about all this for years, and finally I just decided to be myself, ogre or not. It was the only way for me to live. That was after a particularly sad love affair I had in Paris one spring." He chuckled to himself. "Oh, everything was all set up for love, that time. The background was just right. The trees were green and it was cool, and I was in Paris, and Paris was a beautiful dream, just made for love, built for it." He grinned and shook his head. "The object of my affections then was a jockey, a wiry little guy with a sad face and a Kentucky drawl. I brought him over with me and we lived together in a big, plush right-bank hotel, in a suite with mirrors and pink comforters, and toile de Jouy. He was a wonderful little guy. Not much to look at. Rather revolting, as a matter of fact, when you saw him getting up in the morning in his underwear, with his skinny legs sticking out, scratching his scrawny little tail. But in the afternoons it was all different . . . at Longchamps, or St. Cloud, when he'd walk out into the saddling paddock in his colors, and his neat little boots. Then they'd lift him on a horse, and love would start to sing. Just the way he sat there, Pete, and tucked his crop under his leg while he tried the girth, and then they'd start out of the paddock and the bells would be ringing up in the tribune, and I'd get my glasses on him and watch him ride. God damn, it was always something. Win or lose, I'd wind up with my heart in my mouth, just to see Jackie out there, coming up between horses, or riding away from the pack.

"It wasn't that he was good; it was more than that. He

made it look simple, clean. And he never bent your ear with the details of what he did. From steam room, to saddling paddock, to the winner's circle, he was always a neat little guy who kept his mouth shut and his eyes open. A real pro. That's what made me admire him, love him. . . . You get what I mean?"

I waited patiently for him to go on. It was just like him to start a long rambling story at this time, all part of his vague, mystic, half-phony philosophy. He turned and started walking slowly down the road.

"There was no sex, of course," he went on, "because I'm not built that way and neither was he; but I loved him all right, make no mistake about that. The kind of love you don't forget, the rare article, the unusual thing." I was trying to see his face in order to understand what sort of satire this was, what purpose there was behind it. Was he mocking me or himself? But it was impossible to tell by looking at him.

"You've been to the track in Paris, haven't you, kid? When the trees are that clear green, before the exhausts of the cars poison them, or the sun dries the edges. And the gravel is almost white in the sun, and the sky that special blue, and the characters you see are all those strange, wonderful-looking guys who are trying to win a little more of that flimsy money, playing with their rent and their grocery bills, betting what they already owe against what may come. Well, after the races, we used to do the town." He sighed nostalgically. "The bistros and the boîtes."

"And what made that particular passion of yours cool?" I asked.

"Well, as you say, I'm a spoiler, and the spoiler was there, too, in Paris that spring. We went out a lot, Jackie and I, just because I can't stay home in a hotel room in a city, unless I'm shacked up with a dame. We went to all the joints and ate that wonderful food they have there, and swilled the champagne, and Jackie started putting on weight. Not just a little weight, mind you, but quite a lot. Then three days before he had to ride, he'd stop eating, and the day before he'd spend ten hours in a Turkish bath, and his legs would be shaking when they lifted him up on a horse.

"Now I knew what I was doing, but I couldn't stop. Because, what the hell, I wasn't riding, I didn't have to make the weight. Why should I live a jockey's life, just because I had a jockey for a friend? Egocentricity, as you say. I suppose I was at fault, and I suppose I did spoil him. He finally fell off a winner a hundred feet in front of the wire, with no other horse even close, and downhill he went, in one glorious slide. My love for the little guy seemed to go with it, for he got sour, and nasty, and I didn't like to have him around any more. He was always squawking and taunting me. Sounds familiar, doesn't it? Well, finally he went back to the States, broke. He was a game little guy, the gamest I ever met, until I ran into Kivu. As a matter of fact Jackie was a lot like this little jig. I guess that's what made me think of him. He wasn't out hunting big game with a spear, but he was doing just as tough a job. And when he went on his ass, he went all the way." He paused. "I guess the really good guys are like that," he said. "When they fall, well, they go right to the bottom, and there are no stops, no net to save them. They die the way they lived . . . or at least they go into oblivion the same way. Hard and fast. And that's what happened to my jockey. He never got up in the big time again. He tried everything, but he never made it. He was through, finished, washed up as a direct result of Paris in the spring."

"What's the moral of the tale?" I asked patiently.

"Well, it seems to me to be this. Or, let me say I understand it this way, interpret it so. You can't spoil anybody unless they go along at least halfway. Just like you can't con anyone unless they're part crook, or willing to play along in a shady deal. So what the hell, a man's responsibility is really limited to himself. If you found out, through me, that you're not as brave as you think you are, well, that's not my fault. You would have found out ultimately anyway. Oh, I admit, it's nasty of me to have helped that discovery find the light of day in your soul, but God damn it, I didn't put caution there in the first place and I didn't make you find out. Just as I didn't force anybody to sign for this movie you're afraid I'm going to blow out of my nose. Just as I haven't ever forced any dame to marry me, or sleep with me. I've always taken care of my end, and I've always gone along just the way I've wanted to, without thinking of what the final result might be."

"And that's not immoral, I suppose."

"Oh, sure it is," he said quickly. "But I'm not running as a moral guy. *You* are. So you should be the one to behave morally, because you're fond of making moral judgments. I'm not interested in that. I'm just going along, trying to live a little before I die."

"I've just made a moral judgment," I said, "and I'm even going to act on it."

He seemed to agree completely. "Well, that's O.K.; perfectly all right. Just as it's O.K. for you to leave tomorrow. Just as it's O.K. for you to judge me, and condemn me, and even laugh like crazy if an elephant stomps me to death. But make goddam sure you learn something from me, kid. Make goddam sure of that."

"I think I have," I said. But I wasn't sure; not at the time.

"Well, that's all right, then," Wilson said. "That's the important point. Get something out of everything you do, especially if you're a writer."

"O.K."

"You want to say anything else?"

"Oh . . . go to hell . . ." I said, lamely.

He smiled delightedly, and clapped me on the back. "Pete," he said, "you had me worried. Now I'm sure that we're really still friends."

I pulled away from him. He had succeeded in making what I had to say sound ridiculous. "The gripe's bigger than that," I said. "That's just the personal side, and what you say is probably right. It's not only your honey-sweet charm that draws people in. Their self-interest is usually at fault as well. But never mind. I find that mildly disgusting, that's all. What I find worse is your own irresponsibility to yourself, to your job, your art, if you want to get highbrow. You're always pushing it aside and devoting your main efforts to a horse, or a jockey, or some outside passion, and you never really level with what you're truly involved in. Maybe it's to have an excuse if the pictures don't turn out, I don't know, but that's what you do. And this time it's worse than ever before. This time you're risking the success of the whole venture, just to satisfy a peculiar personal appetite of your own. Forget about spitting on your craft. Forget never really doing something that's close and that might hurt as it comes out. This time you're even letting the pure mechanical job you have to do go by the boards. Really producing something you feel strongly about has been abandoned long ago. And what for? Why are you doing this? To kill an elephant. To kill a marvelous thing, one of the rarest, most noble beings that walks this crummy world. You're being a louse—to do a lousy thing. Because I've seen them now outside the circus, John, where they look a little ridiculous, and I know what I'm talking about. Well, in order to kill one of them, you're ready to forget the rest of us, and let the whole goddam show go down the drain. It's not a passion this time that's guiding you, that's pulling you away from your responsibility. A passion would be an excuse. This time it's a crime. Because it's a crime to kill an elephant. And in order to commit this crime you're willing to ruin everyone else. If you were running out on the picture because of a woman, or a better offer, or because you'd suddenly gotten bored with the whole thing, I'd go along. But this way, it's even too rough for my taste."

Wilson looked intensely serious for a minute. He drew reflectively on his cigarette. I knew something I had said had made an impression on him. Most of it, I realized, had gone past him into the warm African night, but something had struck him in that strange way it occasionally did, had pierced into his armor-plated process of thought. He was pausing now to give his answer weight. I knew him so well, I thought.

"Kid," he said, after a long pause, "you're wrong. It's not a crime to kill an elephant. It's bigger than that. A crime . . . what the hell, that isn't much. And that isn't it. It's a *sin* to kill an elephant, you understand, a sin. As basic as that. The only sin you can buy a license for and then go out and commit. And that's why I want to do it before I do anything else. You understand?"

33

It was a smooth take-off. Hodkins turned and nodded to us as we rose up over the town of Tatsumu and the surrounding countryside.

"We're getting an early start," he said. "Have time to go down to the lake and take a look at what the boys are doing."

"All right," I said. "It's the safest way to go hunting with John."

He grinned and banked to the right. We were up about a thousand feet, and we rose higher now and passed over the mountains that bordered the lake. Then we started down once again toward the tree-covered plain. Hodkins pointed out the hunting camp. The neat rows of huts lay placid in the morning sun. There was no trace of life. We flew up along the shore, following the road we had taken so often, and found the truck. It was parked among the trees. There was no sign of Wilson and his companions. A herd of antelope was grazing not a hundred yards from the lone vehicle. We flew on toward the mountains again until they seemed much too close, and then Hodkins turned. He stared down at the ground, his small eyes searching everywhere. Suddenly he smiled and nodded. He cut the engine and we swooped lower. There among the trees was Wilson, the fat elephant hunter, and Kivu. They looked up angrily. Wilson waved for us to go away.

"He's afraid we'll scare the game," Hodkins said, "but there isn't an elephant in sight." He shrugged and pushed down on the throttle. We rose and flew back toward the lake. "Now we'll go up toward the Semliki," he said, "and see if there's anything there."

In ten minutes we were over the mouth of the river. The country was swampland, flat water-soaked fields, with the brown muddy river water showing everywhere between the bushes. The plane banked hard to the left and we stared down on a small herd of buffalo charging through the shallow water. Their hoofs splashed among the weeds as they ran. Hodkins circled lower and passed over the herd once more. The leader, a huge bull, stopped and glared angrily up at our plane. We flew on. A family of hippos took to the deeper water as we passed over them, and then we saw our first Semliki elephants.

The cows were bathing their young. They turned and crashed through the brush when they saw our shadow. We were down at about two hundred feet above the swamps, and we saw another herd of elephant on the opposite side of the river. There was a large elephant bull with huge tusks, very much like the one we had seen the previous evening. We circled and came back in a power-off glide, flying within fifty feet of the huge bull. He lifted his trunk and I knew that he was trumpeting the alarm signal. The small herd under his command turned inland, following the riverbank.

"I guess the old boy was right," Hodkins said. "Lots of game here."

Delville looked unhappy. He had been clinging to his seat throughout all of the acrobatics. "There is game here," he said, his voice apologetic as always, "but it is hard to approach. This swampland . . . it is difficult even for a boat."

"I'm glad we stayed where we did," I said.

Hodkins turned the plane back into the direction from which we had come. In a few minutes we were over the edge of the lake again. The country changed back to the same kind of vegetation that we had found at the hunting camp, twenty miles farther on. We rose higher, climbing toward the clear, smooth air.

The objects on the ground below us grew smaller until they had lost their meanings, and then in a little while the black expanse of the forest lay ahead of us, as ominous as ever. We flew toward it and soon it surrounded us again, held us prisoner with its endless borders which stretched out below us once more in every direction.

It was late afternoon when we landed in Stanleyville. Delville's wife drove out onto the runway.

"I was worried about you," she said. "Where is Mr. Wilson?"

"He stayed on for a couple more days," I explained.

She looked surprised. "Was it a good trip, René?"

Delville shrugged. "Not so good," he said. "We had no luck."

"But that happens," she said. "Even in Africa you do not always find game."

"We found it," Delville said sadly. "But we shot nothing."

"Well, if everybody is all right, that is all that matters." She shrugged. "You do not agree, Mr. Verrill?"

"I most certainly do."

"You know, you had better phone the Sans Souci," Mrs. Delville said. "Some of your people have arrived from London."

We drove over to the Sabena Hotel, where I telephoned. I spoke to the room clerk at the Sans Souci and explained who I was. The next voice I heard was Landau's.

"Pete?" He sounded worried. Just the way he said my name made me realize that he suspected the worst.

"Welcome to Africa, Paul."

"Where are you? Where's John? What's happening?"

"I'm at the Sabena. I'll come over and explain things to you in a little while."

"Come right away," he said.

"I'd like to take a shower first. We've just arrived."

"Well, come in half an hour. And don't be late, please."

I found him on the porch of the Sans Souci. He was dressed in a checkered shirt and slacks, exactly what he would have worn in Santa Monica at his beach house. He looked grave, but he managed to smile as he shook my hand.

"It's good to see you, Pete."

"Good to see you, Paul."

"You frightened me when you spoke to me on the phone. You sounded ominous."

"I'm sorry. I didn't mean to," I said. Landau snapped his fingers and a boy came running. "What would you like to drink? An iced tea?"

"God, no," I said, horrified. "Anything but that."

He looked surprised. "Why not iced tea? It's a good thing to drink in the tropics."

"I have memories, Paul."

He shrugged and ordered a gin fizz for me. The waiter responded with a spirit of amazing willingness.

"What have you done to them?" I asked. "I've never seen them move that fast for anyone before."

Landau grinned, very pleased with himself. "My good manners," he said, "and my obviously exalted station in life tend to influence servants everywhere."

That was true. No matter where he appeared, he had the same effect on the hired help; they hung around in droves, seeing to it that he was well served. Headwaiters, hotel managers, and butlers immediately recognized him as a king.

"Now then, tell me everything," he said.

"I can't, Paul. It's much too long. Let me just say that I've found out that what you told me in London was no exaggeration. You were right. I should have listened to you then."

"What did I tell you in London?" he asked. He seemed puzzled. "Come on, now, don't make a mystery of things."

"You said Wilson was insane, or heading in that direction. Well, you were right. One hundred per cent right."

"Why do you say that? Where is he, anyway?"

"He's at the mouth of the Semliki River hunting elephants," I said. "And chances are he won't be back here for quite a while."

"What?" he looked amazed. Then he was immediately on guard. "Now, please don't make jokes, Pete. Please. Things are complicated enough, and I'm in no mood for it."

"It's no joke. That's where he is, with a native tracker and an elephant hunter, and he probably won't come back until he's killed a big tusker."

"That's incredible. You mean he won't be here tomorrow when the rest of the company arrives?"

"Not a chance in the world," I said. "He's half a day's journey from the nearest road and eight hours' drive from an airfield the big plane can land at, and there's no phone or telegraph service, even if he wanted to come back, that is."

He stared at me with an open mouth. "But we're supposed to start shooting in five days," he said. "He knows that."

"He doesn't care. He's almost forgotten all about the picture. All he thinks about are elephants, and how to kill them."

His agile mind skipped ahead. "Are you no longer friends?" he asked.

I shook my head. "The love affair is over. I've told him what I think of him, and he's indicated what his feelings are about me."

"Good God," he said.

"I want to go back to London as soon as possible. I don't ever want to see him again if I can avoid it. I'm fed up. I know . . . I've let you down, I haven't done the job you sent me here to do, but that's just one of those things. I'm through."

"What about the script?" he asked.

"I sent that to you from Entebbe," I said. "Didn't you get it?"

"We got half of the corrected final draft, but that's all," he replied, the horror in his voice growing.

"Well, I sent the rest. It's probably following you back here now."

"And you want to leave?"

"That's right. Tomorrow, if there's a plane."

He grew calm. I suppose he realized that he must deal with each problem as it arose. "You can't do that," he said. "Just think of what it would do to the morale of the company if you went back. They'd think something terrible was wrong. I can't start the picture that way."

"Something terrible is wrong, Paul."

He started to answer me and then changed his mind. "Look," he said, "I have other worries now. Don't add to them. A few days of waiting won't hurt you. There's so much to do here. The equipment hasn't arrived. The camp near Pontiaville isn't ready. Nothing's organized. Don't make my work even more complicated by bringing your personal problems into it now."

Basil Owen arrived at our table. He looked even thinner and more worried than when I had last seen him. "I must speak to you, Mr. Landau," he said. "About the trucks. There's been no word from Lockhart."

Landau held him off. "In just a minute," he said. "Let's take a little walk, Pete."

We went through the lobby of the hotel, down to the side of the river. Native women were doing their washing in the brown water, while on a small wooden pier in front of us, sixty or seventy Negroes were waiting for the long canoe which served as a ferry. Landau walked majestically along the waterfront, surveying the shabby confusion of life on the Congo River. I was astonished how very much at home he felt here. I had always believed that outside of Hollywood and New York he would not be able to exist. I realized right then and there that that was a foolish notion. He had obviously lived in every kind of wild background, in poverty and splendor, and somehow he had managed to push his way through it all.

"I'll tell you about the equipment, Paul," I said. "First things first."

"There seems to be a good deal that you can tell me," he said.

We walked slowly among the palm trees while I told him the story of our safari. Strangely enough, it sounded rather mild. Again and again he asked me what specific thing Wilson had done to antagonize me, and my answers sounded surprisingly feeble even to me.

"He made you the victim of a stupid practical joke, and he shot at a doe. That's all not very sporting, I know, but it doesn't sound like a thing that could break up a friendship."

"The doe was just finishing a nap," I explained, "and he shot at it from a truck. He steadied the rifle on a bar on the truck's side."

Landau shrugged. The ethics of hunting were obviously not very important to him. "All right, it sounds fairly lousy. But what specifically did he do to you?"

"Actually nothing, I suppose. But his manner, that strange, superior taunting attitude he can assume. The way of ignoring you that he has, outside of all the insults."

He smiled faintly. "You talk about insults," he said, "when I'm worrying about starting a picture in five days without a director and without equipment." He stopped and watched the heavily laden pirogue start out across the river.

"Aren't they worried about tipping over?" he asked, his attention straying.

"No, Paul. Anyway, what have they got to lose?"

"H'm, that's true." He returned to our problems. "I think you should relax a little," he said. "We'll get together with the pilot and Owen tonight and discuss everything, point by point."

"But what is there for me to do?" I asked. "I want to get out of here, Paul. I never want to see Wilson again, or Africa, for that matter."

He looked thoughtfully at the surrounding jungle. Then, very slowly, he mopped his brow. "I can understand how you feel," he said patiently. "I warned you about him, if you'll remember. But still I say you've got to stay. You've got to help."

"How, Paul? Just tell me how, short of shooting him in the head."

"Well, for one thing you've got to help me get him back here," he said. "Because if he's not back here in three days we'll all be ruined."

"My God. You're asking for the impossible."

"We'll see, we'll see. I've faced tougher problems in my life."

"Have you? Well, go out and lead Wilson to an elephant and fix it so that his rifle shoots the beast through the brain. Then you'll have solved what you're up against today."

34

We sat in the bar of the hotel, each one of us equipped with one of Landau's cigars. I had the place of honor, on the producer's right. Hodkins was across the table from us, explaining the logistics of the thing, trying to make it all sound less hopeless.

"There's only one thing I could do," he concluded, "and that's fly over the village or wherever John is and drop him a message to meet me at the Lake Albert air strip. That is, if we get Mike to fly down from Entebbe in the Beechcraft and take the Rapide back from Tatsumu."

"That can be arranged," Landau said impatiently. "I'll have him here tomorrow afternoon."

Hodkins glanced dubiously at his watch. "I rather doubt that, sir," he said. "You see, a telegram will take a day to get to Nairobi, and they're closed now. But let's say you got it off in an hour and Alec received it in Nairobi in the morning . . . Mike could still only get as far as Tatsumu by tomorrow afternoon. It's a big risk flying in the late afternoon over that forest in a single-engined plane."

Landau puffed on his cigar. "And you must have a single-engined plane to get John?"

"At that field, yes. If we can get him to drive to Tatsumu, I could get him in the Rapide."

"He won't drive to Tatsumu unless he's shot his elephant," I said once again. "He might drive an hour to come and talk to you but that's the most he'd do."

"All right, then let's proceed on that basis," Landau replied. "What can we do about Lockhart and the equipment?"

"Well, I could fly over the hunting camp and drop a note for Paget to come and meet me at the landing strip as well. You'd get the answers to all of your questions then."

"Good idea, Hod," Landau said. He turned to me with his most friendly smile. "Mr. Hodkins is quite a help, isn't he?"

"He's our eyes, ears, and brains, that's all," I said. "If it weren't for him John would still probably be straying through the African brush."

Landau nodded pensively. "Let me ask you something, Hod," he said after a pause. "Why couldn't you leave today in the Rapide and drop all the messages? Get that done?"

"Because the Rapide's overdue for a checkup, and one trip over the forest is all we should risk," Hodkins replied.

Landau shook his head, like a confused field marshal assuming a new command. "Everything is so complicated here. No communications of any kind, no transport . . ."

"And no director," Basil Owen said. "It would have been a lot simpler to shoot the entire thing in Kenya."

"Or in Florida," Landau sighed. "We could all go to Miami on week ends."

Hodkins excused himself. He had fulfilled his functions

admirably; whatever other problems there were, he wanted no part of them. Landau asked me to step outside onto the veranda for a moment. He had learned a long time ago that open covenants, openly arrived at, were a luxury only major powers could afford.

"What do you think?" he asked, as we stood in the darkness, looking out at the quiet river.

"About what?"

"About who should go down with Hod to see Wilson."

I looked at him with surprise. I knew what he was going to suggest. "I'm damned if I know," I said. "I guess you're the logical choice. You're his partner."

"Please don't remind me of that," he answered. "In any case, I don't think I can. There'll have to be someone here when the company arrives."

"I'll take over for you."

"You've tried to do that once and failed," he said bitterly.

"Well, then I guess I'd better not try to represent you with Wilson, either. Send Basil down there with Hodkins."

He got suddenly angry. The strain was beginning to tell on him. "What an idiotic thing to suggest," he said. "Basil has no influence with John. None whatsoever."

"Neither have I."

"But you could carry my message, and you could argue with him. I don't think he knows how serious the situation is. We have a budget on this picture, you know."

"Why don't you send Kay?" I said. "She's a woman and a star, and she has a strong will of her own."

He shook his head even more forcefully. "Come on, Pete," he said. "Stop it. You know that if she sees him in this condition she'll take the first plane back to the States. Her contract hasn't been completely approved yet, and that would be all the excuse she would need."

"All right," I said. "Suppose I go and threaten and plead with him to come back, and suppose he tells me to go to hell. Then what?"

"Then we'll see. Let's not answer that question until we come to it. I think he'll listen to you. If you apologize to him, and tell him that you want to keep your friendship going, I think he'll . . ."

"Apologize to him? What the hell for? He should apologize to me."

"Pete, Pete, for God's sake. Use your head. What'll it cost you to say, 'I'm sorry'?"

"Nothing. Not a cent. I'll do it under one condition."

"What's that?"

"That I take the plane home not more than a week after I get back."

"You've got a deal," Landau said. Those were always fateful words in the picture business, and I should have been on my guard. But I wasn't. I had been in Africa too long.

A Sabena DC-4 arrived the next day, carrying the entire company. The entrance to the airfield was crowded with the citizens of Stanleyville who had come to see the stars. A few had even climbed up into the neighboring palm trees to get an unobstructed view of our actors. They were rather disappointed as the technicians and crew members appeared.

"What do you do?" I heard an aggressive boy of about ten ask Fielding, our cameraman.

"I try not to get in the way," Fielding answered proudly.

Finally the Duncans and Kay Gibson came down the ladder. A cheer went up. Duncan waved. Landau and I hurried forward to help Kay into a waiting car and we drove off at high speed toward the Sans Souci.

"Well, Peter," Kay said enthusiastically. "It's nice to see you alive. I thought you'd be trampled by a charging buffalo by now."

"We didn't meet any, or I would have been."

"Where's the ogre?" Duncan asked. "Why wasn't he there to meet us? I bet he's shacked up with one of these black ladies and has forgotten all about us."

"He isn't here," I replied.

"He's out looking for locations," Landau said hurriedly.

"Locations? Haven't you got them all picked yet? What have these guys been doing down here all the time?"

"Working on the script," I explained.

"I hope it's better," Kay said.

"What she wants to know is, if her part's any larger," Duncan said. "She feels she's just a foil for me the way it is now. She just listens and I do all the talking."

"I don't mind your doing the talking," Kay Gibson said pertly. "I just feel I'd like to have some inkling of what my character is about. I don't mind if I don't say anything throughout the whole film, as long as I'm playing the part of a human being."

"You're absolutely right," Landau agreed, from the front seat. "And you'll see . . . the changes the boys have made have taken care of that."

Duncan winked broadly at me. "As long as you haven't taken away any of my best lines," he said.

They were shown to their rooms in the hotel, and a few adjustments had to be made. Kay's suite was dark and moist and had to be changed. We moved Wilson's belongings out of his room, and peace was restored.

Landau took me aside once more while the others were unpacking. "Be sure and not let on the nature of your mission tomorrow," he said. "And warn Hodkins to keep quiet at dinner tonight."

"I'm not as big an idiot as you think," I told him. Kay Gibson appeared, dressed in sharkskin trousers and a big straw hat. She declared herself ready to see the town, and I volunteered to be her guide. The Duncans and Landau joined us and we went shopping in Stanleyville. Everyone bought huge supplies of tomato juice, and pork and beans, so that they might be prepared for any catastrophe. While Landau paid, Duncan's wife took me aside.

"What's it like?" she asked. "What kind of a camp have they built? What about the houseboat Paul has rented?"

"It's all fine," I said. "You'll love it."

"Oh yeah," she said. "Don't give me that double-talk. Have you seen it?"

"No," I said, "but I trust implicitly in the efficiency of the company."

"I don't," she declared.

"Oh, don't worry about any of it," Kay Gibson declared. "It won't be heaven but it'll be all right." She beamed at me. I felt all of the adoration of my youth returning. "I can't tell you how I've been looking forward to all of this." She took a deep breath. "Africa! I've always wanted to come here."

I smiled feebly. "It's something to see, all right," I said.

The morale was quite high at dinner that night. The hotel was more comfortable than anyone had expected, and the food was quite good. Fielding, the cameraman, had joined us at the Sans Souci, and he added the only sour note. "The vegetation," he said at least five times during the meal. "It's so thick. I keep looking at it through my finder, and it loses its value. The shores of the Congo look like any river in southern England."

"But we're not shooting here, Ralph," Landau said hurriedly. "The country's different where we're going."

"I'm sure it is," Mrs. Duncan interrupted. "If John had anything to do with choosing the locations, it's going to be just dandy."

"Where *are* we going, Paul?" Kay asked.

"South," Landau said vaguely. "A hundred miles from here. And then to Masindi."

"Where's that?" Duncan asked.

"On the shore of Lake Albert," Hodkins replied.

"Is that nice?" Kay asked.

Hodkins and I exchanged silent glances. "It's interesting country," he replied. "All of Africa is, for that matter." He was covering himself with glory.

"Oh, I'm sure it is," Kay Gibson said heartily. "And I want to see as much of it as I can while I'm here. Don't you feel that way, Peter?"

"Well, I've been here quite a while," I said, thinking of my imminent departure. "And I've seen a lot." Entebbe, Tatsumu, Lake Albert, and the jungle. That was enough, as far as I was concerned.

"Oh, I don't feel that way," she said. "I'd like to stay here for years and see it all."

"You may," I said in a very low voice, so that Landau couldn't overhear me, but she was much too excited to listen to any warning.

It was a little after eleven when we drove back to the Sabena Hotel. The porch was crowded with members of our British crew. They looked strangely out of place, with their predominantly blond hair and pink skin. In direct contrast to the optimistic mood that had prevailed at the Sans Souci, there was a general tone of bitterness here. The first shipment of the crew's jungle clothing had arrived, and the hats that had been bought for them were the main bone of discontentment. They were all the same size, all too large, all made of heavy dark brown felt. As we walked across the crowded porch, several members of the crew angrily clapped their hats on. They looked like figures out of a Disney cartoon, white-skinned dwarfs, with huge, brown mushroom heads.

"Oh, something will be done about it," I declared grandly, when detained. "Don't worry about a thing."

"Something better be done about it," the sound man said. I knew that whatever revolution might ultimately take place, it would be caused by some small incompetence of this kind.

It started to rain. The first fat drops fell with a great noise onto the leaves of the palm trees, and as I reached the door of my room it began to pour. There was the sound of thunder and the water came down in sheets. It bounced off the cement porch of the hotel and formed swift rivers along the paths.

"The little rains have started," Hodkins said. "Right on schedule."

"Can you imagine what it's like in Kivu's village?" I said. "No cement floors there, you know."

Hodkins grinned happily. "Wilson is sitting in the mud, protecting his rifle. The natives are singing the rain song, and the leopards are prowling around outside," he said. "He may actually be rather anxious to come back tomorrow. It may all solve itself."

"It may at that," I answered doubtfully. I thought of Wilson out there in the rain and the wilderness, cooped up in a native hut, planning the death of countless wild beasts, letting his madness run on unchecked, and I felt certain of one thing. Whatever else might be running through his head, he was certainly not thinking of us. He had had Hollywood long ago. He was having Africa now.

35

It was still raining when Hodkins and I took off the next morning. We carried one passenger, a friend of Delville's, who was going to Tatsumu on business. When he saw our flimsy, old-fashioned plane, he almost turned back, but as the alternative was a three-day drive through the jungle, he decided to come along. He said nothing all throughout the trip; he just sat and stared down at his feet, a thin, nervous little man in a white uniform with bright green shoulder boards. I spoke briefly to him after we had landed in Tatsumu. He was the census taker and tax collector, and he was on his way out into the forest.

"Who is there to tax there?" I asked him. Hodkins was arguing with the customs official inside the bamboo hut, trying to explain that we were not leaving the Congo, but that the plane was.

"The natives," the little man replied, as if mine had been a foolish question. "Why, even the Pygmies pay a head tax."

"Well, I don't envy you the job, trying to collect from them."

"It is not difficult," he said. "The only difficult thing is trying to find them."

There was the noise of a plane passing overhead, and I followed Hodkins outside. The Beechcraft circled and landed. Landau's master plan was unfolding step by step.

Looschen grinned as he shook hands with us. "Let's go inside, fellows," he said. "I'm not quite as fit as you are. Haven't been on safari, you know."

"Well, you missed something," Hodkins replied. "It was a wonderful trip."

"I bet it was. What's the deal now? I take your old boat back to Nairobi, and you go on with mine and collect more medals."

"That's it, I guess." Hodkins smiled. "Unless you want to relieve me right now."

"Oh no, old boy. It's quite all right. You carry on. I'll relieve you when they get Jenny all sewed up again."

Hodkins turned to me. "Say, that reminds me," he said. "We'd better get some cloth and tailor our messages. We've got to do it right, don't you know."

The customs man supplied us with string and Looschen produced an old undershirt that had been forgotten in the baggage compartment of the Beechcraft. I tore it into long thin strips. Then Hodkins made small neat pockets out of each end with a needle and thread and we rolled up Landau's messages and put them inside. A .256 Mannlicher shell served as a weight in each one. Looschen was watching us, an amused smile on his face.

"You chaps are awfully clever," he said. "But I'd like to know just whom you've lost."

"Wilson," I said. "He's gone off with a she-elephant. We're dropping him a lock of his wife's hair just to remind him of his obligation to the human race."

"Doesn't sound too unlikely from what Alec tells me." The pilot grinned. He followed us to the edge of the runway. "Well, take care, boys, don't fly too low over those trees. You've only got one fan on that kite, you know."

Hodkins and I got inside the Beechcraft and fastened our safety belts. Looschen waved casually and hurried back into the hut. It was raining steadily. The wheels of the plane made deep tracks in the red clay as we taxied up to the end of the runway. Hodkins winked at me and put his thumb up. We were a very "pukka" crew by now. I unfolded the map across my knees. The messages were on the floor, under my legs.

We rose very quickly through the rain. The speed of our flight kept the windscreen clear, as we banked steeply among the clouds. In half an hour we were over the hunting camp.

Hodkins flew very low over the huts, but there was no sign of life. He circled out over the lake and we passed over the camp once more.

"No truck, is there?"

I looked at my watch. It was a little after one o'clock. Normally no one was out hunting at that time of day, but as the rain had done away with the heat, it was quite possible that Wilson had decided to stay out in the field.

"There's the Pole," Hodkins said. We turned sharply once more and flew past the main hut. Zibelinsky was standing in the doorway of his hut waving to us. "Guess they're all gone," Hodkins shouted. "We'll fly up toward the Semliki." He tipped his wings quickly from side to side as a recognition signal and we flew on.

The ceiling was very low along the shore line, and we were forced down to an altitude of a hundred feet. The winding road passed constantly from his side of the plane to mine, and he banked sharply every few seconds to keep it in view. I started to sweat. The warm air inside the cabin and the constant twisting motion of the plane were having an effect on my empty stomach. I put my head down in my hands.

"The loving cup's right under the seat," Hodkins said cheerfully. He had a cigarette stuck in his mouth, and he sat very straight in his seat, peering out of the windows.

"Never use one," I said. We banked sharply to the right, doubling back in a tight circle.

"Trucks," Hodkins said. "Take a look at them, will you?"

We were diving down toward the road again. The ground was rushing up at me at a strange angle, and I caught a glimpse of a row of trucks stopped at the side of the road. A figure in khaki jumped out of the lead vehicle and waved a large, battered hat.

"Paget," I said. I couldn't say much more.

"I do believe it is," Hodkins said. "We'll drop Message A. Have to make a new approach first." We circled back. Hodkins put down his flaps into the approach position and I handed him two of our streamers.

"We'll cut our air speed a little for a more accurate bombing run." He smiled. "You all right?"

"I'm alive," I groaned.

"Awfully close in here, isn't it?" He seemed unperturbed. "By Jove, I do think it's strange seeing old Paget on this road. He must be going down to the village to pick up John."

"With all of the trucks. That sounds fairly unlikely."

"Well, this road leads nowhere else, you know.'" We were flying very slowly now, the plane hovering over the tops of the trees. Hodkins opened the small window next to his elbow, and held one of the streamers in his fist. Then he dipped the wings and released his package. I could see it floating down into the road just ahead of the lead truck.

"Jolly good shot, what?" He beamed. He seemed very pleased with himself. I sat watching his hands pull back on the wheel. I didn't trust myself to look outside. He gave the plane a little more throttle and we circled back.

"Drop another one just like that," he said. "Always make sure." The second streamer caught in the branches of a tree. We rose a little and turned back once more. Paget was ordering one of the native drivers to climb up in the tree after the message. Hodkins signaled with his wings and we went on. I noticed that he was looking at the motor-temperature gauge, and that he was frowning. "Gets a little hot when you fly her like that with the flaps down," he said. "We'll go upstairs and cool her off a little before we start after old John."

We climbed up through the dense clouds, and Hodkins retracted the flaps. I could see nothing but white mist on all sides of us. I took a cigarette and lit it. I was feeling a little better now that we were flying on an even keel. "Awfully strange," Hodkins said, shaking his head. "All those trucks down there on the wrong road. Can't imagine what Vic's doing."

I didn't care. I was trying to recover. A few minutes later the engine had cooled sufficiently and we started down through the clouds again. We found the lake and then the road and passed over Paget's convoy. They had gotten under way once more. I could see the wheels of the trucks bouncing over the rough terrain.

"Watch the road," Hodkins said. "It's over on your side again."

I did as I was told. The road twisted back to the left. "Over on your side now."

Hodkins nodded. We flew on. In a few minutes we caught sight of the village. "We'll buzz them now and then drop Message B."

"Right you are." The village passed quickly under our wings. There were a handful of native children standing in the rain.

"The truck's there," Hodkins said as we pulled away. His quick little eyes seemed to be capable of seeing everything at once. We circled back and then made our first slow run over the tops of the grass huts. I caught sight of a white man towering over the crowd of natives.

"That was John, wasn't it?" I asked, once we were climbing away again.

"John and the fat fellow both. They looked pretty muddy."

"The whole place looks muddy to me."

"It is, I believe. Pass them under your wing this time."

I nodded. The motor-temperature gauge was rising out of the yellow field and approaching the red once more. If we crash and burn, I thought, Wilson will have had his way after all. He'll have spoiled us by remote control.

"There they are. Take a good look now."

I pressed my face against the side window. Wilson was standing ankle-deep in mud in the center of the small village square. He didn't bother to wave. He was squinting up at the plane, his hat pulled down low over his face to protect him against the rain.

"It's John all right," I said.

"Looks like a bloody great albino witch doctor, there among the blacks, doesn't he?"

"I guess that's what he is by now."

We circled back and dropped the duplicate message. The needle of the temperature gauge was well inside the red field. Hodkins was looking back at the receding village.

"Got them both," he said. "Jolly good bombing, what?"

"Jolly good," I answered weakly. I pointed at the gauge. Hodkins grinned and nodded.

"Upstairs we go," he chirped. "Have to cool her off before we try to land."

We flew around for over ten minutes in the white soup, and then went down again to look for the landing strip. We found it near the lake, halfway between the hunting camp and Kivu's village. We touched down in a sea of mud, and Hodkins cut the motors.

"Cluster for you, old boy. Pin it on your chest as soon as I have a smoke."

"Do the same for you, Hod."

He shook his head. "I'll get mine from old Landau when I get back. I want a big ceremony. None of this informal stuff. The whole bloody troupe and a brass band."

We waited for half an hour on the empty field. Then the first truck arrived. It was Paget.

"Well," he said, "quite a surprise to see you chaps."

"Pleasure is all yours," Hodkins said. "Say, you're on the wrong road, aren't you?"

Paget grinned maliciously. "There's been a change in plans. Sent you a telegram from Tatsumu this morning. Mr. Wilson's decided to start shooting the picture here."

"What?" I couldn't believe it. He was obviously a partner in John's latest practical joke.

"Yes, that's it. The new gen. Made up his mind yesterday when we finally cleared the trucks through customs. Wants to start shooting here instead of at Masindi. Says the village is every bit as good. The company can live at the hunting camp. Lockhart's laying it on right now. For the grub and all that."

"Holy God! What about Masindi? The village is already built there. It cost a fortune."

"But it's not as authentic as this one," Paget said, smiling falsely. "And then it would mean clearing all the equipment again to get it back into Uganda. So he decided to write the village off there. Plans to shoot the destruction sequence in Masindi and that's all. Once he's all through in the Congo, that is. Quite logical, don't you think?"

"The logic of a madman. How does he know the two villages will match? How does he know we can all live at the hunting camp? Good God Almighty. Didn't Lockhart argue with him? He's the assistant unit manager . . ."

"Take it easy, old boy," Paget said happily. "Everything will be all right. He's the boss, you know. We're all just employees. Lockhart, me, you . . . even Hod here . . . all cogs in the great machine . . . not paid to think . . . just do what you're told."

"Didn't John think of asking Landau's advice? That's the least he could do."

Paget was grinning even more broadly now. "He didn't think of that," he said. "Didn't have time. He made his decision and then he went out with old Ogilvy again. Looking for his big tusker, don't you know?"

"Be a bit of a shock for old Paul," Hodkins muttered.

"What about the hunting?" I asked weakly. "Have they shot anything?"

"Nothing yet," Paget chirped. "Wilson's waiting to get a really good elephant. Hasn't seen anything worth his while as yet. I must say, he's quite a game bloke. Lives right there in a native hut like a nigger king."

"Good God." I thought of Landau and the company. To bring them here sounded like the final insanity. Tatsumu and the endless dusty road and then the hunting camp. It was too much to ask of anyone.

"It's really not such a bad idea, Pete," Hodkins said, trying to see the brighter side. "If the bloody Belgians would only allow us to come in here with the Rapide. Sabena could fly the company to Tatsumu in a DC-3 and then ferry them right to this place in short hops. It's logical all right."

"What about the weather?" I groaned. "You couldn't shoot in this rain."

"Weather's bad all over," Paget said. "Road through the jungel to Stanleyville would be hell. Take a week, maybe more. Anyway, as I said before, and as I believe you said once or twice, he's the boss, isn't he?"

"I suppose so."

Paget climbed inside the Beechcraft to get out of the pelting rain, while Hodkins tramped around the field, inspecting the ground. He hurried back when he heard the sound of a truck approaching.

"The field's all right," he said. "I'd land a DC-3 here if they'd let me."

The familiar vehicle we had used so much on our "safari" drove up to the plane. Oglivy got out. There was no sign of Wilson.

"John is very put out," he said, without a word of greeting. "You'll scare all the game if you buzz the area like that."

"He's not coming here, then?" I asked, amazed.

"No, he sent me. I've got all the instructions."

Paget's story was confirmed. Wilson had made his command decision and would accept no alterations or discussions.

"Think there's any sense in my going to see him?" I asked Hodkins.

The pilot shook his head. "Don't think you'll accomplish much, Pete, and if we waste all that time we won't be able to make Stanleyville again tonight. Have to stay in Tatsumu. Probably worry everybody to death doing that."

"Do you think we can get back through this weather?"

"Oh, I think so. If we get started now."

"Well then, let's go," I said. "We've done our duty."

"Oh, just one more thing," Ogilvy said. "Mr. Wilson would like more gun oil and ammunition the next time you fellows come. He said to be sure to give you the message."

"Is that all?" I asked.

"That's all. And don't forget about the game. Fly around our area if you have to come over this way."

Paget crawled out of the plane, and Hodkins started the motor. We rose up out of a sea of mud. I sat for a long time watching the rain wash the red clay off our silver wings.

36

I had often wondered just how Landau would behave in a real crisis. I had really never seen him confronted by anything more serious than a violent disagreement during a story conference, or a complicated business transaction, or an argument over a gin rummy score. I remembered that he had an unpleasant way of losing his temper with nearby inferiors when things went wrong, but that is a common failing and only an overtone to a man's reaction to trouble. Landau's attacks on waiters and secretaries were no worse than anyone else's explosions. On the whole, he usually seemed to stand up pretty well when in danger of losing money or prestige. He was logical and fairly controlled, and accepted the worst, when it finally came, with great coolness and elegance.

However, this was different. This was no disaster involving a calculable loss. This was the end; not necessarily for Wilson, who was bringing it about, but it was certainly the end for Landau, his unwilling partner. He would undoubtedly be the one to receive the largest share of the blame, just as Wilson would certainly have received whatever glory might have been won. If everything went wrong, and the chances were strong that it would, people would merely associate Wilson with the disaster in a good-natured, tolerant way. "Well, that's the ogre for you," they would say with a smile. "Everything withers under his hand." And they would hurry off to sign a new contract with him. He had his talent, and I was sure that it would stand up above the charred ruins. That was not true of Landau. A unified cry would go up against him from all sides, and he would be declared basically at fault, solely responsible. I felt sorry for him as we flew back now with our news of defeat. A financial calamity coupled with a scandal was the correct formula for the end of a Hollywood career. One was bad enough, but a combination of both was almost always fatal.

We passed over Stanleyville and made our approach. There were large puddles on the runway, and it was still raining steadily. Great sheets of water rose on both sides of us as the wheels touched. In the distance I could see two figures standing in the open doorway of a hangar.

"There he is," Hodkins said. We taxied toward the hangar. I saw Landau step out into the rain and start toward us. A very military-looking trench coat was draped across his shoulders, and a large pipe jutted out from under the brim of his white tropical helmet. Basil Owen was walking next to him, wearing one of the enormous brown felt hats.

"Poor old Paul," Hodkins said. "I don't envy him his job."

"Neither do I."

"He might as well go and join up with a Pygmy tax collector . . . the way things are going now."

The propeller stopped. We opened the doors and crawled weakly out of the plane. Landau caught my elbow in his most paternal manner and steadied me as I stepped off the wing. He glanced apprehensively at both of us, at our greenish faces that must have corroborated his worst suspicions.

"Well, give us the news, boys," he said.

"Right here, Paul? Wouldn't you rather wait till we get back to the hotel?"

"I can't wait that long," Landau said. He looked suddenly amused. "It's what I said in 1938 when someone told me Hitler was going to be finished in one year. I hope you've got kinder words for me."

"No, we haven't," I said.

"Well, don't milk the scene," he said good-naturedly. "It's raining, and you know how that raises the price of any sequence."

We started toward the shelter of the hotel veranda on the other side of the road. "Your partner is crazy as a coot," I said slowly. "He wouldn't come to the air strip, but I saw him from the plane. There's no doubt about his madness any more."

"Where was he?"

"In a native village, a few miles from the shores of Lake

Albert. He didn't wave to us. He was sore because he thought we were scaring the game in the surrounding country."

"Did you drop the messages?" Owen asked. He was quiet and reserved.

"Sure. But Wilson didn't come to meet us. He sent his hunter to the field." I patted Landau on the shoulder. "Now prepare yourself for a shock, Paul," I said. "He's changed everything. He wants the principals and a skeleton crew to come to the hunting camp near the village, and he wants to shoot there instead of at the Masindi location."

"Is that true, Hod?" Landau asked quietly.

"Yes, sir. I'm afraid so."

He closed his eyes for a second and took a deep breath.

"He thinks the village where he is now is a better location."

"But the village is already built at Masindi," Landau said in a controlled voice.

"He wants to use that set for the destruction sequence," I replied. "The actual slave sequences he wants to do where he is now."

Landau's mouth closed firmly. His teeth ground down on the stem of his pipe. "Well, that's not so hard to talk him out of," he said. "We'll get the equipment started down here, and then his hands will be tied."

Hodkins shook his head. "The equipment is there with him, right now. He got hold of Paget yesterday and made him reroute it to the village."

Landau stopped in the middle of the street. The rain beat down on his hat and fell in small rivulets from the shoulders of his coat. "I don't believe it," he said. "I just don't believe it."

"We saw it, Paul," I told him gently. "Come on, let's get in out of the rain."

He refused to move. "But it can't be true. Doesn't he know he's risking the lives of the company and the crew? Doesn't he ever think of anyone but himself? Doesn't he realize . . ."

"Paul, come on."

He stood for another minute or two in the pouring rain. His long, dark face was covered with beads of perspiration. Then he started toward the porch. "What's it like there?" he asked, in a new voice. He had accepted the worst and was trying to get used to it.

"A mud flat, covered with squat, brown straw huts," I answered. "The surrounding country is like Masindi and Butiaba. A little less jungle growth. It's raining there . . ."

"But where would we live?" Landau asked. "God damn it!" He controlled himself once more. He closed his eyes, and shook his head, as if he were trying to shake himself out of a bad dream. "He knows that even a skeleton crew will involve at least twenty people. Where will they sleep and eat?"

"In the hunting camp. Lockhart is supposed to be making the arrangements right now," Hodkins said.

"Can one live there? I mean, can one live there and survive?" the unit manager asked.

"Yes, for a week or two, it's bearable."

"What's the food like?" Landau asked.

"Quite good. It gets better as the marksmanship improves. What *we* ate was lousy."

"Please don't make one, single, solitary joke today," Landau pleaded. We sat down among the northbound passengers of Sabena. A good many squalling children seemed to be headed for Belgium that night. "That goes for everybody," he continued. "No wisecracks, no sarcastic remarks. Only straight answers and questions." He looked out at the rain-soaked jungle all around him. "Oh, my God, why did I ever choose that maniac to be my partner?"

He shook his head, wiped the sweat off his brow, and leaned back in his chair. "Will someone bring me a map," he said to Owen. "A map and a tall glass of water."

"We've still got a chance, Paul," I said. "If the rains stop we *could* shoot down there. It would look very real, you know, the natives and the mud. Probably help the picture."

He shook his head. "I'm not going to let him do it," he said. "The crew is my responsibility, and so is the cast. I'm not going to send them to a place like that."

"But what can you do?" Owen asked. "We must start, you know."

"I'll call off the picture," Landau said gravely.

"But you can't. We've already spent a hundred thousand pounds."

"I'll pay that back. I don't know how, but I'll manage. It may take years, but it's better than having someone's life on your conscience."

He sounded very dramatic. I could see him now as a very old man, working as a cashier in an Indian general store in Kampala, going to the bank and depositing the last fifty pounds of a lifetime of labor into a London account, and then walking very slowly along the arcades to a small, hot room, knowing that at least he had behaved honorably and had paid off the debt incurred by his insane partner. It would be like the last shot in one of those old German movies, the gray-haired, broken-down bum, walking slowly home, stopping to pause in front of the local movie theater and staring at a marquee which would, of course, be carrying the real villain's name in large, glorious letters.

"It would take you the rest of your life to pay back a hundred thousand pounds, Paul," I said.

He shrugged. "What do you want me to do? Send everyone down there, knowing that they're going off to their doom?"

"Oh, it isn't as bad as that," Hodkins said. "It might be a little uncomfortable for ten days or so, but I don't think anyone's going to die."

"Anyway, you can put it up to them," I suggested. "Tell them the truth. That it'll be rough, but that it undoubtedly will make for a very distinguished film."

"No," Landau said slowly, "we can't do that. Either we call it off, or we play along with Wilson. We can be honorable or crooked. There's no middle road."

"But why not tell them the truth?" I asked. "It seems the sensible thing to do."

"Because then they will be obligated to helping us. They will want to behave honorably because we're in trouble and we've been honorable with them." He scratched his nose with the mouthpiece of his pipe. "No, there are only two things to do. Call it off and accept disaster, or lie to them and hope some stroke of luck will help us through it."

"That's much too complicated for me," I said. "I think it's always better to tell the truth, Paul."

He smiled for the first time since he had arrived in Africa, and with the smile, a shrewd, intensely human expression passed over his face. "If I had always told the truth, Pete," he said, "I would now be a cake of soap."

The laughter of the others offended me. I knew that it was a funny reply, but it seemed to me to have such an overwhelmingly sad ring to it.

Landau rose abruptly. Duncan and his wife had just driven up to the veranda in a taxi. They were both wearing white pith helmets. Kay Gibson arrived an instant later in another car. Landau waved to them and then stood watching their approach. It made me nervous to have to face them, not knowing what plan we were to follow.

"What'll we say, Paul?" I asked. "Come on, you've got to make up your mind."

He waved my question aside with an outstretched palm. "Never mind, never mind. Not now."

"But, Paul, Kay knows we went out on a reconnaissance flight."

"I said, never mind."

Kay Gibson and the Duncans were involved in a mild quarrel as they crossed the crowded veranda.

"Why didn't you wait?" Kay asked. "I told you I'd only be a minute more."

"Phillip hates to wait. . . . You know that, Kay," Mrs. Duncan said. "And we knew there was another car. . . ." They came up to our table. Hodkins and Owen supplied more wicker armchairs.

"Well, what about it, Pete?" Duncan asked aggressively. "What's the ogre up to?"

"Nothing has changed much," Landau said.

"We're asking Pete, Paul," Mrs. Duncan said, adopting her husband's aggressive tone of voice.

"And he'll answer you, only I'm giving you a brief résumé of the situation."

"That's just what we don't want," Kay said. "We want to know it all, the whole horrible truth. When do we start? Where do we go? How do we get there? Where is the new version of the script? How long will we be where we're going?"

"I'm only the hired man, you know," I answered. I looked at Paul, hoping he would soon come to my rescue.

"Ask Hodkins," Duncan said. "He's not in the picture business, so he's not apt to be quite such a foul liar."

"Oh, I wouldn't know how to answer any of those questions," Hodkins said.

"What about Basil?" Mrs. Duncan said, glowering.

"Please, no," Owen replied.

"Come on, Paul," Duncan said harshly. "Enough of this crap. What cooks? What's going to happen? We all going back to London tonight, or are we going to make this picture?"

"Yes, Paul," Kay added pointedly. "Stop all this nonsense. We're not children, you know."

Landau emptied his pipe into the ash tray in front of him on the table. I could see that he was busy with his decision. They had been fairly unpleasant with him, just at the instant when he had felt protective. They had threatened him, not knowing that they were entirely in his hands, perched on his large palms, helpless and exposed. He stuck the empty pipe into his coat pocket and passed his forefinger, like a windshield wiper, across his brow. "Everything is under control," he said. "As soon as the rain lets up a little, the cast and a skeleton crew are going to be flown to a location selected by John on the shore of Lake Albert, and we will start working."

"Is this the truth now, Paul?" Duncan asked apprehensively.

"My word of honor," Landau said. Once more he had used his old methods to fight against the threatening forces. There was an open door somewhere ahead of him that led out of the heat and the jungle back to a saner land; to the terrace at Fouquet's; to the bar at Twenty-one, or the ultimate haven: Romanoff's. One door, one opening in the borders that were steadily being closed. He had no passport and very little money. He had only his wits to help him escape.

"Well, that sounds better," Duncan said. "Now we'll be off and resume our shopping. Are you coming, Kay?"

"I most certainly am. In your car."

They rose, smiled acidly, and left. Landau looked slowly at the rest of us. "Do you think we have a chance to make it?" he asked. "One single solitary chance? Or are we all proverbial snowballs in hell?"

"I think we have a chance," I said.

"I certainly hope so," Owen allowed stiffly.

"Everything will be all right. We just have to get those

Belgian fellows to close their eyes a little and we'll fly everyone in there without a hitch," Hodkins said.

"Leave the general closing of eyes to me," Landau told him. We all agreed to that. Hodkins and I started back to our rooms.

"It'll all work out," the pilot said. "You'll see. It's not nearly as risky a place as the old boy thinks. Everything in life always appears to be ten times worse than it really is, don't you know."

"I haven't always found that to be true," I said.

"Oh, I certainly have," Hodkins said. "In any case it's the only way a fellow can keep going."

Now that the die had been cast, there was only one hero in Stanleyville, and that was Landau. He did everything. He was a perspiring Napoleon planning his hundred days. He took care of the officials. He dropped the necessary messages to Wilson and Lockhart so that everything would be in order once the company arrived. He pacified the crew by presiding over endless meetings in which they were given an opportunity to air their complaints. He made the actors feel secure by giving a caviar and champagne dinner for them. He organized the departure of trucks and planes. And finally he even solved the greatest thorn in everyone's thigh. He found a solution to the hat problem by discovering that the large brown felt hats were actually two in one, and that they could be separated with the help of a razor blade and made quite serviceable. Beyond all that, he seemed at the last moment to receive the help of those powers to whom he usually addressed his most agonized words of despair. The rains subsided. The sky cleared momentarily, and the expedition got under way.

I had one more brief discussion with him the day before they left. It happened that he discovered I had made reservations to fly back to Europe, and he immediately summoned me to his command post, the bar of the Sans Souci.

"Are you really going to leave me to face John alone?" he asked, once I had been served a drink. "Are you really going to do this to me, Pete?"

"That was our agreement, Paul. Remember? One more week. . . ."

"I didn't ask that," he interrupted. "I asked are you going to leave me to face him alone."

"But what help would I be?"

"If you don't know," he said in a tired voice, "well, then I can't tell you."

"But, Paul . . ."

"It's all right. You can go. I won't argue about it."

"I just don't know what good I'd be doing."

"All the good in the world," he said heatedly. "That's all. You'd be supporting me. Backing me up. Doing all the things friends are supposed to do for each other."

I felt very weary. "For how long do you feel you need support?" I asked.

"Until the day we start shooting."

"That's all? You're sure? This will be my final contribution."

"I give you my word of honor," he said.

"Please don't, Paul," I said. "I'll go."

He looked hurt. "Have I ever abused my word in dealing with you?" he asked. "Have I?" He seemed to have forgotten his preachment of a few days ago.

"Well, not exactly. . . ."

"Then why do you say that?" he flared.

"Never mind. To hell with it."

The journey was uneventful. I was used to the jungle at a low altitude, or in a storm, in a small plane that responded to every current and thermal. Sitting in a comfortable seat in a DC-3 was an experience I forgot as soon as we landed in Tatsumu. I took a few pictures of the company standing in front of the bamboo customs shack, and then Looschen arrived in the Rapide. Hodkins had preceded us by a few hours in the Beechcraft, and he now changed planes with Mike. He had accepted the risk of landing the Rapide on the small strip near the hunting camp, and it was up to him to carry out his word. I flew with Mike and Landau in the Bonanza.

It was late afternoon when we landed on the strip. As soon as we had unloaded our luggage, Looschen took off for Tatsumu to help ferry the rest of the crew to the landing strip. The trucks from the camp had not yet arrived. Landau walked nervously up and down in the late heat of the day. I tried to calm him by telling him that we still had two hours of daylight, and that it would take at least two trips before the whole company was assembled.

"But suppose they don't get here?" he asked.

"They're bound to get here. It's less than an hour's drive."

"But suppose they don't. What happens to us? Do we sleep here? John never thought of that, I'm sure."

"Paul, relax. We could walk to the hunting camp if we had to."

The Rapide circled the field. We watched Hodkins make his approach with a good deal of apprehension, but he proved to be absolutely correct in his calculations. The plane landed with at least a third of the runway to spare. Fielding and his camera crew got out and kissed the ground. Landau barely smiled at their antics. He continued to pace up and down along the edge of the runway. Only when the truck convoy arrived did he quiet down a little. He supervised the loading of the camera gear, getting in Fielding's way most of the time, and then took his place in the cab of the lead vehicle. Everyone except the sound man had arrived, and as the light was failing, we presumed Looschen would bring him the first thing in the morning.

We drove along the winding road into the hazy evening light that hung in a wide pink belt over the lake. Hodkins stood next to me, leaning on the roof of the cab.

"Familiar, isn't it?" he said.

"Like coming back to a horrible home you thought you had left forever," I said. "But I'm afraid it's going to turn out to be a disappointment. Wilson will prove to be right and everything will work smoothly and splendidly."

"Well, let's hope for the best."

It was almost dark when we arrived at the camp and everyone was dusty and tired. No one said anything. They didn't even try to make out their surroundings. They merely picked up their hand luggage and turned to look for instructions.

"Where do we go, Paul?" Duncan bellowed. His face was covered with a thick layer of dust, and only his angry eyes were visible.

"I don't know. I've never been here either."

"I'll show you," I said. I led them down the familiar road that bordered the lake. The main hut was less than fifty yards away, yet I could hear quite a few of the crew members grumbling as we walked through the deep sand. Outside the doorway of the hut I stopped and turned back to the others. "Now you're in for quite a pleasant surprise," I said.

"Lead on, Pete, God damn it," Duncan groaned. "I'm ready for anything."

We stepped inside the hut, pushing past the straw curtain that covered the entrance. It was quite dark. The table was set as if for a large banquet. There were burning candles everywhere that gave the place a dim, festive light, and standing at the bar we saw Wilson. He was alone, dressed in a dinner jacket, wearing a black tie. He turned, as if surprised by our entrance, and only then did I see that he had a small monkey perched on his shoulder.

"Oh, do come in, chaps," he said in a broad British accent, smiling his snake charmer's smile. "I've been so looking forward to seeing all of you again."

37

It was one of Wilson's elaborate jokes, the kind of thing he loved to plan and carry out. But as it continued, I began to feel that there was a basic truth underneath it. Paget appeared in a white shirt with a black bow tie, and so did Ogilvy. They had been rehearsed in their parts and they performed them reasonably well. Drinks were served with more elaborate bowing and scraping, and although we all laughed and enjoyed ourselves, it didn't stop there. It went on, Wilson playing the English gentleman in the jungle, and Paget and Ogilvy aping him, obeying his commands. I realized that, with it all, he was telling us that he was king here.

Movie directors usually raise themselves to princely station by the power they temporarily wield, but Wilson was more than a prince now. He moved as if a powerful light were trained on him, was tracking his every step, and as he overplayed it strenuously, he ultimately succeeded in making everyone uncomfortable. The crew stared at him as if he had completely lost his mind. The Duncans, Kay Gibson, and the rest of us played along with him all through dinner, asking him questions in the most courteous phrases, and constantly excusing ourselves for the way we were dressed. Duncan made the most of his role.

"I'm really horribly put out, old boy," he said again and again, "but some bloody fool, excuse me, ladies, insisted on loading the plane with cameras and sound gear. You know the sort of thing, old boy. And they just didn't take our dinner clothes along."

"Shocking." Wilson frowned.

"Savages," Kay said archly. "Well, nothing is the same any more today, is it? Life . . . the way it used to be, well, it just *is* no more. Graciousness, manners, dress . . . all that is gone, I'm afraid. Forever."

"The war," Wilson said. "My deah . . . we should all have died long before it was over. We should be peacefully resting in our graves, and we wouldn't have to witness this . . . this burial of our way of life."

I was watching Landau as they went on. He had laughed good-naturedly in the beginning and had avoided the monkey on John's shoulder as much as possible, but now he was getting nervous. He felt embarrassed in front of the crew, who had started to withdraw, one by one, to their huts. We were almost alone. Paget and Ogilvy sat stiffly smoking cigarettes with extremely long bamboo holders. The rest of us, in our dirty safari clothes, kept to one side. Landau coughed and cleared his throat.

"John, shall we stop the kidding now?" he asked.

"Kidding? My dear boy . . . I don't understand, I'm afraid."

"I'm serious, John. We have to get started tomorrow. Fielding's got to go out to the location and you've got to look at the costumes . . ."

"I'm perfectly prepared to do anything you suggest, old boy," Wilson said. Hodkins laughed happily; Wilson looked very coolly in his direction. "The airplane driver . . . he's in a revoltingly good mood tonight, isn't he?"

"John, please," Landau wailed. "I'm serious."

"Well, what is it, Paul? Do anything you like, within limits, of course."

Landau tried to control his temper. "Well, first of all, drop that phony accent, and then please, for God's sake, abandon your role of the great white hunter and become a movie director once again."

Wilson looked at him for a long time with his most poisonous stare.

"Listen, you Balkan rug peddler," he began, shedding his British accent. "My role of great white hunter, as you put it, is entirely my own business. It doesn't concern you one goddam bit. It's a holy thing, you understand? Like the sex life of my mother. You will refrain from talking about it, even thinking about it. Because it's much too serious and important a subject for your low mind to try to grasp. It's a passion that's beyond you. I'd have to explain the smell of the woods and the sound of the wind to you. I'd have to make you over again, blot out all the years you've spent on pavements in cramped shoes . . ."

"I'm not interested in your hunting," Landau managed to say. "It doesn't mean a thing to me. Only when it interferes with the picture . . ."

"How has it interfered? When?" Wilson asked.

"Why, I haven't even got the ending of the new script yet," Landau said.

"You haven't?" Wilson's manner changed again, as if he were remembering another part of his act. "Oh, dear me," he said. He turned toward the entrance of the hut. "Kivu!" he called loudly. "Kivu!"

The tracker appeared.

"The script, Kivu. You've been correcting it, haven't you?"

"*Ndio, bwana.*" Even *he* had been carefully rehearsed. He disappeared once more.

"It has to be typed and copies have to be made. We're losing precious time," Landau pleaded.

"Of course, of course."

Kivu re-entered the hut. He was carrying the last fifty pages of the script in one hand and his spear in the other.

"That'll be all, Kivu," Wilson said archly. "See you tomorrow at five."

The tracker nodded and tossed the script onto the cleared dining table. Landau rose and started toward it, but as he did so an unexpected thing happened. The small monkey on Wilson's shoulder had been attracted by the rustling of the papers, and he leaped down toward the script simultaneously with Landau.

"The ape," Landau said, terror in his voice. "Somebody hold the goddam ape."

But no one moved. It was too comic, too bizarre. Landau took hold of one end of the manuscript and the monkey clutched the other. For an instant they both pulled, and then, very quickly, the monkey reached out and tried to scratch Landau with his free hand. The man released his hold on the script and stepped back, leaving the monkey the master of the situation. In an instant the small animal was swinging around the rafters of the hut, grasping his prize. He leaped from the antlers of a Thompson gazelle to the horns of the buffalo skull. Two or three pages of the script fluttered to the floor, and then he went on, the speed of his acrobatics increasing. Hodkins and I rushed after him. He was distributing the pages we had slaved over, like a little boy dropping leaflets at a fair. Wilson and the others roared. Paget had taken one of the rifles and was aiming it at the monkey, offering to shoot him down.

"The frontal brain shot," Ogilvy shouted. "And don't, for God's sake, miss."

Landau stood glaring at Wilson, and then turned abruptly and left the hut. The laughter of the others rose to an even higher pitch. Hodkins caught the monkey and forced the papers out of his hand. Wilson was doubled up with laughter, coughing violently. "Oh, God, oh, God. This makes it all worth while," he roared.

"You better go after Paul," Hodkins said. He gave me the manuscript. Paget had collected the stray pages.

"Yes, you must tell him everything is all right," Kay said. "He's apt to walk right out into the lake, the poor man."

I left the bar. Landau was in his hut, unpacking his things. He looked up as I entered. "I was wrong," he said. "I should have called the whole thing off and sent for a strait jacket."

"Oh, I don't think so, Paul. This is kind of a good sign. He's almost himself again if he's devoting his time to practical jokes."

Landau glared at me. "I can't take it any more," he said. "I'm through, washed up. I'm going back to Stanleyville in the morning and cable Reissar. He can come down here and take over."

But at breakfast the next morning he seemed restored to his usual self. He spoke to Wilson as if nothing had happened. When Kivu brought the monkey, he got up and left and went outside to supervise the loading of the trucks. Half an hour later, seated with Wilson in the lead vehicle, he led the procession out of camp.

We drove through the cool early morning air and arrived at the village. The sun was just coming up. Again we realized that Wilson had prepared things for our arrival. A quarter of a mile before we drove into the village square, we saw natives lining the road. They cheered when they saw Wilson and ran after him. And once his truck had stopped in the village, they clustered around, shouting and dancing. An old man began to beat on a wooden drum, and a long line of girls issued out of one of the grass huts. They started to dance, holding onto each other's waists, moving rhythmically with the drumbeat. In spite of the fact that it had been ordered long beforehand, the dance had a wonderful quality of improvisation. It was a conga line; only the real thing. The dust rose around the shuffling feet. The round, smooth faces shone in the sun. The full-fleshed shoulders tipped back and forth. The drumbeat grew faster. Another smaller drum joined in. Then Wilson moved out into the center of the square, waving his hat.

They screamed with joy. Wilson stood there, grinning, among the sweating bodies of the dancers, turning and smiling at them all. A small black child ran out to him and he caught it up in his arms, while cameras were clicking all around us.

"He's not insane," Landau said. "He's far beyond that. A strait jacket alone wouldn't do. A strait jacket and a padded cell would be the minimum I'd settle for."

In another corner of the square, a native cockfight had started. Four of the young men of the village had been painted white and adorned with feathers, and now they circled each other, swinging long knives. Wilson moved out of the center of the square of dancers with the native child in his arms, and went over to watch them. A swarm of natives followed him, cheering wildly.

"Isn't this something?" I heard him say to Kay Gibson. "Isn't this just something?"

"It's wonderful, John," she agreed.

It took an hour for the festivities to subside. Then Wilson devoted himself briefly to Fielding and the camera crew. He ambled around the village, followed by a swarm of Negroes, planning the week's work.

"God, what a performance," Duncan said to me. "They really love him."

"Why shouldn't they? Everyone does in the beginning."

Wilson came over to us. "Well, Pete, I was certainly surprised to see you again," he said. "The bitter moralist . . . what the hell are you doing here?"

"I just came to witness the beginning of the end," I said.

He shook his head. "You should be back in Paris, kid," he said, "devoting yourself to literature, writing all the things you know nothing about."

"Did you get your big tusker?" I asked him.

"I'll get him, don't you worry."

"Maybe you weren't meant to sin. Did you ever think of that?"

He shrugged. "Just stick around," he said. "If you can't live yourself, you might get a kick out of watching someone else do it."

The next day he was greeted again by hordes of cheering natives. But the weather changed just as the cameras were being unpacked and it started to rain. It grew dark and lightning flashed across the sky. We took shelter in the bamboo huts where we waited until lunchtime. Then it was decided to return to the hunting camp and try again in the afternoon.

But the rain continued. Only at night did it subside. At daybreak the next morning it started to pour once again. Wilson, Paget, and Ogilvy decided to continue their hunting. The rain did not affect that, and now I understood why Wilson had insisted on changing the site of the location. He could utilize the rainy days here, continue his quest.

"No work today, guys," he would call out on each of the following rainy mornings, and then in a heroic voice: "Hunters, man your spears."

The truck with the hunting equipment would appear then, driven by Paget, and Wilson and Ogilvy would climb into the back of it. It went on for four miserable days, the same procedure. Landau was in despair, while Wilson was frankly delighted. The discomfort of the entire company made up somehow for the lack of game. Everyone was suffering, which seemed to make his frustration more bearable. He was not getting his "big tusker," but they were not getting their movie made either.

On the fifth morning there were patches of clear sky over the lake, although it was still drizzling. Wilson decided to stay in camp, thinking that the weather might clear. He sat in the main hut with Paget and Ogilvy, cleaning his rifle. I was reading quietly in a distant corner. Hodkins joined them.

"No luck yet? No elephants?"

"Oh, we've seen quite a few, Hod," Wilson said. "Just not a big tusker. Not the kind I want."

"We'll get one," Ogilvy said. He rubbed his callused naked feet. "We have time. Another week yet, before these rains really let up."

"You think so?" Wilson asked hopefully.

The fat hunter nodded slowly. He was completely unconscious of the actual venture that existed all around him. He had no interest of any kind in the film. The actors and the technicians seemed to be there quite by chance as far as he was concerned. He never spoke to them, never really looked at their faces. They were not hunters, so there was no purpose in considering them. Landau he avoided, sensing a natural enemy. He looked up briefly now as the producer pushed the bamboo mat aside and came through the door. Landau nodded to the hunters and sat down near me with a copy of the schedule.

"Too hot to work in my hut," he said. "It's damp like the inside of a Turkish bath." He looked over at Wilson and then spoke to me out of the corner of his mouth. "He never looks at the script in his spare time, does he?" he said.

"He's afraid to lose his artistic spontaneity."

"Is that it?"

"Oh, sure. He gets much more inspiration out of squinting down the barrel of his rifle."

"Interesting character, isn't he?"

"Fascinating."

"If he only weren't such a goddam bore."

Wilson looked over at us. "What are you two grousing about now? Aren't you happy, Paul, for Christ's sake? You're on the spot, the weather's clearing, and I'm standing by to rush out with my camera and start making you rich. What the hell is the matter with you?"

"Nothing," Landau said, and turned away.

Wilson got up and started pacing up and down. "A swell couple of friends I have," he said. "I'm risking my neck to make them rich and famous and they sit stewing in their fat and grumbling. God damn, what a sad lot! My companions, my home-town buddies!" He spat. "Come to Africa and find out who's on your side. Come into the wilderness and learn about civilized man."

"Turn the record over, will you, John," Landau said. Hodkins got up and left the hut.

Wilson shook his head and looked over at us. "No guts, no sense of humor, no comradeship," he said. "Well, I'm glad I've found out about both of you. I won't have to drag you along any more."

"That's for sure," Landau said, anger creeping into his voice. "This is my last association with you."

"Will you sign a paper to that effect?"

"Any time."

Wilson turned to the others. "You heard him. You're witnesses. We've just dissolved Sunrise Productions, this date, this place. A great American corporation falls by the wayside." He laughed dryly. "Oh, Jesus Christ, am I glad. This is the happiest day of my whole life."

A native had come up to the entrance of the hut. He knocked on the bamboo mat and stood waiting patiently in the rain.

"There's a boy outside, John," Paget said.

"Well, ask him to come in. He can be another witness for us."

The boy came in and stood at attention in front of Ogilvy. He muttered something in Swahili and the fat elephant hunter replied.

"What is it, Ogilvy?" Wilson asked.

"Kivu sent him. He's out at the village. He's seen something. Elephant."

Wilson cocked his head to one side. "Is that right?" he asked. "Where'd he see them?"

"A couple of miles from the village. But that was two hours ago. The boy came back here on foot."

"Well, let's go," Wilson said. "What are we waiting for?"

"They're probably a good way off by now, John," Paget said.

"We've got nothing else to do." He had already picked up his hat and rifle.

"The weather's clearing, John," Landau said. "We might be able to work this afternoon."

"And we might not. Come on, let's get going."

Landau rose, his entire face trembling. "We could maybe get half a day's work if it clears. John, for God's sake be reasonable."

"It won't clear," Wilson said. Paget and Ogilvy were putting their rifles together. "Anyway, if it does, you can bring the company out to the village and we'll come back too."

"But you'll be miles away somewhere in the brush."

"We'll get back," Wilson said irritably. "You just stand by here and get the company together. You're supposed to be doing something, you know, except sit on your fat ass."

"But you won't be there," Landau said. "We've been waiting for days to start the picture, and now just as our luck is about to change, you take off."

"My luck may change too, you know," Wilson said angrily.

"John, please," Landau pleaded. "The sun will come out and you'll be miles away . . ."

"Don't tell me where I'll be," Wilson shouted. "Hell, send your boy Pete along to make sure I know when it clears up if you don't trust my judgment."

"Will you go with him and see to it that he doesn't forget that we're waiting to start our movie?" Landau asked me.

"He doesn't need me."

"That's right. And it might be risky," Wilson crowed.

Landau looked imploringly at me. "Please, Pete, go with them."

"Sure, Pete," Wilson crowed. "Paul will take care of your family if anything happens."

"I'll go," I said. "I'd just like to have a rifle, that's all."

Wilson grinned. "You won't need one on the truck," he said. "Because that's where you'll be anyway."

"All right, John," I said. "Come on. With God's help this may be our last afternoon together. That'll make anything worth while."

"If it clears up we'll be there," Landau called after us. "Don't forget."

We went out into the rain. The native followed us, mumbling Swahili to Ogilvy.

"Maybe we'll get our elephant today, John," Paget said hopefully. "I've got a funny feeling . . ."

"Well, we'll see, Vic. We'll see. Stranger things have happened, you know," Wilson said. Then he fell silent. The strained look had come over his face once more.

38

He stood there in the rain, as I had so often seen him during the past weeks, his hat pulled down low on his forehead, his bony face wrinkled as he squinted through his glasses, one long, thin arm stretched out holding onto the side of the truck, and the other hand curled around the barrel of his rifle. He seemed unconscious of anything around him, of the green hills crowned with white, mushy clouds, and the gray expanse of the lake on the other side of us. He didn't seem to notice the rain splashing against the lenses of his glasses, or the clean smell of the moist air, or the constant movement of the truck bed under his feet. He was lost again. The torturer within him was forgotten, or had retired at least temporarily, had been suppressed as had the many other facets of his personality: the pretentious side, the snob side, the humane side, the comic, clowning side, as well as the practical, intelligent side he could sometimes display. And as I watched him, I decided that he was as much a stranger to me as he had ever been. I knew what he might say at any given moment, but what he really felt, what he really might do under a given set of circumstances, was still a mystery to me.

And as is usual when one looks for a long time at a face that has been friendly on a good many occasions, I started remembering all of my original liking for him. He'd changed a lot this last month, I thought. He'd gotten vaguer when he was vague, and sharper when he was sharp, and meaner when he was mean. Africa had made him more pronounced in every respect, had underlined every one of his characteristics. He had somehow become a caricature of himself, the sometimes benevolent, sometimes spiteful, and often boring favorite uncle on whose whims everyone's fortunes depended. That was why my liking for him had vanished. He was an unbearable extreme now. And the fact that he had allowed this to happen, had rather enjoyed the process, made it seem worse. He had been self-indulgent, which is something he had never been before. He had stopped looking at himself from an outside viewpoint. He had just let himself go, had abandoned himself to his appetites; what he had said about Hollywood had become true of him. He was the walking expression of the radical climates of an overly ardent man.

"There's the village," he said curtly to Paget, pointing out through the rain.

We passed the first row of grass huts and rolled into the village square. The natives stood in the shelter of their doorways, grinning at us, out in the pouring rain. A few children ran out and stood staring up at us, as brown and naked as the mud under their feet. Ogilvy was talking to the oldest one of them. He turned to Wilson, his fat pasty face glistening with raindrops.

"Kivu's not here. He's out tracking the elephants. Two of the other hunters are out with him."

"Find out in which direction they've gone," Wilson commanded.

"Out toward the Semliki," Ogilvy translated. "One of the boys says he'll show us the way."

"Is he sure he knows?" Wilson asked.

"He says he does."

"Well, you'd better ask him to make sure. He might just be trying to be nice to us."

The boy nodded energetically. He had already climbed up on the running board of the truck and was peering eagerly inside.

"He says he knows exactly where they went."

"All right, then," Wilson said. "A little child shall lead them." He nodded to the boy, and the little Negro got into the cab next to the other two natives. We drove out of the village again. An old woman waved feebly from the doorway of her hovel. She was naked to the waist, and she had long flat breasts that looked as if they were drying up.

"Good-by, Mother," Wilson nodded and smiled. "You old bitch."

Paget roared with laughter. Ogilvy nodded wisely. "I bet she's given a lot of boys a good bit of trouble, that one."

"I hope she has," Wilson said.

The ground was very moist, and the truck left deep tracks in the tall grass. Occasionally the wheels spun and we hung momentarily in place, but then we ground on again. There were large patches of water covering the low ground and we had to pick our way through them. Every once in a while the little boy's brown arm would point out of the window and we would follow in the direction he had chosen.

The rain stopped, and the heavy clouds moved more quickly through the sky. We passed through a patch of sunlight.

"It's clearing up," I said.

Wilson didn't answer. He looked briefly up at the blue sky, and then went on staring out at the country in front of us. After a few more minutes, the truck stopped.

"What's the matter now?" Wilson asked Ogilvy.

"There's a boy out there," the hunter said. "He's coming over this way."

A native, dressed in khaki shorts and carrying a spear, was running slowly through the shallow water toward us. His figure was reflected in the surface and he seemed to be stepping across the clouds that were mirrored around his feet. Once he had arrived next to the truck, Ogilvy spoke briefly to him in the language of the region.

"It's not far now. We'd better walk."

"What about the company, John? It's clearing."

Wilson hesitated an instant. Then he climbed down off the truck. "They can wait," he said. "This won't take long. And *I've* been waiting a good deal longer."

"Better ask him if the elephants are still around," Paget said to Ogilvy.

The fat hunter scowled. "You think I'd have us walking through this water if they weren't?" he said. He turned and spoke brusquely to the native. The man nodded and got up on the running board of the truck, where the little boy was standing, watching Wilson and Paget go.

"Don't want a whole gang of them around," Ogilvy scowled. "Just get in the way."

I caught up with Wilson.

"John, are you sure we shouldn't go back?" I asked. "It might clear for only one afternoon and then go on raining for days."

"You go back if you like," he said. "You can shoot the scene."

"But you told Paul . . ."

"Forget it, will you." He broke his rifle at the breech and inserted two shells. "You coming along?" he asked, sounding surprised.

"Sure. I guess I'll be all right as long as I stay close to Ogilvy."

The water was well up over our ankles. It soaked quickly through my mosquito boots. Once inside, it stayed there and grew warm. The native led straight across three huge puddles into the higher grassland. The vegetation was thick. There were more bushes than any place where we had hunted, but no trees.

"Buffalo country," Paget said. He was chewing on a straw. I glanced quickly at him. He looked nervous. A tsetse fly droned around our heads, and we all followed its course. Finally it lit on Ogilvy's bare leg. He slapped it quickly, but there was a tiny red mark when it fell away.

"Bastard," he said under his breath.

We went on, following a spur of high ground. A few minutes later we saw Kivu. He was squatting on his naked heels, his spear buried deep in the soft ground. He rose as we approached. On his brown, shining face there was a look of pride and eagerness, the look of a man who has almost accomplished a long, difficult task, who has suddenly found the end to be in sight and who is able to report this news to a chief he admires.

"*Mingi tembo. Mingi.*" He pointed out through the brush and rattled on in Swahili to Ogilvy.

"He says there's a big fellow," the hunter translated. "Tusks down to the deck. But there are cows and young ones with him."

Wilson's face was very pale. The skin covering his jaws was wet, and seemed to be clinging to his jawbones. The edges of his mouth were lined with a dry crust. "What do we do, Ogilvy?" he asked. "You're the boss."

The fat man scratched the bite on his leg. It was bleeding slightly. He made a smudge out of the blood with his thick fingers. I looked quickly up at his face. He was thinking, his eyes passing over the flat, treeless country in front of us, as he looked for a logical answer to the problem that confronted him.

"I don't know," he said. "It's got me worried. Bloody cows. And this grass is awful high."

"Not a tree to climb in about twenty miles," Paget whispered.

Kivu's eyes went from one to the other as they spoke. He looked impatiently at Wilson.

"We've got three guns," Wilson said. "And it's not hard to hide in this grass."

Still Ogilvy seemed to be hesitating. "Hate to shoot a cow when she's got a little one. Always an awful fuss made about that."

Wilson scratched his thin chest. "Why don't we take a look? We've been waiting for this for a week now. How many chances do you think a guy gets?"

Ogilvy nodded. Despite the fat that covered his face, he looked strained and wan. "All right, Mr. Wilson," he said. "We can take a look. But you're wrong about getting only a couple of chances. And even if it were so, it's never a reason to do something that's wrong."

"You make me think of Delville," John said softly. "You're acting just like him, and after all those explanations of how dumb he was."

Ogilvy didn't answer. He spoke briefly to Kivu and we started forward in single file. The ground rose slightly once more, and we found ourselves on the top of another rounded ridge line. Kivu squatted down in the grass and we followed suit. In the distance I could see a white tick-bird flying very slowly toward our right. Then there were others, circling against the blue sky. Ogilvy rose very slowly, and peered out, his legs bent, his huge body hovering in a strained, awkward position. He nodded once more, and Kivu started moving again. I felt Paget's hand on my arm, and turned with surprise.

"Stay back," he said in a low whisper.

"What about you?"

"I've got a gun. I'll go on a little way."

"I'll go as far as you do."

He swallowed and brushed the sweat away from his lip with a nervous hand. "We'll stay back a little. Too many's no good."

Kivu was crawling on his hands and knees now. I could see his green skullcap, and the tan soles of his feet. Wilson and Ogilvy were directly behind him, crawling steadily forward. Paget stopped and sat down on the path the others had beaten out for us. He pointed off to the right. There were two elephants not more than a hundred yards away, their sagging sides visible above the top of the grass. Ogilvy and the others had stopped too, and were sitting in the shelter of the weeds.

We crawled toward them. Wilson was on his knees next to the fat hunter. Kivu was ten yards farther on. There was the sudden sound of trumpeting, very shrill and high. One of the cows had begun to sense trouble.

"It's no good," Ogilvy was saying. "Believe me, it's no good. I don't like it."

Wilson didn't look at him. He was staring down at the ground. "What does Kivu say?" he asked.

"Don't care what he says," Ogilvy replied. "I don't like it. I've killed over five hundred of them and I tell you this is not the day."

"Ask him," Wilson said. He was trying to control his temper. His head was still down, hanging from his long, thin neck.

Ogilvy waved to the tracker, and he crawled back toward us. He looked up questioningly, the whites of his eyes standing out from the dark skin of his face. The fat man whispered to him, and the tracker replied immediately, without hesitation.

"He's willing to try," Ogilvy said. "It's his word against mine, Mr. Wilson."

Wilson didn't look up. His right hand gripped the flattened reeds of grass next to his knee. "Will you go?" he asked. "That's all I want to know."

Ogilvy nodded. "I have no choice," he said.

"All right," Wilson said. He looked over at Paget. "You don't have to," he whispered.

Paget didn't move. He just sat there, biting on the

straw between his teeth. Wilson turned to the tracker. "All right, Kivu," he said.

For one moment the tracker seemed to smile, but it was impossible to know whether it was as simple an expression as that. There seemed to be a fleeting look of fear mixed in with his delight, fear, and triumph. Then he turned quickly on his hands and knees and crawled on. The two white men followed him. I looked over at Paget. He was still sitting there, biting the straw. All at once he spat it out, and turned back toward the high ground from which we had come. I followed him.

We crawled up through the alley until we were on the top of the ridge again, and there we stopped. For a long time we lay in silence in the tall grass. Paget was breathing hard; he spoke with difficulty, the words sounding indistinct and blurred.

"Watch them better from here. See the whole herd."

I nodded. There was a bush ahead of us, its dark brown branches and green leaves standing out sharply against the sky line. We circled back below the other side of the ridge until we were directly behind it, and then climbed up to the high ground again. The entire herd was there in front of us, the cows and the small elephants nearest us, and the big bull Kivu had reported, farthest away. He turned as we stood there watching him, and I saw the sweep of his tusks that went down out of sight into the grass, and then very quickly his trunk came up and started moving through the air like a periscope, its small end twisting in all directions, sniffing the air. Then his distant trumpeting floated across to us, fighting its way against the wind. For an instant I caught sight of Wilson and Ogilvy. They were in the center of the herd, incredibly close to one of the cows, and they seemed not to be moving.

Paget looked over at me, and then turned back to the fields in front of us. There was a terrible expression on his face, an expression of complete defeat, and I wondered if I looked that way too, for there was a strange uncomfortable feeling inside me, a gnawing at the lining of my stomach, a pressing down on my lungs, and I knew that what I felt was a desire to be there among the elephants with the others. It was nothing like what I had experienced the first time we had seen them, when I had stayed behind on the truck. I felt no fear now. It was envy and despair, and the feeling of having lost something eternally, as if a death had occurred inside me, a death that had been a long time in coming.

The trunks of some of the other elephants were high up above the grass now, and the trumpeting that floated toward us was constant. They were starting to move in all directions, searching for the danger that they sensed was among them, their trunks high in the air, like periscopes, searching the wind. They looked pathetic and blind, and yet huge and indestructible. I caught sight once more of one of the hunters, but it was only for an instant, and then all at once there was the flat sound of an explosion. The big bull stopped in his tracks, his ears flared out, and he trumpeted once again. There was another shot, and he stepped backwards, a slow recoiling step away from danger, and then he fell back suddenly into lifelessness.

"He's got him," Paget shouted. The phrase seemed to hang in the air like one of the explosions, meaningless and past, for tumult had started in the high grass in front of us. The elephants were moving fast now, in confusion, trumpeting, thrashing with their trunks, their ears flaring as they trotted toward each other and then fanned out once more. For one second I thought I saw a spot of green among them, and then it seemed that a body was being lifted and flung through the hazy air. Then there was the sound of another shot and another. One of the cows slid forward into the grass. The rest of the herd turned, and started moving very quickly in a uniform direction, cutting wide paths through the grass as they rushed off in full flight.

Paget shouted to me and started toward the place where we had seen the bull elephant fall. I followed him, but we had gone only about seventy-five yards when Ogilvy rose up slowly in front of us. He glanced at us, and turned away. His face was white. Paget and I stopped and followed him at a walk. He was cursing, in a low, angry voice, cursing steadily as he made his way to the place where the bull had gone down. An instant later I saw Wilson. He was sitting in the grass, throwing up. He got slowly to his feet and stepped over his rifle. I caught sight of his face; there was no sign of triumph, only complete and final despair.

"You got him, John," Paget shouted.

Wilson turned on him viciously. "Shut up," he screamed. "Shut up. All of you."

He moved wildly through the thick grass, walking with large, spiderlike steps. The dead bull lay twenty yards to his left, but he went on, moving away from it. I glanced over at the corpse of the elephant. The sprawled body of the huge beast had a terrible look of uselessness about it, as if it had never been alive, had never been able to move under its own power. But his feet looked even more tragic than the rest of him. Their size and familiar shape had a final look of sadness, of hopeless death. There were millions of flies on his bleeding head, millions of dirty little bodies spoiling the face's last look of nobility. I had stopped without noticing it. Now as I looked up I could see the others thirty yards away, standing very still above the swaying tops of the weeds. I hurried after them, and then I saw what lay in front of them. There was a dead cow on her side with a bullet hole just behind her front leg, and not ten feet away the twisted body of Kivu. His small, creased face was half buried in the sand. The rest of him was smashed beyond recognition. I looked away quickly, but the picture of brown skin covered with blood and dust clung to the inside of my head.

"My God, John," I mumbled.

He shook his head. Tears were streaming out of his eyes. He pushed past Ogilvy and Paget and started off across the fields. We stood watching him go, the thin, khaki-clad figure walking rapidly toward the ridge line behind us, with the golden grass up around his hips, and the clear blue of the sky beyond his head.

"Poor, bloody nigger," Paget said.

Ogilvy scratched his leg. "No," he said. "It isn't the day for it. It isn't the day for a man to die." He stepped back very slowly, his eyes on the body in front of him. Only when he was deep in the surrounding field again did he turn and walk forward. We followed him back to the truck in silence.

He was sitting on the truck bed with his back resting against the cab when we arrived. The two natives and the boy were standing in front of the hood. They looked frightened. Ogilvy went over to Wilson.

"We've got to tell them, John," he said quietly. "They'll have to go after him."

"And what about the ivory?" Paget asked. The horror

had already left him. The tracker was dead, but that was not such an unusual thing to happen on safari.

"Never mind that," Ogilvy said irritably. Wilson had still not answered. "I'm going to tell them now," the hunter went on. "The driver can take us back to the village and then come back for them."

"Go ahead," Wilson said.

Ogilvy still hesitated. "He knew what he was up against," he said finally; but it sounded forced. "Especially as I told him it was a mistake to go on."

"He wanted to please me," Wilson said slowly. He bit his lip. "Game little jig. He just didn't know any better."

"More likely he had his eye on a bonus," Ogilvy muttered. Wilson looked up at him with an abrupt movement of his head.

"You think that was it?"

The hunter shrugged. "What difference does it make? He's bought it, and that's that."

"What do you think, Pete?" Wilson asked. He stared dazedly at me. I felt sure that I knew what he was after. He wanted to hear the truth. He wanted to hear someone else say the same thing that was running through his mind.

"I think he was just like Jackie," I said slowly. "The same story, the same pattern, only quicker and rougher."

"Go on."

"What for? You know the rest. You saw him. He didn't fall off a winner, and he didn't go broke. He just got stamped to death."

"For God's sake, Pete," Paget started.

I turned on him angrily. "You'll notice I'm not worried about the ivory, or whether he wanted a bonus or not, Vic. That sounded worse to me than what I've just said."

They stood there for a long time, the fat hunter on one side of the truck, and Paget on the other. I climbed up on the truck bed with Wilson. He glanced over at me.

"It's a shame you can't talk Swahili, isn't it?" he said. "You could tell the boys all about me."

"They'll see for themselves," I said.

Ogilvy turned abruptly, as if someone had wakened him out of a deep slumber, and then he walked around to the front of the truck and spoke to the two natives. They stared at him, wide-eyed. Then they turned and ran off in the direction in which we had come. We watched them go. They were about a hundred yards away from the truck before they slowed down to a walk, and we saw them moving close together, starting to walk side by side. Even at that extreme distance we could see that they had taken each other by the hand.

The little boy had crawled into the cab. We could hear him whimpering. "Tell him to shut up, will you, Vic?" Wilson said.

Paget nodded. He got in behind the wheel, and we could hear him speaking softly to the little boy.

"You want to ride back there?" Ogilvy asked.

Wilson nodded. The fat hunter crawled into the cab with Paget. The starter ground noisily, and then the engine caught. I held onto the wooden sides of the vehicle as it started to sway and tip. I hadn't noticed how rough the country was on the way out, but now I was very conscious of it. Wilson lit a cigarette. His knees rolled back and forth with the movement of the truck, and he had to hold onto one side to steady himself. We reached the road, and the dust rose around us on all sides. Wilson started coughing, but his fit didn't last nearly as long as it usually did. Somehow he managed to control it. He shook his head, and swallowed. "You know, the funny thing is," he said in a low voice, "that I started out to be a nice guy. Just like you. The way everyone starts out, I guess. Nothing ever went wrong, nobody was ever unhappy." The noise of the motor ground on. "Not for years and years," Wilson muttered. "Then all at once it started. People I knew getting into trouble, getting sick, dying. All kinds of lousy things happening all around me. All the hell of life. I tried not to see it for a while, tried to look away, but that didn't work; and so I started changing with it, getting calloused, selfish, not feeling anything as strongly any more. I could sense it happening to me. Just a slow change, and pretty soon I was no longer what I started out to be. And nothing else was either. Like you're on a train passing through the country, leaving hayfields and farms and coming into the gray, dirty outskirts of a crummy town. God damn, how I hated it. Hated life for changing, hated myself for going along. Nothing solved itself any more. Nothing worked out. Still, all I thought I could do was just keep living. And I didn't know until too late that that wasn't enough. Because by that time there was no way to change back, and so I just had to let myself slide and keep going along. You know what I'm talking about, kid?"

"Yeah, I guess so, John."

He shook his head slowly, and then he went on: "What you said about Jackie was right," he said. "This little guy was just like him. Jesus Christ, kid. Just exactly like him." He pulled at his hat, and got up, his big-knuckled hands clutching the railing next to him. The wind blew back the brim of his hat. The dust bit into his eyes. "A little soul's been stamped out, Pete. D'you understand? A little soul." He was shouting against the wind, like a deaf man.

I didn't answer. We drove into the village. The company trucks were parked in the square, and the camera was set up. Paget stopped. All of the natives had been hunched together on one side of the square. They were sitting on the ground waiting for the picture to start. I saw Landau and the others turning toward us.

"Go on, Paget," Wilson shouted. "I'm not getting off here."

But it was too late. Ogilvy had already opened the door on his side and the native boy had jumped out. He ran screaming across the square. I could understand only one word of what he said: Kivu. The natives rose to their feet. For an instant they stood in awed silence, and then they broke out in all directions, wailing and shouting. Three or four of the younger men ran to the chief's tent and sat down behind the long wooden drums, and began to pound on them.

"Go on, Vic," Wilson shouted once more. He grabbed his rifle and smacked the stock against the steel side of the cab.

Paget ducked back inside. Ogilvy slammed the door and we drove out of the village again. A chicken ran across our path and I could feel the front wheel pressing over its body. Then we turned sharply to the right and started down the road toward the hunting camp. Wilson threw his rifle into a corner, and turned his back toward the breeze. We drove on. The only noise was the whining of the gears and the churning of the motor. We joined the main road that ran along the edge of the lake. From very far away we could hear the faint beating of the drums.

"Stop," Wilson shouted. "God damn it, stop."

The brakes squealed. The cloud of dust grew thicker

and thicker until it obscured the sun and the sky. We were left choking in a golden-brown fog. It is strange when I think of that moment now, now that it's all in the past, all the hard, bitter work that followed, with Wilson a changed man, a gaunt, silent scarecrow, moving among the actors and the lights and the crew, doing his job, and his job only, the job that he hated to do, the movie he had to start when everything else was over, creating the foolish make-believe when his mind was still burdened by the reality he could not stamp out; a gaunt, empty man who never spoke to anyone unless it was necessary, never smiled, never looked anything but haunted and troubled. And that moment seems even stranger now when I think back and remember the success that greeted the release of the picture, the success that everyone connected with it basked in. Everyone except Wilson, that is, for he never saw the film.

We were so far away from cities and theatres then, so remote from it all, from box offices and queues, from fame and failure, from people and film and money. We stood there in the hot dust, and everything seemed pointless and lost, and Wilson leaned down and spoke to the men in the cab in front of us.

"What are the drums saying, Ogilvy?" he asked.

There was a long silence and then the answer came in a deep voice from behind the brown steel wall in front of us. "The drums? Oh, just about what you'd expect, I suppose."

"What's that, Ogilvy?"

"They're telling everybody what happened, that's all. The bad news." He paused. "It always starts with the same words," he went on. There was a strange, malicious sound in his voice.

"What are they?" Wilson asked.

Ogilvy coughed, and then when he spoke he sounded as if he were savoring each word, as if somehow he wanted to slide them deftly into Wilson's brain. "White hunter, black heart," he replied. "White hunter, black heart."

Wilson nodded slowly. It seemed that he had suddenly felt the need to make sure that it had all really happened, and now he appeared to be satisfied that none of it was a dream.

"Drive on," he said.